Praise for John Gilstrap
and His Thrillers

"A page-turning
exciting

AGAINST ALL ENEMIES

"Any John Gilstrap novel packs the punch of a rocket-propelled grenade—on steroids! Tentacles of intrigue reach into FBI headquarters and military hierarchy. Lines are crossed and new ones drawn. The philosophy of killing to preserve life takes on new meaning. Gilstrap grabs the reader's attention in a literary vise grip. Each installment of the Jonathan Grave series is a *force majeure* of covert incursions, and a damn good read."
—BookReporter.com

"Tense, clever . . . series enthusiasts are bound to enjoy this new thriller."
—*Library Journal*

END GAME
AN AMAZON EDITORS' FAVORITE BOOK OF THE YEAR

"Gilstrap's new Jonathan Grave thriller is his best novel to date—even considering his enviable bibliography. *End Game* starts off explosively and keeps on rolling. Gilstrap puts you in the moment as very few authors can. And there are many vignettes that will stay with you long after you have finished the book."
—Joe Hartlaub, BookReporter.com

DAMAGE CONTROL

"Takes you full force right away and doesn't let go until the very last page . . . has enough full-bore action to take your breath away, barely giving you time to inhale. The action is nonstop. Gilstrap knows his technology and weaponry. *Damage Control* will blow you away."
—*Suspense Magazine*

THREAT WARNING

"If you are a fan of thriller novels, I hope you've been reading John Gilstrap's Jonathan Grave series. *Threat Warning* is a character-driven work where the vehicle has four on the floor and horsepower to burn. From beginning to end, it is dripping with excitement."
—**Joe Hartlaub, BookReporter.com**

"If you like Vince Flynn–style action, with a strong, incorruptible hero, this series deserves to be in your reading diet. *Threat Warning* reconfirms Gilstrap as a master of jaw-dropping action and heart-squeezing suspense."
—**Austin Camacho, *The Big Thrill***

HOSTAGE ZERO

"Jonathan Grave, my favorite freelance peacemaker, problem-solver, and tough guy hero, is back—and in particularly fine form. *Hostage Zero* is classic Gilstrap: the people are utterly real, the action's foot to the floor, and the writing's fluid as a well-oiled machine gun. A tour de force!"
—**Jeffery Deaver**

NATHAN'S RUN

JOHN GILSTRAP

A JONATHAN GRAVE THRILLER

FRIENDLY FIRE

PINNACLE BOOKS

Kensington Publishing Corp.

www.kensingtonbooks.com

PINNACLE BOOKS are published by

Kensington Publishing Corp.
119 West 40th Street
New York, NY 10018

All Kensington titles, imprints, and distributed lines are available at special quantity discounts for bulk purchases for sales promotions, premiums, fund-raising, educational, or institutional use. Special book excerpts or customized printings can also be created to fit specific needs. For details, write or phone the office of the Kensington sales manager: Kensington Publishing Corp., 119 West 40th Street, New York, NY 10018, attn: Sales Department; phone 1-800-221-2647.

First printing: July 2016

10 9 8 7 6 5 4 3 2 1

ISBN-13: 978-0-7860-3507-6
ISBN-10: 0-7860-3507-2

Printed in the United States of America

First electronic edition: July 2016

ISBN-13: 978-0-7860-3508-3
ISBN-10: 0-7860-3508-0

To Joy

Chapter One

Ethan Falk recognized the monster's voice before he saw his face. The voice in combination with the phraseology. "Be quick about it, if you don't mind."

Be quick about it.

With lightning speed—the speed of imagination—Ethan was once again eleven years old, his ankles shackled by a chain that barely allowed for a full step, that prevented him from climbing a ladder without hopping. The pain was all there. The humiliation and the fear were *all there.*

It had been eleven years. The monster's hair had turned gray at the temples, and hugged his head more closely. The features had sagged some and his jaw had softened, but the hook in the nose was the same, as was the slightly cross-toothed overbite. There was a way he carried himself, too—a square set to his shoulders that a decade had done nothing to diminish.

Ethan felt his face flush as something horrible stirred in his gut, a putrid, malignant stew of bile and hate and shame. "Look at me," he whispered. He needed the confirmation.

An old woman's voice startled him. "Are you even listening to me, young man?"

No, he wasn't listening to her. She stood there, a silver thermos extended in the air, dangling from two fingers. "You're out of half-and-half," she said. Her clipped tone told him that she'd said it before.

Because reality had morphed into the past with such sudden violence, the request registered as a non sequitur. "Huh?"

"My God, are you deaf? I said—"

The monster turned. Raven, Ethan's nominal girl-friend and fellow barista, handed the man his drip coffee, and as the monster turned, Ethan caught a glimpse of him, full-face. His heart skipped. It might have stopped.

The lady with the thermos continued to yammer.

Please need cream or sugar, Ethan pleaded silently. That would put him face-to-face with the man who'd ruined so much. The man who'd beaten him, torn him.

But apparently the monster preferred his coffee black. He headed straight to the door, not casting a look toward anyone. Whatever his thoughts, they had nothing to do with the sins of his past.

Perhaps they had only to do with the sins of his future.

". . . speak to your supervisor. I have never—"

"No," Ethan said. The monster could not be allowed to leave. He could not be allowed to torture others.

He could not be allowed to dominate Ethan's life any more through recalled horrors.

Another customer said something to him, but the words—if they were words at all—could not penetrate his wall of rage.

Ethan needed to stop him. Stop the monster. Kill the monster.

He dropped the stuff he'd been holding—a tiny pitcher for the steamed milk and the spoon through which to sift it—and was deaf to the sound of them hitting the floor. People looked at him, though. Raven at first looked confused, and then she looked frightened.

"My God, Ethan, what's wrong?"

Ethan said nothing. There wasn't time. The monster was on the loose, out in the world, preying on other people. On other children.

Raven tried to step out in front of him to stop him— *how could she know?*—but he shouldered past her. He moved fast, not quite a run, but close to it. Fast enough to catch the attention of every pair of eyes in the shop.

As he passed the pastry case, he snagged the knife they used to cut bagels. It had always been the wrong style for slicing bread, with a straight edge instead of a serrated one, but they'd learned as a crew that if you kept a straight edge sharp enough, it would cut anything.

The whole rhythm of the shop changed as he emerged from behind the counter with the knife. The old lady with the thermos put it down on the counter and collapsed into a fetal ball on the floor, covering her head and yelling, "I'm sorry, I'm sorry! I'm so sorry!"

In a distant part of his brain, Ethan felt bad that he'd scared the poor lady—all she'd wanted was a little customer service—but in the readily accessible portion of his brain, he didn't give a shit. Maybe next time she wouldn't be such a bitch.

The crowd parted as Ethan approached the door with

his knife. He didn't slow as he reached the glass door, choosing instead to power through it as if it weren't there. The blast of autumn air felt refreshing after the stuffiness of the coffee shop. Invigorating. Head-clearing.

Where is he?

The shop lay in a suburban strip mall. There weren't many people milling about, but this was lunch time, so there were more than a few. The monster could only have gone but so far. He had to be here somewhere.

He saw a guy from a Subway sandwich shop chatting on the corner with a hot girl from the quick-quack medical place next store. She wore a checkerboard scrub suit that strained in all the right places. Ahead and to the left, a lady in a red jacket carried a take-out order from the ribs joint. ("You bring your appetite, we'll provide the bib.") Beyond that lady, tail lights flashed on the back end of a pickup truck, followed by the white reverse lights.

Shit, he's getting away.

He stopped himself from chasing, though, because he knew that the monster wouldn't be in the pickup. It was too far away. He wouldn't have had time to get that far.

Ethan pivoted to look the other way. He stepped around the corner of the coffee shop to look past the drive-through traffic.

There he was.

The monster walked easily, as if not a care in the world, on his way to the rest of his day.

Ethan took off at a run. He'd changed a lot, too, in the past eleven years. His shoulders had broadened, and he'd grown to six-two. The monster no longer had a chance of holding him down with a hand on his chest and a knee in his belly.

The monster had no chance of winning this fight.

Ethan ran at a full sprint, closing the distance in just a few seconds. When he was only ten or fifteen feet away, the monster seemed to awaken to the danger and turned.

Good, Ethan thought. *Get a good look at me you son of a—*

The monster led with a punch that came from nowhere and caught Ethan with withering force just in front of his ear. Light flashed behind his eyes.

But Ethan still had the momentum, and the collision took both of them to the ground between parked cars. The monster's head sheared a side-view mirror from its mounts, and then pounded hard against the pavement.

They landed in a tangle, with Ethan on top, in the command position. As his vision swam from the punch and the fall, he knew that quick action meant survival. The monster bucked beneath him, trying to throw him off. The guy didn't seem scared at all. He seemed angry. If he got free—

Be quick about it.

Despite the squirming and writhing, Ethan's right hand was still free, and it still grasped the knife. He raised it high.

In that instant, the monster seemed to understand what was going to happen.

In the next, Ethan drove the blade through the monster's left eye and into his brain.

"All units in the vicinity of the Antebellum Shopping Center, respond to the report of an assault in progress. Code three."

Detective Pam Hastings pulled her microphone from its clamp on the dash and brought it to her lips, keying the mike. "Detective One-four-three responding." With the white mike still in her grasp, she used the first three fingers of her right hand on the rocker switches to light up the grill lights and their counterparts in her back window. She cranked the siren switch all the way to the right—to the Wail setting.

Known throughout the Braddock County Police Department as a lead-foot (with the Internal Affairs reports in her record to show it), she didn't think about the future paperwork as she mashed the accelerator to the floor and let herself be thrown into her seat back as the 305-horsepower Ford Police Interceptor accelerated from cruising to holy-shit-fast in zero-point-few seconds. In that same amount of time, at least four other units likewise marked responding. Nothing drew a crowd of cops quite like violence in progress.

Pam didn't know where the other units were coming from, but she knew that she was only a quarter-mile away, and that almost certainly meant that she would be first on the scene.

"Units responding be advised that we've received multiple calls on this. Callers report a man in the parking lot next to the Caf-Fiend Coffee House with a knife in his hand. One victim appears to be down."

That raised the stakes. If the callers were right—and when multiple callers had the same story, the situation was almost always as reported—Pam was at best cruising into the middle of an attempted murder in progress. At worst, well, there was no ceiling on what the worst might be. She used her right thumb to release the snap on her thumb-break holster. If she was going to need her weapon, she was going to need it quickly. Milliseconds counted.

Peripheral vision became a blur as Pam pushed the speedometer to its limit down Little Creek Turnpike, switching the siren to Yelp as she approached intersections. She'd learned over her thirteen years on the job that if you move with enough conviction—whether on foot or in a vehicle—people will get out of your way.

As Fair Haven Shopping Center whizzed past her on the left—a blur of colorful signage and logos—she lifted her foot off the gas to prepare for the hard left onto Pickett Lane, named after a Civil War loser who led thousands of his men to slaughter at the Battle of Gettysburg. She couldn't live with the irony of dying on a road named after such a man. She tapped the brakes, but didn't jam them, taking the turn twenty miles an hour faster than the intersection was designed for, but a solid fifteen miles an hour slower than her tires could handle. Her seat belt kept her from being launched into the passenger seat.

The ass end of her cruiser tried to kick out from her, but Pam wrestled it back in line with gentle pressure on the wheel. The casual observer wouldn't have seen even the slightest fishtail.

Straightaway. The engine growled as she pressed the accelerator to the floor. Up ahead, as far as she could see, the traffic somehow knew to pull over. She saw cars in the median, a truck up on the curb on the right. This was the part of the job that she loved more than any other.

The Antebellum Shopping Center was now in sight, ahead and on the right, and she slowed. It was one thing to get to the scene quickly; it was something else to rush into an ambush. Because weapons were involved, county protocols required that she wait for backup. But because someone was in the process of being murdered, she decided to disobey the rules. The fact that the murderer had a knife and she had both a .40 caliber handgun and a 12 gauge shotgun within easy reach made the decision a little easier.

Pam cut her siren and slowed to twenty miles an hour as she turned into the shopping center. She pulled the mike from its clamp again and keyed it. "Detective One-four-three on the scene."

"Four-four-seven. Hold what you've got. I'm ninety seconds out." That would be Josh Levine, a cool kid with a big heart and a bigger crush.

Pam opted not to reply. A crowd had gathered in the parking lot outside the Caf-Fiend Coffee House, naturally forming the kind of semicircle that directed Pam's eye to the threat. The closest gawkers beckoned her forward, while the ones who were farther away continued to stare and point at the hazard.

"The situation is critical," Pam said into the radio. Translation: *I'm triggering the backup protocol's exception clause.* "Other units expedite." Translation: *Run over anybody in your way if you want a piece of the fun.*

She threw the transmission into Park, kept the engine running, and stepped out of the cruiser.

"He's up there!" a lady yelled. "Shoot him!"

Pam ignored her. In fact, she ignored everything but the events she saw play out before her. With her Glock 23 at low-ready, she approached carefully yet steadily, sweeping her eyes left and right, vigilant for an unseen threat, perhaps an accomplice. She tried to focus on her tactical breathing—four seconds in, four seconds held, then four seconds to exhale. It made all the sense in the world when she learned about it in the classroom, but it was pretty damned hard to do in real life. The combined energy from all the people watching her created its own form of heat.

Crime scene gawkers were a funny lot. Roughly a third of them thought you were a God, a second third thought you were Satan incarnate, and the rest didn't give a shit. They were the ones with the cell phone cameras. She saw three on her periphery, one of which hovered in the air at the end of a selfie stick. Of the thirty or so people who had gathered, none of them had pressed forward to help the victim or to confront the attacker. That was her job. The crowd's job was to film it and to offer criticism after the fact.

She'd nearly made it to the front when she caught her first glimpse of the gore. Two cars were painted with it, as was a tall, rail thin, terrified young man in the apron of a Caf-Fiend barista. The kid seemed confused. His artificially blond hair dangled in his eyes as he looked at the knife in his hands. It was as if he wondered where the knife had come from.

Pam raised her Glock to high ready and rested the front sight at the center of the attacker's chest. "Police officer!" she yelled. Her voice cracked a little. She hoped it wasn't obvious to anyone else that she was in way over her head. "Put the knife down or I will shoot you!"

The attacker held out his free hand as if to ward her off. "No!" he said. "I'm not the killer. He's the killer. He's a kidnapper. A rapist, and a killer!"

"Put the knife down!"

"You don't understand. I'm the victim here. He's . . ." The kid's face seemed to clear, and he looked at his hand. At the blood. "Oh, my God." Then he looked at the bloody man who lay motionless at his feet. "Oh God, oh God, oh God."

Pam moved her finger lower on the trigger guard. The experts all agreed that inside of twenty-one feet, a man with a knife could kill a cop before the cop could pull a firearm from its holster. Correcting for the fact that she was scared shitless, but that her gun was already trained on the bad guy, a finger only a quarter inch from the trigger pretty much canceled out that research. If he took a step toward her, she was going to blast his heart out through his spine.

"Listen to me!" Pam yelled. Her voice was firm and strong this time. "Put the knife down and lie down on the ground."

"I'm the victim!"

"You're the victim with a knife," she replied. "You're putting me in danger, and you're putting all these other people in danger, too. Put the knife down. Do what I tell you, and then I'll listen to your side of the story."

In the distance, the sound of sirens crescendoed. One of them would be Josh Levine. If he thought she was in mortal danger, he would shoot before talking.

The assailant didn't move.

"What's your name?" Pam shouted.

The kid seemed confused. Perhaps it was the ordinariness of the question.

"Your name," Pam prompted. "What is it?"

"Um, Ethan. Ethan Falk."

Pam lowered her weapon a few degrees. "Nice to meet you, Ethan Falk. I am Detective Hastings, and I am here to arrest you. Whether you're innocent or guilty, victim or perpetrator, is not my concern. All I know is that right now, there's a man on the ground at your feet, and you're standing over him with a bloody knife. What would you assume if you were in my position?"

"It looks bad, doesn't it?"

The comment struck Pam as funny and she smiled. "Yes, it looks bad. So how about you put the knife—"

"But I didn't do—"

"Listen to me, Ethan! Do you hear those sirens? Those are other cops, and when they arrive, they're going to see you still standing there with a knife. They're going to see the blood, and there's going to be many more guns pointing at you. You don't want that. Please just drop the knife and—"

He dropped it. The knife landed flat on the victim's belly. Baby steps.

"Thank you, Ethan," Pam said. "Now, keeping your hands where I can see them, I need you to step forward into the road—"

Just then, a Toyota driven by a soccer mom in a pink top sped down the parking lot aisle that separated cop from felon.

"Jesus," Pam cursed. "Really?" Refocus. She stepped out into the roadway and pivoted to her right, keeping more or less the same distance between herself and her suspect.

"Four-four-seven is on the scene." Josh Levine had arrived.

Pam's portable radio was out of reach while she was

covering the killer. She wished she could tell everyone to come in easy. To her suspect, she said, "Ethan, I need you to take two giant steps forward into the street and lie flat on your face, your hands out to the side."

He seemed to be caught between reality and some-place else.

"Come on, Ethan, I know you can do it."

"Don't shoot me."

"I won't shoot you if you don't threaten anyone. Come on, two big steps forward, and then just sprawl on the ground. We'll get past this one step, and then everything else will be easy."

Josh Levine burst out of the crowd on Pam's left, Mossberg shotgun pressed to his shoulder. "You heard her!" he shouted. "Get on the ground! Now!" He pressed in three steps too close, ruining the safe zone that Pam had been trying to create. "I said now!"

"Josh, shut up!" Pam shouted. The words were out before she had a chance to stop them. But once out, they needed to be followed up. "I've got this. Step back." She was distantly aware that she was making some great video for the cell phone crowd.

"Look at me, Ethan," she said. "Not at him, at me. He won't hurt you. But do you see how nervous you're mak-ing everyone?" She dared a couple of steps forward, if only to earn the frightened glances that were going to-ward Levine. More sirens approached, and more units marked on the scene. The entire Braddock County Police Department would be in the parking lot soon.

Ethan took two exaggerated steps forward, taking care not to step on the body, and ostentatiously avoid-ing the stream of blood, to stand in the middle of the street. If the Toyota had come by then, he'd have been launched over the hood. He walked with his hands out to the side, cruciform, his finger splayed.

"You're doing great, Ethan," Pam said. "Now, I just need you to—"

Levine rushed him. With the shotgun one-armed into his shoulder, he closed the distance in two or three quick strides. Grabbing the back of the kid's shirt at the collar, he kicked his right foot from underneath him while driving him forward and down. Ethan barely had enough time to get his hands out in front to prevent his face from being smashed into the pavement.

With the kid down, Levine kneeled on the small of his back and pressed the muzzle of the shotgun against the base of the kid's skull. "I've got him!" he announced. He used expert technique to cuff the kid.

Pam's shoulders sagged. She holstered her Glock and approached the two men on the ground. "You didn't have to do that," she said when she was within easy earshot. "I had this under control."

"Yeah, but I have him under arrest," Josh said. "You're not going anywhere," he said to Ethan Falk.

Anger boiled in Pam's gut, but she swallowed it down. The kid had been one hundred percent compliant.

Josh cocked his head. "Are you pissed?"

"You didn't have to hurt him," she said.

"You know he killed a guy, right?"

Pam didn't answer. She helped Ethan to his feet and Mirandized him. She did her best to ignore the citizens who crowded her as she escorted her prisoner to Levine's cruiser, and she didn't acknowledge any of the other officers. It was the damn cameras. She just wanted to be out of their range.

"Watch your head," she said as Ethan lowered his butt into the backseat.

"Detective Hastings?" They were Ethan's first words since he'd been pressed into the pavement.

Pam made eye contact.

"That man kidnapped me when I was eleven years old. You look it up. It was terrible. He was a monster. I'm sorry for what I did, but he was . . . a *monster.*"

Just from his tone, Pam believed him. "Okay," she said. "Make sure you tell your lawyer. And the prosecutor if you decide to talk to him. The FBI will have a record of your rescue, and that will surely help. We'll talk again in a little while—"

"But I wasn't rescued by the FBI," Ethan said.

"Then how did you get away? Did you escape?"

Ethan shook his head. "No, I was rescued, but not by the FBI. I was rescued by a guy named Scorpion."

"Who?"

"That's all I know. His name was Scorpion."

"That's not a name."

"Of course it's not a name. But that's what he called himself. He saved my life."

Chapter Two

The Sleeping Genie Motel seemed to get its own joke. Nestled behind a strip mall in an unincorporated stretch of Route 1 between Woodbridge and Quantico, Virginia, the seedy low-rise 1960s-vintage motor court had a reputation. Let's just say that precious few of the genies in residence did much sleeping, and that the rooms turned over two or three times on a good night.

Jonathan Grave had seen places like this in every military town. The forty-dollars-per-night marquee was a dead giveaway. He'd fail a lie detector if he swore he'd never frequented such a place, but it had been a long, long time—back when most of the promiscuity-related diseases could be cured with penicillin.

"Hey, look, Dig," Boxers said, pointing through the windshield as they cruised into the crumbling parking lot. "The genie wants you. She's winking."

Indeed, the circle of neon that made up the busty sign's left eye had started to wear out, and it looked for all the world like she was flirting. "I'm saving myself for that special genie," Jonathan said.

"Looking like that, she wouldn't have you anyway,"

Boxers said. In deference to the daylight hours, Jonathan had done what he could to change his appearance. His nose was slightly larger than normal, and he sported teeth that gave him an overbite. A specially designed T-shirt gave him a paunch that wasn't real, and he wore a pair of taped-up glasses over his normally blue eyes that were now brown. In general, people overestimated the capabilities of face-recognition software, and nine times out of ten, if police interviewed the people with whom he and Boxers interacted, all they'd remember was the tape on the glasses and sheer size of Boxers, who'd similarly altered his features. In general, Jonathan hated disguises, but sometimes, they were the smart move.

Jonathan waved his hand to the right—at the edge of the lot closest to the highway. "Pull over here while we work things out." He lifted his portable radio from where he'd placed it on the center console and pressed the Transmit button. "Mother Hen, Scorpion," he said.

He knew that Venice Alexander would be monitoring everything from the office in Fisherman's Cove, Virginia, about fifty miles to the south and east of here. She pronounced her name Ven-EE-chay, and she was the person every NSA recruiter would sell his left arm to add to his staff.

"Go ahead."

"Do we have any stronger confirmation on the room number?"

Islamist nutjobs had snatched nine-year-old Mindy Johnson, a congressman's daughter, from the parking lot of a shopping mall north of here in Montgomery County, Maryland, and had declared that any attempts to contact the police would result in her execution. The bad guys wanted $1.3 million in cash to get her back. Her father—Congressman William H. Johnson of Massachusetts—had opted to invest in Jonathan's services instead. Mindy had been visiting her father for the weekend, and had been on her way home from hanging out at a theater in Rockville, where she'd seen a movie with friends.

Apparently Congressman Dad knew neither that she had gone to a movie nor that she hadn't come home. The first he heard of it was when the kidnapper contacted him at work.

Reaching out to Jonathan was a difficult thing to do, what with all the blind e-mails and cutouts that made him nearly impossible to find. The fact that the congressman had been able to do so within the first eight hours of his daughter's kidnapping told Jonathan that the guy had leveraged some inside information. This was not the first time Jonathan had done work for very important people in Washington.

That initial contact with Jonathan had been nearly eighteen hours ago, and in the interim, Jonathan and his team had been working all angles to find the kid. As often was the case, the big break had lain buried in the electronic metadata that piloted e-mails through cyberspace. With that head start, followed by a lot of phone calls and shoe leather, they'd narrowed the options down to this motel. They had everything but the room number.

"Nothing much has changed since we last spoke," Venice said. "I'm ninety percent sure that this is the right place. And if that's the case, then I am eighty percent sure that they're in room one twenty-four."

Jonathan looked to Boxers for an opinion. At six-foot-huge, Boxers, who was born Brian Van de Muelebroecke, was hands-down the largest, most intelligent, and most lethal person Jonathan had ever known. "What say you, Big Guy?" Jonathan asked.

Boxers rumbled out a laugh. "Eighty percent stacked against ninety percent. I can't do that math in my head, but it sounds an awful lot like a guess."

Jonathan agreed. Given the stakes, if only from the firepower they were about to bring to bear, they needed better than that.

"Okay, I copy," Jonathan said into the microphone.

"Does that mean you're about to go hot?" Venice asked.

"I'll let you know when I do," he replied. He looked across the console. "We need more, don't we?"

"You're the boss," Boxers said. "But if I were the boss, I'd want more." Big Guy had a special way with non-deferential deference.

Hostage rescue was a delicate balance of finesse and violence. Methodical research and stunning speed. It left no room for mistakes. Cops could get away with raiding the wrong house and killing the wrong people because they had friendly prosecutors in their corner. Jonathan had friends, but not in those spaces. Besides, he didn't know if he could live with himself if he killed an innocent.

"We need eyes on," Jonathan said.

Boxers eyed him. "We need world peace, too. And let's throw in eternal sunshine. The devil is in the details of getting it."

Jonathan had an idea. "Find me a liquor store."

Boxers laughed again. "Are we going to have a party?"

"Sort of," Jonathan said. Sometimes it was more fun to be cryptic than to be forthcoming. "This is a military town. How far can the nearest booze vendor be?"

"You forget that you're still in the Commonwealth of Virginia." The state ran all of the liquor stores—and had just raised the tax to be paid on top of the sales over which they had a monopoly. Without the worry of competition, the Virginia Alcoholic Beverage Control Board put liquor stores however far apart they wanted, and charged whatever they pleased.

Boxers cruised their recently purchased, old and smelly SUV out of the parking lot, and back down Route 1 in search of the familiar red, white, and blue sign of an ABC Store. This POS vehicle would be dumped when the mission was done, and they would drive back to Fisherman's Cove in the Batmobile—Boxers' name for the heavily customized and armored Hummer that was their real transportation. It never made sense to let security cameras see your getaway car.

The liquor store resided in a strip mall that looked just like every other strip mall on that stretch of highway. "You're really not going to tell me what you're up to, are you?" Boxers asked as he nosed into the space.

"I'm going to make myself stink," Jonathan said, and he let himself out. Inside the store, he chose a pint of cheap bourbon, and paid in cash. Back in the vehicle with Boxers, he said, "Okay, let's go back and see the genie."

"Not until you tell me what you're doing."

Jonathan winked at him. He stripped the cap off of the bottle, pulled his shirt away from his body and poured about half the contents down the front of his chest.

"What the hell?"

"I need to smell like a drunk," Jonathan said.

Big Guy winced and raised a hand to his nose. "Well, that'll do it. Jesus. Why?"

Jonathan explained while they drove back to the Sleeping Genie.

Ethan went through the motions as if in a dream. A nightmare. His bruises had all congealed into a single body ache. Once they had shoved him into the back of the police cruiser in the parking lot, right in front of Raven and so many of his coworkers who had all filed out to see what the commotion was about, they shut the door and left him there for what felt like an hour. He wondered if maybe that was all about setting the humiliation hook as deeply as possible.

He tried to ignore reporters' camera lenses as they were pressed against the window. But he couldn't miss the look that Raven had in her eyes when they locked glances. Her gaze cut him like diamond on glass. It was a look of utter disappointment, of betrayal. She broke the look off after an instant, but for Ethan the damage was done.

So many faces stared at him. The clerks and customers from so many different stores pointed and said things, but he couldn't hear and he told himself that he didn't care. They didn't know him and he didn't know them, so what did they matter? They were no different than the kids that gathered around his schoolyard fights back in the day, just hungry to see the blood of the guy who lost and to cheer the winner. A few regular citizens tried to come in closer for a better look at him, but the police kept them all at bay.

Among the crowd of cops who mingled between Ethan and the onlookers, Ethan could see the monster's feet sticking out between parked cars. No attempt was made to resuscitate him or to take him off to the hospital. Ethan figured that that meant the Earth was finally free of one more child molester. He hoped that that meant his night terrors might go away.

Detective Hastings opened the door of the police cruiser and leaned in. A smear of blood marked her arm. "Your name is Ethan Falk, is that right?"

He nodded.

"Where do you live?"

He told her, and as he watched her read along from his confiscated driver's license, he figured that she was verifying what it said.

"Do you live there alone?"

"No, ma'am. There's a whole other family there. I just rent a room. That's all I can afford."

"Are there weapons in the house?"

"I have no idea. None in my room. Am I really under arrest?"

The question seemed to confuse the detective. "You killed a man," she said. "That's a surefire way to get arrested."

"But it was self-defense. I already told you that."

"I'm not saying it wasn't. But that's not for me to decide. That's for the judge and jury."

"So, I'm going to *jail*?" The realization that should have been so obvious barreled at him.

Hastings smiled, might have even chuckled a little.

"I can't exactly let you just walk away, can I? You already told me that you killed that man. Do you expect me to just look the other way?"

Ethan's heart slammed itself against his chest. "You're arresting me for *murder*?"

Hastings cocked her head. Her eyes showed kindness that he hadn't been expecting. "You know, Ethan, I'm just a cop. I'm not a lawyer and I'm not a priest. That means I'm not in the business of giving advice that people listen to. Having said that, I do have a word of advice in case you're interested."

Ethan felt his shields come up. This was her opportunity to tell him to go to hell. He waited for it.

"If I were you," she said, "I wouldn't say anything to anyone on any subject until I was sitting across the table from my attorney."

"But I don't have an attorney."

"You will," Hastings said.

Oh-three-hundred missions—hostage rescues—presented infinite variations on thousands of variables, all of which posed their own unique dangers. Each of these were directly linked to the fact that people were unpredictable even in the best of times. Once they felt threatened, their unpredictability often rose to the level of frenzy, and frenzied people often did stupid things such as shooting at hostage rescuers in spite of the rescuers' superior firepower and skills.

As a hedge, Jonathan and his team stacked the odds in their favor through the use of advanced weaponry, body armor, high-tech surveillance techniques, and flawless marksmanship. One of their most effective force multipliers was their ability to function in the night as effectively as if it were midday, thanks to night vision technologies. The darkness more often than not disoriented their opposing forces—OpFor—making even talented fighters less effective.

In an operation such as the one that was unfolding at the Sleeping Genie, darkness posed an even greater advantage—that of being invisible to the surrounding general public. Even though Jonathan's team was working at the request of a member of Congress, they had no legal authority to perform any of the operations they undertook. By statute, it was illegal to discharge a firearm in this part of Prince William County, and if those shots killed or injured someone, then Jonathan would have committed a homicide, and it would be left to a jury to decide whether or not the crime was justified. But first the police would have to catch him.

His team always wore gloves on an operation, but as a practical matter it was virtually impossible to eliminate all traces of fingerprints, and with DNA technology being what it was, he couldn't rule out leaving behind a drop of blood or sweat. The good news was that a trace of such typical forensic indicators would lead nowhere. Neither Jonathan nor Boxers existed anywhere in the real world, thanks to efforts by highly placed friends in the government for whom he occasionally did work that for a number of reasons could not afford to be traced back to the officials who'd ordered it.

Long-term survival in Jonathan's world was all about managing the tiny details.

Today, those details were all working against him. While a nine-year-old girl was in the grasp of kidnappers, every second of captivity was an opportunity for serious harm, but the smart call remained to await darkness and the advantages it brought. First, they needed to verify that they had the right place. Once that was done, they could set up surveillance—even deploy a small camera to watch what was going on—and from that develop a scoop-and-swoop plan that would mean the smallest amount of harm to the fewest number of people.

As Boxers drove the rattletrap Ford back toward the Sleeping Genie, he said, "I don't believe I'm about to say this, but if you can verify that she's there, maybe this is one we need to report to the cops and let them handle it."

Jonathan swiveled his head to look at his friend across the center console. "And what would we tell them?"

"Don't look at me like that," Boxers said. "I know the drill. They'll ask questions we can't answer, but we don't have to fill in all the blanks. We can just make an anonymous report and step away."

"That's not what we've been hired to do. If we tell the local cops about this, they're going to check with the FBI. Congressman Johnson seems to think that the bad guys have a source inside the FBI. If the jihadists get word, they'll kill the kid. This is why we get the big bucks."

Boxers drove past the motel, presumably because he wanted to continue talking. "Don't make it sound like I'm trying to pussy out of this," he said. "If the PC is in there, how the hell can we wait till dark to pull her out? But if we try it during the day, the entire world will see what we're up to. That's too dangerous for us."

Big Guy's point was a valid one, but the job was the job. "Tell you what," Jonathan said. "After I scope it out, if I can confirm that Mindy Johnson is inside, then we'll talk. Maybe we can contact the congressman and let him make the call. Tell him the stakes and our limitations, and he can decide."

"What do you think he's going to say? He's going to want us to go in and grab her now."

"We'll just have to tell him that's not how we do things. We'll tell him we have to wait till dark."

Boxers weighed the idea. "You know he won't go for that," he said.

"And that's why we don't ask others for their opinions, and we don't invite LEOs into our operations." LEO stood for law enforcement officer. Jonathan had never intended to call them in, but sometimes it was easier to let Big Guy arrive at his own answers in his own way.

Boxers pulled a legal U-turn at the next light and drove the Ford back toward the Sleeping Genie. "How do you want to handle it?" he asked as they pulled into the lot.

"I'm going to be the drunk looking for his missing girlfriend. When they open the door, I'll see what I can see."

"What if they don't open the door?"

Jonathan flashed a knowing smile. "I really don't think that will be an issue."

Chapter Three

Ethan sat in that damned car for a long time—long enough for his left hand to go numb from the handcuffs. Finally, a uniformed cop slid in behind the wheel, glanced at Ethan in the rearview mirror, and then dropped the transmission into gear and drove off. The fact that the cop never asked him any questions made Ethan wonder if Hastings had shared with the others her advice for him to stay silent.

The ride to the police station was short, maybe ten minutes. The cop drove around to the back, where they waited for a garage door to open. They pulled through, and then waited for the door to come back down before the driver got out, walked around to the back of the cruiser, and opened Ethan's door.

"Come on," he said. "Time to get you processed."

Processed is what you do with sausage, not with people, Ethan thought, but he said nothing. As he shifted position to get out of the vehicle, he realized how full his bladder was. "I need to pee," he said as he swung his legs around to stand up.

"Go ahead," the cop said. "They're not my pants."

He put a hand around Ethan's right biceps and helped him to his feet. "Thanks for the warning, though. Most prisoners aren't that courteous. They just piss on you without notice."

Ethan considered asking the cop for a little help, but as soon as the image formed in his mind of a cop messing with his zipper, he knew it was a stupid idea. As was the idea of letting him out of the cuffs just long enough to do what needed to be done. He'd just have to endure.

Saying nothing, he allowed himself to be led from the garage and into the basement of what he assumed was the local jail. The door through which he passed certainly looked thick enough and heavy enough to be part of a jail. And Ethan knew what he was talking about. This wasn't his first rodeo, after all. The cops would soon find out about his previous history of breaking and entering and his two DUIs. A few abortive attempts at drugs, but the drugs never bent reality enough to be worth the risks. The high wasn't worth the expense. Not when you could buy beer by the quart for a couple of bucks at 7-Eleven.

He'd done this processing thing in each of those cases, but he'd been released on his own recognizance on the B and E, and let go from the DUIs after the mandatory six-hour stint in the drunk tank. The judge had warned him of dire consequences if he didn't straighten up and fly right, and he'd been trying. Really, he had. He even thought maybe his life was back on a normal track.

Until the monster. Until this nightmare. It was all still very new, but looking back on it from the perspective of a couple of hours downrange, he'd have done it again. The monster had to die. *Had* to. Surely these people would understand that.

The heavy door slammed shut. Beige concrete blocks surrounded him on both sides as the cop led him across gleaming white linoleum that reflected and multiplied the glare of overhead fluorescent light. Fisheye cameras on the ceiling watched their every step. The hallway was narrow, and it terminated at another door, as heavy as the first, but this one sported a thick glass window.

"Don't move," the arresting officer said. He stepped away from Ethan to what looked like a bank of safe deposit boxes. The cop punched numbers into an electronic pad and a metal door dropped open. The cop drew his pistol from his holster, slid it into the box, then locked the door with another code.

The cop made eye contact with a guard at a desk on the other side of a heavy glass window, and the door buzzed. The cop pushed it open, and Ethan felt hope evaporate. He sensed that he'd breathed his last breath of fresh air for a very long time.

In that vacuum of hope, he felt the hot urine stream down his right leg. It soaked his socks before it showed through his pants, and it streamed over his shoes. "I'm sorry," he said.

"Don't worry about it," the cop replied. "It happens more than you might imagine. At least you don't have to feel like you're going to explode."

"It's embarrassing."

"It's jail," the cop said. "There's a lot more embarrassment to come. Just try to keep it in perspective."

A man at the end of the hallway sat at another window, reminding Ethan of a receptionist in the ugliest medical practice in the world. He wore the same uniform as the cop who escorted him. The receptionist cop smiled as they approached.

"So, I see we've got a bed-wetter," he said. "I'll make a note for rubber sheets."

"Give him a break, Vince," the cop said. "This is Ethan Allen Falk. We're booking him on a homicide."

"Ah, the big one!" Vince declared with a smile. "Bring him in and sit him down so we can get down to business." The door next to the window buzzed.

"Can I change clothes?" Ethan asked his escort at a whisper.

"Soon enough," the cop said. "Really, don't worry about the little stuff." Ethan glanced at the cop's name tag. He wanted to remember the nice cops. There was Hastings out there in the parking lot, and now this one. His name tag read, Bailey.

The open door revealed an elaborate warren of doors and concrete-block walls. The light in here was dimmer, and there was a lot more noise—the sound of many people at work doing many things. Officer Bailey led Ethan to a long metal bench. "Have a seat," he said. "This will take awhile."

"Nathan, I haven't seen you in what, a week?" Vince said. "You been on vacation?"

"I took the kids to see Mickey down in Florida," Bailey said. "Fifty thousand screaming tourists. I'm back to take a vacation from my vacation."

The small talk went on for twenty minutes as Ethan sat on his bench, crossing and re-crossing his legs as he tried to find a comfortable posture. Nothing seemed to work. By the time he was called up to the tall desk, the bench had filled with five more men in handcuffs. They all looked way tougher than he, and none of them had pissed their pants.

Officer Bailey gripped Ethan's biceps and helped him to his feet. "Sometimes balance is a little hard when you don't have your hands."

"Okay," Officer Vince said, "I know that you're on the record not wanting to answer any questions, and that's fine, but these are just for information's sake. Nothing about the charges against you."

Ethan gave his name (again) and his address (again). No, he didn't have any medical conditions, and no, he was not on any prescriptions. No, he was not addicted to any drugs, and no, he wasn't intoxicated—as if they wouldn't find that out for themselves. And finally, no, he was not experiencing suicidal ideations. He wondered what percentage of the people Vince processed had any idea what that term even meant.

Officer Bailey donned a pair of black latex gloves and Ethan stood still as the cop rummaged through his pockets yet another time. They'd already stripped him of everything out at the scene of the attack, and he didn't wear any jewelry. Bailey unfastened Ethan's belt and pulled it free of the loops. He wrapped the leather strip around his fist to make a loop, and then stuffed the loop into a plastic bag that was then inserted into the other plastic bag that contained his stuff.

Officer Bailey left after that, handing Ethan off to a towering cop whose name tag read Taylor, and who his colleagues called Bob. "Promise me you're not going to be a problem," Officer Taylor said.

Ethan didn't answer because he didn't think the cop needed one. He allowed himself to be led farther down the concrete hallway. Next came the mug shot—full-face and profile—followed by fingerprinting. Ethan was surprised that they did the printing behind his back while he was still cuffed, manipulating his fingers one at a time while instructing him which digits to extend. How big a risk did they think he was?

"You're doing fine, Ethan," Taylor said. They turned left and were buzzed through another door. The room was small, maybe ten by ten feet, and it smelled wet. An industrial-looking Dutch door dominated the left wall, heavy metal, with a panel at the top that swung away from Ethan, exposing bank-teller bars that had a half-moon slot along its lower edge. Another cop stood on the other side. He looked unhappy.

"Remember your promise not to be a problem," Officer Taylor said. He moved behind Ethan and fumbled with the handcuffs. "Just hold still."

Ethan didn't bother mentioning that he had never promised anything, though he had no intention of fighting anyone. As the handcuffs fell away, he brought his hands around to the front and rubbed his wrists. The bracelets had left red grooves in his skin.

"Now we need you to take your clothes off."

Ethan's guts stiffened. "Excuse me?"

"Get naked," said the guy behind the bars.

"Why?"

"Every new guest gets a shower," Taylor said in a light tone. "And then you get your new wardrobe."

"It'll prevent diaper rash," added the cop in the window.

Ethan felt his heart race. He wondered if color had drained from his face. He felt a rush of dizziness.

Take your clothes off and be quick about it.

I don't want to.

I don't care. Don't make me hurt you.

That was *before,* he told himself. That was not now. The monster was not here. The monster was dead. He knew that because he'd witnessed the blood spray.

"Look," said the guy behind the cage. "There's an easy way to do this, and there's a hard way. You can shower and be clean, or you can shower and be bloody. Your choice."

Taylor seemed to sense something. He cocked his head. "You okay?"

Ethan didn't answer. He opened the three buttons at the top of his polo shirt, and pulled it over his head. He dangled it in the air, unsure what to do with it.

The cop at the window tapped the top edge of the lower door. "Right here."

Ethan draped the shirt, and then kicked out of his shoes. Reeboks, the most expensive shoes he'd ever bought, purchased four months ago in celebration of his first real job. He picked those up and placed them on top of the shirt. They were still damp with his piss. He bent at the waist to pull up his pants legs and get at his socks.

"You can sit on the bench if you want," Taylor said.

Sit on the bed if you want. I can help you.

Ethan sat. He took his time, pulling each sock down below his ankle bones before scooping them off his feet one at a time.

"Oh, for Christ's sake, we don't have all day," Window-man said.

Be quick about it.

He unbuttoned his jeans. Unzipped them. Paused.

"We're not going to hurt you, Ethan," Taylor said.

I'll go easy. It won't hurt. I promise.

He lifted his butt from the chair and pulled his legs out of the holes. He folded the pants vertically at the seam, wet leg over dry leg, and then folded them again, and then again, creating a nearly perfect square.

Those tight little underpants, too.

"What?" His head shot to Taylor.

"What what? I didn't say anything. But we need to get on with this."

Ethan hadn't worn tight underwear in eleven years. Not since that day. He stepped out of his soaked boxer shorts, folded them, and placed them on the bench atop the rest of his clothes. He felt tears pressing behind his eyes, and he saw that his hands were shaking.

"Over here." Window-man beckoned Ethan with two fingers.

Naked now, Ethan carried his clothes to the deputy and placed them next to his shirt and his shoes.

"Try not to gain or lose too much weight over the next twenty years," the window cop said with a chuckle. "These are your go-home clothes, too. And holy crap are they gonna stink by then."

Ethan hated the man behind the bars. He was a shit-head bully with a badge. An asshole who sensed weakness in others and preyed upon it. He was a predator.

"This way," Taylor said. He beckoned for the next door. This one was wooden and needed no buzzer to pass through. On the other side, a row of three shower heads protruded from the wall, dripping water onto iron-stained once-green tiles. Taylor gestured to them with an open hand. "There's soap in the dispensers on the wall. I advise you to be thorough. After this, once we transfer you to the Adult Detention Center, you'll be limited to two showers a week."

Ethan hesitated, his hands covering himself. "Are you going to watch?"

"'Fraid I have to. Believe me, there are other things I'd much rather be doing."

Ethan moved hesitantly, haltingly. With his hands still cupping his genitals, he stepped over the two-inch curb that marked the edge of the shower and shivered as his feet hit the ages-old accumulation of water. The water spigots were a knurled wheel-and-spoke design that looked more appropriate to an outdoor hose bib. They were unmarked, but Ethan bet on the standard arrangement of hot on the left. Standing to the side, he cracked the knob, heard a rush of air, and then dodged a formless spray of frigid water that hit him even from his offset of ninety degrees. The chill took his breath away. Five seconds later, the temperature transitioned to scalding. After fifteen or twenty seconds of balancing with the knobs, the spray was tolerable.

Eyes closed, Ethan took his time. He tried to recall the tricks the psychologists had taught him about focusing away from the demons and toward the positive. He needed to find that boat dock in the woods that he'd never actually visited, but that he'd conjured as his place to retreat mentally. If he could make it to the dock, the bad thoughts could be kept at bay.

It had worked so well then. But back at that point, after he'd been rescued and returned, the reality of his life was indeed safe. Now, he was back in the hands of—

"Okay, that's enough," Taylor said. "Rinse off and let's get going."

Ethan leaned forward into the wall, into the spigots, and let the water flood for just a few more seconds over his face and hair. Down his back. Then he shut the water off.

Keeping his back turned to the deputy, he said, "Where is my towel?"

"That comes in another two minutes. Turn around and look at me, please."

Covering himself again, Ethan turned. Taylor had donned a pair of blue rubber gloves.

It won't hurt. Just imagine you're at the doctor's.

Ethan's heart rate doubled. "No," he said.

"It's procedure," Taylor said. "Nobody enjoys the cavity search, but—"

It did hurt. Oh, my God, it hurt so bad. And the monster laughed as Ethan yelled.

"No!" Ethan shouted it this time.

Taylor seemed startled. "Come on, Ethan, don't—"

—make this any harder than it needs to be.

The color in the room changed in Ethan's head. Reality transformed into something unreal—unrooted. He knew it was impossible, but he was eleven years old again. But now he was big. Now he could defend himself.

He launched himself at the cop. Not the shithead predator cop, but the nice one. The one named Taylor. Like Andy Taylor from Mayberry, the show that played without end on TV Land. The deputy was taller by a head, but Ethan knew a trick to make up the difference. As he lunged forward, he tucked his chin just a little and then on contact, thrust his head up under the deputy's jaw. He heard a snap, and he heard someone yell. It might have been Ethan's own howling, but he couldn't be sure.

They were on the wet floor now, bare skin against leather and hardware. Ethan threw punches and he received them, but he didn't feel anything. This was *not* going to happen to him again.

The space around him reverberated with noise and he saw more shoes and he felt more hands. He swung at as many of them as he could. His guts exploded as someone landed a kick, and then he saw the stick coming.

Darkness.

Chapter Four

"**W**here do you want me?" Boxers asked.

Jonathan pointed ahead and to the right. "Take the red-black corner." The right rear corner. "I don't expect they'll run away from a knock at the door, but we might as well be prepared."

"Just sidearms, I presume?"

"And keep it concealed. Like I said, I don't anticipate a panic response from a knock at the door."

Boxers backed into a parking space across the lot from room 124, threw the transmission into Park, and sat, his massive hands poised at ten and two on the steering wheel. "This doesn't feel right, Boss."

Jonathan pulled on the door handle. "Let's see what happens."

Playing drunk was a tricky thing. The staggering, slurring caricature drunk wouldn't fool anyone. In fact, the average drunk tried very hard *not* to look drunk when he was at his drunkest, which was a doubly difficult act to pull off when the person trying to look sober was in fact sober, trying to look sober while drunk. It was about understatement, and the stink of booze should go a long way toward selling the bluff. If room 124 was indeed the right place, then alcohol would be against the occupants' religion, triggering an even greater level of disgust.

Jonathan's plan was simple. He would knock on the door, and when someone answered, he'd eyeball them to see if they matched the description of the kidnappers. He'd apologize for the interruption, and then evaluate the options to rescue the little girl. Boxers monitored the action from the shadows of the building's right rear corner, where he could simultaneously see if anyone bolted out the back, while keeping an eye on Jonathan.

"Is everybody on the channel?" Jonathan asked softly as he approached the door.

"Big Guy's here," Boxers said.

"And Mother Hen." Venice monitored most of their ops when they went hot. Sometimes, Jonathan wore a body cam to give her a more complete view, but there was no place to hide it on this disguise.

"Here we go," Jonathan said. He settled his shoulders and sagged his knees a little. He let his eyelids droop just a bit, and then rapped on the door with the knuckle of his left middle finger.

He heard motion on the other side. Multiple voices. It took nearly ten seconds for one voice to say what is normally said immediately. "Who is it?"

Jonathan said nothing. Noting the motion of the curtains as someone peeked out, he knocked again.

More motion, more voices. They sounded angsty.

Jonathan whispered, "I think you might be getting some business after all, Big Guy."

"You're making my nipples hard," Boxers replied.

Jonathan smiled and kept knocking. Not hard—not

a search-warrant pound—just a steady, annoying-as-hell thump with his knuckle. The whole point was to get them to open the damn door.

"Go away!" a voice said. It carried an accent, but these days, in this neighborhood, unaccented English was more the exception than the rule.

He heard a little yip—maybe squeak was a better term. Was it a little girl being hurt?

Jonathan kept knocking.

Finally, he heard the chain move on the back of the door, and the knob turned. The door cracked a few inches, enough to reveal a man's left eye. It looked like a pissed-off left eye. "I said go away!"

"Dude!" Jonathan said. He wedged his body closer to the door. "Whatcha doin' in there? This is the party room, right?" He pushed on the door, opening it just enough to see the shadow of a second man wedged behind the door panel. He was hiding. In the mirror on the wall over the dresser, Jonathan saw a seam of light around the closed bathroom door. That made at least three targets. And the one he could see looked Middle Eastern. Check, check, and check.

"There is no party here," the man at the door insisted. "You need to leave."

When Jonathan saw what appeared to be blood on the floor, he decided it was time to call an audible. "Dude, look, I'm sorry, man. Can I just use your pisser?" He pressed in tighter.

The doorman pressed his hand to Jonathan's chest. "No, you may not. You are drunk. You do not belong—"

"Hey, Mindy, are you there?" Jonathan shouted.

The doorman's eyes flashed fear as commotion rose behind the closed bathroom door. The doorman's hand whipped around to the back of his trousers. It was all the confession Jonathan needed.

Jonathan shouldered the door hard and drove the heel of his left hand into the other man's nose. Knocked off balance, the guy staggered back three steps. Jonathan hammered the door again, harder this time, to unbalance the guy in the shadow. In one smooth, practiced move, he lifted his T-shirt with his left hand, pulled his 1911 from its holster, and thumbed the safety off.

The man he'd driven back into the room recovered enough to draw a pistol, and had nearly brought it to bear when Jonathan fired two one-handed shots into the gunman's chest. The guy was still collapsing when Jonathan pivoted left to encounter the hider behind the door. He never saw the man's face, but he saw the gun in the man's hand. A pistol-grip pump shotgun with a shortened barrel. Jonathan fired three times into the shadow's center of mass, and both the weapon and its owner fell like bricks.

When Jonathan turned back to the first guy, he saw that he still sat upright, bleeding from his chest, his face a mask of confusion. Jonathan shot the mask through the eye.

"Mindy, are you in the bathroom?" As he spoke, he pulled a fresh mag for the Colt out of its pouch on the left side of his belt, and brought it up the pistol's grip.

"Help! I—" The young voice was silenced by a slap.

He dropped the partially spent mag into the space between the middle and ring fingers of his left hand and jammed the new one home. The whole maneuver took less than two seconds. He dropped the mostly empty mag into his pocket. Never enter a new gunfight with old ammo.

Jonathan fired a kick that landed square on the bathroom door's flimsy brass-colored knob.

The panel exploded inward, launching a shower of splintered mirror.

Mindy screamed. Her kidnapper held her by her flaming red hair, lifting her off her feet as he cowered behind, trying to get a bead on Jonathan. Black zip ties bound Mindy's hands in front of her. Motel bathrooms were not big spaces, and old shitty ones were even smaller. At a range of maybe three feet, the worst marksmen in the world would have a hard time missing.

Jonathan went for the gun. It was a Glock—either a 19 or a 23. He grabbed the weapon at the slide, behind the front sight, and he twisted it inward and up. If it fired, it wouldn't hit anyone. As the kidnapper's finger snapped inside the trigger guard, the guy lost his concentration on Mindy's hair. As she moved, she opened a space that revealed the bad guy's face. Jonathan thrust his Colt through the opening till he felt hard contact with the guy's forehead, and he pulled the trigger, opening a star-shaped hole in flesh and bone. The kidnapper left a crimson arc on the shattered green tile wall as he slid sideways into the bathtub, pulling the shower curtain and rod with him.

"We're clear," Jonathan said, holstering his Colt. "Three sleeping. PC is secure."

"Holy shit, Scorpion, what did you just do?" Boxers nearly shouted. The cadence of his words told Jonathan that Big Guy was running.

Without saying a word, Jonathan grabbed Mindy

around the middle and lifted her off her feet. She struggled. "Leave me alone!" she yelled. "Let me go!" She swung her bound fists as a single unit, as if chopping wood.

Jonathan used a second arm to pinion her hands to her side. "Don't look at the bodies," he said, as he maneuvered her out of the bathroom. "I'm here to take you back to your parents."

"Put me down!"

She'd been through a lot. Jonathan didn't expect her to understand what was going on, and this was no time to go into detail. He just gripped her tighter and hustled across the parking lot toward the Ford. He carried her sideways to avoid getting kicked by her pedaling feet, and was a little ashamed at how quickly his grip had begun to slip. Apparently, kids are born with a wriggle instinct, and young Mindy was particularly gifted. He picked up his pace.

Boxers was already in the cab and cranking the engine when Jonathan was still twenty feet away. Reading the situation for what it was, Big Guy swung back out of the vehicle and opened the back door on the driver's side. Jonathan ducked his head, stepped high, and sort of leaped onto the back bench seat, while at the same time turning to keep from landing atop the squirming little girl. Knowing that a door slam was coming, he tucked his knees up to prevent losing his feet at the ankles.

Five seconds later, they were on their way.

"Leave me alone! Let go of me!"

Boxers shouted, "Hey! Mindy, shut up! We just saved your life! Show some respect!" When Big Guy wanted to be loud, he could be seismic. They were harsh words, but they worked. Mindy fell silent, and even Jonathan felt a little stunned.

He unwrapped his arms from around the PC and helped her sit up straight. "Are you hurt?"

"They hit me," she said. Some of the wind had left her sails, but she was still spun tight. Clotted blood mixed with her red hair.

"Well, they can't hit you anymore," Jonathan said.

"You killed those men."

"Yes, I did. They'll never hurt anyone ever again."

"I didn't ask you to do that."

Jonathan didn't know how to read the emotion in her words, and he didn't much try. At this point in a mission, his job was simple. He needed to return the precious cargo to her family and move on. He was not a counselor and he was not a soother of souls. In his experience, those who were so drawn were born with a radically different skill set than his.

"I didn't ask you to do that," Mindy repeated.

"I heard you the first time," Jonathan said. "But it's done anyway. Here, let me see your hands. I'll take those ties off." As he spoke, he lifted out the three-inch folding blade that was clipped to the pocket of his jeans and opened it with a one-handed flourish.

The suddenness startled Mindy. She retreated from him.

"I'm not going to hurt you," Jonathan said. "I'm just going to cut the plastic away."

"Stay away from me."

Jonathan sighed. "Fine." He folded the knife and put it back in his pocket.

"Who are you? You're not the police."

"That is true," Jonathan said with what he hoped was a friendly smile. "We are definitely not the police. But we are on your side. We came here just to save you."

"Why?"

"Because we're the good guys," Jonathan said. She didn't need to know anything about his business arrangement with her father, and she didn't need to know anything about his operations. These were the times when he most missed his days with the Unit, doing the official bidding of Uncle Sam. Back then, the Army psychologists would take care of the emotional damage, and all he had to concentrate on was the physical stuff.

Right now, their biggest concern was to get rid of this vehicle and transfer over to the Batmobile. All the screaming and shooting almost certainly attracted attention, and if anyone saw them hustling Mindy into the backseat of the Ford, they would conclude that Jonathan and Boxers were the bad guys. So far, he heard no sirens or indicators that word of the shoot-out had made it to the authorities, but any delay would buy him only minutes.

They'd stashed the Batmobile in the bay of a body shop owned by Marcus Glenning, a former MARSOC operator who'd lost a leg in Afghanistan and retired on disability to pursue his passion for cars in the community of residents who would most appreciate his sacrifice. Marcus and Jonathan had crossed paths a few times back in the day, and Marcus was willing to do his old friend a favor without asking too many questions. Within an hour of trading the Ford for the Hummer, the Explorer would be a pile of parts awaiting resale.

Jonathan pressed his transmit button. "Mother Hen, Scorpion. Call the hammer man and tell him we're two minutes out."

"Calling now," Venice said.

Jonathan turned to his precious cargo. "Mindy, I need you to listen to me. I need you to trust me. Your father sent my friend and me to rescue you from those bad men—the ones who hit you and tied your hands. Can I cut that band off your wrist now?"

She held her hands out. He opened his knife again and carefully slid the razor-sharp blade under the plastic band, near her thumbs, and sliced it away. The deep red lines in her skin angered him. Mindy pulled her hands back and rubbed her wrists.

Jonathan continued, "In a few minutes, we're going to pull into a garage and we're all going to transfer to another truck. That's the truck we're going to use to take you home."

"How do I know I can believe you?"

"I don't know how to answer that. Let's start with the fact that I killed the men who hurt you. That's got to buy me something." He smiled, showing off his fake buck teeth. "I need you to cooperate with the transfer, okay? No more kicking and screaming, no trying to run away. We're still in danger, and need to move quickly. Will you do that for me?"

"Are you going to kill anybody else?"

Jonathan scowled. It was an odd question. "I hope not. I'll certainly try not to." From the way she pulled back, he saw that it was not the right answer. "Let me put it this way. The only way I would kill anyone else would be to protect you from harm."

Something clicked behind her eyes. "So, you're, like, my bodyguards?"

He winked. "We are exactly like your bodyguards."

"Promise you're telling the truth?"

He drew an X across his chest with his finger. "Cross my heart."

Mindy thought some more, then nodded. "Okay, then. I'll trust you."

Jonathan bladed his hand and held it out. "Let's shake on it."

She smiled as she took his hand and shook it.

"Great," Jonathan said. "Now, one more thing. Don't talk to anyone other than Big Guy and me. There might be people in the garage, and I don't want you getting involved in conversations."

Her eyes grew larger. Jonathan took that as a yes.

"Hey, Boss," Big Guy said from the front seat. "We're here."

They pulled around to the back of the body shop, where Marcus Glenning had left two bay doors open. The one on the right was empty, and the nose of the Batmobile peeked out of the one on the left. Jonathan wasn't sure what Glenning had done with his employees—or with himself, for that matter—but the place was devoid of people. Boxers slipped the Ford through the opening and pulled to a stop.

"Okay, Mindy, here we go," Jonathan said. He opened the door on the driver's side and Mindy slipped out right after him. Ten seconds later, they were inside the rolling fortress. Ten seconds after that, Boxers cranked the engine and they were on their way.

"Score another one for the good guys," Boxers said.

They drove north and west for over an hour to a roadside

rest stop near the foothills of the Blue Ridge Mountains. Mindy said nothing along the way, and Jonathan made no effort to get her to talk. She'd seen a lot and endured a lot, and the fact that she was safe now—a fact that she likely did not believe one hundred percent—wouldn't do much to diminish the nightmares that lay in her future.

Big Guy pulled into one of the regular slots and threw the transmission into Park. Only one other car sat in the lot.

"We're almost done, Mindy," Jonathan said. "I'm going to introduce you to one more person, and that person is going to take you to your parents. Are you ready?"

Mindy stared at the back of the seat in front of her. If she'd heard him, she made no indication.

"Mindy?"

"I heard you." She turned her head to face him. "Why is this happening to me?"

Jonathan recognized his cue to say something wise and soothing. If only he owned those words. "You know what, Mindy?" he said with a sigh. "There are a lot of bad people in the world. You just happened to cross paths with them. Sometimes, there is no why."

Her eyes filled with tears. "You *killed* those men."

Jonathan let the words hang. Then he opened his door. "Come on," he said. "I'm going to introduce you to one of the nicest men in the world, and he'll be much better at answering your questions." As he spoke, one of Jonathan's oldest and dearest friends unfolded himself from a slightly worse-for-wear Kia sedan and walked toward the Batmobile. The man wore a black suit, a clerical collar, and a big, kind smile. His name was Father Dom D'Angelo.

Jonathan stepped down out of the Hummer and turned to help Mindy do the same. She looked frightened again. "Mindy, this is Father O'Malley, a man I've known since I was in college."

With a trim build, thick black hair, and dark brown eyes, Dom looked like an Italian movie star. He stooped to get eye-to-eye with the little girl. He didn't reach out a hand, and he kept his distance. In addition to his role as a priest and pastor of Saint Katherine's Church in Fisherman's Cove, he was also a licensed psychologist. Jonathan figured that the distance he kept had something to do with the psychologist part.

"Hello, Mindy," Dom said. "I know you've had a really rough few days. Are you ready to go home?"

Mindy looked up to Jonathan. "I thought *you* were going to take me home."

Jonathan stooped down, too. "That's not something I can do," he said. "That's for Father O'Malley to do."

"Is it because you killed those men?"

Jonathan glanced to Dom, who arched his eyebrows. *You're on your own.*

Jonathan said, "Sort of. Besides, Father O is a much nicer man." He sold it with a smile.

Without warning, Mindy threw her arms around Jonathan's neck and hugged him. "I want you to take me."

Jonathan was stunned—both by the suddenness of her move and by the pressure he felt behind his eyes. He returned the hug. "You're safe now, sweetie, I promise," he said. He kissed the top of her head and eased her away. "Do you think for a minute that I would put you in the care of someone I didn't trust?"

"Please?" Her lip trembled.

"I can't," Jonathan said.

"Hey, Mindy," Dom said, rising to his full height. "Time to say good-bye to Scorpion and say hello again to your parents. We're only about an hour away."

Jonathan stood, too, and turned away. It made no sense to prolong the inevitable. Besides, if he ended up shedding a tear, Boxers would never let him hear the end of it.

Chapter Five

Of all the Northern Virginia police jurisdictions, defense attorney German P. Culligan respected Braddock County the most. Of all the prosecutors, however, theirs resided on the bottom of the list. J. Daniel Petrelli could not stand in front of enough television cameras, couldn't spout enough crush-the-criminals rhetoric, and couldn't play hardball any more aggressively in the courtroom. Elected in the standard four-year voting cycle, he'd wormed his way into office six times now.

Combined with the limp-wristed board of supervisors that governed the county, Petrelli had begun to think of himself in somewhat Caesarean terms, consistently filing the toughest charges against even minor infractions. The assistant Commonwealth's attorneys who worked for him were well aware that the sole path to promotion lay in being equally intractable. It all played so well with the voters.

It didn't, however, play very well with the police department. The chief, Warren Michaels, famously despised J. Daniel, and he encouraged his police officers to serve as a kind of Petrelli antidote, at least to the extent that they could. That cooperative attitude often inured to benefit German Culligan and his clients. He was hoping that would be the case today. The court had appointed him to represent a crazy kid named Ethan Falk, who'd apparently attacked a man without reason and stabbed him with a carving knife. Fifteen times.

The uniformed cop in the greeting window smiled as he approached. "Good afternoon, Counselor," she said.

"Hello, Gloria. You're looking well as always. I have appointment with Lieutenant Hackner and a Detective Pam Hastings."

Gloria buzzed the security door. Culligan walked through it and into the hallway that led to the department's administrative offices. Five years ago, the police department had relocated from its dingy digs near the old courthouse into this brightly lit cube farm. Lots of blues and greens gave Culligan the feel that the county had spent a dollar or two on an industrial psychologist to design the décor, and he was certain that in ten years that same décor would make the place look dated as hell.

"Just wait in the conference room, Mr. Culligan," Gloria said, but he was already on his way. He waited in the same conference room every time he visited. On the way, he stopped at the communal coffeepot and helped himself to a cup. Two sugars, and a teaspoon of the white poison that they called creamer. Then he headed to the fishbowl that was the conference room.

The detective and her lieutenant arrived together after about five minutes. Culligan had known Jed Hackner for years, but Detective Hastings was a new face to him. Tallish and blondish, she looked a little like a cheerleader poured into a pantsuit. He sensed that she knew that, thus explaining the hard set of her mouth and the stiffness of her bearing. Overcompensation.

After the obligatory dance of introductions, they got down to business. "How did you get this dog of a case, German?" Hackner asked.

"Beats me. The judge spins the Rolodex and my card pops to the top." As a sole practitioner, Culligan looked to court appointments the way senior citizens look at a Social Security check: Not really enough to live on, but a reliable source of cash. "How big a dog is it?"

Hackner deferred to Pam Hastings. "We've got at least two dozen eyewitnesses who saw Ethan Falk race out of a coffee shop, tackle a man in the parking lot, and stab him fifteen times."

"Don't forget about the confession," Hackner prompted.

Pam chuckled. "Oh, yeah. And he confessed to the whole thing."

Culligan couldn't keep himself from smiling. "I presume you jumped through all the proper hoops?"

"Mirandized him and everything," Pam said. "Twice, actually. Once when it was just the two of us, and then a second time in front of a witness."

Culligan took a note, not that there was much to forget. "When I meet with Mr. . . ."

"Falk." The cops said it together.

"When I meet with Mr. Falk, I'm not going to see a lot of bruising from where you beat the confession out of him?" He'd meant the statement as a joke, an allusion to the growing media-driven zeitgeist that badge-bearers were bad guys, but what he saw in their faces gave him pause. "What?"

"He attacked one of the officers downstairs as they were processing him," Hackner said. "It got pretty violent. It took more than a couple of stick-hits to get him to settle down."

"Bones broken?"

Hackner said, "Not that we know of."

"Has he seen a doctor?"

"He refused," Pam said.

"But you offered medical treatment?"

"He refused," she repeated. "We can show you the security tapes if you want."

Culligan shook his head. "Maybe in time." Culligan never saw the prosecution team as enemies. Adversaries in the courtroom, sure, but at least in Braddock County, everyone pulled on the same oar in favor of justice. Even J. Daniel Petrelli, though his version of justice always came with a harsh spin and five exclamation points.

"When he confessed, did he tell you why he attacked the guy?"

"Some bullshit story about a kidnapping when he was eleven years old," Hackner said.

Culligan's head snapped up. "I'm sorry, how old did you say Ethan is?"

"Twenty-three."

"I don't understand. Did the victim—what's his name?"

"We don't know," Hackner said. "John Doe for now."

"Did Mr. Doe just get out of prison or something? Was there a vendetta against him?"

"Not that we know of."

Culligan put his pen down and shifted in his seat.

"Please don't be difficult. Why did Ethan allegedly kill a man twelve years after he was kidnapped?"

"The suspect just had a birthday," Hackner clarified. "So, it was closer to eleven years ago, or so he claims. That's the bullshit part. There never was a kidnapping."

"He made it up?"

"It's not a complicated thing to look up kidnappings," Hackner said. "He gave us a date and a place, and we checked both local and federal records, and there's nothing there."

"Why would he make something like that up?" Culligan asked. It made no sense.

Hackner rolled his eyes. "Maybe when you look down at yourself and you see your hands and legs covered in someone else's blood, you feel the urge to make up a quick story. How the hell should I know?"

Culligan looked to Pam, whose eyes were somewhere other than the conversation. "Is that what my client told you at the time of his arrest?" he asked. "That he was kidnapped?" If he didn't have as solid a relationship with Hackner as he did, the lieutenant might have taken offense at being second-guessed. As it was, Hackner looked away. "Detective Hastings?"

She scowled as she inhaled deeply through her nose. "That is what he told me."

"But?" There seemed clearly to be more.

"It was the *way* he told me," she said. "He seemed genuinely flabbergasted to be put under arrest. Like killing the John Doe was the most obvious thing in the world."

Culligan scratched the back of his head. It seemed

that every new answer deepened his sense of confusion. "What are you telling me?" he asked. "Or maybe
what are you *not* telling me is the better question. I'm
kind of lost here."

"I'm telling you that I believe him."

Culligan looked to Hackner. "You said no such kidnapping ever happened."

"Let me restate it then," Pam said. "I think that
Ethan Falk really *believes* it happened."

"Just as he might *believe* that he's Santa Claus,"
Hackner said. "Believing doesn't make it true."

Pam wouldn't back down. "You asked."

"Because I need to know."

"He could be delusional, of course," Pam said. She
seemed to be arguing with herself. "That'll take a
shrink to figure out. But I saw the raw emotion in the
heat of the moment, and I'll bet everything that if you
could climb into his head and look around, you'll see
pictures that are scary as hell."

Culligan looked over to Hackner, and then back to
Pam. "Okay, then. Anything else I need to know?"

"Nope," Hackner said, and he stood. The meeting
was over.

Ethan Falk did not look like a murderer. In Culligan's experience, only sixty percent of criminals had
the criminal look about them—a much lower number
than it used to be, now that tattoo sleeves were no longer
the markers solely of prisoners and gangbangers—but
precious few had the look of innocence that this kid
projected. He was terrified. And with good reason.

Blood still seeped through the bandage on his cheek, and Culligan had seen raccoons with lighter coon's eyes than Ethan.

"I don't belong here," Ethan said after the introductions were finished. The guards had refused the attorney's request to remove the shackles that held the kid's hands to the chain around his waist.

"You killed a guy," Culligan said. "He wasn't shooting at you, and he wasn't actually kidnapping you, your story notwithstanding."

"But he—"

Culligan silenced him with a raised hand. "Nope, not yet," he said. "I've heard what you told the police when you were arrested. What part of 'you have a right to remain silent' and 'anything you say can and will be used against you in court' confused you?"

"I needed to make them understand—"

"No, you didn't." Culligan wasn't trying to be mean, but he needed to get his client to understand that admitting to a murder was not a trivial thing. "From this point forward, up until the day you step into a courtroom, everything that transpires will be driven by perceived facts. Right now, there's a growing list of witnesses who saw you charge out of a coffee shop, tackle a guy who's smaller than you, and then stab him about a million times. Are you following me so far?"

Ethan's head twitched a noncommittal yes.

"I prefer verbal responses," Culligan said.

"Yes, I'm following you."

"Excellent. Thanks to the legions of eyewitnesses, your confession doesn't do as much harm as it otherwise might have. But quit telling yourself that you don't belong in jail. For now, here's exactly where you belong. What you need to consider—the thought that needs to consume your heart and soul—is whether you ought to die by lethal injection. Or worse, in my personal opinion, whether you deserve to spend the rest of your life in prison."

Ethan blanched—all but his eyes, which remained just as purple and bruised as they were before.

Culligan pressed on. "From this point forward, you have no friends in this place—except for me and one other, but I'll get to her in a minute. Say as little as you can to as few people as possible when you're in here. There are some biker dudes in this place who could eat you whole in one bite and not even burp. You don't talk to them because they're sensitive to nuances that haven't even occurred to you."

"I've been in jail before," Ethan said somewhat defiantly.

"Have you, now. And is that a point of pride? I've seen your jacket, Ethan, and no, you haven't. The drunk tank ain't what we in the business call real jail. You're not getting out of here tomorrow, and you're not getting out of here in a month. If everything goes right and with the gods smiling upon us, you might get out of here in twelve to *fourteen* months. That's a long time to live with anybody, but when your roomies are mean sons of bitches who could kill you without breaking a sweat, the time gets particularly long."

Ethan's jaw set as a swell of anger returned color to his face.

"I'm not done yet," Culligan said, sensing that the kid was about to say something. "That's why you don't talk to other inmates unless you have to. And in not talking to them, find a way to show respect. Don't know what to tell you specifically on that one, but you'll be happy if you figure it out. The other people you don't talk to is anyone in a uniform. I'll say it again. *Anyone in a uniform.* Good morning, please, and thank you are fine, but 'have a good day' crosses the line. Everything you say and do in this place is on the record. It's watched and it's recorded. Whatever you confide and whoever you confide it to are all admissible in court."

Concern returned to Ethan's face. "Not this, right?"

"No, not this. Attorney-client privilege is still the rule. What you tell your psychologist is also protected."

Confusion. "I don't have a psychologist anymore."

"Might not have been a bad continuing investment," Culligan said. He tried selling the line with a smile, but it was too little too late. "Anyway, you're going to."

"I don't want one."

"Oh, yes, you do. Her name is Wendy Adams, and you're going to tell her everything. Even stuff you don't want to tell me, you want to tell her."

"Why?"

"Because from where I sit, you being a little touched in the head is the most viable strategy to get you sprung before you're eighty."

"Not guilty by reason of insanity?"

Culligan weighed his answer. "I'm not sure if that's what the exact wording would be, but that's the general theme, yes."

"So, I'll spend the rest of my life with the world thinking I'm crazy?"

"Baby steps, Ethan. Consider the relative merits of people thinking you're a bit psycho as opposed to being convinced that you're a murderer."

"But I'm not crazy."

"And you say you're not a murderer, either." Culligan sensed that the conversation was turning darker than he wanted it to, so he waved the topic away as if shooing a fly. "Put all of that on a back burner. All of those considerations are for later. Wendy will be visiting you in the next couple of days. Just promise me you'll talk to her."

"I can't afford to pay her."

"Don't worry about that. She's done pro bono work for me before, and she'll do it for me again. Won't cost you a penny."

Ethan scowled. "Why would someone do that for me?"

Culligan matched the angle of the kid's head exactly. "Well, if it's important, and you really need to know, she won't do it for you. She'll do it for me."

"Why?"

Culligan waited for it.

"Oh. You two are . . . friends."

Culligan let it go. "So, are we good? You'll talk with Doctor Wendy when she shows up?"

A shrug, the ultimate gesture of noncommitment. "Sure."

"Good. One last thing. The Commonwealth is likely to send a shrink of their own to evaluate you. Don't know who it's going to be, but whoever it is, they'll give you some line about being on your side, and about being off the record, but don't believe it."

"The cops can lie to me in here and it'll stand up in court?"

"Absolutely," Culligan said. "Cops, guards, lawyers, psychologists, every one of them can lie, and everything you say will still be held against you." He felt a pang of guilt and backed up a little. "Well, okay, the prosecution's psychologist won't reveal the specific things you say, but what they will do is report to the court whether or not, in their professional opinion, you are competent to stand trial." He leaned in closer. "Hint: Everybody is always competent to stand trial in their eyes. And then that shrink will work with the prosecution on ways to counter everything and anything we try to put together for your defense."

"So, what am I supposed to say?"

"You answer the questions that anyone else would answer, but if the shrink starts sniffing around the details of your past, or the kidnapping you allege, I need you to lock up and tell them you want to see your lawyer before you answer any questions."

"And they'll do that?"

"Yes. Well, they might sniff around your answer a couple of times, but once you invoke your right to speak to your lawyer, they'll stop."

"But you said they can lie."

"Not about this." Culligan smiled. "Yeah, I know," he said. "It gets confusing."

Jonathan Grave loved his office atop the converted firehouse in Fisherman's Cove, Virginia. Featuring dark woods and leather furniture, it had the feel and the look of a gentlemen's club. The windows looked out on the marina, where the masts of pleasure boats seemed to be engaged in a slow-motion sword fight. Down to the right, maybe four blocks from the front door, crews of commercial fishing vessels and dock workers toiled to keep the residents of Virginia's Northern Neck—and parts beyond—stocked with seafood. Jonathan wished sometimes that he was more of a boat person than he was. It seemed wasteful to possess such a view yet enjoy so little of the activities. He found peace in the rhythms of the waves and the masts and in the foreverness of the horizon.

Much as he enjoyed the view of the world through the windows behind him, he desperately hated the view of the piles of papers that cluttered his desk. As president of Security Solutions, a major player in the world of high-end private investigations, he had to stay at least reasonably versed in various ongoing investigations, and he most certainly had to sign all the checks, though even that was something of a formality.

While most of the administrative matters were handled by Venice Alexander, and most of the standard investigatory issues were expertly managed by Gail Bonneville—his one-time nemesis and subsequent lover (until they broke up—no awkwardness there!)—Jonathan had learned from his father a long time ago that one should never cede control of one's money to a third party. It was one thing to write the checks—any bookkeeper could do that—but it was something else entirely to sign them. He kept that duty for himself.

And there were *a lot* of checks to be signed. Between the 0300 mission to rescue the Johnson girl, and an op right before that to separate a Mexican banker from some mean-spirited drug lords, he'd been away from the office for ten days, and he was shocked by the speed with which administrivia could stack up. The good news was that Venice and Gail both had arranged their respective stacks of paper more or less in the order of their importance.

Security Solutions was in every sense a legitimate private investigation firm, providing confidential services to some of the world's most recognizable companies, none of which knew anything about the covert side of the business which interested Jonathan infinitely more. The firm's name was not well-known to the private investigations industry, but it was known among the quarters where it mattered. Security Solutions specialized in obtaining the most sensitive kinds of information through means that were always successful and rarely discussed. That meant the kinds of fees that allowed him to pay his employees very, very well.

Jonathan's office resided in a corner suite that he called The Cave. He shared the space with Venice and Boxers, the latter of whom rarely spent much time in the office. Of everyone on the payroll, Boxers was the most . . . action-oriented.

A light rapping on his open office door pulled his eyes from his papers, happy for some relief. Venice stood in the doorway with Dom D'Angelo. "Have you got a minute?" Venice asked.

He didn't like the expression on her face. "What's wrong?"

"We need to talk," Dom said.

"Uh-oh." Jonathan had known Venice since he was a teenager and she was a little girl with a crush. Her mother—Mama Alexander—had officially been Jonathan's family housekeeper, but in reality became Jonathan's surrogate mother after his own mom died when he was very young. He'd known Venice long enough to translate her facial expressions into emotions, and she was upset. Dom had been Jonathan's roommate through college, and close friend ever since.

They started for the guest chairs in front of his desk, but he stood and diverted them to the conversation group in front of the fireplace. "Let's get comfortable," he said. "My back's beginning to ache anyway." That's what happened when you spent a career jumping out of perfectly good airplanes. His chair of choice was a wooden Hitchcock rocker marked with the Seal of the College of William and Mary in Virginia, his and Dom's alma mater. He swung it around a few degrees so he could face them as they sat next to each other on the green leather love seat.

"Who died?" Jonathan asked. Sometimes, the quickest, most merciful way to the point was to steal the punchline.

They seemed startled. "No one," Venice said. "It's not like that."

"Well, sort of," Dom corrected. As was his habit when off duty, Dom wore a regular collared shirt and jeans.

"Someone is sort of dead?"

"I mean that's not the point," Venice said.

"Then how 'bout you get to the point," Jonathan said.

"Do you remember Ethan Falk?" Venice asked.

Jonathan looked to Dom and scowled. "Why does that name ring such a loud bell?"

"He was the precious cargo on a rescue mission about ten, eleven years ago."

Jonathan winced, feeling busted. He'd made it a

point over the years not to think much about the people he rescued. They were all just PCs—precious cargo— the points of the missions for which he would risk his life. To get too close was to lose perspective, and getting distracted was the surest way to come home dead.

"James Stepahin," Dom said.

And that did it. Jonathan rarely forgot a bad guy. "Kid-toucher, right? Sold boys into slavery?"

"That's the guy," Dom confirmed.

"And Ethan was the PC we snatched."

"Exactly."

"Okay. What about him?"

"James Stepahin was killed yesterday," Venice explained.

"Good," Jonathan said. The details of the operation were coming back to him. "He and his buddies were sick sons of bitches. I think we toasted one of them and one got away. That was Stepahin, right?"

"Three were killed and one got away," Venice corrected. Jonathan admired that she had just pulled that detail from memory.

"So, why the long faces? Where's the champagne?" Jonathan shot an uncomfortable glance toward Dom. "Meaning no disrespect, but I think we can agree that Stepahin won't be impacting Saint Peter's day."

"This is where Ethan Falk comes in," Venice said. "He's the one who killed him."

Jonathan laughed. "Really? Well, good for him. Justice the way it's supposed to be done."

"The kid is being charged with murder," Dom said.

Something snagged in Jonathan's gut. He said nothing, choosing instead for them to play the rest of their hand.

"He's trying to claim self-defense," Venice explained. "He told the police about his kidnapping and his rescue, but no one's listening."

Jonathan brought both hands to his head and pulled his hair back from his forehead. "Because there's no record," he said.

The others nodded in unison.

"Well, shit," Jonathan said.

Chapter Six

At Jonathan's request, Venice summoned Boxers from his home in Washington, and within two hours, the team sat in the War Room, a teak conference room that sported every high-tech gadget that Venice thought worthwhile to own. She sat at the end of the long oval table, at what Jonathan called the command center, directly across from the enormous screen that dominated the far wall. Jonathan sat at the long side to her right, his back to the door. Boxers sat directly across, and Dom sat on Jonathan's right.

The big screen displayed images of four men who looked only vaguely familiar. They were black-and-white mug shots of four tired-looking white guys, aged between twenty-five and thirty-five, their images displayed as a grid, Brady Bunch style. They all wore the same sullen expression of every mug shot.

"Which one's our boy?" Jonathan asked.

"The one on the bottom right," Venice said. That guy fell between the others age-wise, and he by far looked like the most intelligent of the lot. The measurement scroll on the wall in the background showed him to be just a touch over six feet tall, and he sported a shock of blond hair combed straight back in a style reminiscent of old greaser movies. "The other three are Gabriel Potts, Raymond Stanns, and Samuel Din-klage."

"They're the ones we killed, right?" Boxers asked.

"Better be careful, Box," Dom said. "When you've killed so many that you can't remember what they looked like, it might mean you have a problem."

"People look a lot different when parts of their heads are missing, Padre," Boxers fired back. "Judge not lest ye be judged, remember?"

Dom held up his hands in surrender. "No offense intended."

"Those assholes were slave traders," Big Guy pressed. "They sold kids to the highest bidder. My bullets let them off better than they deserved."

Dom looked to Jonathan. "Slave traders? Is that right?"

Jonathan looked down at the table. "Some of the baddest bad guys we've ever run across."

"But we didn't know that at the beginning," Venice prompted.

"No, not at the beginning," Jonathan concurred. "The case came to us as they usually do, through the normal cutouts."

"We were a lot easier to reach back then, too," Boxers said.

"True." The higher their profile got, the thicker and more numerous the safeguards. "We got word through the kid's father that he'd been kidnapped."

"Lawyer," Venice said.

"What?"

"The father didn't contact us, his lawyer did."

Jonathan shrugged. "Fine, his lawyer." A memory bell dinged. "There was something strange about the contact." He looked to Venice.

She clicked a few keys on her computer to bring up whatever she was using for notes. "The first contact was to make a phone call, but when we made the call, they pretended that we had the wrong number. Then they tried to call that number back and were stymied by the rolling numbers we use to prevent detection."

"That's right," Jonathan said. "I got pissed off that they were trying to double-cross us somehow. At least that's what I thought at the time."

"Another day passed before they reached out again," Venice said, picking up her momentum. "I suggested we ignore them, but you insisted that we give them a second chance."

"We were still trying to learn our own business," Jonathan explained. He heard the apology in his voice. "Jeeze, that really was a long time ago."

"They wanted a face-to-face, but you drew the line on that," Venice continued. "It turned out that eleven-year-old Ethan Falk left school on his own to walk to football practice. His folks didn't know he was missing until he didn't come home for dinner."

"Did he show up at the football practice?" Dom asked.

Venice shook her head. "No. And the coach didn't call because why would he? Kids miss practice all the time."

Venice explained, "The kidnapper called Porter Falk from a payphone along the highway and made a ransom demand for five hundred thousand dollars—more money than the Falks could possibly pull together—with the standard threat not to involve the police. Porter called his lawyer, and then they put the wheels in motion to get Security Solutions involved."

"What were the directions for ransom delivery?" Dom asked.

"They were bogus, as I recall," Jonathan said. "A suitcase of money left under a tree in some park in rural New York."

"In three days," Boxers added. "That was the real warning bell. They didn't want the money right by God now the way most assholes do. They gave us too much time."

"That made me think that it wasn't about the ransom at all," Jonathan said. "That was just a delaying tactic."

"Delaying for what?" Dom asked.

"Sex trade," Boxers said. "When it comes to kidnapped kids, if it ain't about ransom, then it's about sex."

"We moved heaven and earth on that case," Venice recalled. "We even got help from Doug Kramer. He wasn't chief yet, but he pulled some strings for us." Currently, Doug Kramer was the chief of the Fisherman's Cove Police Department. Jonathan wasn't sure exactly how much Kramer understood of the details of Security Solutions's covert activities, but over the years, Jonathan had seen indicators that the chief knew more than he let on.

"Actually the entire company got involved in that," Jonathan said. "We worked a lot of leads, wore out a lot of shoe leather. A fingerprint from that payphone— one of many fingerprints—led us to look into Stepahin."

"The guy was sort of a nobody," Venice read from her notes. "Petty criminal, in and out of jail seven, eight times. He was the beneficiary of bad police work, lazy prosecutors, and generous juries. I don't think we knew about the others in the mug shots until after the fact, did we?"

"No, we just pretty much stayed focused on Stepahin," Jonathan said. "The harder we pushed, the closer we got to him. We finally tracked him down to a crappy little farmhouse in the middle of a field outside of Nowhere, Ohio."

"They tried to put up a fight," Boxers remembered. "It was in the mix that Stepahin got away. We found the boy in a stone cellar that was accessible through a hatch in the basement floor."

"How was he?" Dom asked.

Boxers looked away. "I don't want to talk about it."

Dom looked to Jonathan, who warned him away with a flash from his eyes. *Don't go there.*

"Okay," Dom pressed, "you said there was a sex ring. Did you find other kids there as well?"

"Jesus, Padre, let it go, will you?" Boxers said.

Jonathan explained, "Apparently, we missed a few others by a couple of hours. But we had our PC, so it was mission accomplished."

"And the others?"

Boxers was turning red.

"I called Wolverine to let her know, and then we declared victory."

"We should have kept investigating," Boxers said. His voice resonated with barely controlled fury.

Jonathan didn't bother to reply. What was done was done, and that was a long time ago. He decided to change the subject. "So, Ven, do we have any idea why Stepahin was back in town?"

Venice leaned back in her Aeron chair and crossed her arms. "That's not the question you should be asking."

"Oh?"

"Yeah. He's something of a miracle man."

Jonathan recognized that she was dangling bait, but he chose not to go for it. Given a few seconds, Venice would explode if she didn't share whatever the interesting tidbit was.

She grinned. "He died nine years ago."

Jed Hackner cocked his head and scowled. "I don't understand what you're trying to tell me."

"What's not to understand?" Pam said. She'd stopped by his office to update him on the results of the shoe leather she'd been eroding in her search for answers in the Ethan Falk case. "There are no records of the man he killed. None."

Hackner offered a tired glare. "Anything more on the kid?"

Hastings shook her head. "Now that he's lawyered up, it's tough to get much beyond his juvie record. Petty stuff. Acting out. His parents divorced when he was thirteen, and by the time he was seventeen, they were both dead. Dad of suicide and mom of breast cancer. With Ethan being as old as he was, he aged out of foster care before he could really even get into it. Not that it mattered because by all accounts, he was what you might call a free spirit."

"Thus the record," Hackner said.

"Exactly." Pam took a deep breath. "I'll tell you what, though. There is nothing in that kid's past that even hints at violence."

"He certainly made up for lost time." Hackner's body language said that he was ready to move on to something else. This case was something north of a slam dunk, and he'd started to shift papers on his desk. Then he looked up at Pam, who continued to watch him. "What?"

"What do you mean, what?" Pam said, matching his tone. "This case reeks of bad things."

Hackner sat up straight, then leaned back in his chair, crossing his arms. "What it reeks of is a closed case. We've got about a million eyewitnesses and a confession. I'm not a lawyer, but I think that's all very good for us."

"I mean the rest of his story. About the kidnapping, and the rescue and the abuse? Where is that all coming from?"

"I don't know. Delusions, maybe? Wasn't it David Berkowitz whose dog told him to kill? Maybe Ethan Falk has a talking dog. Or a goldfish. I never did meet a trustworthy goldfish."

Pam smacked his desk with her palm. "Are you seriously going to tell me that your inner Sherlock is not going nuts over this?"

Hackner smiled. He wasn't a bad guy when he wasn't being an arrogant asshole. Presently, he was skating through the no man's land in between. "My inner Sherlock is a pragmatist. We build the prosecution's case. Let the defense fend for itself."

Pam recognized a lost cause when she saw it. She stood.

"Don't look so glum," Hackner said. "There are plenty more cases to solve."

The details of this case bothered her. She'd *seen* the look in the kid's face when she arrested him. If she was going to be a party to sending a young man away to become an old man in prison, then she owed it to him to dig a little deeper.

A bizarre childhood story combined with the lack of identity for the man he killed was at least two too many levels of oddity. Plus, she believed Ethan's story.

If the kidnapping happened, then it left evidence. All she needed to do was find it.

Jonathan caught himself gaping, his mouth open just wide enough that he was sure he looked stupid. Venice laughed at what she saw, and he snapped his jaw shut again.

She continued, "Okay, *died* is the wrong word. *Evaporated* is better. According to what I've pulled together off of ICIS, the decedent in Braddock County is in fact no one. He never existed. His fingerprints trace to nothing."

"What about facial recognition software?" Jonathan asked.

Venice shrugged with a single shoulder. "Death does funny things to a face, as you know," she said. She tapped her keyboard. "I can pull up the death photo for you." The screen blinked and a dead guy appeared, the standard naked shoulders-and-head photo from every autopsy. His eyes drooped, one an unfocused slit and the other a bloody hole, and his facial features sagged from lack of muscle tone.

"Look familiar to you?" Dom asked.

Jonathan looked to Boxers, whose scowl spoke for him. *What, are you kidding me?*

"I don't know," Jonathan said. "I could be talked into either a yes or a no. That was a long time ago."

"That was a lot of people ago," Boxers added with a chuckle.

"This gets better," Venice said. She leaned in toward the table, as if to reveal a secret. "According to official documents and records, even the guy we know to have been Stepahin in fact never existed."

Dom rattled his head. "Okay, I'm lost. How can you know that if there's no record? I mean, how can you prove the negative?"

Venice beamed as her fingers returned to her keyboard and started to fly. "Because I'm a thorough researcher," she said. She hit enter with a flourish, and the big screen blinked to reveal a list of a bazillion files.

Jonathan's shoulders sagged. With all the windup he'd expected a bigger delivery. "Um, what is that?"

"Those, Mr. Grave, are copies I made of all the research we did on Stepahin." She widened her eyes and leaned in again, as if expecting applause. Exasperated, she pointed to the screen with both arms outstretched. "This is all the stuff that no longer exists. Wiping it from the Interwebs doesn't delete anything from my files and my backups."

Jonathan smiled. Yet more evidence that all the countless thousands of dollars he'd spent over the years to build Venice's Fortress of Solitude hadn't been wasted. "And if I know you as well as I think I do, one of those files is a summary of what you gleaned from all the other files."

"Indeed," she said.

"How about a photo?" Boxers asked. "Before we go too deeply down a rabbit hole, do you have a picture of the guy from eleven years ago? One that's not a mug shot?"

"Of course I do," she said. More clicks, and there was the photo of a man who looked nothing like the monster that he was. "This is from his driver's license."

"The one for which there is no longer any record," Dom said. He looked like he may have been on the verge of understanding.

"Exactly," Venice said.

Dom looked at Jonathan. "Can someone actually do that? Make all traces disappear? I mean, that must involve hundreds of thousands of records, and then there's the tangents off of those primary records. How could anyone do that?"

"Not just anyone could," Jonathan said. "But we both know someone with the skill set and resources to make it happen." He kept his glare burning on Dom.

"Wolverine?" the priest guessed aloud.

"The one and only," Jonathan said. "Give her a call for me, will you? Let her choose the meeting spot, but don't tip your hand too far."

"Since when don't you trust Wolverine?"

"I trust her just fine," Jonathan said. "I just think that if she knew where my head was taking me, she might refuse to show up."

Chapter Seven

In the hierarchy of Catholic cathedrals, Saint Matthew's in Washington wouldn't fall into anyone's top ten. It wasn't even the most majestic in the Nation's Capital, dwarfed as it was by the Washington National Cathedral in the Upper Northwest. Jonathan often wondered how the Vatican sat still while the Episcopalians won the contest for the most beautiful house of God in town. Still, a cathedral was a cathedral, and this dark stone structure on Rhode Island Avenue was impressive, but it had a dreary look about it. Perhaps its most famous moment occurred on November 25, 1963, when the cathedral served as the setting for President John F. Kennedy's state funeral. Fifty years was a long intermission between big moments.

Or so the public thought. If walls could talk, right? The Our Lady Chapel inside the cathedral was in fact one of the spookiest—read *clandestine*—locations in all of Washington. Some years ago, Irene Rivers, director of the FBI and affectionately known to Jonathan as Wolverine, had spent hundreds of thousands of unaccounted-for taxpayer dollars to make the chapel a black hole for surveillance teams. DC was a town of alphabet agencies that didn't trust each other. Irene believed that Bureau headquarters had been infiltrated years ago by the CIA and the NSA, with listening devices in every corner. For the most part, that didn't matter—more times than not federal agencies pulled on the same oar in more or less the same direction—but some things and some assignments were so secret that the information needed to be one hundred percent contained.

Accordingly, Jonathan had spent a fair amount of time here in the chapel, learning the details of things he wished he didn't know, all under the watchful glare of the Blessed Virgin.

Jonathan was what Dom D'Angelo liked to call a convenience Catholic. Raised in the faith by a single father who was now serving a life sentence in a supermax prison, cynicism ran like blood through his veins. He found comfort in the thought of a God who created the universe and sent His Son to die for mankind's sins, but often his faith was strained by his up-close familiarity with all the evil that escaped God's notice. On those occasions when Jonathan was dispatched to set things straight—often dispatched from this very chapel—he felt confident that he was doing the work of the angels, but the Rite of Confession gave him reassurance. Still, given the number of people who had died at his hand—irrespective of the fact that they were evil and needed to die—his disdain for hypocrisy would not allow him to attend Mass anymore. He hoped that God understood.

The chairs in the Our Lady Chapel served as a kind of penance in their own right. Wooden and wobbly, the blond bentwood chairs provided no support for your arms, and felt like they might collapse at any moment. Jonathan considered standing, but realized that while awaiting the arrival of a famous personality for a clandestine meeting, it was best not to look too anxious.

Jonathan had met Irene Rivers a long time ago, back during her days as a special agent. She'd had a family emergency, and she'd reached out to Dom for assistance. Dom, in turn, reached out to Jonathan, and bad things happened to the bad guys. Since then, as Irene advanced through the ranks in the Bureau and all of her communications were subject to public review, Father Dom had become their communications pipeline. Even the director of the FBI was afforded privacy when it came to communications with her priest.

Wolverine leaned on Jonathan frequently to do jobs that no government could ever confess were necessary, and for which the legal penalties were huge. Jonathan trusted her with his life not just because she had proven herself to be scrupulously trustworthy, but also because their shared dirty laundry was of a nature and scope that would bring both of them down if either betrayed the other.

Jonathan had arrived at their appointment twenty-five minutes early—not because he'd planned to, but because the vagaries of traffic between here and his home in Fisherman's Cove made more specific planning difficult. More times than not, he wound up being as much as twenty minutes late. He'd considered killing time out on the street for a while, but between the chill, his lack of hunger, and the fact that he was already pretty tweaked on coffee, he decided it was better just to sit and wait.

When he heard the massive front door open behind

him at precisely two o'clock, he knew that Wolverine had arrived. She was a precise kind of lady. He fought the urge to stand and greet her because, again, this was supposed to be a meeting that never happened. The church wasn't full, but it wasn't empty, and reunion scenes attracted attention.

Besides, some choreography was so carefully scripted that it needn't be watched to be seen. Wolverine would be preceded and followed into the church by her security detail, all in dark suits with pigtails cascading from their ears and expressions that hinted at constipation.

Jonathan listened as the footsteps grew near. Then they stopped.

"Excuse me, sir," a stern voice said from behind.

Jonathan turned in his chair to look up at exactly the image he'd been expecting. "Hi," he said.

"I need to see some identification," the agent said.

Jonathan hated this element of the law enforcement community. He was tougher than they would ever be, and had endured more life-threatening situations than they could imagine even in their wettest dreams, but he understood that his role was to be deferential. More specifically, his role was to appear intimidated, but that was a step too far. The deference soothed their ego, and at the end of the day made everything go more smoothly.

Jonathan reached to his back pocket, withdrew his wallet, and produced a driver's license that identified him as Richard Horgan. A different pocket held a set of FBI credentials that were as real as his missions for Uncle Sam, but it was never a good idea to flash them in the presence of agents whose creds were official all the time.

The agent took more time than was necessary to review the driver's license, his eyes dancing back and forth between the picture and Jonathan's face. It was another intimidation move.

And Jonathan had had enough. "Are you having trouble with the big words?" he asked.

Cue the icy glare. Good lord, these guys were predictable.

"Are you carrying a firearm, Mr. Horgan?"

Jonathan shifted his eyes from the questioner to his partner, who looked familiar. They'd danced this tune together in the past. "Really?" Jonathan said.

"It's all right, gentlemen," said a familiar voice from beyond the guards.

"Forgive me, Director Rivers," the first guy said. "But I saw something under his jacket that looked like the printing of a firearm."

Irene Rivers smiled in a tolerant way. Jonathan recognized it as her tell for being about to lose it. "He is the man we're here to meet," she said. "That means you show him all the courtesy and consideration that you would show me."

Security-boy looked wounded. An aspect of government service that Jonathan did not miss was the ease with which a single oh-shit could wipe out a lifetime of attaboys. Even the gentlest rebukes could end up derailing a career.

"I know you're just doing your job," Irene said, backing off on the sharpness of her tone. "Rest assured that Mr. Horgan is a friend of mine." She sealed it with a smile. "Now, take your positions, both of you."

In unison, the security detail turned their backs and took on the posture of toy soldiers, standing close enough to block others from entering the space, but far enough away that the discussion would not be overheard. Jonathan found it significant that Irene trusted her security detail little more than she trusted the general public.

Jonathan stood as she crossed the threshold into the Our Lady Chapel. In a different circumstance, he'd have greeted her with a friendly hug, but where the wall had eyes, a professional handshake was a better choice. "Hi, Wolfie," he said. "It's been not nearly as long as either of us would like."

The words brought the laugh he'd been trolling for. "Truer words," she said. She indicated the chairs as if they belonged to her—and at one level he supposed they did. "Let's sit down for a little devotional."

Irene led the way to a spot as far away as possible from the threshold and sat. She crossed her legs and somehow managed to look comfortable. Jonathan had always found something undeniably hot about Wolverine, and it wasn't just the fact that as FBI director she still kicked the occasional door. He knew better than to guess her age, but he suspected that she was older than she looked. The strawberry blond hair looked natural enough to his eye, and she had terrific legs. Unfortunately for her, cameras deeply disliked her, projecting the image of a nineteenth-century schoolmarm, cursed with whatever is the obverse of hotness.

He selected a chair two away from hers and twisted ninety degrees so that he could speak to her directly.

"So, tell me," Irene said, taking the lead. "When did you start drinking on the job?" A harsh question delivered with a twinkle of humor.

"Excuse me?"

The twinkle grew to a smirk. "Of course. Plausible

deniability. Well suffice to say that a certain congressman is wildly impressed and deeply grateful to have
his daughter back."

Jonathan kept his poker face.

"He wanted me to tell whoever this Scorpion guy is,
the congressman considers himself indebted, and both
willing and anxious to confer whatever repayment he
can offer."

"If I had any idea what you were talking about, I
would of course be thrilled to hear the news," Jonathan
said.

Irene leaned in closer. "Would it have killed you to
clue me in?" she whispered. "Hypothetically, of course.
He's a congressman, for heaven's sake."

"One who hypothetically does not trust the Bureau,"
Jonathan said. "Rules are rules, Madam Director."

"You put me in a very awkward position, Digger.
Good thing this had a happy ending."

"My hypothetical operations always deliver happy
endings. You know that." Jonathan shifted his position
in his chair. "How did you know it was me?"

Irene rolled her eyes with a dramatic flourish. "Oh,
please. A guy named Scorpion who has a friend the
size of a sequoia. Some dots are easy to connect." She
glanced at her watch. "I believe this is your meeting."

"I believe you're right," Jonathan said. "Did Mother
Hen send you a name and a picture?"

"Indeed she did."

"And what did you discover when you ran him?"

Irene inhaled noisily through her nose and glanced
to the floor. Jonathan sensed that she'd been searching
for a way to say what was on her mind, but hadn't yet
decided on a strategy.

"Tell you what," she said at last. "Why don't you tell me what you're looking for specifically?"

"Is that really better than just dealing the cards from the top of the deck?" Jonathan's tolerance for bullshit was limited on a good day. When it came to government-sponsored bullshit, his reservoir had overflowed years ago.

"In this case, yes," Irene said. He saw a flash of anger. "And friendship notwithstanding, it wouldn't hurt you from time to remember just who the hell you're talking to."

Jonathan reared back in his seat. "Whoa. Where did that come from? We're always on the same side, you know."

"No, we're not," she snapped. "Your world is vastly less complicated than mine. While you're venturing the save the world one injustice at a time, I'm balancing about a million of them every second of every day. The fact is that I am entitled to know things that I can never share with you or anyone else."

This was new territory for the two of them. Jonathan had for a while been questioning Irene's wisdom when agreeing to a second ten-year stint as FBI director, and now it seemed that his concerns were justified. It was not in his nature to cower, however. "So, why are we here? You knew what I wanted to talk about, but you could have blown me off to Dom over the phone."

Her back stiffened as he drew in another big breath, and gathered herself. "Jonathan Grave, we have known each other for a very, very long time. You ask me over and over again to trust you. And I do. How about you return the favor this once and trust me? Tell me why you need to have information on Mr. James Stepahin."

Fair enough. "He was the focus of an op we conducted over a decade ago—"

"You mean a hypothetical op, right?" Her eyes danced.

Jonathan smiled. The previous tension had been defused. "Yes, of course. He showed up on our radar again, and when I try to run his background, we find that he literally never existed. That feels to me like the involvement of your shop."

Irene stood and rubbed a spot on the small of her back. "These chairs are killers," she said. She was looking up at the Blessed Virgin when she asked, "In what context did the alleged Mr. Stepahin appear on your radar?"

It felt ungentlemanly to sit while a lady stood, but he sensed that she preferred it this way. The lack of eye contact was another tell. "Well, let's start with the fact that he's dead."

Irene's head whipped around. "What? Where?"

"A little south and west of here. In Braddock County. He's a John Doe. Killed yesterday in what the local PD is calling a murder."

Irene opened her mouth to speak, but then closed it. The furrow in her brow spoke of multiple levels of confusion. "Who killed him?"

"A kid. Twenty-three."

"Was it a professional job?"

Now there's a clue to what she's not telling me. "Hardly. The killer is a coffee shop barista."

Irene stifled a laugh, brought a hand to her forehead. Whatever pieces she was waiting for were apparently not falling into place. "Wait. How do you know the identity of a John Doe? Especially if he, as you say, never existed?"

"That's complicated."

"I imagine it is."

Jonathan stood and joined Wolverine at the feet of the Virgin. "I told you that Stepahin was the focus of an op eleven years ago. Well, as it turns out, his killer— the kid's name is Ethan Falk—was Stepahin's victim. Ethan's father was our client. Stepahin ran away, and we didn't chase him because we had our PC." He paused to let the details sink in, and for Irene's memory to be triggered. "You should remember the case. It was during the period of your transition into the directorship. That was a sex ring—"

"I remember it," Irene snapped.

"We rescued Ethan before he could be sold," Jonathan said. "When he was arrested for the murder—which he committed in a friggin' parking lot in front of countless witnesses—he tried to tell the story of this guy being his abuser, but of course—"

"There's no record of anything because you were the rescuer." Irene was already ahead of him.

"Exactly," Jonathan said. He lowered his voice. "If I can't figure out a way make Stepahin real again, this kid won't have a chance. This is a death penalty case."

"It most definitely is," Irene agreed. "I've dealt with the prosecutor down there before—a jackass named Petrelli. He goes for the death penalty on jaywalking cases. But the public keeps reelecting him."

"So now you understand my dilemma," Jonathan said.

"You killed people during that op, right?"

"Yep."

"So stepping forward isn't an option."

"Well, for me, maybe," he joked, "but you know how Big Guy hates tight spaces."

"And lethal injections."

"Those, too." Most of what Jonathan did carried a death penalty if he was ever caught, but that algebra worked for him. What was the point of living a safe life if endangered people went unprotected? "The stakes are as high as they've ever been for me personally, Wolfie. What can you do to help? I'll take anything you can give me."

Something changed in Irene when he asked that question. Her demeanor relaxed, her features softened. "Let's go for a walk," she said.

Avenues rarely crossed in Washington. Numbered streets ran north and south, and lettered streets ran east and west. Avenues, on the other hand, were granted the freedom to go wherever the hell they wanted to, and it just so happened that Rhode Island Avenue, where Saint Matthew's resided, lay only a couple hundred feet east of Connecticut Avenue. Irene led Jonathan down the stairs of the cathedral, and then made the right-hand turn onto Connecticut. This was a huge breach of security as far as Jonathan was concerned, and Irene's detail seemed to share his interpretation. And just in case the world wasn't paying close enough attention to the movements of the FBI director, they were tailed by a caravan of two massive armored SUVs.

"I need to breathe fresh air as I dig into the places

where I'm about to go," Irene said, answering Jonathan's question before he could ask it.

Her words tugged at Jonathan. He put his hand on her arm. "Hey, are you okay?"

She turned to look him in the eye. "If I could un-learn half the things I know, and un-see three-quarters of what I've seen since taking this job, I'd be one happy camper."

"So, why did you re-up? You put in your ten years. You could've just walked away and lived off your retirement."

"Because I love it," she said. Then she smiled. "Color me a blind patriot."

"That's exactly the reason why I like you so much," Jonathan said.

"James Stepahin," Irene said through a forced smile. She looked to the sky. "Not my finest hour, I'm afraid." They walked together another ten paces. "We never knew him to be a sex offender." More silence.

More, in fact, than Jonathan could tolerate. "We?"

"Okay, I," Irene said. "The standard profile for a pedophile is a man who believes that his obsession with children—whether boys or girls—is a form of love. When they hug them or fondle them, or . . . worse, they think their actions are about compassion and caring. They don't see the violence in it." As she spoke, she frequently looked skyward, as if searching for a source of strength.

She nodded to the approaching intersection. "We'll go Eighteenth Street and avoid the Circle." The lunch crowd had thinned, but the early-departure bar crowd had started to form, making DuPont Circle a place to avoid. Certainly, the guys in the SUV would be happy.

"On the other end of the spectrum are the serial killers who victimize children just for the thrill of it, the release."

"I don't understand why you're telling me this," Jonathan said.

"I'm answering your question," Irene said. "Under the specialness of this circumstance, I'm breaking my personal rule about sharing shit that you don't need to know."

His feathers appropriately singed, Jonathan backed off, committed to let her take her time and bear as much of her soul as she felt necessary.

"Both of those personality types—whether organized or disorganized—tend to be focused on their purpose. James Stepahin was apparently the rare exception. I didn't know that when I hired him."

Chapter Eight

"You'll recall that the wreckage of the Twin Towers and the Pentagon was still warm when I took on the job of director," Irene explained as they crossed N Street, Northwest. "A lot of things needed doing that we didn't have the legal authority to do. I won't say we shredded the Constitution, but it got pretty heavily creased. The good news is that the folks at Langley took most of the heat, and God bless them, they never ratted us out."

"About what?" Jonathan asked. So much for staying quiet and letting her talk.

"You remember those black site prisons the agency created all over the world?"

"I do." He resisted the urge to tell her that he'd delivered more than a few of their occupants.

"Well, we had them here, too," Irene said. "And I'll tell you right now that at the time, I was a big supporter of them. There were a lot more cells of bad guys here on U.S. soil than the press ever knew—even more than congressional overseers knew. Frankly, when the news broke about the foreign black sites, I was shocked that no one connected the dots domestically."

"Do we still have them?"

She gave him a glare.

"Chalk that question up to stuff I have no need to know," Jonathan said. Though he could name at least two off the top of his head. He just wanted to see how far this walking confession had weakened her walls. Answer: not a bit.

"Well, just as you helped to fill sites abroad, we needed similar help stateside, and that was one job for which we had no takers. Overseas, at the end of the day, SF and Agency people had cover back home if things went wrong. Here, that was not the case. I could not ask sworn agents to break the law, and if I tried and worked leaked out, it would have been a disaster."

"So you turned to contractors," Jonathan guessed aloud. Ahead and to the left, on the opposite side of the street, stood the beige-brick Federal-style town house that was the Albanian Embassy, situated unobtrusively next to a café that sported outdoor seating shaded by beer-sponsored umbrellas.

"Exactly. About that time, Mister James Stepahin was arrested for a drug infraction that barely cracked the floor of a felony. I don't remember precisely how his name came all the way up the ladder to my desk, but I recognized him from the heads-up you gave me after your rescue operation. It turned out that his job was to kidnap people."

"For sex rings."

"For the highest bidder," Irene corrected. "And he was good at it. After he lawyered up, we made a deal. And as I explained before, it never occurred to me that a professional criminal and a child molester would be two sides of a single personality. Maybe I was rationalizing, but what's done is done."

Jonathan of all people had no business casting stones at others whose best intentions had turned out to be misguided. If a book were to be written on the subject, it would be his autobiography.

"You might not like to hear this," Irene continued, "but he was really, really good at what he did. He found the people we wanted him to, and he brought them in."

"Was it wet work?" Jonathan asked, knowing that she would understand his question.

"Nope, not an assassin, though God forgive me, we have a few of those as well." She gave him a friendly poke in the ribs with her elbow. "Don't be jealous now. You'll always be my favorite felon-contractor."

He knew a joke when he heard it.

"Because Stepahin delivered everyone we asked for, Uncle Sam officially forgot that he was ever a criminal."

"Is that when you scrubbed his file?"

Irene coughed out a bitter laugh. "I wish. All we did was expunge his criminal record. Stepahin did the rest. I always figured it had something to do with the frenzy over the black sites overseas. The media was calling for criminal prosecutions for the soldiers and contractors who staffed those sites, but thank God Darmond wasn't in the White House yet to give them up. If I were Stepahin at the time, though, I think I would have begun to feel awfully lonely and exposed."

"Shouldn't he have?" It went unsaid that everything Jonathan did for Uncle Sam these days was done under a veil of one hundred percent deniability.

"Of course he should have. That's why you guys get

the big bucks. And as I said before, I was shocked that the domestic sites were never revealed. Anyway, one day, he just ceased to exist. No birth records, no anything. Just poof."

"Did you ever try to trace him down?"

Irene wrinkled her nose as she shook her head. "Nah. What would be the point? The post-nine-eleven frenzy was calming down by then, and he'd done everything we'd asked him to do. Deep inside, I think I figured maybe he'd earned an anonymous retirement." She drilled him with a glare. "So have you, you know."

Jonathan chuckled. "I'm living the dream." They turned right onto Massachusetts Avenue, and Jonathan glanced over his shoulder to see if the security guys were still there. He'd been in their spot enough times to feel sorry for them. If they'd fallen back, he'd have waited for them, but they were right where they were supposed to be.

"Do you really mean that?" Irene asked. "Living the dream?"

Jonathan scowled. "I did when I said it, but that look in your eye makes me want to take it back."

"Perhaps you just know me too well," she said.

"Are you going to make me ask? And before you answer, how in the world does Uzbekistan rate a cooler building than Albania?" Just ahead, the Uzbek embassy looked like an old-money mansion, with a sculptured edifice and a circular driveway in front.

"Open the index of things I don't give a crap about," Irene said. "You'll find that one there."

Jonathan laughed. Irene's no-bullshit persona vastly magnified her inherent hotness as a woman.

"Okay, here's the deal," Irene said. "In recent weeks, we've heard a lot of chatter over the scary channels. Have you ever heard of al-Amin? It means 'the trustworthy.'"

"No. But it sounds jihadist."

Irene explained, "They're the current crop of terrorists to grow out of the Muddled East. One group on a list that keeps getting bigger. Building on the success of the Mexican model of terror-funding, al-Amin's revenue stream comes largely through ransoms paid for high-profile kidnappings. The basic theme is that you pay to get your loved one back, or you get to watch a video on the Internet of his head being sawed off with a butter knife."

Jonathan inhaled sharply. He'd seen too many such videos, and in each case, wished that he could un-see them.

"The thing with al-Amin, from everything we can figure out, is that they're pissed that the US government still won't bargain for hostages."

"Except we do," Jonathan corrected. "In fact, we just did."

"Moving on," Irene said, "the backchannel chatter leads us to believe that al-Amin may be on the verge of forcing our hand. We believe that they're planning to target high-value assets here on American soil."

Something fluttered in Jonathan's gut. "You mean, like kidnapping a congressman's daughter?"

"Something very much like that," Irene confirmed. "The plan, as far as we can tell, is to target a subject, snatch him—or her—and then boogey them off to the Sandbox. It's entirely possible that embassies are cooperating with the bad guys, but we cannot confirm that as yet. What we *have* been able to confirm from multiple assets is that the targets will be elected officials—either themselves or their loved ones. Actually, until your op down on I-95, we thought it was exclusively the actual elected officials. Now it seems that they've cast a wider net."

Jonathan thought it through as they strolled toward the embassies of the Republic of Trinidad and Tobago and Peru. Up ahead, on the other side of Seventeenth Street, he could see the flag of the Philippines flying above their embassy as well. But he doubted that they would walk that far.

"You're thinking that Stepahin was here as part of that plot, don't you? Al-whatever."

"Al-Amin," Irene said. "What would you think if you were in my pumps?"

The phrasing made Jonathan laugh. "I would think that the thing that looks like a duck and quacks like a duck might very well not be a sparrow."

"Bingo. The stars aligned too closely to be a purely random event. I've seen the reports coming out of Prince William County, and while the news media will likely never get the information to report it, those guys you killed in the motel room—we can drop the *hypothetical* trope, right?—were in fact part of an al-Amin cell. To have Stepahin in the same sphere at the same time tells me that he was planning some kind of operation. Hell, for all I know, there are five hundred thirty-five separate assault teams—one for every member of Congress. Now, throw in the cabinet and the Supremes, and that's a lot of people to frighten and then guard."

Something in the hypothesis wasn't working for Jonathan. "Let's stipulate that you're right," he said. "We'll assume for the sake of argument that Stepahin—

professional bad guy—was here for nefarious purposes. How on God's half-acre does a coffee shop kid take out a trained asset?"

"From everything I've read, the kid cold-cocked him," Irene said. "Stepahin had let his guard down, and why wouldn't he? Who's going to be afraid of a coffee shop kid?"

Another bell rang in Jonathan's head. "You seem to know a lot about this case"

Irene pointed ahead and to the right. "Let's go back down Seventeenth," she said, proving Jonathan correct: they weren't going to make it as far as the Philippines. "While we didn't know he still existed until Mother Hen sent me the name, we're trying a forensic effort to figure out what he was up to." Irene gave him a knowing smirk. Now that they were on their way back to the cathedral, their meeting was likely coming to an end. "I cannot afford to have a record of any of this," she said. "Those renditions back in the day were simply too dirty. The whole reason we used criminals in the first place was to prevent a record from ever being established. I sure as hell don't want one established now."

And there it was. Wolverine had played her hand perfectly. "You're hiring me, aren't you?" Jonathan asked.

"Can you think of a more motivated contractor?" She gave him her most demure smile.

Jonathan bowed his head, silently acknowledging that he'd been had. "Okay, boss," he said, "what exactly do you want me to do?"

"I want you to find out why Stepahin was here, what he was doing."

"Is this al-Amin group affiliated with al Qaeda?"

"Who knows? Anymore, it matters less and less. Boko Haram affiliated with ISIL, ISIL affiliated with al Qaeda, who's joined at one level with the Taliban. They all stand for the same murder, so I personally don't get lost in the distinctions. And I don't think they'll prove to be all that relevant to you."

"What about the guys we offed at the Sleeping Genie Motel? You said they were al . . . Amini. Is that even how you say it?"

"I have no idea how they say it. I said they were affiliated. That doesn't necessarily mean they were believers. This wasn't their first kidnapping."

Jonathan scowled.

She did the eyebrow thing again, indicating that he was being dense.

"Ah," Jonathan said. "Previous contractors?"

"Bingo. Born and bred in the USA," Irene said. "Which makes Stepahin all the more interesting. If I'm right, then al-Amin isn't depending on zealots to accomplish their goals. They're using local talent pursuing a very capitalistic agenda."

Jonathan laughed at the absurdity. "Doesn't matter who triggers the body count so long as the body count happens." They'd barely made the turn onto Connecticut Avenue for a second time when Jonathan started to recap the conversation in his head. "So, let's be clear," he said. "You want me to poke around and find out why James Stepahin resurfaced. I'm going to need a back door to some difficult-to-access files. The kind of files that you don't like to show people."

Irene nudged him with an elbow. "If you need it, you can have it."

Jonathan thought through the logistics. Finding an

unknown among the unknown was a monumental undertaking.

"Do what you have to do," Irene said. "But I cannot overstate how on your own you will be if this somehow goes public. I'll hang you out to dry like a laundry sheet."

The harshness of Wolverine's words startled him. Not the content—the rules were the rules—but the vehemence with which she stated them.

"This Stepahin stuff is a real source of shame for you, isn't it?" Jonathan kept his tone soft.

"Beyond any words I can use to describe it," Irene said. "But such is the nature of the job I signed on for. Twice."

Jonathan returned her elbow-nudge. If a van hadn't been following them, he might have offered a hug. Or probably not. Theirs was a complicated relationship. Always all-business, but always something more. He'd volunteered more than once to take a bullet for her, and he sensed that he was about to do it again.

"Don't you dare feel sorry for me," Irene said, as if reading his mind. "No one thrust this bullshit onto me. I'm here of my own free will."

Jonathan raised his hands in playful surrender.

"This thing with Ethan Falk," Irene continued. Her tone was softer, and she'd slowed her pace. "That's not your responsibility. You gave him his freedom, and he chose to kill a man. Those are two entirely different transactions. Your obligations are fulfilled."

Jonathan appreciated the words, but he rejected them. "He killed the predator that I allowed to live," he said. "I didn't finish the job I started. Are we done here?"

"I'm not," Irene said. "One of the things I've always

admired about you, Digger, is the line you draw in the sand about what you do. If I've heard it once, I've heard it five hundred times. You are not an assassin. Ring any bells?"

Of course it did, but Jonathan didn't acknowledge.

"Your mission with Ethan Falk was reunite the boy with his family. You did that. That's a victory. Don't you scoff at me."

She'd read his response for exactly what it was.

"Some stories just don't have happy endings, Dig. Cut yourself a break."

Jonathan appreciated her words. But in his world, justice often wasn't measured in what was reasonable. He preferred to measure it in terms of what was *right*.

Jonathan pulled to a halt and offered his hand. "Wolfie, in a city that's full of shitheads, you're one of the finest people I know. I'll do what I can to get to the bottom of what Stepahin was up to."

Irene cocked her head as she accepted his hand. "You're going to go jousting at windmills, aren't you?"

He winked and flashed his most charming smile.

Chapter Nine

Wendy Adams stood as she heard the lock turn in the heavy steel door—a bit of an effort since her chair, like the other three chairs and the steel table, was bolted to the concrete floor. A glance through the wire-reinforced window in the door revealed a frail-looking skinny young man in an orange jumpsuit. She could only assume that the unseen person with the key was one of the deputies.

The door opened outward into the dingy hallway of the Braddock County Adult Detention Center, and there stood her first head-to-toe vision of her newest patient. After only four days in custody, he'd already taken on the institutional pallor that was so common among incarcerated people. She'd noticed that the pale skin was more common among younger prisoners than older ones, and more prevalent among males than females. At first glance, she noticed that his hair appeared greasy and stringy, and that his fingernails were uncut and dirty. An array of zits dotted his forehead. They looked a little like the outline of Florida, but tipped over on its side.

"Go on in," said a male voice from the hallway outside her view.

Wendy knew from the file that this prisoner was twenty-three years old, but he looked eighteen. She hoped that would play to his favor in the eventual trial. "Hello, Ethan," she said. "My name is Dr. Wendy Adams. I believe that your attorney, Mr. Culligan, told you to expect me." She stepped forward to shake his hand, then saw that his handcuffs were attached to a restraining belt around his waist. Another chain ran from the belt to the shackles around his ankles.

"Deputy?" Wendy said.

A middle-aged bald guy with a beer gut and a brown uniform stepped into view.

"Keep my patient's hands cuffed if you must, but I insist that you release them from the belt."

The deputy started to argue.

"I've had this argument before with your supervisor," she preempted. "Let's not do it again. I'm not asking you to set him free. I'm merely asking you to give him the ability to scratch his nose if he so desires."

"Ah," the deputy said, reaching for a key that he'd stuffed into his Sam Browne belt. "You're *that* one." Ten seconds later, Ethan had use of his hands, though they were still bound together.

"Are the cuffs loose enough, Ethan?" Wendy asked.

The prisoner looked wary. "I suppose. You get used to them after a while."

"We good?" the deputy asked.

Wendy nodded, and the deputy nudged Ethan farther into the room and pushed the door closed.

She tried the handshake thing again, and Ethan begrudgingly returned the gesture. "That thing with the handcuffs," he said. "Was that you being the good cop?"

Wendy gestured to the chair opposite hers, and turned. "I'm not a cop at all," she said. "I'm not an investigator, I'm not a lawyer, and I'm not a federal agent, either. I'm a psychologist." She sat, but Ethan hadn't moved. That was fine.

"So, I guess we're going for an insanity defense?" Ethan said.

"I have no idea. Like I said, I'm not a lawyer."

The kid's eyes narrowed. "But Culligan told you to come."

"He *asked* me," Wendy corrected. At this stage of the doctor-patient tarantella, words mattered.

"Why would he do that if he wasn't trying to get me declared insane? I'm not, you know. Insane, I mean."

Wendy sat erect in her seat, her hands folded on the gray steel table. "Okay," she said.

"Okay, what?"

"Okay, we'll stipulate that you're not insane."

"Then I guess you can go home now," Ethan said. His posture read tough, but his eyes read terrified.

"You'd rather be locked in your cell?"

"I don't want to be manipulated," Ethan said. "I'm tired of people telling me what to do."

"I'm not here to do that."

"What, then?"

Wendy pointed to the chair opposite hers. "Have a seat and I'll tell you." God, how she hated this place. In her heart, she didn't understand how any prisoners kept their sanity in here. The aromas of cleaning solvents and dirty feet combined in a toxic stench that never changed, and that never dulled for the duration of every visit, and there had been many. Fluorescent light tubes that had no doubt been purchased from a low bidder provided the only light, and it was at once glaring and dull, thanks in no part to the yellowed wire-reinforced glass that covered them.

Ethan's chains rattled as he shuffled to the chair and sat down. "Thanks," he said. "For the hands, I mean." He held up his cuffed wrists.

She bowed her head to acknowledge.

"Just so you know, whatever this is, I can't afford to pay you," he said.

"Don't worry about that."

"Is Culligan paying you?"

"Don't worry about that, either," Wendy said. "And frankly—not to be unfriendly—that's none of your business."

"I need to know who your allegiance is to," Ethan said. "How do I know you're on my side if I'm not paying you?"

It was a savvy question, and not unreasonable. It just was not relevant in this case. "You are my patient," Wendy said. "What you say to me cannot be reported outside of this room."

"Suppose I threaten to murder someone?" Ethan asked through a deep scowl.

Wendy knew she was being tested. Clearly this kid had been around the block a few times, and had learned to trust no one. "Well, in that case, I'd be ethically bound to rat you out."

He weighed her words for a few seconds. "Right answer," he said.

"I knew that."

Then he clammed up. He sat in his chair, shoulders slumped, elbows resting on the table, watching her with casual disinterest.

Wendy read his posture as a power play, a way to maintain control. If the circumstances were different, she might have just stared back at him, testing to see who would break first. Not this time, though. "I guess this is my meeting, isn't it?" she asked.

He looked at his hands. Couldn't care less.

"Have you read the police narrative of your incident in the parking lot?" Wendy asked.

"I've read it and retold the story a thousand times. You gonna ask me to do it again?

"I don't know. Is the report accurate?"

Another shrug. "More or less."

"What's the less part?"

Another few seconds of silence, followed by a smirk. "Okay, you got me. It's accurate."

Wendy tapped the table with her fingertips. "Very well, then. No need to recap it again here."

Ethan started to stand. "Short meeting," he said.

"Not done yet," Wendy said, holding out a hand. "In fact, we haven't really begun. Have a seat."

This time, he didn't resist. He just sat. And waited for the rest.

"I want you to tell me more about your previous encounter with the man you killed."

"Nobody believes that part," Ethan said.

"Because it's hard to believe," Wendy countered. "I mean, think about it. A kidnapping that didn't happen, with a nameless kidnapper who just happened to be in the same spot as you, eleven years after the fact."

Ethan locked up again. His posture said that he wanted to cross his arms, but of course that was not possible with cuffed hands.

"Don't misunderstand," Wendy said. "I want to believe you."

"So you can get me declared crazy when I stabbed the guy."

"So German Culligan can get you exonerated of any wrongdoing," she fired back.

He recoiled. Clearly, that wasn't what he was expecting.

"Ethan, you need to divorce yourself of this notion that everyone is your enemy. I don't know what all you've endured in the past, but I'm telling you that you have an ally in me, and in German."

"Why?"

"Why should you trust us, or why are we your ally?"

"Both, I guess."

"The simple answer is because that's our job," Wendy said. She sensed that Ethan had a finely tuned bullshit meter, and she wanted to stay far away from any trip wires. "But that's not really it. I can't speak for German, but I *want* to believe you. It makes no sense to me that a young man such as yourself—no angel as far as the law is concerned, but no history of this kind of violence—would go all Rambo on a stranger. There has to be a reason for something like that to happen."

"So, I'm your research project."

Wendy sighed. "If it makes you feel better to be cynical, then yes, you're my research project. And if I do my job right, maybe—just maybe—we can put your life on the track that it's supposed to be on."

"And if you're wrong?"

She fired straight from the shoulder. "Then this does not end well for you. I don't know what you've heard of J. Daniel Petrelli, but he's the most vicious prosecutor in the Commonwealth, perhaps in the nation. If you're convicted, he'll do everything he can to see you with a needle in your arm."

Ethan looked stunned.

"Young man, if you're looking for someone to sugarcoat your situation, I'm the wrong person. And unfortunately, you're stuck with me. I want this to be the beginning of a relationship that is blunt, direct, and truthful. You impress me as someone who would appreciate that. Am I right?"

He took his time answering. "It would be a refreshing change from the bullshit artists in this place."

"That was too easy," Wendy said. She kept her tone dead serious. "I want a real answer from you. Are you willing to do your best to work with me? To help me help you?"

"I don't have much choice, do I?"

"You certainly do," Wendy said. "Drop that victim crap when you're dealing with me, or we'll be done before we start. You may have no choice where you live at present, but you have infinite choices on *how* you live. This is one of them. Do you promise to work with me, or not?"

Ethan's head bobbed.

"Say it."

He rolled his eyes. "Okay, I—"

"Without the eye roll and without the attitude."

His scowl deepened as he weighed what was happening. His eyes reddened. "I promise to work with you."

Wendy gave the tabletop a triumphant pat with both palms. "Excellent. Let's get started."

Ethan had spent a decade trying to forget the events of that afternoon. At times, he thought maybe he'd even been successful, and at other times, when the memories sneaked in anyway, the self-medication could help. Until it didn't. Often those were the worst times of all. It seemed that the drugs worked both ways. When they were helpful, they kept the memories at bay. But then there were the times when they made it impossible for him to turn them off.

The doctor's question wasn't really a question at all, but rather an opening—the same shit that shrinks pulled all the time. *Tell me about what happened eleven years ago.*

"It's got to be in that report you read," Ethan said.

The doctor did a weird thing with her face. Half smiling and half pained, she cocked her head to the left and seemed to look straight through him—all the way to his spine. "The report says you claimed to have been kidnapped eleven years ago. That's the exact language— you *claimed* to have been kidnapped."

Translation: They don't believe me. "Well, there you go," he said.

"You know better," the doctor said. "Even dismissing the conditional language—the poisonous *claimed*—saying that you were kidnapped is like saying of World War Two that the Nazis and the allies had a spat. I need to know the details."

"I have no idea what happened in World War Two."

Her eyes flashed anger. "Really? Is that how you're going to honor our agreement that is not yet five minutes old? Passive-aggressiveness is the strategy of cowards. And trust me, you are nowhere as good at it as other patients I've dealt with."

Ethan felt heat rising in his face. "What do you want from me?" he said, louder than he'd intended. "I don't know who the hell you are. You say you're a doctor—a shrink. Well, okay, I'll tell you that I'm an astrophysicist. Are you ready for me to map the universe for you? I don't even remember your name!"

"Dr. Wendy Adams," she said. She'd made her voice quieter, an old standard in shrink strategies to get him to lower his own. "You can call me Wendy. And the fact of the matter, young man, is that I am likely your last hope. Even if I made all of that up, tell me where the downside is for you trusting me."

Ethan had lost count of the number of shrinks who had tried to drill into his brain over the years. *Hey, crazy boy. Do you have nightmares? Do you have violent fantasies? Can we trust you not to bring a bazooka into your school and blow everybody away?* While those might not have been the actual questions, they were always the subtext, and the easiest route to be excused from the exercise was to lie. Tell them that you sleep like a baby every night, that your only thoughts were about roses and springtime, and that your life's ambition was to save whales or children—or both—and they scribble good things in your chart and you get your life back. The last thing any psychiatrist wanted was to deal with a problem that needed to be fixed.

They wanted to give you a handful of pills and call it a closed case.

Something about this shrink, though, felt different. For one, she didn't talk to him in that singsongy pitiful voice that the others used. And she didn't bow to his bullshit. She didn't close the file and say, *if you want to be that way, fine. I'm done.* Plus, she didn't *look* like a shrink. Instead of some precious professional business suit, she wore blue jeans, a pink top and a sport coat—or whatever the hell ladies called a sport coat. She looked both athletic and feminine, a combination that was difficult to pull off. Maybe forty-five years old, he didn't believe that the platinum blond hair was natural, but she wore it well, cropped close to her head without looking butch. Maybe it was time for him to roll the dice. Like she said, there wasn't a lot to lose at this point.

Well, except his life. But that wasn't on such a bright course as it was.

"Okay," he said. "You're right. I have to trust someone and you're it."

"I was stupid," Ethan said. "You hear all that stranger-danger bullshit from your parents and from teachers, and you just let it roll out of your head unheard, you know?"

"There's nothing stupid in being a victim," the doctor said.

Ethan felt a swell of anger. "Been a victim much yourself, Doc?" he snapped. He didn't want to be rude—in fact, he really wanted to like this one—but that was such a shrink-like thing to say. "I know what I did, and I know it was stupid. I'm not making excuses for the shit-heads who did what they did to me, but I was there, and you were not."

Dr. Adams seemed startled. "I was just—"

"You were just trying to get ahead of me. You were just preventing that moment when I say something self-destructive. I've been to this well before, you know. How about you let me talk and you sit there and listen?" That was a lot of anger—much more than the situation warranted—and he didn't know where it came from. He considered apologizing, but that impulse came and went.

"I was supposed to be at football practice," Ethan explained. Only he decided to skip out on it. It was too hot out and more and more, he just wasn't that much into football. The friends he'd known for as long as he'd known anyone had all started to grow at twice the rate that he was, and where he used to be the best ath-lete among them, now he could barely hold his own. It was embarrassing. His mom had tried to tell him that it was all so very natural—he was at that *awkward age*—but that was embarrassing, too.

So, he'd pedaled his bike from the house to the end of the street, and then off to the 7-Eleven down on Hawkins Turnpike, way the hell and gone from any-place he was ever supposed to be. Times were tough back at the house with Mom and Dad tearing at each other over whatever it was that parents who love each other hate each other about. Ethan wasn't in much of a mood to keep them happy, so this was the afternoon of his rebellion. Not just skipping out on practice, but then going to a place he wasn't supposed to be to buy the most enormous, highest-sugar Big Gulp that he could afford. It was the stuff of his mother's nightmares, and that was just fine.

Once he got to the 7-Eleven, it was Slurpee time. He was drawn to the blue raspberry flavor, until he realized what color that was going to turn his mouth. It was fine to take chances and risk getting in trouble, but it would have been stupid to stain your lips and teeth and tongue, and therefore guarantee trouble when he got home. Lemon-lime would have been the smartest bet, but it made no sense to be a pussy about it. He chose the Coke, a Slurpee that was only slightly smaller than the galvanized trash can he had to drag back and forth from the curb every Sunday and Thursday night.

"The owner was an old fart," he explained, drawing a smile from Wendy. "I tried to hang around to drink it, but he said I couldn't loiter, and that I had to leave the store. I could stand outside if I wanted to, but I couldn't take up space inside."

The problem was, it was still hot as hell outside and he had five pints of flavored ice chips to get down before they melted. After a brain freeze that felt like his skull had been cleaved with a dull hatchet, he surrendered his mission as a lost cause. Plus, he still had a half hour of pedaling to do to get home by anything close to the dinner hour. To be home later than seven o'clock was the Falk family equivalent of treason, and the penalties were similar.

"Mom would go ape shit if I was even a minute late. It was my responsibility to call in. She said that one minute of worry on her part was more of a problem than any inconvenience I might have in finding a pay phone to call home."

"No cell phone, then?" the doc asked.

Ethan coughed out a laugh. "Clearly, you never met my mom. No, no son of hers was going to be distracted from his school work by a phone." That sounded too harsh under the circumstances. "But remember, this was a long time ago. Pay phones actually existed back then."

"But you didn't call," Wendy said. "Surely there was a phone at the 7-Eleven."

"What was I going to say?" Ethan countered. "By then, it was a little after six, I guess, so I still had time to roll the dice."

What he hadn't counted on was running over a nail in the road. In all his years of biking, he'd never had a blowout. He'd never even thought about one. And he sure as hell had not been prepared to lose a front tire going downhill. He didn't remember a *bang* or even a *pop* when it blew. All he knew was that the steering wobbled for maybe two seconds, and then the handlebars jerked hard to the left, and he was airborne.

"All that talk about accidents happening in slow motion is bullshit," Ethan said. "I mean, it was like a snap. I was in my seat, and then I was flying. And then I was on the ground, half on the gravel and half on the grass."

By some miracle of good luck, he flipped in flight, landing on his back and shoulders, thereby sparing his face and his teeth. That was the first time he'd ever had the wind knocked out of him. As he struggled for the next breath, he remembered thinking that he was about to die.

"I was scared," he said. "Really, really scared."

"Were you badly hurt?"

"Nothing broken," he said. "And I don't think I hit my head all that hard, but I had a lot of road rash. Even that, though, wasn't horrible. No streaming blood anywhere."

"You were lucky," Wendy said, and immediately tried to pull the words back.

Ethan gave a genuine laugh. "Yeah, lucky. And you've even read ahead in my story."

She was pretty when she blushed. "I'm so sorry. That's not what I meant."

"I know what you meant. So, now I was stuck on the side of this road with a broken bicycle, skinned up everywhere, and with only one shoe."

"What happened to the other shoe?"

"I have no idea," Ethan said. "Weird, the things you remember. Somehow, I got blasted out of my shoe, and I couldn't find it anywhere."

"Was there any traffic?" Wendy asked. "Didn't anyone try to help you?"

"Just one car," Ethan said, and his mood darkened. "One goddamn car."

Chapter Ten

It was getting late, and Ethan was getting scared. The window of opportunity for arriving home without punishment had closed, and the sun was beginning to dip low. You'd think that a place with the word turnpike in its name would have more cars driving down it, but that was not the case for the Hawkins. This was a country road where no one who lived along it had any place to go, and knew no one who wanted to visit them. A long stretch of loneliness.

As he pushed his crippled bicycle down the shoulder, its front wheel all but useless, Ethan considered several times dragging the bike down a long driveway to one of the houses that lay nestled in the trees, but the same vexing question kept him moving along: What am I going to tell my parents?

Ethan heard the engine before he sensed the presence of the car. It was a throaty sound, a more powerful engine than most. He felt the vibration in his feet. He turned to look at the approaching vehicle, and as he did, it slowed. As it passed, he didn't recognize the logo on the hood, but it was a hot-looking beast. A two-door hardtop, it looked like something Batman would drive. It slowed as it passed, and for a brief instant, Ethan thought that his savior had arrived. Then it pulled away, only to pull over to the shoulder and stop a few dozen yards farther down the street. Its hazard flashers popped on.

Finally, the vehicle's door opened and a man unfolded himself from the driver's seat. He was of the age that Ethan had a hard time identifying. Roughly the age of his parents, maybe a year or two older. The most striking thing Ethan noticed was the darkness of his dark beard. His height was hard to judge, too, because of the squattiness of the car.

"Are you okay?" the driver called.

"I'm fine," Ethan said, despite the fact that he was anything but.

"What happened to your bike?"

"I wrecked it."

The stranger laughed. "Well, I can see that. Are you hurt?" He checked over his shoulder and started to approach.

At that moment, Ethan felt no fear at all. Instead, he felt relief that someone was there to help. "Not really. Skinned up a little, but not really hurt."

Maybe twenty-five feet separated them. "How old are you?"

"Eleven," Ethan said. "Almost twelve. My birthday's in two months."

"Eleven and five-sixths, then." His smile widened. "What's your name?" Ten feet.

"Ethan Falk."

The man offered his hand. "Pleased to make your acquaintance, Ethan Falk. My name is Joey. Joey Mc-Fadden."

Ethan shook the man's hand, and in retrospect, the contact lingered just a few beats too long. His first inkling of trouble.

"Let's take a look at you," Joey said, and he stooped to look closer at the boy's bare legs. He touched one of the scrapes, and Ethan jumped. "Sorry," he said. "It doesn't look too bad. He stood. "Lift your shirt and we'll see if you're hurt there."

"I'm not," Ethan said, and he took a step back. "I already checked."

Joey mirrored his step back. "I frightened you," he said. "I'm sorry. I can see how that would make you . . . Well, you know. Sorry."

"That's okay."

Joey looked at his watch. "It's getting late. Do your parents know where you are?"

Ethan's face got hot. "No."

"Uh-oh. They're going to be worried, aren't they?"

"More like pissed."

"I guess that kind of worry always leads to pissed," Joey said. "Why don't you go to one of these houses and call home? They can pick you up."

Ethan pivoted his head to look down one of the driveways. "That's complicated," he said.

"Look, they're not going to get any less pissed the longer you wait."

Ethan took a long, deep breath. The guy had a point. Anger had to peak someplace, right? By now, Mom was going to be ready to declare war. She'd be calling the cops soon. If he called, at least he could cap the worry. Maybe the relief would even give him some points in the good column.

"It's the only smart move," Joey said. "Look, I've got kids, and it hasn't been that long since I was one. Tell you what. Put your bike down there off the road for a second, and I'll let you use my phone. It's in the car." He started walking back to his vehicle.

Something didn't feel right. Ethan hesitated, but there's no way he could have articulated why. Joey seemed nice enough. It wasn't as if he—

Joey turned. "Are you calling, or aren't you?" Ethan caught the exasperation in the man's voice, the subtext of, Dude, I'm doing you a freaking favor here.

Ethan pushed his bike to the side of the road, into the ditch, where he propped it more or less upright. When he turned back, Joey was still waiting for him, beckoning him with an extended arm, wiggling his fingers in the darkening shadows. "Don't look so glum, for God's sake," he said. "This will all pass."

He waited till Ethan was astride, and then placed his hand on his shoulder. He squeezed. Just a little. "Whoa. Muscles. You must be an athlete."

Ethan smiled. "Football. That's where I was supposed to be."

Joey guided him to the passenger-side door and opened it. "There's the phone," he said. It was on the center console. "Help yourself."

"I guess that's when he hit me," Ethan concluded. "I remember it as a flash of light and the smell you get when you hit your head really hard. Blood, I guess."

Dr. Wendy's face had folded into a raisiny scowl. He couldn't tell if it was sympathy or distrust. She hadn't said anything in a long time.

"What?" Ethan said. "You don't look like you believe me."

"Is it safe for me to assume that Joey was in fact the man you killed in the parking lot?"

Ethan inhaled to answer, but something broke free in his head—an image he hadn't thought of until this very minute. "No!" he proclaimed. He could hear the excitement in his own voice, and he could see that it startled her. "No, he wasn't. That guy—the guy I killed—called himself Bill. I never believed that that was his name, but that's what he called himself."

Now Wendy looked confused. "I don't remember any mention of someone named Bill," she said. "Not in as many times as you've told the story."

"I know!" Ethan said. His heart pounded. "I just now remembered that. There was more than one guy involved. There were a bunch. Maybe four. I guess they just ran together in my head."

"Bill," Wendy said. There was that look again.

"You *don't* believe me."

"It's not that I don't believe you. I just haven't heard any mention of Bill before."

"We've never spoken before. Plus, I just told you."

"Suppressed memory," Wendy said. "You've told your story to a lot of other people, though. You've never mentioned a Bill, but now in a flash, you do. At just the right time to start building that insanity defense that you said you didn't want."

Anger boiled in Ethan's gut. He was being played. "I thought you said you were the one I could trust."

Wendy's features didn't change a bit. "I am," she said.

"But you don't believe me."

She rolled her eyes. "And you keep coming back to that. Do I believe you? I'm trying to, but every word you say is fantastic—in the sense of the word that it has no basis in verifiable fact. It's fantasy."

The anger bloomed larger. Ethan felt himself shutting down.

"You're getting pissed," Wendy said. "Your body language says that you're done talking, that you're going to punish me by keeping your story to yourself."

"What's the sense of telling it?"

"As opposed to which alternative?" Still, her face showed nothing. Not disinterest, exactly, but in-your-face brutality.

Then an internal switch flipped or something. She abruptly sat up straight, and patted the table with both palms. "Nope, we're not doing this," she declared. "We're getting unnecessarily crosswise. Hand to God, I don't know yet whether or not your story is credible, but I can tell you this: I am one hundred percent convinced that you one hundred percent believe every word you're telling me. You're not spouting a line of bullshit—at least I don't think so. How's that?"

Ethan remained passive. It was too early to commit.

"Okay, fine, hold your cards tight," Wendy went on. "I get it. You're angry, and you're frustrated. Not just about this, but about a lot of things in your life. If you let me, we can explore all of that, and I promise that I will try to help you cope with whatever you need to cope with. But the first step is to be forthcoming, and that's the ball that you seem particularly adept at dropping. I said at the beginning of this meeting that I wanted you to trust me. That means giving me a break."

Ethan was tired of the lecture, so he took a breath to speak.

"I'm not done yet," Wendy said, cutting him off. "You, young man, need to recognize that this is a two-way street. You can't treat every question as an affront. This interview process is in fact how truth is discovered. That means not getting pissy at every other sentence."

"This is hard," Ethan said. "This is shit that I've spent the past eleven years trying to forget, and you and the others are doing everything you can to bring it back to life."

"You want exculpatory evidence, don't you?"

"I want it all to be a bad dream!" He knew he'd said the words too loud, but she needed to adjust, too. "Those assholes ruined everything. They ruined . . ." He was surprised when his voice disappeared. He took a moment. "They ruined *me*."

The words just hung there. Neither of them said anything for the better part of fifteen seconds.

"So, do you want to know what happened next?" Ethan asked.

"No," Wendy said. "We'll get to that in time. Tell me about your previous encounters with mental health professionals."

Ethan's shields flew up. "Why?"

She waited for the answer.

"Okay, they were bullshit," he said. "Nobody really wanted to hear what happened—well, okay, at first, I wasn't willing to share what happened—but folks don't want to hear about an eleven-year-old boy getting ass-raped. You bring that up, and they reach for their prescription pads. But there's a world of difference between dulling a memory and coping with it."

"Why do you think you weren't willing to share?" Wendy asked.

Ethan fought the instinct to throw out an I-don't-know. "Because it hurt, I suppose."

She waited for more.

"And because I was afraid."

"Of?"

Ethan's mind raced. Did he want to go here? It was the room in his memory that he'd promised years ago never to open. And when he did, there'd be no going back. But if not now, then when?

He settled himself with a breath, and looked over his shoulders to verify that they were still alone. "How much time do we have?"

"As long as you need." Dr. Wendy looked like she was preparing herself for an interesting story. She had no idea.

"Ask me what happened to Joey," Ethan said. "Ask me what happened to all the others."

Chapter Eleven

When Jonathan was done with his recap of his conversation with Wolverine, Dom rose from his chair around the War Room's teak conference table and walked to the door. "I don't think I need to hear any more of this," he said. "As much as I admire your ability to compartmentalize information, I'm afraid I don't share it."

"Really, Padre?" Boxers asked, clearly surprised. "You hear confessions all day."

"From people who want forgiveness, Big Guy," Dom said, placing a hand on Boxers' shoulder. "The way this is going, I don't see a lot of contrition in the immediate future. Besides, I don't want to steal Digger's thunder from a future meeting." He winked at Jonathan, whose last steps in closing out most operations was to seek absolution from God via Dom.

After the door closed, Boxers said, "I'm not sure why he was here to begin with."

"Because I asked him," Jonathan said.

"Why?"

"Because I wanted him here." Jonathan engineered

his tone to cut off all further discussion. Fact was, Dom was a solid source of strength for him during the first dance with Ethan Falk, and Jonathan felt comfort in his presence.

"So, what exactly is our mission?" Venice asked.

"I want to know why Stepahin was back in town," Jonathan said.

"And how are we going to do that?" Boxers asked.

"Well . . ." Venice drew the word out to fill three seconds as she typed. "The Braddock County Police Department will do a fair amount of our heavy lifting for us on that one," she said. "The ICIS entries make it clear that they're trying to retrace his steps. For what it's worth, they're as confused and concerned as we are by the fact that he's a John Doe."

"What all are they doing?" Jonathan asked.

"Everything I would, but they're doing it with permissions and warrants."

"How boring," Boxers said with a rumble of a laugh.

Jonathan stood and moved to a window, where he could look out toward the swaying masts of boats moored at the marina. "Let's think this through," he said. "They're going to trace where he's been. They'll tap into every security camera they can find. If he was using a false cover for credit cards, they'll have that trail, too."

"He had twelve thousand dollars in cash," Venice said. "I doubt that he'll have needed to use credit."

"And he'd have been a fool if he did," Boxers agreed.

"Still," Jonathan said. "My point is that the police will take care of tracking where he went. All we need to figure out is why he went there."

Boxers laughed again. "Well, okay, if that's *all* we have to do, we'll have lots of spare time to cure cancer and uncover the secrets of Area 51."

Jonathan acknowledged the irony with a smile. "Okay, maybe it won't be easy."

"Do you think that the BCPD will have access to Stepahin's secret past?"

"Absolutely not," Jonathan said.

"So, when they put together their trail, they're going to try to connect dots that don't exist."

"Which means they'll make them up," Boxers said. "That won't be good for our pal Ethan."

"No, it won't," Jonathan said. It was the job of a police detective to stitch strands of evidence into a narrative that will make sense for a prosecutor, and ultimately for a jury. Since they were starting with the supposition that Ethan Falk was a cold-blooded murderer, Jonathan had every expectation that the evidence trail would demonstrate to the police that their John Doe had spent a lifetime merely minding his own business.

"How do you intend to bridge that information gap?" Boxers asked.

"I have no idea," Jonathan said. "Let's find the new information before we worry too much about bridging the gaps." When he turned away from the window, he saw a faraway expression in Venice's face that intrigued him. "Okay, Ven, what aren't you saying?" He was particularly intrigued that her thoughtfulness involved neither typing nor staring into her computer screen.

"I'm a little confused as to which case we're working," she said. "Are we doing Wolverine's bidding and finding out what Stepahin's mission was, or are we trying to build a case that will help Ethan Falk?"

"As far as I'm concerned, a little bit of both," Jonathan said.

"The kid's a lost cause, Dig," Boxers said. "I mean, even if we paint the perfect picture of Stepahin being the monster that he was, that wouldn't justify a cold-blooded attack in the middle of a parking lot."

Jonathan glared. "Whose side are you on?"

Boxers' features darkened. "I'm going to pretend you didn't ask such a stupid question."

Jonathan felt instant regret. "Sorry," he said. "This guilt thing is new territory for me." He returned to his seat. "Okay, then, what's our next step?"

"In which direction?" Venice asked.

"Let's deal with Wolfie's request first," Jonathan said. "How are we going to figure out if Stepahin was here to kidnap somebody, and if so, who that some-body might be?"

Silence prevailed for a solid half minute as they each worked the problem. "There's no string to pull," Boxers said, finally.

Venice agreed. "We don't have direct access to the evidence from the stabbing, and we don't have direct access to the body, though I can't imagine what they would show. The electronic trail lies in the hands of the Braddock County PD, and until they update ICIS—which they've been pretty good about doing so far—I don't think we can get an angle to leverage."

"I'm hearing a lot of defeatism," Jonathan said.

"I believe the word you're searching for is *reality*," Boxers said.

"All we need is a little nudge," Jonathan said. "Just enough to get some momentum, and from there, to get some enthusiasm." He stood again and returned to the window. If he craned his neck to look through to the right, he could see the near edge of the beginning of the commercial fishing pier.

"We're missing something," he mused aloud. "Somebody give me a different angle to consider," he said.

"I have no idea what you mean," Venice said.

"We're obviously running down the wrong alley." When his team fell silent like this, Jonathan knew that they were humoring him. It was not uncommon for him to utter non sequiturs when he was thinking aloud, and he'd come to appreciate their hesitance to keep saying, "Huh?" as he worked the problem.

"Let's assume that Wolfie is correct," he said. "Let's assume that there is an organized effort to kidnap high-profile Americans. Who are the players?"

"Holy crap," Boxers said. "How do you begin to count?"

"Let's start," Jonathan pressed. "You've got four hundred thirty-five members of the House, plus another hundred from the Senate."

"Plus their spouses and children," Venice said. "And their grandchildren. In some cases, great-grandchildren. Big Guy's right. The list is too high to count."

"And there's no way to provide security for all of them," Boxers added. "Is Wolfie even making them aware that they might be in danger?"

Jonathan looked at him and made a pained face. "I doubt it. I hope not. They're dysfunctional enough as it is without being driven to panic."

"She's not even sure that such a plot exists, right?" Venice said. "Isn't that one of the things we're supposed to find out?"

"Exactly," Jonathan said. "That's why it wouldn't make sense to alert them."

"What about Congressman Johnson?" Boxers said. "Surely, he's going to tell his colleagues what happened."

Jonathan dismissed that. "Given the events of the rescue, I'm not sure he'll want to come forward with his use of nongovernment assets to get his daughter back. If he does, he does, but as far as he knows, this was just a one-off."

The door to the War Room rattled from a soft impact from the other side. Boxers rolled his chair back and reached for the knob. As soon as the door was ajar, JoeDog entered the space, her tail wagging hard enough to unbalance her back end. A stray black lab who had adopted Jonathan some years ago as her nominal master, JoeDog had unfettered access to wherever she wanted to go.

Jonathan beamed. "Hey, sweetheart," he said, clapping his hands softly, "I haven't seen you in days."

She hit him with a running hug, her forepaws stretching nearly to his shoulders. She exchanged a chin lick for a quick ear rub, and then she was done. She curled up under the conference table and was snoring within fifteen seconds.

"It occurs to me that we haven't looked at this world from the bad guy's point of view," Jonathan said.

Boxers and Venice exchanged looks of confusion.

"Think about it," Jonathan said. He could hear the excitement in his own voice. "If you're the al-Amin group, and you paid a bunch of guys to kidnap the Johnson girl, how are you going to feel if you never hear anything about it? It's not on the news, and the girl hasn't been delivered. How's that going to sit with you?"

"I'm gonna be pissed," Boxers said.

Jonathan shot him with an extended forefinger. "Exactly. Now, let's say you find out that another kidnapper you hired ends up dead in a parking lot. How are you going to feel then?"

Venice said, "A little desperate, I would imagine."

"Or a lot desperate," Jonathan said. "You're going to wonder just what the hell is going on. You're going to start feeling paranoid. And then what are you going to do?"

They stared back at him.

"You're going to make a phone call!" Jonathan proclaimed. "If not literally, then figuratively. You're going to reach out to whoever you reach out to, to find out just how deep a shit storm is on its way."

Venice's eyes got wider. "You're suggesting there's a record."

Jonathan grinned. "NSA's got a record of every call made by every citizen. If those calls—or e-mails or texts or whatever—originated with a known asset of al-Amin, they're especially likely to have something."

Venice's smile turned to a wince. "I'm among the best at hacking, Dig, but NSA files are a bit beyond my league. And my one source locked down tight after that business in Mexico."

Jonathan looked to Boxers. "Who do we know who just announced on the Unit message boards that he'd taken an analyst spot at No Such Agency?"

Boxers' perpetual scowl deepened. "How 'just'?"

"Within the last three months. He was on C Squadron, I think. At least at the end."

Big Guy shook his head. "This isn't ringing a . . . wait. Was it Konan?"

Jonathan snapped his fingers. "Yes. That's him."

"Konan?" Venice said. "Like the Barbarian?"

"Exactly like him," Boxers said with a laugh.

"His real name is Henry West. The man was a beast," Jonathan said. "His biceps were the size of my thighs. A hell of a war fighter, too."

"Took a bullet, didn't he?" Boxers asked.

"I think so. Through-and-through gut shot. It's good that he got to stay in the Community. He had skills." Jonathan nodded toward Venice. "You'd have been particularly impressed."

"He's a hacker?" Venice guessed.

"Of the nth degree."

"Do you think he'd help us out?" Boxers asked. "I mean, he's pretty new to his spot."

"We'll be especially charming," Jonathan said.

"They kept us in a dungeon," Ethan explained.

"Us?" Over the past few minutes, Dr. Wendy had become deeply engaged in the conversation. "Who is 'us'?"

"I wasn't always alone in there. There were other boys, about my age. I knew their names at one point, but I don't remember them anymore."

"How many?"

Ethan pursed his lips and looked to the ceiling. "Over the time I was there—which they told me was only eight days, but I don't believe it—there were three others. Two were there when I got there, but they left early. Then I was alone for a while, and then there was one who came in and was gone really fast after that."

"What happened to them?" Wendy asked.

"Don't you already have all this? I told—"

"I want to hear it from you," she said. Her voice was softer, kinder.

Ethan took a deep breath and closed his eyes against the memory. "I think they were sold," he said. "I was telling you that they kept us in a dungeon. It was a room carved out from under the floor of the basement. The basement floor was concrete—which meant that the dungeon's ceiling was concrete—but the floor was dirt. Lots of rocks and stuff. They'd dug a pit in the back corner about this big." He made a circle with his arms, maybe two and a half feet in diameter. That's where we'd shit and piss. You can imagine what it smelled like."

Wendy watched Ethan as he spoke. When he opened his eyes, the intensity of her glare startled him.

He chuckled and scratched his head. "You know what's funny? They gave us toilet paper. Lots of it, probably thirty rolls of it."

"Why is that funny?"

"Think about it," Ethan said. "They kept us naked on a dirt floor that smelled like shit—literally—they did unspeakable things to us, but they made sure that we used soft toilet paper." He felt his eyes redden and he wiped them. "It makes no goddamn sense."

"Why do you think the other boys were sold?" Wendy prompted as she looked down and made a note in her book.

"I assume it was for sex."

She looked up, momentarily confused. "No, that's not what I meant. What happened that made you think they were sold?"

"Oh. Every now and then, the trap door in the ceiling would open, and one of them—usually it was Bill— would stick his head down and call for the other boys to come upstairs."

"But not you?"

Ethan shook his head. "No. From the very beginning, they said that they had somebody special in mind for me. I have no idea what that meant. Looking back, I figure I was somehow a perfect match for a specific customer. Jesus, those guys were disgusting." He didn't realize that he was crying until he sniffed.

"Are you okay to go on?" Wendy asked.

"I'm good if you are," he said. "This is the part where all you shrink types start getting squirmy. Don't worry, I won't go into the gory details."

"You can go into as much detail as you're comfortable with."

Ethan suppressed a smirk. Honestly, head doctors were as predictable as sunrises. They put the aggression in passive-aggressiveness. "So the kids would climb up the ladder—hop, actually, because they kept our feet cuffed, and then I wouldn't see them again. In one case, two of them went up but only one of them came back. He told me that there was an Asian guy up there who looked them both over, and then picked the other one. The one they didn't choose was sent back into the hole. He was gone for a long time, though, and when he came back, he didn't say anything. He sat on the opposite side and cried." Ethan waited to see if Dr. Wendy could read between the lines, or if she would ask the obvious. Her silence won her some points.

"The others, when they went up, they were by themselves, and I never saw them again. It's a shame that the last one—I do remember his name now, it was Pierre, such a weird name—disappeared maybe half a day before I was rescued. Just a few hours."

Ethan watched as Wendy wrote more notes. He waited for her nod before he picked up the story again.

"Tell me what happened to Joey," she said.

It was both the best and worst memory of the entire nightmare.

Ethan wondered what made the dangling light move. The single bulb provided just enough light to see—maybe even enough to read if you really wanted, but there was nothing to read, so that meant nothing. There was also enough light to create shadows, and the shadows made the dark spots where monsters lived. He knew that there was no such thing as monsters, but knowing it didn't make it any less scary. And because the bulb was always swaying, the shadows never stopped moving. Even when he closed his eyes, he could still see the darkness swirling.

The aloneness was beginning to get to him. He heard himself thinking thoughts that he shouldn't think, about maybe killing himself, or about fashioning a weapon out of something, and fighting back. Something sharp, so next time Joey told him it was time to earn his supper—

The trap door moved and Ethan's heart rate tripled. It must be suppertime, and there was no weapon. The door must have been heavy as hell because when it opened, it made a concrete-on-concrete scratching sound. It would lift slowly at first, and no matter who it was, they always groaned and cussed while they were doing it. The concrete hatch would crack open, and then they'd cuss, and when the hatch finally heaved over, it shook the whole ceiling.

Dust fell, as did a patch of light from the basement above. Ethan prayed—actually begged God—for it to be Bill, coming to sell him off. Anybody other than—

"Step back, kid," Joey said. "Time for you to earn your supper."

"I'm not hungry," Ethan said. He scrambled to his feet and backed away from the ladder.

"Oh, but I am," Joey said. The stink of cigarettes somehow washed away the stink of the shit pot. "I am very, very hungry." He climbed down the ladder, and smiled as he turned to face his prey. He carried no food. "And I see exactly what I want." His hands moved to his belt.

Ethan couldn't do this again. He wouldn't do this again. Joey hadn't taken two steps forward when Ethan launched a shriek from his throat. It was a girly sound, high-pitched and impossibly loud in this small a space. He didn't speak any words. It was just noise, the sound of panic and disgust and hate and pain.

Joey stopped in his tracks, seemingly stunned. "What—"

From upstairs, a voice yelled, "What the hell is going on? My God."

Ethan retreated further toward the shit pit.

"Do it again, kid, and I'll break that throat," Joey said.

From upstairs, the voice—Ethan recognized it now as Bill's—said, "Oh, for Christ's sake, you sick bastard! Leave him alone. You're going to ruin him."

"You'd like that, wouldn't you, boy?" Joey said. *"You'd like a little ruining, wouldn't you?"* He advanced.

Ethan shrieked even louder.

Joey's face turned crimson. "Don't say I didn't warn—"

The entire world came apart over the course of just a few seconds. First, the lights went out, and then half a second later, the house shook from an explosion. A real explosion—not like a slamming door, but an explosion, complete with a flash, though the flash seemed far away.

Someone yelled, "Hands, hands, hands!" and then there was a rapid series of gunshots. Bang-bang-bang. Bang-bang-bang. *Bursts of three in less than a second.*

Ethan moved quickly to his left, trying to put distance and an angle between him and Joey with the distended pants.

The air filled with cussing, yelling. "Hands!" Bang-bang-bang.

And then the most magic of all magic words: "Ethan Falk! Shout out! We're here to take you home!"

"Here!" Ethan shouted. *"Under the basement! Help! I'm—"*

Joey was on him. Ethan couldn't see him, but he could smell him. And he could feel his hands, one down low, and one up high. "Shut up, you shit. Shut up or I swear to God—"

"Help!" Ethan shouted. "Oh, God, help me!"

The world erupted again, only this time from an impossibly short distance. The blinding light and the deafening blast arrived together. The pressure wave took Ethan's breath away, and suddenly, he was on the ground, in the dirt, trying to breathe and struggling to hear.

Then hands were on him again, and Joey's stink was like a part of his skin. "Stay back!" he yelled. Ethan couldn't see anything. The world was like black velvet at midnight, but with a big honkin' white spot where the explosion had burned a hole in his retinas.

"Put him down, shithead," someone said. It was a deep voice, deep enough to make the floor vibrate.

"I swear to God—"

BANG!

Another flash of light, this one not as bright, but somehow much louder, and then Ethan was on the ground, and hotness flooded over his naked flesh. He knew it was blood, and he knew he should have been horrified, but all he felt was relief.

"Are you Ethan Falk?" asked another voice.

"Yes!" Ethan shouted it because he wasn't one hundred percent sure he could make noise with all this weight on his back. Plus, his ears felt as if they'd been stuffed with cotton. "I'm Ethan! I'm right here!"

"PC secure," the voice said, though Ethan wasn't sure who the man was talking to. "One more sleeping."

The weight lifted from atop Ethan, and he clearly smelled blood. "Hey, kid," said the man with the deep voice. "We're here to take you home. Did that shithead hurt you?"

* * *

"And I couldn't answer him," Ethan said. "I just started to sob." As he was about to do again right now. "It was over. I still couldn't see anything, but the big one slung me over his shoulder like a sack and he carried me up the ladder. He wore all of this equipment. Like a soldier. The stuff on him—ammunition and shit—all dug into me and I remember complaining about that. He told me that it wouldn't be much longer."

"What did he look like?" Wendy asked.

"I told you. He was big. And I mean *huge*. And he was dressed like a soldier, only all in black. He had night vision goggles on him, too. I mean, I guess that's what they were. They looked like binoculars fixed to a helmet, the same kind that you see in the news reports from Iraq. The guy dripped guns and ammunition. When he finally put me down, we were up on the main floor of the house, and there was some light up there, through the windows, I guess. He put me on a chair in the living room and told me not to move, that he'd get something to wrap me in. A few seconds later, he wrapped a blanket around my shoulders and when he pulled the binocular things out of the way, he still didn't have a face. Everything but his eyes was covered with a ski mask."

"How long were you on that chair?"

"I have no idea," Ethan said. "Honestly, it could have been five minutes, it could have been fifteen. I don't think it was as long as an hour."

"What did the big man do then?"

"He just stood there. He kept his rifle up, like he was ready to shoot, but not at me. Like at anything else. Looking back, it was like being guarded by a big dog."

"Did he talk to you?"

"No, not really. Not after he put me down and wrapped me up. Every now and then, he'd press a button on his chest and say something—I imagine it was a radio—but he never talked to me. After a while, the other guy came upstairs. He was dressed just like the big one, but he was a lot smaller. His face was covered, too, but I remember he had blue eyes. Not just regular blue eyes, but *intensely* blue eyes. He came over to me and kneeled down directly in front. He asked me if I was okay, and I said yes, and then he told me that I was out of danger, but he wanted to know if there was anyone else in the house. Any other kids. I told him no, that I was the last one. He took the cuffs off my ankles and asked me if I could walk, and when I said yes, he said they could carry me if I wanted, but I said that I wanted to walk. I didn't tell him that it was mostly because of the way their stuff poked at me. So, we left."

It took a few seconds for Wendy's note-taking to catch up with real time. "Just like that? You just left?"

Ethan answered with an extended shrug because he didn't know what she was looking for.

"How did you leave?"

"Through the front door."

"Don't be obtuse, Ethan. In a car, by helicopter? How did you leave?"

That was a good question, not a part of the ordeal that he thought about very often. "By several cars," he said. "First, they hustled me into like a station wagon, a real beater of a car. We were only in that for a couple of miles, and then we switched to a bigger one. An SUV, I think. Maybe a van. Then we drove for a long ways. It was still dark when we pulled into this big empty parking lot. We parked, and then they handed me off to another guy. This one looked normal. Dark hair, wore a suit. He then drove me to another parking lot, where my dad was waiting for me."

More note taking. She was writing a book, apparently. "Were you frightened during this trip?" She asked that without looking up.

"No." The strength of his answer startled him.

It startled Wendy, too. Her head snapped up from her journal. "No? Face masks, guns, ammunition, shooting, death, and you're telling me you weren't frightened?"

Ethan felt continually off-balance speaking with this lady. What did she want from him? "When the shooting was going on, of course I was scared. I was startled by the noise, but I never felt in danger once Scorpion had me."

"Scorpion is the big man?"

"No, he's the littler one. And he wasn't what you'd call little. But next to the other one, *everybody* is little. When they were dropping me off with the guy in the parking lot, I asked him who he was, and he said I should call him Scorpion." Ethan smiled at a memory. "He said it's 'a cool name for a scary insect that strikes fast.'"

Wendy wrote some more.

Ethan went on, "So, after my dad picked me up—"

Wendy raised her hand for silence. "No," she said. "That's all I need for now."

Ethan gaped. There was a lot more story to tell.

Wendy closed her notebook and clicked her pen closed with a flourish. "It's been a long session. Almost an hour and a half. We'll pick up here next time."

Ethan's stomach fluttered. He didn't want to go back to his cell. "When will the next time be?"

"How's day after tomorrow?" She stood. This was not a negotiable decision.

Ethan said, "My schedule is wide open."

Chapter Twelve

Like most associations of retirees, former Special Forces operators enjoyed a number of gossip lines. The best ones were heavily encrypted and shared the kind of unvarnished opinions that would cause politicians to shit pickles.

One such encrypted site was a listserv called Do or Die. Through it, Jonathan was able to keep track of the truth behind the worldwide terror threat. Hint: It was way, way worse than the general public comprehended. Jonathan's listserv handle was Detn8or4life, and by tweaking a few known contacts, he was able to find out that Konan's avatar was PipSqueak1. With a little help from Venice, he was able to find an e-mail address for Henry West. Two hours later, Jonathan spoke with him on the phone, and three hours after that, Jonathan was sitting in his BMW M6 in the lot at Edgewater Park in Edgewater, Maryland, awaiting the arrival of a white Lexus with Maryland tags ending in the number 856.

And there it was. The man behind the driver's seat appeared to have changed little, and he waved as he passed. The spot next to Jonathan's was open, but Konan chose a spot two rows over, and probably ten slots down. It was good tradecraft to take one's time when establishing a contact.

Since it was Jonathan's meeting, he moved first, unfolding himself from his sports car and strolling across the paved lot toward a paved path that led to a collection of four baseball fields. Ahead of him lay a squatty white building with a gray roof. He figured it to be restrooms, but by the time he approached closely enough to see the sign on the door, his interest had evaporated. Beyond the building, and between the fields, the park's designers had left a thick grove of trees, which Jonathan imagined were intended to provide a buffer between the noise of the park and the saltbox houses that surrounded it.

Jonathan entered the woods, walked maybe twenty-five yards, then turned and waited. This was the time of year when the Washington Metropolitan Area was at its most beautiful. The brilliance of the autumn leaves had faded, but color remained, and the thermometer registered chilly but not yet cold. Jonathan's jacket concealed a Colt Commander on his belt, making him a felon only ten miles from the other side of the Potomac River, where no one would raise an eyebrow.

Konan took long enough to join him that Jonathan wondered if maybe the man had changed his mind. When he finally did push his way into the woods, Konan greeted his old friend with a big smile and an extended hand.

"Digger Grave," he said. "Man, it's been a long time." Henry West had softened a bit since Jonathan last saw him, but he remained an imposing man. At six-three, he still had a broad chest and narrow waist, and his biceps still challenged the fabric of his shirt, but there was just enough jiggle to show that civilian life had reduced his maniacal workout regimen. Plus, he was wearing a white shirt and Republican tie—a look that defied every memory Jonathan had of the man.

"How ya doin', Konan?" Jonathan said, accepting the gesture of friendship. "Actually, it hasn't been as many years as you probably think."

"Where's Big Guy? I thought you two were joined at the hip."

"I keep him home sometimes," Jonathan said with a chuckle. "In public places like this, he sometimes can draw a little bit too much attention." He didn't like talking about Boxers with others from the Unit. All too often, they allowed themselves to confuse Big Guy's overt aggressiveness and overall quiet tone as a sign of limited intellect, and nothing could have been farther from the truth.

Jonathan made a show of looking at his watch. "I know you have work to do, so—"

Konan held up a hand for silence. "Before you get to what you want to talk about, I want to tell you how much I appreciate all that you do."

Jonathan's shields came up. He knew that some elements of his post-Army work had made it into the rumor mill, but he didn't know how much was known by how many. The correct answer was as little as possible by as few as possible.

"What's that look?" Konan asked.

"I'm not sure what you're talking about."

"Yeah, right." He laughed, but when Jonathan didn't, he dialed it back. "Okay, fine. Play it coy. Certainly neither confirm nor deny, but we all know how you went to bat for Boomer and his family—twice—and that kind of loyalty means a shitload to everyone in the Community."

Boomer—real name Dylan Nasbe—had gotten cross-ways with some of the wrong people not too long ago, and Jonathan had reached out in friendship when the rest of the world seemed committed to being Boomer's enemy.

Jonathan remained poker-faced.

"Yeah, fine," Konan said. "We've also heard rumors about some pretty wild freelance antics that we lay at your feet. If the rumors aren't true, please don't tell me, because I really want them to be. Anyway, you need to know that there's a whole lot of snake eaters out there who'd walk through fire for you. Number me among them. Now, what can I do for you?"

"I need you to bend some laws for me," Jonathan said.

Konan snorted a laugh. "Yeah, I kinda figured that out when you spelled out that you wanted to meet in the woods in a public park."

"What do you know about a group called al-Amin?"

Konan cocked his head and tucked his hands in his pants pockets as a smirk grew on his face. "So that *was* you, huh? That business on Route One a few days ago?"

"Jesus."

"Looking at the elements, you were the first person I thought of when I heard that no one could figure out who the shooters were."

Jonathan didn't have the energy to go through the whole denial charade again. "So, the bad guys . . . ?"

"Freelancers, as far as we can tell."

"For whose side?"

Konan chuckled. "Well, that's the problem with free-lancers, isn't it? It's hard to know. Tell me who their target was, and I'll give you my opinion on where their allegiances lie."

Jonathan cocked his head, trying to see the other man's angle.

"What?" Konan asked. He sounded defensive.

"Are you playing straight?" Jonathan asked. "You really don't know who the kidnapping target was?"

Konan drew an exaggerated X on his chest with his finger. "Cross my heart. I figure it had to be somebody important, but we haven't yet been able to figure out who."

"Then how did you even know it happened?"

"Because guys we were watching ended up dead. Even the local cops have figured out that it was probably a foiled kidnapping. You must have seen that on the news."

"I haven't watched the news since it became info-tainment," Jonathan said. "But you're right. It was an important person. Mindy Johnson, daughter of William H. Johnson of Massachusetts."

"The congressman?"

"The very one," Jonathan said. "Now, what's the tie to al-Amin?"

Konan pointed to the meandering trail through the woods. "Let's keep moving," he said. "I don't like standing still when I talk about this."

"There's a lot of that going around," Jonathan quipped, recalling his stroll through DC with Wolverine.

"Huh?"

"Don't worry about it." Jonathan glanced over his shoulder to make sure they were alone.

"The connections are all fuzzy, and they're not pointing in an identifiable direction yet. But if you close one eye and look at them is just a certain way, you can talk yourself into seeing something pretty scary." He looked to Jonathan for a reaction.

"You're not really going to make me ask, are you?"

"Fine," Konan joked. "Ruin the fun. Now, I caution you that I have analysts working for me who would argue I'm wrong—"

"Oh, for God's sake."

"It's important," Konan insisted. "Given the stakes, it needs to be clear where the space is that separates fact from supposition."

Jonathan decided to let him run. It seemed like the fastest route to the punch line.

"There's been chatter," Konan said. "Not much that could be considered actionable, but it's interesting nonetheless. For years, we've dealt with fundamentalists from the Sandbox and the 'Stans who dream of bringing the fight to the Great Satan on our own turf, but we've done a pretty good job of keeping a cap on the crazies. When al Qaeda or ISIL start to reorganize, we're pretty good at finding the leadership and droning the shit out of them. Those efforts have kept the worst of the terror threat fenced in between the big oceans.

"Al-Amin, from what we can tell, is a Western Hemisphere offshoot. Our borders are so porous that the bad guys don't even have to fake a passport anymore to get in. They just walk. Or ride, or take a boat. My guys estimate that as much as fifty percent are miscreants of one form or another, and that a solid twelve percent are either terrorists or wannabes."

"I've heard there are over five hundred known terrorist cells within the US," Jonathan said.

"That's a low number. Within a two-hour drive of this park, I could show you two al Qaeda cells and three Hezbollah cells. The Fibbies try to watch them and eavesdrop on them, but there are limits to their resources."

Jonathan said, "I know plenty of people who think those known cells are just noise to distract us from the real threats that we don't yet know about."

"And I agree with them," Konan said. "If there's anything that I lose sleep over, it's all the splinter pop-ups that we won't know about until they open up on a county fair or a shopping mall. I wonder sometimes if ISIL deliberately fat-fingers their cyber security so that we can keep such good tabs on them. That's how we've stopped their much-hyped intention to spill blood on American soil."

Their path through the woods ended on the edge of a baseball diamond where some local kids were engaged in what appeared to be a pickup game. Their ages ran from ten to thirteen, and they seemed to be having a good time. Jonathan and Konan stayed on the far side of the outfield fence as they continued to stroll. Jonathan didn't think any of the kids had enough ass to hit a home run, but he kept an eye on the action anyway.

"So, how does al-Amin fit in?" Jonathan asked.

"We don't know yet," Konan said. "Not exactly, anyway. They're definitely the new kid on the block, but they're learning from the mistakes of the big boys. Their Internet footprint is virtually zero, and they've learned to communicate mostly via burner phones. They make two, maybe three calls per phone before they toss them. They've got a good technical guy on their side, because they've actually figured out how to mask their phones' locations, so even when they do dial in, the cell towers are confused."

"What's their mission?"

"We don't really know that, either," Konan said. "I know you're tired of hearing that, but I'm just being honest. The evidence you bring today confirms that high-profile kidnappings are on the list, but to what end?"

"I know at least one well-placed source who thinks that the end is to raise money and awareness," Jonathan said.

"But to what *end*? Money is a tool for something else. That's what we need to know. Once they have the money and publicity, what are they going to do with it?"

"I presume they'll take it on a jihading spree," Jonathan said.

"Well, there's another thing." Konan had dropped his tone five decibels and had stopped walking.

Jonathan leaned in to hear.

"My team isn't convinced that al-Amin is Islamist. We've heard no serious mention of them from any of our known sources. And these are talkative sources."

"Who, then?" Jonathan asked, and as Konan opened his mouth to answer, he beat him to the punch. "You're not sure."

"Bingo."

Jonathan smiled. "You've kept my interest by guessing so far. Keep going."

"Take those guys you killed at the motel," Konan

said. "They were as American as you and me. They were also homicidal nutcases who hired out to the highest bidders. Certainly there was no Internet radicalization. God, I hate that phrase. We know of no connection to al-Amin beyond a single phone contact two months ago."

"A call from a known burner?"

"Exactly. The content of the call wasn't much—in fact they spoke in codes, numbers instead of letters. My bosses didn't think it was high profile enough to put a team of decoders on it, but from the duration, I imagine it was some kind of directions."

"Why were you watching the guys from the motel in the first place?"

Konan waved him off. "We weren't," he said. "It was the fact of the phone call that put them on our radar. It wasn't until we floated that data back upstream that we identified Muhammed and Kamta and Amal. Those were their names, by the way."

"I didn't need to know that," Jonathan said. What difference would it make to know the names of someone he'd been forced to kill?

"Hereinafter known as Motel Guys, then," Konan said. "They likewise used a burner phone, but they made the mistake of *a,* not turning it off before they burned it, and *b,* throwing it in the trashcan behind the apartment building where they lived. We looked into them and found out that they had done some work for the Agency in the past, and frankly that cut them a little bit of slack. We didn't let them off the hook, but we didn't watch them as closely as we probably should have." Interpreting Jonathan's look of horror for what it was, he added, "Limited resources, Dig. My three letters of the alphabet don't have a lot of ground pounders to depend on. Those come from other alphabet agencies, and they all have their own priorities. Shit happens, dude."

Jonathan turned and started walking back toward the woods and their vehicles beyond. "So until their names ended up in the news after our unpleasantness at the motel—"

"We had no idea where they'd evaporated to."

Jonathan gave a bitter chuckle. "My God, if Middle America had any clue how screwed up the government really is—"

"Maybe they'd pay more attention to issues at the ballot box, and less on slogans and handouts," Konan said, finishing Jonathan's sentence for him. "And no, I'm not the least bit insulted by your indictment of my work."

"Anytime."

"But all of this brings me to a new development that I bet you will find interesting. The al-Amin network— if that's what you could actually call it—has come alive in the last couple of days. They seem to think that they've been made, and that they are under attack. This is particularly interesting because we still have no idea who they really are. But in their swirl of communications, we picked up what we think is a reference to four operatives being killed. *Four,* not three. Do you have any idea who the fourth one might be?"

Jonathan felt his heart rate quicken. "I think I might, yes."

Konan's features darkened. "Don't you dare play coy with me. I just committed half a dozen felonies by telling you what I have."

While Jonathan despised showing any of his cards, Konan had earned a right to see this one. "There's a John Doe in the morgue in Braddock County," he said. "I happen to know that Mr. Doe's real name was James Stepahin, and don't ask me how or why I know this, but he used to be a freelancer for a different part of the alphabet."

"CIA?"

"I neither confirm nor deny. And don't bother checking because you'll only get frustrated. Believe me or don't, but I know what I'm talking about." Jonathan couldn't imagine a circumstance where he would betray Wolverine's confidence.

"Now that's interesting," Konan said. "How did he die?"

"Murdered in a parking lot. By a coffee shop barista."

"You're shitting me."

"It's a long story. What's the chatter saying?"

"They think they're under assault. I suspect they're going to the mattresses, as it were."

Jonathan caught the reference to Mob-speak for preparing for a siege. "That's good, isn't it?"

"Not necessarily. If they drive themselves too far underground, we'll lose them completely. We do know that they continue to recruit, but their model is far less based on jihadist principles than it is on wreaking havoc and getting revenge."

"Revenge for what?"

"That's the brilliance of their model," Konan said. As they crossed back into the cover of the foliage, tension visibly drained from his shoulders. "It's not a focused anger, but rather an all-purpose anger. Against cops, against politicians, against your next door neighbor."

"It's an anarchy site, then."

Konan weighed the word. "I suppose. I prefer revenge."

"I guess that makes sense," Jonathan said, thinking aloud.

"Think about it," Konan pressed. "I mean, if you can attack all the underpinnings of what Middle America finds to be a source of comfort, you create terror in the most literal meaning of the word."

"And we can't get ahead of it," Jonathan said.

"That would seem to be the case," Konan agreed. "Certainly, people like me continue to get paychecks because of the anticipation of terror, and contractors make shit pots of money, but after trillions of dollars spent since nine-eleven, I can't testify that we're demonstrably safer than we were on nine-ten."

It was a depressing reality that everyone in the Community accepted as fact.

"And you know what scares the living shit out of me?" Konan asked.

Jonathan waited for it.

"It will take only one hardcore, seriously coordinated hit to send the country into a panic. I think the American psyche is *that* unprepared for another attack."

Jonathan sensed so much negative energy emanating from his old friend that he offered a softer version of the truth. "You know, it's not like we've accomplished nothing. We've reunited tens of thousands of bad guys with their maker. At seventy-two apiece, the price of virgins must be skyrocketing."

"For every one we kill, another ten step up to take their place. The bad news is, it's not just Muslims anymore."

Now *that* was a point to which Jonathan could personally testify. "Are you always this upbeat and cheerful?" he quipped.

"Nah," Konan said with a laugh. "Sometimes I get a little down. Especially around the holidays."

Chapter Thirteen

Pam Hastings recognized the expression in Jed Hackner's face the instant she saw it. The best label she could conjure was annoyance. "I'm not building a defense strategy for your newest pet prisoner," he said.

Pam ignored his words and helped herself to the chair in front of his desk. "You're going to thank me for this," she said.

"Is it about Ethan Falk?"

"It is. But—"

"I don't want to hear it. Not unless it makes our case stronger."

"How about if I can help you close a triple homicide?" She'd been preparing for that line, and it launched and landed exactly as she'd hoped.

"I don't remember a triple homicide," Hackner said, but she'd clearly piqued his curiosity.

"That's because it was outside of Ashland, Ohio."

"Get out of my office." Hackner dipped his head to return to his paperwork.

"It happened eleven years ago." Pam put a singsongy lilt into her voice. Unspoken temptation.

"And?"

"And it's still an open, unsolved case." The hook hadn't sunk yet, but she could see him sniffing at it.

"I thought Ethan Falk said he was kidnapped from someplace in upstate New York."

"Geneseo."

"I don't care. What does Gen-whatever in New York have to do with Pikeville, Ohio?"

"Ashland."

"I don't care about that either. What's the connection?"

"The connection is three bodies, all shot at close range with two-two-three caliber bullets, plus signs of explosive entry."

Hackner put his pen down and shifted back in his seat. He was a trim man, but his ancient chair creaked anyway. "That's what Ethan described."

"Exactly. But there's more. When the Ashland detectives did their investigation, they found what they called a dungeon in a space under the basement. It showed signs of having been occupied."

"What kind of signs?"

"That's where the reports get fuzzy," Pam said. "Much of the record has been sealed."

"Why?"

"That's part of the fuzziness. I don't know."

"Was it part of a court order?"

"More fuzz."

"Well, dammit, Hastings, there's nothing there to work with."

"Not true," Pam said, and she opened her binder to a bookmarked page. "I have the name of the investigating officer. He's still in Ohio."

"Have you talked with him?"

"I tried. But he hung up on me."

"Why?" Hackner blushed as he realized the stupidity of his question. "Hard to find out after a guy hangs up."

"Yeah, kind of."

"Have you tried again?"

"I want to talk to him in person," Pam said. "I'm more persuasive eye-to-eye."

Hackner's eyes narrowed. "You want me to give you permission to go to Ohio, don't you? You want me to help you spring your sociology experiment."

"I want you to help me solve a case," she insisted.

"For the good people of Ashford, Ohio."

"Ashland."

"I still don't care."

"Come on, Lieutenant. Don't you—"

"Go."

Pam paused, feeling a little stunned. "Excuse me?"

"It's only one word, Detective. Go. It means git. Run away. Call if you need to shoot anyone."

She saw the smile as he spoke, and knew better than to sell to the sold. "Thank you," she said.

"You're still here." Jed Hackner returned to his paperwork.

Twenty-seven days, four hours, and thirty-seven minutes. Calendar days, mind you, not work days. When the clock turned that many times, Cletus Bankstrom would be a man of leisure and luxury. On that day, at that time, he would have been an employee of Braddock County for exactly thirty years, and that meant he would no longer be an employee at all. Retirement, baby. And not a retirement where he had to pay himself out of his own savings—though he'd done a pretty good job stuffing cash away over the years. Instead, because he was damned old, he qualified for the county's old-school pension. The one where they owed him a fat check every month for the rest of his life, no matter how much money he had in the bank. If he closed his eyes, he could already see the boat in the lake, feel the weight of the fishing pole in his hands as the water gently rocked him to the purest form of peace there was.

The county had exactly that much time to find and train his replacement, or the police department's property room would have to live without a manager. He'd heard of guys who punch out of a career only to return as a "consultant" to help with "transitions" and other such bullshit business speak, but that wasn't him. When Cletus was out, he was out. It had been a good run, but he was done.

His wife told him that he would miss the people when he left, but he wasn't so sure. The guys were nice enough—and Chief Michaels was a man that Cletus admired—but as a civilian employee, he could never enjoy full status in the cop club. No one was rude to him—at least not per se—but he sensed a silent disdain for the work he did. And the rules he had to follow.

Cletus was the guy who had to tell ate-up young, studly, world-saving rookie cops that they were allowed exactly four magazines for their duty weapons, and that for a new one to be issued, an old one needed to be turned in. The same was true of ASPs, nightsticks, MagLites and holsters. And shirts and vests, and, and, and . . . Yes, he got that the sworn officers were risking their lives every day out on the streets, but let's be honest: Braddock County wasn't exactly the Bronx. It wasn't even DC or Baltimore. Sure, they had their crime, but the way some of these younger cops wanted to kit up, you'd think they were in Baghdad.

And if you wanted to know Cletus's thoughts on things, that was exactly the problem: More than a few of the kids had in fact served in Baghdad. And Kabul and God knew how many other damned scary places. They were so used to getting shot at that they prepared for a new firefight every day.

But as luck would have it, no one in fact did want his views, so he largely kept them to himself, and counted the days.

He'd be lying, though, if he said he didn't enjoy handling some of the toys he got to play with. Cletus figured there was a little boy inside every man—didn't matter how old he was—and every little boy liked to play with rifles and pistols and bullets and ballistic armor. Plus, there were the electronics, everything from listening devices to night vision to their most recent acquisition: their own fleet of three drones that no one yet knew how to fly. The Department of Homeland Security had been most benevolent these past few years, throwing so much money at police departments that it was darned near impossible to spend it all.

And every item that came to BCPD arrived through Cletus. He opened the crates and the packages, he cataloged the serial numbers and the property tags, and he made sure that everything ended up exactly where it was supposed to be. Let's see one of those eager-beaver cruiser jockeys keep everything together with that level of detail.

The more he thought about it—and he'd been thinking a lot these past few months, ever since he'd announced his retirement date—the more he realized that the time was right for him to leave. Too much had changed in too short a time for him to keep up with it all. It wasn't just the new computer system and the other bullshit efficiency measures, either.

In the past few years, there'd been a palpable change in the atmosphere of the BCPD that he didn't like one bit. Yes, the cops were more paranoid and trigger-happy, but the society they protected had become angrier than they'd ever been in the past. It was as if the general public no longer looked at the police as providers of peace, but rather as the enemy. Cletus had reached the point where he avoided telling people he met that he worked for the department at all. He told them that he was a county employee, and then he avoided the rest.

It didn't help that the sworn officers' daily garb had switched from the long-standing light blue shirts atop dark blue trousers to an ensemble of black-on-black that made every one of them look like they were part of an assault force. The guys loved it because it made them look tougher—cooler—but who wanted to approach a storm trooper for directions? Who wanted to seek assistance from a soldier festooned with weapons and ballistic gear? The officers would say they wore the new kit because the streets were getting tougher for them, but they never saw a connection with the fact that cops these days projected malice.

Cletus understood the viciousness of the circle, but the world he lived in was many times more nuanced than that which was imagined by many of the cops with whom he interacted. These were same cops who continuously pressured him to break the rules and allow them to have special favors that the department would never allow. He'd lost count of how many times he'd heard, "I won't tell, and if you don't tell, there's no way anyone can be the wiser. Come on, Clete, be part of the team."

No, sir, Cletus Bankstrom had lived sixty-six years on the right side of honesty, and he wasn't about to start crossing that line now. If only his was not such a minority commitment. It used to be that pilferage was never a problem, that you could trust cops to be trustworthy. And for the most part, they were, but there again, something about the current crop of newcomers—something about the way they were wired—apparently made it okay to steal. For the past year, year and a quarter, inventories that used to balance one hundred percent had begun to show losses. Nothing huge, maybe five thousand dollars total over that period, but that was a huge increase over a baseline of zero, and Cletus lost sleep over even the little stuff.

Now he was reviewing the incoming receipts from the laundry service, and he could see that Sergeant Dale had signed for thirty uniform blouses and thirty pairs of trousers when in fact there were only twenty-five of each on the racks that had just been delivered to his storage room. Good lord, how was Cletus supposed to do his job if he couldn't even get the supervisory officers to count before they signed? This was the last straw.

Cletus was not a confrontational guy—and he for sure didn't want to spend his waning days with the department in conflict—but he had to do something about this.

Sergeant Dale sat down the hall in an office that allowed barely enough room for a desk and chair. In charge of logistics and planning, he was seen by many as a suck-up and finger-pointer. Cletus always figured that Dale had another job on the side, else how could he afford to drive a Maserati? The official version of things was that he'd won a settlement in a lawsuit over a traffic accident. Cletus didn't believe the story, probably because he didn't like the guy, but that was for Internal Affairs to referee, not him.

As Cletus turned the corner into the office, he caught the sergeant in the middle of a conversation with Yolanda Pierce, a pretty young thing who knew she was hot as hell and flaunted it everywhere she went. Yet another member of this generation who didn't understand the meaning of propriety. Short skirts and dipping blouses were for the dance floor, not for the office. But again, that was not his job. She worked in the IT department, and that meant Cletus had very little interaction with her.

"Oh, I'm sorry to interrupt," Cletus said.

"No, that's okay," Dale said. "We're about done here."

Yolanda looked startled. She turned quickly to see who'd entered behind her, and as soon as she made eye contact, she broke it off. "Yes," she said. "I was just about to leave."

Something happened between them in the three seconds that passed as she pushed her chair out and stood. Cletus had always prided himself in his ability to read people—to read their expressions—and what he saw from Dale was an eye twitch that said, "Don't worry about it."

About what? Cletus wondered.

As she left, Yolanda said nothing to Cletus. She just edged past and left.

"What was that?" Cletus asked.

Dale feigned shock. "What was what?"

"I got an odd vibe."

The sergeant shrugged. "You felt what you felt," he said. "Doesn't mean it was there. What do you need, Clete?"

Cletus brandished the uniform receipt. "You signed this," he said.

Dale leaned forward and squinted. "Uniforms?"

"Exactly."

"I frequently sign for laundered uniforms."

"You signed for thirty," Cletus said. "Thirty complete sets—blouses and trousers. There were only twenty-five."

Dale's eyes narrowed. "What are you suggesting?" he said.

"With all due respect, Sergeant, it doesn't help me do my job if you don't do yours."

"And what, exactly, do you perceive my job to be?"

There was a menace in Dale's tone and posture that gave Cletus a chill. This was a man capable of violence. Rumor had it, in fact, that the reason Dale had a desk job instead of being on the street was because he'd beaten the tar out of a kid who had done nothing wrong.

Cletus broke the sergeant's gaze and instead focused on the receipt as he spoke. "Sergeant, sir, I expect you to count the items you sign for, before you sign for them."

"Why would Destin Uniform Company want to short us five sets of uniforms?"

"Wait. What?"

"Why would the uniform company want to short us

on our delivery? They always deliver what they say they're going to. Did you call Destin and ask them?"

"Of course I did," Cletus said. "And of course they maintain that they shipped us thirty uniform sets. What else are they going to say?"

"There you go, then. And I agree. From where I sit, there are only so many different places that uniforms can go after they're here."

"You're telling me that you did in fact count the shipment?"

"Of course I did," Dale said. "And I'm more than a little insulted that you would have thought otherwise. Those uniforms went someplace else, but not from my hand."

"Then by whose hand?" Cletus said. He heard his voice rising and he lowered it. No sense shouting at one another.

"You tell me," Dale said. "As far as I know, there's a direct line between my contact with the shipment and yours. What have you been doing with the uniforms?"

Cletus was dumbstruck. "You think *I* took them?"

"No," Dale said. He leaned back in his chair and smiled. He looked smug as hell. "But I'm saying that if you really want to push this, the burden is going to fall on you to prove that you're as on top of things as you pretend to be."

Cletus gaped.

"And it's not just uniforms, is it, Bangstrom? Over the past year or so, there's been a steady trickle of stuff getting lost in the system."

"You know that because I told you!" Cletus said— nearly shouted. "I've told you all along. It's pilferage."

"But whose?" The smile went away as Dale leaned forward and planted his elbows on the edge of his desk. "Have you been helping yourself to the company store?"

"How dare you!"

"How dare I what? Your inventories *come up short*"—he used finger quotes—"and you need to deflect the blame. You report it to me and blame unknown parties. Today, you try to lay it at my feet. You work with cops, you know. We're not stupid about how crimes are committed."

Cletus's heart raced. There was absolutely no truth in anything Dale was saying.

"I get it," Dale said. "Or at least I think I do. You're only a few weeks from no longer having a paycheck, and you're trying to feather the nest a little. I imagine that's a hard temptation to resist."

"I did not steal anything!" This time it was definitely a shout, and he startled himself. He dialed it back in. "I never have."

"And in a few weeks, you'll never even have the opportunity again," Dale said. "I'm willing to let it slide. And I'm not accusing you of anything. I'm really not. If I was, then I'd be obliged to investigate more deeply, and I don't think either one of us wants that, do we?"

"I didn't steal."

"Fine," Dale said. "Let's just leave it at that. Now, if you don't mind, I have to get back to work."

Chapter Fourteen

Jonathan Grave considered himself to be a gourmet cook. At his core, he had a taste for fine food, and in his travels over the years he'd picked up a taste for cuisine from all over the world. Even England had fine cuisine, he'd found, though most of it was found in Indian restaurants in London.

Over the years, he'd developed a tradition where on every third Thursday, as long as he was in town, he'd have people to his house for dinner. The invitations were more often than not spontaneous, driven by what was going on at the time. If there were no pressing issues to be discussed from the covert side of Security Solutions, he might invite some of the junior investigators, and he often included friends like Dom D'Angelo or Doug Kramer.

Tonight, though, the topic for table discussion was destined to be compartmented, so the guest list was the one that was most typical: Boxers and Venice. It was a list that brought tactical advantages, too. For too many years, Big Guy and Mother Hen had been crossways with each other—for any number of reasons—and Jonathan felt that by breaking bread, they could develop a bridge that would help them get along better. At least that's what he told himself.

Every good meal began for Jonathan with a good martini, a delicate balance of six parts Beefeater gin, one part dry vermouth, and two olives. Boxers' meals began as they ended, with one very large part scotch whisky—the more expensive the better, especially if it came from Jonathan's liquor cabinet. Venice was a moving target, most often bouncing between a glass of sauvignon blanc or a Kir Royal, but tonight was one of her wild card nights of a cosmopolitan, poured with Ketel One vodka, Cointreau, and cranberry juice.

Years ago, when Jonathan bought the old firehouse and converted it into his home and offices, he did little to change the layout of the kitchen from the way it was when he was a boy and he hung out here with the fire crews. All the appliances and finishings had been upgraded, of course, but he maintained more or less the same footprint, with the main fridge, cooking, and prep surfaces occupying the long wall on the left, and the longer-term storage along the corresponding wall on the right. The far end of the rectangular room was left for the pantry, sink, dishwashers, and drain board. Down the middle of the eighteen-by-twenty-four-foot space, where the guys back in the day had tucked three picnic tables end to end, Jonathan had installed a granite-topped table capable of comfortably seating sixteen people in butt-friendly padded wooden chairs that had been designed specifically for the space. He had a formal dining room as well—what used to be the day room for the fire-fighters—but he could count on two hands the number of times he'd used it. Let's face it: no matter how much space you had, people always gathered in the kitchen.

JoeDog hovered at the base of the cooking area. Jonathan took a pull on his martini, then opened the fridge and removed the sea scallops that had been soaking in milk for the past fifteen minutes. The beast shadowed every step as he walked them over to the pan where the hot unsalted butter and olive oil were waiting.

"Okay, Ven," Jonathan said. "What do we know now that we didn't know a couple of hours ago?" The scallops were big—nearly the size of a half-dollar—and they sizzled perfectly as he placed them into the pan. He looked at the clock. He need three minutes per side. JoeDog needed a miracle where a scallop would abandon the pan and jump to the floor. It had never happened, but hope sprang eternal.

"Your friend Henry is a very nice man," Venice said.

"Konan?" Boxers asked.

"Right. But that's for you to call him, not me. In fact, he called himself Henry on the phone. Anyway, he called me on my encrypted line—please tell me you gave him the number, that he didn't just figure it out for himself."

Jonathan laughed. "Yes, I gave him the number. But now that you mention it, he *is* NSA."

"So, he called me, and shared some very interesting news." It was Venice's way to set bait when revealing details, enticing her listeners to ask for more. Jonathan knew it was the one habit of hers that evoked the greatest and most frequent ire from Boxers.

"And what might that be?" Jonathan asked. It was a

reflex. He turned his attention to the bed of sunflower sprouts he had prepared as the garnish for his scallops appetizer.

"One of the burner phones the NSA had been tracking was found in Stepahin's pocket."

"So that confirms Dig's theory," Boxers said. "The asshole was here to kidnap somebody."

"Seems that way to me," Venice said.

Jonathan said, "How does that help us advance what we know?" He returned to the pan and lifted a scallop to see how it was advancing. Almost time to turn it.

"Try to control your enthusiasm," Venice said.

He'd hurt her feelings. That was not a hard thing to do. "I don't mean to offend, but confirming what I already know doesn't exactly move the ball down the field." He turned the first scallop and was delighted to see perfect caramelization. He turned the others.

"At least we know more for sure than we did before," Venice said.

Jonathan shot her a look and smiled. "Yes, we do. Thank you."

"So how do we figure out who he was trying to snatch?" Boxers asked. "Or, that he was trying to snatch anybody at all? Bad guys don't necessarily have to specialize."

"No," Jonathan said, taking another sip of martini. "They don't have to specialize, but most of them do. If he were a shooter, we wouldn't expect him to snatch somebody. I don't want to close down the possibility, but I also don't want us to get distracted." Another check. Almost time to serve. "Is there a way to track where that phone went while he had it on him?"

"There are ways," Venice said, "but they're very

low probability when you're dealing with a burner. He did have another phone on him, though, and the BCPD are trying to follow his steps through that, but for whatever reason, they're not putting it up on ICIS."

Jonathan lifted the first scallop out of the pan and plated it on the sprouts. Two scallops per plate. "Joe-Dog," Jonathan snapped. "Git. Out of the kitchen." Head and tail both hanging low, the beast retreated to the threshold that separated the kitchen from the living room.

Jonathan served the plates.

"What, am I on a diet?" Boxers grumped with a smile to sell the fact that he was kidding.

"There have been worse ideas," Jonathan said without dropping a beat. "And there are three more courses after this one."

"It looks delicious," Venice said. It's what she always said. Funny how routines like this develop their own script over time.

Jonathan set the third plate on the table for himself, retrieved his martini, and sat down. A freshly opened sauvignon blanc sat between them for anyone who needed more hydration.

"The phone," Jonathan said, getting the conversation back on track. "Is there a way for *you* to track it? Do we need to depend on ICIS?"

Venice took her first bite. "Oh, my God, this is delicious."

Jonathan smiled his appreciation. She was right. He did scallops better than most.

"If I had more information about the phone I could," she said.

"If only we knew someone in the most effective

eavesdropping organization on the planet," Boxers said. His scallops were already gone. In another sip, he'd be able to say the same about his scotch.

Venice looked to Jonathan. "How many times can we go to that well?"

He shrugged. "As many times as it takes until he cries uncle. I don't think we're close to that point yet. Did he give you a way to contact him?"

"Yes, but with rules."

There were always rules when it came to clandestine contacts. "Follow them and reach out," Jonathan said. "The worst he can tell you is no."

"Actually," Boxers said, "the worst he can do is mark you for death and order a drone strike. Just sayin'."

Jonathan pretended to ponder that. "Don't you think rendition and torture would be worse than a quick drone strike?"

"You've got a point."

"Okay, boys," Venice said. "Can we move on?"

Jonathan bit into his second scallop. Every bit as good as the first. "You've got more?"

"I've always got more."

"How about more food?" Boxers grumped. "Contrary to popular opinion, a mouthful is in fact not a meal."

"Savor and listen," Jonathan said. "Ven, you're on."

"I've been keeping an eye on ICIS to see how the Braddock County PD are developing their case against Ethan Falk," she said. "They're beginning to make me uncomfortable."

She had both men's full attention.

"The detective in charge out there—a Pamela Hastings—is a pretty tenacious researcher. She keeps pushing until she finds answers."

"I hear admiration in your voice," Jonathan said.

"Of course you do," Venice said. "You have to admire cops who go to the wall for their jobs."

"Gotta fear them, too," Boxers said.

"Yes, you do. This one in particular. Somehow, from the details she's collected by talking with Ethan, she's been able to triangulate back to an unsolved shooting incident eleven years ago in Ashland, Ohio."

Jonathan felt a tug in his gut. "That's where we snatched Ethan from the bad guys."

"Bingo," Venice said. "And we don't know how they've categorized the incident because those were the days before ICIS."

Boxers cocked his head. "What do you mean, how they've categorized it?"

Venice explained, "Well, on some of your ops where you leave bodies behind, the locals are able to put together that there was some kind of freelance rescue thing in play, and they don't push all that hard for answers. Sometimes, they don't connect those dots—or they do and they don't care—and those are the cases I worry about. In those—and I've never pushed too hard to track their progress because no activity on ICIS is truly invisible—there's a good possibility that some cold-case squad will pick them up in the future. I just don't know what conclusions the Ashland Police drew."

"And that's important?" Jonathan asked.

"I think it can be. It's been eleven years, but if Braddock PD reanimates the otherwise dormant case, I think that can be a problem."

Jonathan sucked another layer off his martini. "How do we find out?"

"Are you sure you want to?" Boxers asked. "Knowledge has value only if there's something you can do with it."

"What's the expression?" Venice said. "Forewarned is forearmed?" She finished the last of her scallops and pulled on the cosmo. "There's one note in the ICIS file that says she'll be going to Ashland tomorrow to meet with the detective who investigated the case."

Jonathan exchanged glances with Boxers. "I don't think we're exposed," Big Guy said. "Clearly, we didn't leave any traceable trace behind, or they'd have already nailed us."

Jonathan didn't like it. "Technology has turned over fifteen times in the last ten years. You never know what they can find now that they couldn't find then."

"Plus, there's the triangulation issue," Venice said.

Jonathan scowled.

"You've been told this before," Venice reminded him. "In West Virginia, remember? You get enough incidents documented in police reports about unsolved killings that follow a certain pattern and occasionally include reports of some guy named Scorpion, and a picture starts to form via triangulation."

"They still can't track us," Boxers reminded.

"No, but they know," Jonathan said. "The pressure is building to be more careful."

"The pressure is building to move on to a different line of work," Venice said, punctuating her words with an eye roll. She pulled her laptop computer out of the bag that she'd stashed at her feet. It was her electronic memory. "But since I don't expect you'll be doing that anytime soon, let me fill you in on the details of Detective Hastings' visit to Ohio." She opened the computer, rubbed the mouse pad, and tapped some keys.

Jonathan rose from his chair and picked up the plates. Next up: a rather mundane spinach salad that he'd prepared, which had been sitting in the fridge for the past forty-five minutes. All it needed before serving was some fresh strawberries, which he likewise removed from the fridge and started to slice.

"The detective on the Falk op was a guy named Jim Dooley," Venice said as she read her notes. "Hastings has an appointment with him tomorrow afternoon at two-thirty." She looked up. "I wish we could have ears on that conversation."

"I still don't understand what we'd gain," Boxers said.

"Information," Jonathan said. "Like they said in *Animal House,* knowledge is good. Maybe we can learn more of what they know. Since there are no such things as coincidences, maybe we'll find another connection to Stepahin."

Boxers' face changed to an expression that looked a lot like dread. "You just said that like it was a thing that was going to happen."

"Hey," Jonathan said. "Who in their right mind would turn down a field trip to Ashland, Ohio?"

"Why?" Big Guy asked.

"If nothing else, to meet Detective Pamela Hastings."

"Are you crazy?" Venice and Boxers said that in perfect unison.

Jonathan continued to concentrate on the strawberries. He didn't want to give them the satisfaction of eye contact. "If you want to gather intel, you have to meet with the people who have what you want," he said. "And tomorrow evening, that will be Detective Pamela Hastings. Do you know if she's planning to stay the night?"

Venice typed some more. "She's got a reservation at a Hilton Garden Inn for tomorrow night."

"There you go," Jonathan said. "So, we know where Big Guy and I will be spending the night tomorrow."

"Why do I have to go?" Boxers said.

"Because we're a team," Jonathan said through a smile. "Besides, you love adventure."

"So, what's your plan?" Big Guy asked. "You're just going to charm her into giving you lots of information that you have no right to know? And, not insignificantly, is all about you?"

"She won't know it's about me," Jonathan said. "I'll be there as Rick Horgan tomorrow."

"CIA or FBI?" Venice asked. There were two versions of Jonathan's best alias.

"Depends," he said. "What I need you to do, Ven, is find out everything you can about Detective Hastings. And I mean *everything*."

In his heart, Ethan knew that prison life would define the remainder of his years on the planet, but his brain wouldn't let him give up. Yes, he'd killed that guy, but an even bigger yes was that the guy deserved to die. As it was, his death was too easy, too calm. In a more perfect world, it would have involved more screaming and begging for mercy. But the world wasn't anything close to perfection, was it? In fact, as far as he could tell, the world was one giant booby trap waiting for innocents to turn the wrong corner or talk to the wrong person, with the result being life-altering awfulness.

He'd come *so close* to being past all that bullshit from back then. If only he'd taken the day off, or if he'd been assigned to the drive through, then maybe he wouldn't have heard the voice, and if he hadn't heard the voice, then he wouldn't be in this shit hole of a place, surrounded by the dregs of the gene pool.

Whoever had commissioned the construction of the Braddock County Adult Detention Center had apparently dictated that perpetual discomfort be a primary goal. During the day, inmates were locked out of their cells—because that made sense to somebody—but for twenty-three hours a day, inmates were confined to the indoors. That meant those who had not yet been assigned work details—people like Ethan—were relegated to spending twelve hours in the "day room"—a common area in the center of the cellblock that sported circular steel picnic tables with seating for ten, each seat surrounding the main table like moons, also made of stainless steel. Nothing was padded, and no seat allowed an inmate to lean back. The result was that no one sat for very long, but rather everyone sort of wandered in aimless circles within circles, hanging out with their homies or their fellow gangbangers. In Ethan's mind, every step they took and every syllable they spoke to each other was somehow tied to bringing harm to him.

He didn't really flatter himself to believe that that was true—he was sure there were far juicier targets than he among the general population—but if he assumed only the worst, then he could never be disappointed, right?

A television sat recessed into a wall and covered by a heavy Lexan shield, with speakers on the walls protected by heavy-gauge wire that might have been part of the security fencing. Set perpetually on either sports or religious programming—neither of which appealed to Ethan—they kept the volume at an ear-splitting level. Since no one watched the damn thing, all of the inmates had to raise their voices just to be heard in casual conversation, with the result being a cacophony of noise that put Ethan's teeth on edge.

In his real world, Ethan was a quiet guy who enjoyed quiet people and quiet times. If nothing else drove him bat-shit crazy during his time in the joint, the noise was going to accomplish the mission. Throw into the mix the guys who just loved to make noise for the annoyance value, and the result was a special kind of hell.

Ethan spent his time in an emotional state that bordered on terror. He knew he wasn't tough enough for this place, for any place where survival depended on defending one's turf. He was here on a murder charge, and that gave him some odd bit of deference, but he was so frightened of the other inmates that he knew that deference wouldn't last for long. Eat or be eaten, kill or be killed. He was doomed.

The only reasonable defense he could think of was to stay to himself. He didn't talk to anyone, he didn't occupy anybody else's space. He tried his best to lose himself in one of the paperback novels that had been stacked on shelves in the day room, but between the noise, his churning stomach, and the dozens of pages that were missing from every volume, that wasn't working so well for him, either.

One thing he was sure of was that race was a very big deal here in the Adult Detention Center. Whites stayed with whites, and blacks and Latinos stayed with their own kinds as well. Asians seemed to be the wild card, not particularly cohesive among themselves, but also neither welcome nor unwelcome among the other groups. Ethan watched, took mental notes, but kept his mouth shut about everything and everyone.

No one on earth was any whiter than Ethan Falk, but he avoided the racial divides. It was clear to him that once you sided with your own, you automatically declared war on the others, and he didn't want to be at war with anyone. Problem was, if you didn't choose a side, you didn't have any allies. As foolish a notion as he knew it was, Ethan was rolling the dice on doing his time in in neutrality. Allies were only important if you had enemies, right? So if you just stayed to yourself—

"So, what's with the rod up your ass, Meat?"

The words startled him. Ethan had been lost in his reading when the voice blasted him from close behind. He whirled on his picnic stool to see a heavily tatted and thickly built skinhead hulking over him. The man yanked the book from his hands and Frisbee-threw it across the day room. He planted one foot on the stool next to Ethan and he leaned heavily on his knee, clearly awaiting an answer.

"I-I don't know what you mean," Ethan stammered. It was a statement of fact.

"You give me a vibe that you think you're better than the rest of us. This disturbs me. A sign of disrespect."

Ethan's head raced. Should he stand? Should he try to back away? Should he laugh it off, or maybe apologize?

"I don't think I'm better than anyone," he said. "I'm just quiet."

The Hulk dusted the side of Ethan's hair with his fingers, raising a cowlick over his ear. "I think you're more than just quiet," he said. "I think you're scared shitless." He sold that last part with a smile.

Ethan forced a smile in return. "Yeah, well, there's some of that, too."

"You can't let that happen," Hulk said. "These folks in here are like vampires. But instead of feeding on blood, they feed on fear. Dude, you're like a fountain of fear."

"Um, I'll work on it," he said. Even as the words left his mouth, he could hear the lameness of them himself.

"You're not showing me disrespect, are you, son?" The word *son* can be used in several ways. One is to breed familiarity and make the other party feel more at ease. This was not that way.

"I don't disrespect you," Ethan said. And instead of just leaving it there, he added, "I don't even know you. How can I feel any way about you?"

The Hulk swelled in size and helped himself to the seat next to Ethan. "There," he said. "What you said right there sounded like disrespect to me. Sounded like you think you're smarter than me."

"I don't think I'm smarter than anyone." Ethan struggled to find the sweet spot between fear and calm, but he could hear for himself the underlying tone of disrespect.

"I don't believe you," Hulk said. "What about that black boy over there? Don't you think you're smarter than him?"

"I don't know him, either." Ethan could think of no more terrible an outcome of this than to be dragged into a race war.

Hulk poked his shoulder. Hard. "What about me, then? Do you think that I'm smarter than that black-assed monkey boy?"

The subject of their discussion—Ethan had no idea what his name was—had dialed into the conversation and was paying attention.

"I don't want any of this," Ethan said. "Just leave me alone." Then, perhaps a beat too late: "Please."

"Just leave me alone. Pleeease." Hulk's echo came in a singsong girly falsetto.

Ethan said nothing. Maybe silence would defuse things.

Hulk brushed the other side of Ethan's head, leaving a matching cowlick. "Hey, don't be rude. I'm talking to you. Do you or do you not think that I am smarter that that trained monkey over there?"

I have piss-stained boxer shorts that are smarter than you, Ethan didn't say. What he did say was nothing. *Just let the moment pass.*

The Hulk smacked him again, harder this time. "Pay attention, Meat. Do you or do you not think that whites are smarter than blacks?"

Oh, what the hell? Ethan thought. He might have

even said it aloud. *If you're gonna die, die big.* "There is no standard by which Kim Kardashian could be considered smarter than Martin Luther King."

The Hulk's face reddened. "That's not what I asked you."

"Actually, it kind of is." The smart move at this point would have been to stand up, if only to have some measure of physical leverage. He worried, though, that it would be seen as an act of aggression. If there was any immutable fact in the universe, it was that he had exactly zero chance of winning a fight with this man.

The Hulk settled it by grabbing a fistful of Ethan's orange scrub shirt and pulling him to his feet. "You need to choose a side, asshole," he said. "Are you with your own kind, or with the monkeys?"

The target of all the insults was thinner yet taller than the Hulk, and he'd transformed himself into a menacing shadow, looming over Ethan's table. Everyone else in the unit had evaporated, their absence proving their sanity.

"How about you shut the hell up?" the newcomer said.

"Back up, Chooney," the Hulk said. "We need to know whether this white boy is with his own kind or with you."

Somehow, that seemed to make sense to Chooney— what the hell kind of name was that?—who puffed up as big as the Hulk and seemed to be likewise waiting for an answer.

Ethan knocked Hulk's hands away with an overhand sweep and took a giant step backward. "What do you want from me?" He shouted the question loud enough to reverberate for two seconds through the canyon they called a cellblock. Plenty loud enough to be heard by guards who were nowhere to be seen. "You want me to say shit that will get me killed. I want none of this! Just leave me alone!"

"You need to choose a side," Hulk said.

Ethan took another step back. Call it maneuvering room. "No, I don't," he said, this time modulating his voice. He redirected his eyes to Chooney. "Do I have any shot at joining your side if that's what I wanted to do?"

"Hell no."

He returned his eyes to the Hulk. "That," he said. "You don't want me to choose anything. You want me to pledge allegiance to you. And you want *him* to have reason to hurt me. Why would I do that?"

The Hulk turned redder still. "How 'bout you do it so I don't kick your ass?"

In that second, reality poured over Ethan like a waterfall. He drew a deep breath and settled his shoulders. "You know what?" he said. "You're going to do that no matter what I say. So why don't you just get on with it?"

Three seconds later, it got very, very ugly.

Chapter Fifteen

Detective James Patrick Dooley (retired) lived in a 1950s-era brick rancher on Duff Street, not far from the center of the City of Ashland. A long-unused basketball hoop stood sentry at the top of the concrete driveway, just to the side of the closed one-car garage. What Pam noticed the most was the perfectly cut diamond mower tracks in the browning front yard. In Pam's experience, cops tended to be slobs or super-neat. Clearly, Dooley leaned toward the anal-retentive side of spectrum. An ornamental fruit tree of some sort—Pam supposed cherry, but plants weren't her thing—spread wide with green leaves just to the other side of the driveway, opposite the basketball hoop, and to the left of the tree, an American flag moved in the lazy breeze atop a tall flagpole.

North Central Ohio was further along in autumn than Braddock County, Virginia, and as Pam opened the door to her county car, the chill was refreshing. The four-hundred-mile trip had taken nearly eight hours, and she felt thoroughly wiped. But the BCPD bean counters felt more comfortable spending $600 in gas than buying a $350 plane ticket. A lot of life's niggling problems would evaporate if we could ship the budgeteers to an island.

Pam had walked only halfway up the thirty-foot driveway before the garage door rumbled up, revealing Jim Dooley literally from the feet up.

He wore khaki cargo pants and work boots, along with matching untucked khaki shirt. Somewhere under there, she imagined he carried a firearm. As she got closer, she noticed that the shirt bore the logo for the Ashland Police Department on his left breast. You can take the man away from the cops, but you can never take the cop away from the man. An ample gut testified that he knew his way around pasta and beer, and his face displayed a bright smile as he walked to meet her.

"Detective Hastings?" he said as he extended his hand. His left hand held a small gym bag that rattled as if filled with tools.

"Pam," she said. "Thanks for taking the time to meet me." They shook hands.

"I'm retired," he said. "I got nothing but time. Thanks for making the drive. It must be a long one."

"If police work were easy, everyone would do it," Pam said with a smile.

Dooley pointed to her car. "Do you mind driving some more? We've only got one car and my wife has a mahjong tournament at three."

"The computer game?"

"Nope, the real one. They play it with tiles and I have no idea how it works. But my wife loves it, and you know what they say: A happy wife is a happy life."

Pam forced a chuckle. One of the precious few parts

of the cop's life that she disliked was the constant hus-band-wife bullshit comments. The whole ball-and-chain meme had worn thin to the point of see-through. She got that no one ever meant any harm, but it got wearisome having to always feign amusement.

In a perfect world, she'd have preferred some time to stretch her legs, but Dooley apparently didn't want her to come into the house. If experience was any judge, that meant that the interior was less pristine than the exterior.

She led the way back to her car, pressed the button to unlock the doors, and slid in behind the steering wheel. Dooley helped himself to the shotgun seat and Pam cranked the engine.

"You need to head west," Dooley said. "Maybe ten miles."

She pressed a button on her console-mounted computer screen and pulled up pre-programmed turn-by-turn directions. "Got it right here," she said. She pulled a U-turn in front of the house, and they were on their way.

"So, you think you have a lead on this case?" Dooley said.

"I don't know that I'd call it a lead in the sense that it will bring you any closer to your killers, but I think I've found a connection." She relayed the story that Ethan Falk had told, filling in some of the details she'd left out of the previous conversation on the phone. By the time she was done, they were already on Wells Road, the street where the shoot-out took place eleven years ago.

"It's down there on the left, about three hundred

yards," Dooley said, pointing through the windshield with a bladed hand.

They were in farm country now, but with a feeling that times were tough. White clapboard was the standard for the houses, and she didn't see a single one that didn't need a new paint job.

"Have you talked to the current owner?" Pam asked. "Are they expecting us?"

"Technically, the county is the owner," Dooley said. "Word travels fast out here, and no matter how far you drop the price, it's tough to get rid of a place that hosted a triple murder and has a torture chamber in the basement."

"So it's been empty for eleven years?"

"Yeah. The owner of the place at the time—a guy named Mullins—had taken a job transfer to Cleveland and had hung on to the place as an investment. Back then, he'd rented it to a Robert and Gayle Rancek, but of course those turned out to be fake names. They paid in cash, though, and Mullins never thought to ask any questions."

"So, Mullins built a house with a torture chamber?"

Dooley laughed. "No, that was an addition by the renters. Mullins was freaked out by it when he heard. I'm not sure he ever stepped foot into the house again after that. He put it on the market, couldn't sell it, and then died of the big C about five years ago. The house went into probate, then foreclosure, and finally the bank wrote it off completely. I'm sure the county will give you a good deal if you want to buy it."

"Not today," Pam said.

"This place here."

Pam pulled the left turn onto a long an unmanicured gravel driveway. Ahead lay the drooping remains of a clapboard saltbox with a sagging roof, surrounded by the remains of a picket fence. She found it surprising that the front windows were still intact. "No vandalism," she observed.

"Like I said, word travels fast. You know the place is now haunted, right?"

She shot him a look.

He laughed. "Hey, if enough people say it, it has to be true."

Pam parked her car in front of the remains of the fence gate, and they got out of the car together. "Tell me what you found during your investigation."

Dooley led the way to the front door. "The shooters came in through here and through the back door," he said. "You can still see some of the splintering in the jamb there." He pointed to the scars on the knob side of the door panel, just above a closed padlock. "After the investigation, Mullins paid to have the doors repaired, and once the property reverted to the taxpayers, we paid for the locks and hasps."

"Do you have a key?" Pam asked.

"This is an official investigation, right?"

"Right."

"Cleared through the Ashland chief of police?"

"Yes. I talked to him yesterday."

"Okay, then." Dooley took two steps back and fired a massive kick with the sole of his boot-clad foot. The door moved but it did not open. A second kick moved it more, and the third did the trick. "That was the only key I had," he said with a big smile. "God, it's been a long time since I've gotten to do that." He pulled a long-handled MagLite from his gym bag and clicked it on. "Let's go in."

Pam's MagLite was much smaller, carried in a loop on her belt. She clicked hers on and followed Dooley into the darkness of what had once been a living room. A musty, mildewed odor spoke of an unrepaired water leak somewhere, and judging from the growth of mold on the walls, it had been leaking for a long time. Shag carpeting covered the floor, but it was heavily stained, and no doubt served as the home for all kinds of mites and bugs. The linoleum surface of the tiny square that probably had been called a foyer was covered with hundreds of rodent turds.

"Think of it as a fixer-upper," Dooley said.

"Where's all the furniture?"

"On the heels of the shooting, and in the absence of any evidence, we seized just about all of it for examination. We logged what little we found, and when we offered to return it, Mullins said just to trash it. That's what we did. Like I said, he was pretty freaked out."

"So go back to what happened," Pam said.

Dooley panned his flashlight beam to a burn spot on the far side of the living room where the floor met the wall. "We found a spent flashbang grenade there," he said, "and there's another one on the other side of the wall and down the hall near the back door. We figure that the shooters coordinated their entry front and back and tossed flashbangs to mess with the decedents' heads."

"Are those bullet holes?" Pam asked, pointing to erupted bits of the far wall.

"Yes, but they're exit holes. Here, let me show you."

He led her through an archway to the back part of

the house, to what used to be a kitchen. Only the sink remained, barely balanced atop the rotting remains of wood and Formica cabinetry. The mold was much thicker on the walls here, and the linoleum floors had buckled badly. "Watch your step," Dooley cautioned. "Have you seen any of the crime scene photos yet?"

Pam shook her head. "That's on the agenda for tomorrow when I stop by the station. I wanted to get the lay of the land before I get lost in the photos."

"I get that," Dooley said, as if offering his approval. He walked through the kitchen into another small room, maybe ten by ten feet. A dining room, perhaps? Pam supposed it was possible if you ate off a card table. Dooley pivoted to the wall separating that room from the living room and indicated a vertical space in front of the bullet holes. "A tall chest of drawers sat here," he said. "My wife would call it an *armoire*." The he took a long step backward, into the center of the room. "This is where we found one of the bodies. You'll see it in photos. He was shot at close range—from right there on the other side of the archway—a perfect triple-tap. Chest, chest, forehead. Five-five-six through and through. Those holes in the wall are from where the bullets went through the decedent, through the drawers and then through the wall. Standard ball ammo, we found all but one of the bullets in the cushions of one of the living room chairs. We figure the other just fragmented all to hell."

"Were there shell casings?" Pam asked.

"Exactly three," Dooley replied. He pointed back through the archway toward the kitchen. "They were on the counter, as I recall. Maybe one on the floor, but there were only three."

"Why do you keep emphasizing that it was exactly three?"

He recoiled as if it were the most obvious question in the world. "Three kill shots is good shooting," he said. "And at this range, to select such precise targets—as opposed to yelling, 'oh, shit!' and spraying bullets—says professionalism to me."

"Professionalism," Pam said, tasting the word.

Dooley's confusion deepened. "I thought you said you'd read the reports," he said. "I've made my thoughts on this as clear as crystal since the very beginning. There's no doubt in my mind that this was a hostage rescue of some sort."

She had, indeed, read that in his reports, and that was, indeed, where her inclinations lay, if only because of the vehement testimony of Ethan Falk. But she wanted to know about his reasoning. "What makes you so sure?"

Dooley seemed to sense that he was being gamed, but then he shrugged, as if to say it didn't matter. "Follow me," he said. He edged past her and led the way back through the kitchen toward the back door in the far corner on the right, and then he buttonhooked left.

He addressed a heavy-duty door that stood closed, directly across from the comparatively flimsy back door. "Just so you know, Mullins didn't know anything about this door until we showed him pictures. The occupants at the time installed it on their own."

"The door to the torture chamber?" Pam guessed.

"Well . . . indirectly," Dooley said. "Remember, you wanted this tour."

Something about the way he said that last part chilled Pam's neck at the spot where it attached to the base of her skull. She tried to imagine—while trying not to imagine—what this place would have looked like through the eyes of an eleven-year-old. As that thought formed, she realized that she now undeniably believed every word that Ethan had said.

"Watch your noggin," Dooley cautioned as he rapped a knuckle against the low overhead. Not an especially tall man, he had to cock his head to the side and bend his knees to negotiate the steps. Pam probably could have made it standing upright, but she ducked anyway. The beam of her flashlight reflected straight back from Dooley's shirt, but the beam from his seemed to get consumed by the absoluteness of the dark. Dampness and mildew and rodent shit combined to form a nauseating, toxic stench.

"I know this is pretty awful," Dooley said without looking back at her, "but I'll tell you that it actually smells better now than it did the first time I was here. Coroner estimated that the bodies had been dead for about seven, eight days when we found them."

The low ceiling continued the length of the twelve stairs to the concrete floor of the basement, which was roughly the size of the house's footprint. The stairway more or less split the space. Pam played her light to the right, which revealed a wide open space, concrete floors rimmed with moldy white-painted bricks.

"When you look at the pictures, you'll see that this whole side of the space was lined with hard-backed wooden chairs."

"Lined?"

"Along the walls. Well, those two walls there." He pointed to the back of the room and the far wall that ran perpendicular to it. "They were arranged like they were a dance floor or something."

Or as a place from which to evaluate your next human purchase, Pam thought. She played her light to the left. That view revealed an archway, beyond which there was a narrow hallway whose far wall was lined with four closed heavy doors. The ceiling hung low down here, barely allowing them to stand.

Dooley stepped into the hallway, leaving Pam standing at the base of the stairs. "The shooter who took out the second guy stood about where you are now," he said. "Again, three shell casings, five-five-six, but with different ejector marks."

"A second gun, then," Pam said.

"Exactly. And we found that body right about here." He walked to a spot in front of the second door. "Another perfect triple-tap."

"What's behind these doors?" Pam asked.

"That first one there, in front of you, is the furnace room. Some food storage, too. This second one"—he opened the door and shined his light inside—"we're not sure what it was for, exactly, but I have an idea. There was a mattress on the floor and it was a DNA farm. Blood, semen, saliva, every body juice you can think of. I don't even want to think of what went on in there."

"Jesus."

"Oh, trust me. That's not the worst of it."

Pam was beginning to regret her decision not to look at the photos first. It would have been nice to have some forewarning. Not that she couldn't already figure it out.

Dooley turned the knob on the third door and opened it. He stepped aside so she could see into it. Her MagLite revealed an empty rectangular room, maybe ten by seven, more or less identical to the mattress room, only this one sported a rodent-gnarled braided rug in the middle of the floor. "Ready to see the torture chamber?"

"Not really." That of course meant yes.

Dooley lifted the rug to reveal an etched square in the concrete. Call it three feet on a side.

"What am I looking at?" Pam asked.

Dooley didn't answer. Instead, he handed his light to Pam and reached back into his gym bag, from which he withdrew two T-shaped metal tools. "When we closed this place up after the investigation, the county attorney was terrified that vandals would somehow lock themselves in the hole, so we removed the handles to the hatch and covered it with the rug. I made these special for you when I heard you were coming."

"Why not just seal it up permanently?"

He smiled. "Well, probably the most truthful answer is laziness," he said. "But beyond that, I think I always secretly hoped that the investigation would become active again. Can you hold the light on the hatch?"

Pam sidled into the room to get a better angle, then held the light high for an overhead angle. Dooley bent at the waist, inserted a T tool into each of the two holes that she hadn't seen until he did it. With considerable effort, he lifted the hatch out of the way and slid it off to the side. "There you go," he said as he stood tall again. "Welcome to Hell." He reached for his flashlight, and played the beam down the hole. "I swore I'd never go down there again."

He gathered himself with a deep breath. "Oh, what the hell? Be careful on the ladder. It was rickety eleven years ago."

Pam watched Dooley descend the vertical ladder, doing her best to illuminate more than just the top of his head. When he was at the bottom, he brought his hand to his nose. "Oh, this just keeps getting better and better."

Pam could feel the change in the quality of the air as she descended into the hole. It seemed thicker somehow, and it was certainly colder and moister. The smell of the place was unlike anything she'd encountered in the past. Musty, certainly, but there was an organic element to it, not as pungent as a decomposing body, but on the same spectrum. "What is that stench?"

She'd meant the question as a rhetorical one, but Dooley answered it. "I think of it as the smell of evil. This is the place that the original owner had no idea was here, the space the occupants dug out." The ceiling here couldn't have been six feet higher than the dirt floor.

"We think the decedents kept people down here," Dooley explained as he knelt on the dirt. He pointed to the far corner with his flashlight beam. "There was a pit over there, used as a toilet. Judging from an analysis of the waste in the bucket, this space housed multiple occupants. The third body was found just about where I'm standing."

"Another perfect triple-tap?"

"No. This one was a single shot through the forehead. It's hard to tell exactly where the shot came from, but from the location of the casing—same rifle as the one used to kill the one out in the hallway—I figure that the shooter was either on the ladder or at the base of it. This dead guy had his pants down around his ankles."

Pam's stomach churned. It was entirely possible that she'd just found the limits of her emotional shields.

"For all these reasons," Dooley said, "I'm ninety-nine percent convinced that what went down here was some kind of a rescue operation. I checked with the State PD and with the FBI, and they didn't claim it, so I guess it was vigilantes or something."

"Or maybe a rival criminal operation," Pam said. She wanted to push her own assumptions as much as she wanted to push Dooley's.

Dooley nodded. "Always possible," he said. "Hell, anything is possible. But I've got to tell you. There can't be more than one or two gang guys in the world who deploy flashbangs and have this kind of marksmanship."

"What did your investigation turn up on the shooters?"

"Not a lot. Nothing, actually. But to be honest, we didn't press all that hard."

Pam waited for it.

Dooley prepared with another deep breath, and then winced at the air he inhaled. "You remember that armoire I told you about upstairs?"

"Yeah."

"It was filled with kids' clothing. One drawer was just underpants. The only reason I'd want to catch the people who killed animals like that would be to shake their hands and buy them a drink."

Chapter Sixteen

The Hilton Garden Inn in Ashland, Ohio, housed a nicer bar than Jonathan had expected. A little brighter than he liked, and a little more plastic, the back wall displayed high-end liquors, and the chairs were reasonably comfortable. He preferred seats with backs like these over the traditional bar stools. Too many years of hard landings and parachute jumps. That shit comes back to haunt you way younger than you think it's going to.

He'd been here for nearly ten minutes, having been alerted by Boxers that Detective Hastings was on her way back to the hotel. Big Guy displaced too much air to attend the kind of meeting that lay ahead, but he was the perfect choice for keeping eyes on Pam Hastings while she toured the house on Wells Road.

The phone call had been short and sweet even by Boxers' standards.

"Okay, Boss, she's on the road to the hotel. She's kinda hot, but keep it in your pants. Uncle Box does not want to have to pull you out of a jail cell. I'm gonna go and try to get laid. Wish me luck." He hung up. Jonathan worried about his friend's proclivities toward one-nighters, but lo these many years had demonstrated that it made no sense to try and talk him out of the things he liked to do.

Jonathan took a position at the angle of the bar where he could nurse his martini while keeping an eye on the propped-open etched glass doors. After a half hour and a bowlful of bar snacks, he began to wonder if Venice's research might have been wrong. For sure, it was time to order another drink, this time with a tall glass of club soda on the side. He was easily good for three martinis, but not without some sacrifice in agility. He needed to pace himself in case the evening stretched longer than he was expecting.

The second drink touched down on his cardboard coaster at the same moment when Detective Pamela Hastings arrived at the doors. She'd clearly changed clothes—unless LEOs these days wore jeans and T-shirts on duty—and she'd clearly showered—unless it was raining in the elevator. Her hair wasn't wet, exactly, but another minute or two under the hair dryer would not have been wasted. Back in the day, Jonathan's now-deceased ex-wife, Ellen, had told him that when women traveling on business visited hotel bars on business travel, they did everything they could to make themselves look unattractive in order to keep horny dudes from hitting on them. Jonathan had countered that dudes on travel could get horny enough that looks no longer mattered.

In Detective Hastings's case, on this particular night, it seemed clear that she wanted alone time. She chose a seat on the distant corner of the bar, as far away from Jonathan as possible.

He offered up a silent apology to Venice for ever having doubted her. As if to drive the point home, Hastings ordered a Stoli vodka and tonic, exactly as Venice had predicted she would.

Jonathan made eye contact and toasted hello. She returned the gesture with a thin-lipped grimace then made a show of stirring her drink. Jonathan gave her two minutes of peace before making his move.

He slid off of his stool and walked the length of the bar to man the corner perpendicular to Pam's.

"Oh, please, no," she said with the concomitant eye roll.

"Excuse me?" Jonathan said. The goal of this meeting was to knock her off balance, so he might as well start now.

Pam hitched her shoulders once, relaxed them, then gave Jonathan a condescending glare that he imagined was well practiced. "Look," she said. "Yes, you're a good-looking guy, but nowhere near as good-looking as you think you are. Major brawn is not my type. I don't care how lonely you are, and there is no part of your body that I wish to see unclothed. I've had a very long day, and what I'd like more than anything else is to be left alone."

Jonathan smiled. It was his charming smile, he'd been told, the one that Venice said made his super-blue eyes look even bluer. And he said nothing.

Silence unnerved most cops when they were not manipulating it. "What." She uttered the word as a statement of exasperation, not a question.

"I'm just marveling at the eloquence of that speech,

Detective Hastings," Jonathan said, smile still affixed. "Did you rehearse it, or was it spontaneous?"

He'd intended to startle her, and clearly he'd succeeded. "Do we know each other?"

Jonathan pulled on his drink to buy a few more seconds of silence. "I can't say that we've met, but I certainly know a great deal about you."

Her mind spun behind her eyes, but she continued to show a good poker face. "And who are you?"

"Call me Smith," Jonathan said. "Or Jones, if you'd prefer."

Pam blanched, but just a little—barely enough to demonstrate that Jonathan had scored a point. "If you're from some law enforcement agency, let me see some ID."

Jonathan changed his smile to something ugly—at once condescending and smug. Pam needed to accept that he was in charge. The flow of information would be entirely one-way.

"I don't have time for this," Pam said, and she pushed away from the bar.

"You went to King's Park Elementary School," Jonathan said. "And then on to Lake Braddock Secondary School for grades seven through twelve. Your father had a debilitating stroke when you were seventeen, so you had to abandon your plans to study English literature at NC State and you settled instead for Northern Virginia Community College. That's where you were bitten by the bug for criminal justice. Shall I go on?"

His recitation of Venice's research seemed to stun the detective, paralyze her. The poker face had morphed into a gaping stare.

"We really do need to talk," Jonathan said. "There will be no flashing of credentials because my identity is irrelevant. That's why Smith or Jones will work equally well. I assure you, however, that I am a good guy, not bad guy, and I have no intention of showing you any unclothed body parts."

Pam blushed through obvious confusion. "Who are the bad guys?"

"I can't tell you that," Jonathan replied. He was in large measure playing a bluff here. He needed to know what she knew, and this seemed like the shortest pathway to the goal. "I need to know what you know about the killings on Wells Road."

"Why don't you ask the Ashland Police Department?"

Jonathan needed to play this part carefully. It was the major hole in his bluff. "Because I'm speaking with you," he said.

"Why me instead of the original investigators?"

"Because the Ashland case is only a small part of what I'm interested in."

Pam's gaze bored into him. "What's the other part?"

"I think you know," Jonathan said. "It's about a fellow you know as John Doe. And a young man you know as Ethan Falk." He forced a chuckle as a response to what he saw in her face. "If I knew everything about your past, why on earth would you think I wouldn't know about Ethan?"

"What is your involvement in any of this?" Pam asked.

Jonathan took another sip of martini. He let the question hang for dramatic effect, and then he leaned in closer. "My involvement is inconsequential," he said. "But the facts of the two cases you're looking at are of huge consequence. I come here tonight to make you a deal."

Pam made a quick waving motion. "Oh, no. I don't have any authority to make deals with unnamed government agencies. And not knowing if you are even telling the truth, I'm not inclined to continue this conversation." She gathered her things and started for the door again.

"Act in haste," Jonathan said, "and repent in leisure." He said it loudly enough to be heard, but he didn't look at her as he said it. The charade was all about him having something that Pam needed. To pull it off, he couldn't look anxious. In the polished brass of the beer tap, he saw a contorted image of the detective paused in the doorway. She stayed there long enough to make Jonathan wonder if he'd misplayed his hand.

Then the image moved, and a shadow arrived at his shoulder. "What deal?" she asked.

Jonathan spun away from her on his stool, and pointed to an unoccupied booth in the far corner of the bar. "Let's talk over there," he said. "It's a little more private." He grabbed his drink and led the way, not bothering to look back. When he arrived at the table and turned, there she was. He slid into one of the under-padded bench seats and indicated that she should take the other. "Want another drink?" he asked.

Pam still had not committed to sitting down. "What deal?" she said again.

"We'll talk when you're seated," Jonathan said. "Really, there's no need to be concerned about me. Besides, you're a cop, and that means you're armed. If I get out of line, you can always shoot me." He fired off his charming smile again.

Pam looked over her shoulder and appeared to scan the bar. For what, Jonathan wasn't sure, but he appreciated her situational awareness. Finally, she sat on the bench opposite him. She didn't commit to it, though, staying on the very end on the bench, her right arm still in the aisle. Jonathan interpreted the posture as a way to guarantee free access to her firearm. "No more games," she said.

"Life and death is never a game," Jonathan said. "The deal is this: I answer a question for you, and you answer a question for me. We'll go back and forth until one of us refuses to answer. The only topic off the table is anything having to do with who I am or where I work. Are you in?"

Pam took her time. "How will I know if you're telling the truth?"

Jonathan shrugged. "I could ask the same of you. There are no guarantees, but at least it's a place to start."

Pam's glare intensified as she read his face. Jonathan knew she would get nothing. He'd practiced the nothing look for many years. "Okay," she said, "I've got a question for you."

Jonathan held up his hand. "I go first," he said. "And you have my word that I will answer your first question, so long as it is within the parameters I laid out."

She clearly didn't like it.

"My deal, my rules," Jonathan said. "Or we can pretend that we never met."

A sigh. "Okay, go."

"Ethan Falk has told quite a story. You followed the elements of that story all the way to Ashland, Ohio. Does that mean that you believe him?"

"Should I?"

"A question is not an answer," Jonathan said. "And I wouldn't waste your first question on one like that. Do you believe Ethan Falk's story?"

Again, Pam took her time answering. "There are elements that ring true, and there are elements that strain credulity."

Jonathan waited for more.

"On balance, I believe him more than I don't. But events that happened over a decade ago do not justify murdering a man in cold blood."

"Under the circumstances, how cold could that blood really be?" Jonathan asked.

"That's a second question," Pam said. "It's my turn. Do you know the true identity of our John Doe?"

Jonathan started to answer, but she held up her hand, as if to stop traffic at an intersection.

"No, let me ask it differently," she said. "What is the true identity of our John Doe?"

Jonathan smiled. To ask a yes or no question is to invite a single syllable answer. "Nice catch," he said. "His real name is James Stepahin, and he was everything that Ethan Falk purports him to be. What have you been able to find out about him so far? That's my next question."

"Absolutely nothing," Pam said. "How do you know his real identity?"

Jonathan patted the table lightly with both hands. "And there you have it," he said. "The end of the game. That's the question I won't answer." He stood without offering his hand. "Good night, Detective Hastings," he said.

Chapter Seventeen

Braddock County Police Chief Warren Michaels looked up as Lieutenant Jed Hackner approached his door and knocked.

"Excuse me, Chief," Hackner said. "Have you got a minute?"

From the way Jed asked the question, Warren was inclined to say no. First of all, he and Jed had known each other since they were kids, and the only time he used the honorific instead of his first name was when the officialness of the official business was grim. Second, Warren could see past Jed's shoulder, where German Culligan and Wendy Adams both looked pretty spun up.

"Am I in trouble?" Warren asked.

"It's about the Falk kid," Jed said. "They want to do something that only you can approve."

"Am I going to want to approve it?"

"I think you should hear what they have to say."

"Do they know that I'm busy and cranky?"

"It's a day with a *y* in it, isn't it?"

"And they've already spoken with you?"

"At length."

"And what do you want to do with whatever they're asking?"

"I want to send them to you so you can make the decision."

Warren's expression triggered a smile from his old friend. "Send them in."

Over the course of his nearly thirty-year career with the Braddock County Police Department, Warren had worked hard to build cordial relationships between the many players in the judicial process. Unlike far too many of his counterparts in other cities and counties, he did not see defense attorneys as the enemy, but rather as the necessary counterbalance that forced his police officers to do their job to the best of their ability. Guilt or innocence notwithstanding, if his troops screwed up an investigation, the accused went free. And that sense of fairness was a counterbalance to the political ambitions of the Commonwealth's attorney, J. Daniel Petrelli, a fifth-degree asshole by any measure of the word.

Warren had learned the hard way nearly two decades before about the fallibility of incontrovertible evidence when a twelve-year-old boy named Nathan Bailey was without question a murderer. Only by forcing himself to look at the evidence from a different angle did Warren see the error of the obvious, and in the process of doing that, he'd saved the boy's life. Now that boy was a thirty-year-old patrolman for the BCPD and Warren called him his son.

German P. Culligan, attorney at law, was to Warren's mind one of the best in the business. He pressed hard, fought harder, and somehow managed to fight fair. Warren knew that German had contacts within the department who leaked him information, but he didn't care. That was one more way to counteract Petrelli's exuberance for his job of prosecuting the innocent as well as the guilty.

As for Dr. Wendy Adams, the jury was still out for Warren. He respected the job she had to do, and the zeal with which she did it, but when all was said and done, Warren didn't have a lot of faith in the art of psychology. There was no way he could think of it as a science. An admitted curmudgeon, Warren had little tolerance for insanity defenses or for so-called hate crimes for that matter. No one murders someone they like, after all, and the fact that the decedent was "hated" or not had no effect on his status as a corpse. As for insanity, he'd noted over the years that that defense was usually trotted out as a last resort, and at that, only for the most heinous crimes.

Culligan crossed the threshold first and Warren stepped out from around his desk to greet him. "Nice to see you, Counselor," he said as he shook the man's hand. "And Dr. Adams, to what do I owe the pleasure?" He gestured to the oval conference table near the window. The police department offices today were a hell of a lot more opulent than they were in Warren's early years.

"Are you aware of what happened to Ethan Falk in jail last night?" Culligan said.

Warren looked to Jed.

"He was beaten pretty badly," Jed said.

"What does pretty badly mean?" Warren asked.

Wendy said, "It means two broken teeth, an eye swollen shut, and nearly broken ribs."

"Have you brought it up with the ADC bosses?" Warren asked, referencing the Adult Detention Center.

"They didn't want to have anything to do with it," Wendy said.

Culligan added, "We talked to the lunkhead who runs the place and he washed his hands of it. He said, 'Well, it *is* jail,' and then brushed it off."

Warren cut his eyes to Jed again. "Doesn't he have a point? You put violent people together and violence is likely to happen."

"How could you of all people say that?" Wendy snapped. She appeared totally aghast.

"Excuse me?"

"Your own experience with Nathan Bailey."

Warren bristled. "That was a *juvenile* detention center, and he was twelve years old. And, frankly, that's not a topic I intend to discuss."

"There are similarities," Culligan said. "Falk does not have the skills to cope with jail."

Again to Jed: "Isn't he charged with murder?"

"Yep."

"Admitted to it, right?"

Jed nodded. "And we have about twenty witnesses to the event."

"Well, come on, Counselor," Warren said. "Actions have consequences, you know? One of the downsides of killing people is that you have to learn to get along with other killers."

Wendy started to speak, but Warren interrupted.

"Why are you even here? I don't run the ADC. Go beat up on Sheriff Wallingford." To Jed: "Why are they even here?"

"We want to move him out of the ADC and into one of your holding cells," Wendy said.

Never a very patient man, Warren felt himself slipping toward anger. "They call them holding cells for a reason. The people in them are just a-passin' through. On their way to the Adult Detention Center."

"This is not without precedent," Culligan said. "Alejandro Garcia."

"That's not a precedent," Warren said. "He was a protected witness who would have been whacked in thirteen seconds if people knew where he was."

Wendy started to speak again, and this time it was Culligan who silenced her, with a gentle touch on her arm. He softened his tone. "The precedent lies in the fact of long-term incarceration outside the ADC."

"It was not long-term," Warren objected. "What? Maybe three weeks?" When this meeting was over, he intended to have a discussion with Jed. Some decisions were easy. This should have been one of them.

"It proves that it's possible," Wendy said, seeming pleased to finally be back in the argument.

"Your cells are singles," Culligan said. "You have shower facilities, and the ADC can send over meals."

"Why not just make him a reservation at a motel?" Warren said. "That way he can have clean, crisp sheets every night and maybe a couple of drinks at the bar."

"I fear that we're losing this argument," Culligan said.

"You *fear*? Oh, trust me, you've already lost it. I am not a prison. And by the way, that Garcia case cost a lot of money in terms of extra guard time."

"That was because he was a protected witness," Culligan said. "That would not happen here."

Warren hated it when the other party in an argument was right.

"Before you kick us out of your office, let me make the case," Culligan said. "Give me sixty seconds."

"You've got forty-five." Warren said it because it sounded like the right thing to say. In reality, he'd give the man five minutes if he needed it.

"We have growing reason to believe that the man Ethan Falk killed had in fact brutalized him when he was a child. Detective Hastings is in Ashland, Ohio, as we speak, hoping to triangulate Ethan's story with an unsolved homicide there that meets the time frame. The early indications are that she scored a home run."

"Then you must be thrilled," Warren said. "You've got a perfect argument to take to court. You can claim temporary insanity, or maybe go for jury nullification, but there is nothing in what you have said, what Ethan has said, or what witnesses have said that could possibly justify self-defense. That means he's likely in the environment that he'll have to cope with for the rest of his life. I'll stipulate that it sucks, but jails have long had a reputation for sucking. There's no surprise here."

"If I may," Wendy interjected. "This case is special. That young man—Ethan Falk—is in a very fragile state. It is my professional opinion that the continuing stress of daily violence will leave him permanently wounded, psychologically."

"Then petition the court," Warren said.

"They will deny my petition," Culligan said.

Warren raised his shoulders in an extended shrug.

"This is more than that," Wendy said. "That young man needs counseling, and he desperately needs to feel a sense of safety. At least of marginal safety. Daily beatings from which he cannot defend himself are hardly the way to sanity."

Warren looked to Jed. "Don't they have isolation cells in the ADC anymore?"

"They're all taken, apparently," Jed said.

"And even with isolation, there is still the air of violence that permeates all aspects of that place," Wendy said. "Look, if he gets convicted, then obviously he's going to have to do whatever the system tells him he has to do. But let's at least give him some coping skills. Let's give him an opportunity for some kind of emotional recovery."

"We can make it work," Jed said.

Ah, so there it is, Warren thought. They'd already won Jed over.

"Not to repeat myself," Wendy said, "and not to step on dangerous territory, but you do know more than most how much difference a little rule-bending goes in taking a young man's future from the dark side to the light."

This was a bad idea. Warren knew it in his heart. No matter how you cut it, this was going to add a burden to everyone involved in the incarceration cycle, from the food workers at the ADC all the way down through his own officers who had to keep track of a semipermanent resident. But Wendy had structured her argument in a way that he could not deny it.

"Okay, Lieutenant Hackner," he said to Jed, "make it happen."

The defense team beamed.

"Don't say anything," Warren said with a trace of a smile. "This'll take a couple of hours to put together, and

I can change my mind as quickly as I made it." He'd never do that, of course, but there was no harm in them thinking that he might.

Warren ushered his visitors to the door, and as they left, an older man in civilian clothes stood from the corner of an empty desk he'd been sitting on. He wore a Braddock County Police Department ID tag, and he looked familiar, but Warren couldn't quite place the face.

"Excuse me, Chief," he said in a timid tone. "My name is Cletus Bangstrom, sir, and I really need to talk with you."

Jonathan spent the night ten miles away from the Hilton Garden Inn, at some all-suites place whose management team needed to think seriously about remodeling the rooms and hallways. Jonathan rarely stayed in the kinds of hotels that catered to business travelers, preferring higher-end digs when the situation allowed, but he couldn't imagine that dirty and dreary was anyone's preference. On the other hand, maybe with the economy the way it was, the market would not support the extra twenty or thirty bucks a night that would be needed for what ought to be done.

He'd pulled himself out of the rack at a ridiculous hour so that he and Boxers could meet back at the airport for their return flight to Virginia. Boxers was already pre-flighting the Learjet when Jonathan arrived. He had just a little over a year left on his "lease" agreement with the plane's owner, and as much as Big Guy hated the aircraft's cramped size, Jonathan appreciated

the convenience. If need be, he could always lease another plane through one of his cutout corporations, but
Jonathan enjoyed the anonymity of this arrangement.

Boxers was just alighting the fold-down stairs when
Jonathan approached from behind.

"Good morning, Big Guy," Jonathan said cheer-
fully. It was always a good idea to give Boxers ade-
quate notice when moving up behind him. "Did you
have a successful night of passion?"

"Nah. But I did get laid well and frequently."

"Congratulations," Jonathan said. "Now maybe
you'll be less cranky."

Boxers climbed through the door and turned. "You
know, Boss, you ought to try it some time."

"Stop," Jonathan said. He'd had difficult times with
relationships for as long as he and Big Guy had known
each other. It never failed that just when he thought he
had found a soul mate, she'd let him down. "Are we
ready to go?"

"We've got wings, fuel, and a working engine," Big
Guy said. "Can't think of a thing that can stop us now.
I filed a flight plan back to Virginia, so as far as I'm
concerned, we're all set. Are you riding up front like a
big boy, or are you planning to lounge in the back?"

If only for the optics of having two faces in the
windscreen during takeoffs from real airports—as opposed to some of the less-than-optimum fields they'd
used over the years—Jonathan always rode in the front
seat until the plane was at altitude. More times than
not, he'd stay there to keep Big Guy company during
the flight. As far as Jonathan was concerned, the private
plane was entirely about convenience and not at all
about the creature comforts. Sometimes, though, when

he had things to work on, he would ride in the back and spread out. This would be one of those days.

"Somebody's got to think the big thoughts so we can make the big bucks," Jonathan said.

"That's why you don't mind this piece-of-shit sardine can of an airplane," Big Guy grumbled.

Jonathan didn't answer. He just waited for Boxers to squeeze himself into the pilot's seat—it really was a comical thing to watch, a little like watching a calf crawl back into its mother's womb—but he dared not laugh at the spectacle. For reasons that Jonathan had never cared to explore, Big Guy was oddly sensitive about his size. Once the pilot was in place, Jonathan maneuvered his way around the center console and settled easily into the right-hand seat.

Jonathan wasn't entirely useless on the controls in an emergency. Boxers had taught him enough over the years that he could land the beast in a pinch, but only if the weather was clear. He had no business flying on instruments. And zero desire to do so.

Ten minutes later, they were airborne.

"So what about you?" Boxers asked once the intensity of departure radio traffic had died down. "Did you accomplish anything with the hot young detective?"

"I told her that she was on the right track about Ethan," Jonathan said. "And I gave her the name of her John Doe."

Boxers gave him a look. "Was that wise? I thought Wolfie wanted you to keep that close to the chest."

"You heard Ven the other day. He's been pretty thoroughly disappeared. Having the name isn't going to help them much."

As Jonathan was unfastening his seat belt to head

back to the passenger compartment, Boxers said, "Hey, Boss. What are your intentions with this Falk kid?"

"How do you mean?"

"Well, as an anything-but-disinterested observer, it seems to me that you're as preoccupied with him as you are of doing what we need to do for Wolverine."

"That's because I think we can do both."

"Nope, not buying it. You deliberately showed your face to the detective who's investigating the deaths of people we killed. You know I don't pull your short hairs often, but that was reckless. As the guy on the other gun that night, I want to know what your intentions are. From the very beginning, my single ground rule was that I am not going to jail."

"Nobody's going to jail," Jonathan said. "We are no more traceable now than we've ever been. But I cannot sit still while Ethan Falk is dismissed as a looney tune when I know the reality."

"The reality is that we saved his life," Boxers said. "We gave him eleven years of freedom that he otherwise would not have had. He chose to kill a guy who wasn't doing anything wrong. Not then."

Jonathan sighed loudly. "Are you going to look me in the eye and tell me that you would not have done the same thing?"

"Of course I would have done the same thing. But I wouldn't have taken care of business in front of a world full of witnesses."

"So, he's too much of a rookie at the whole vengeance thing," Jonathan said.

"Clearly." Boxers took a couple of seconds to adjust a control that Jonathan couldn't see. "You know, I'm not even a cheap imitation of Dom, but there's something else. I think you should consider telling me what it is."

"I don't know what you're talking about."

"I'm not here to analyze you, Dig, and I sure as hell am not here to judge you, but I *am* the guy whose life depends on you having a solid head on your shoulders. There's something eating you up. What is it?"

Jonathan kept about a thousand different drawers in his head locked at all times. That was for good reason. Emotions only became real if you spoke of them. Otherwise, they remained fully deniable. Deniability was important to him. On the other hand, no one had a greater stake in Jonathan's activities than Boxers. If there was a chance that he would not perform at one hundred percent when the shit got thick, then he shouldn't be doing what he did.

"You know I love what we do, right?" Jonathan said. "We're damn good at it, and we've saved a lot of lives."

"Yes, we have," Boxers said. "And we've taken a lot of lives, too."

"And I don't give a rat's ass about most of them."

"You're not shedding angst for those assholes you offed at the motel the other day, are you?"

"Oh, hell no," Jonathan said. "Wake 'em up and I'll shoot 'em again." A beat. "Don't you ever worry about this stuff getting too easy?"

Boxers said, "We've never killed anyone who didn't need killing."

"That's not true," Jonathan said. "I wish it was, but it's not. That op in West Virginia was a total goat rope. A lot more people were killed and wounded than needed to be."

"That wasn't us," Boxers said. "That was Jolaine. Who knew she'd turn out to be psycho?"

A while ago, Jonathan and his team—which had expanded to include a former personal security specialist named Jolaine Cage—invaded a terrorist compound in West Virginia, and the resulting slaughter had been nauseating.

"That was my team," Jonathan said. "Our team."

"I thought you settled all of this with Dom," Boxers said. "You kicked her off the team, and now it's all square."

"No, it's not square," Jonathan said. "She's a murderer and she's free. No justice at all." The irony of his own words did not escape him. According to the law, his whole team was an assembly of mass murderers, but that was different. While often outside the law, he was rarely on the wrong side of it.

Boxers took his time asking his next question. "So, do you want to quit?"

"You know better than that."

"I don't know that I do. I mean up until five minutes ago I thought I did, but now I'm wondering. Because you know, if you even consider the possibility of defeat—"

"—defeat is guaranteed," Jonathan said, finishing Big Guy's statement. "Yeah, I know. I'm the one who told you that. This isn't like that."

"What *is* it like, then?"

Jonathan struggled to find the right way to put it. "Remember that snatch-and-grab we did outside of Islamabad? The Puzzle Palace needed a tribal leader to grill?"

Boxers' whole demeanor darkened. He didn't say that he remembered, but thanks to the body language, he didn't have to.

"That little girl—a guard's daughter, we figured—stepped out to protect her father just as your round was leaving the muzzle." The result was a double-kill, but the damage a 7.62 millimeter bullet inflicts on a little girl is far more profound than what it does to an adult. Boxers went to a very, very dark place for quite a while after that incident.

"It's a little like that," Jonathan went on. "Sometimes this shit just slips through the filters. You deal with it and then move on."

Jonathan chose to stay in the cockpit through the ensuing silence. Boxers was probably pissed that he dredged up that old memory, and he didn't want to leave it unresolved.

"So, what does any of that have to do with the Falk kid?" Boxers said after a couple of minutes.

"He's collateral damage. Just like the little girl in Islamabad, and just like those poor souls in West Virginia. Only, unlike those, we have a chance to fix the damage."

Boxers gave him a long, hard look. "How?"

Jonathan gave him a wry smile. "I haven't quite figured that part out yet. But I promise I won't be reckless."

"I don't even know what reckless means in this context," Boxers said.

"It means that I'll figure out a way to help Ethan Falk without you getting sent to jail."

"What about you getting sent to jail?" Big Guy said. He seemed bothered by where this was going.

"I figure I've got nothing to worry about," Jonathan said with a smile as he arose from his seat to head back to the cabin. "If I get sent to jail, I've got you to break me out."

Chapter Eighteen

Three hours later, Jonathan and Boxers were back on the ground in Braddock County, maybe a half mile from the Caf-Fiend Coffee Shop where all of this began. With Konan's help, Venice had done an analysis of Stepahin's movements in the last hours of his life, based on the cell phone data that she'd been able to obtain. It was scary what one could learn from a SIM card, even when the location services were disabled.

Stepahin had spent his last night at the Governor Spotswood Resort about ten miles from here. It wasn't a high-end place, but it was no slouch, either. It was the kind of place a business owner would take mid-range clients to, perhaps the banker who holds his loan. Built in the eighties, the place featured a lot of indoor water features and an elaborate indoor/outdoor pool, but the real pull of the place for most was the golf course. In Jonathan's experience, avid golfers would suffer all means of discomfort and ugliness so long as they got to spend four hours chasing the little white pill around freshly mowed grass. He didn't understand it himself, but he knew that among men his age, he was in the minority.

According to information hacked from the BCPD, Venice learned that Stepahin had used the alias George Magruder when he'd checked in to the hotel, and that he'd stayed there for only the one night. Because he'd opted for automatic checkout, there was no way to know when he'd left. If the police department had determined his departure time, they hadn't posted it to any source that Venice could tap into.

From there, Stepahin had driven around for a while, rather aimlessly, to Jonathan's eye. "I think he was in evasion mode," he said to Boxers as they reviewed the course tracks uploaded to his laptop. They'd traded the Learjet for the Batmobile, and were parked in the far corner of a church parking lot. When looking for a secluded spot on a day that was not Sunday, church parking lots were always reliable. "Look at all the random turns and switchbacks."

The computer displayed Stepahin's route as a bold red line laid over a map. A tiny red dot indicated the places where he'd stopped for more than a minute or so, and by clicking on the dot, you could pull up a time and date stamp. As one with a keen interest in remaining untraceable, Jonathan found it disconcerting that such tracking capability was available on the public market. Venice assured him that their communications were so encrypted that such tracking was not possible, but it still gave him pause. He took solace from the fact that Stepahin's other phone—presumably his business phone—was likewise untraceable.

As for phone calls made from the device Venice had hacked, every one of them seemed innocent. Restaurants, mainly. The data he accessed dealt primarily with news sites and online reservations. It seemed that the murdering asshole was also quite the foodie. The police were wearing out a lot of phone lines and shoe leather tracking those leads down, but in his gut, Jonathan sensed that they would go nowhere.

"Look here," Boxers said, pointing to a spot on the screen where Stepahin had spent a lot of time. The screen in that spot was a red smear. "What is that, a park?"

Jonathan scrolled in closer. "Yeah, but it's not much of one. But you're right. Look how many times he visited it. The time stamps are all over the place."

"And it's four blocks from the coffee shop."

They locked eyes and said it together: "Dead drop."

Spike Catron pulled his cherry 1974 Corvette into a slot in the rear of his headquarters building. The faded sign out front declared this to be a Moose Lodge, but there hadn't been a moose sighting in many a year. Cosmetically, the place looked like it should have been torn down years ago. Weeds and vines had taken over the front lot, and now were threatening to tear apart the brick façade. Located along a once well-traveled road that had been rendered irrelevant by the construction of a cross-county parkway, the lodge was nearly invisible to passersby.

It wasn't until you got close that you'd notice the heavy-duty steel doors and the concrete-set steel bars in the windows. The property belonged to a company called Bright Skies Environmental, Inc., which was a third-level shell belonging to Spike's masters in Yemen. Blue Skies likewise paid for the upgrades and the utilities. Soundproof and bug proof, the headquarters for al-Amin in America was as secure as any bank physically, and many times more secure electronically because electronics were not allowed. No cell phones, no computers, no data terminals.

Spike was first introduced to al-Amin while working as a clandestine asset for the US State Department in Yemen. Like every other beating heart in the Middle East, the members of al-Amin were suspected of planning terrorist strikes in the United States and among our allies. Less affiliated with any religious cause than they were to cash, al-Amin specialized in extortion, with a special emphasis on ransom. They would accept payment from another radical group—hell, from anybody—and in return, they would snatch a target from the street or from their sleep and deliver it to whoever placed the order. They got paid only for live deliveries, though living and injury-free were entirely different things.

At the time, he'd been impressed that a terror organization could operate under such a pure a business model as profit and loss. Operations were much simpler to plan when they were not driven by ideology.

As Spike's time in the Sandbox evolved, he became progressively more familiar with al-Amin's client list, and he was surprised to discover just how much of their kidnapping schedule was driven by the interests of the US government and its allies. It turned out that in the eyes of the Alphabet Agencies, the drawdown of American assets did nothing to reduce the need for intelligence data obtained the hard way, occasionally one fingernail at a time. Anyone who received a paycheck from Uncle Sam would face prison time for doing such a thing, but with enough attention to detail, it wasn't that difficult to sub the dirty work out to guys who had been in that business for the last two thousand years.

About two years ago, a fact crystalized in Spike's mind, and clarified his worldview. War was about money. It was about the cash paid to mullahs and warlords for their ever-negotiable loyalty. It was about the money paid to the Beltway contractors, and about the money in campaign war chests on both sides of the conflict. Al-Amin existed in large part because of secret money paid to them by Uncle Sam.

Spike figured what was good for his Uncle was good for him as well, so why not follow the boss's lead and offer to extend al-Amin's reach to American soil for a fee? Those Arab assholes would sell their left nut to get their hands on Americans snatched from US soil and cut off their heads—or drown them, or burn them alive, or whatever sick method of killing they could think of. But it wasn't worth the risk of trying to set up shop here.

Guys like Spike—and Bill Jones and Phil Marks and Paul Maroni, and the rest of his oh, so red-blooded American team—had no trouble getting as close as they needed to pull off whatever needed to be done. Up until now, they'd focused mainly on abducting corporate bigwigs and sending them to Mexico, where al-Amin was tight with a couple of the cartels, but now the heat was ramping up, and with it, the audacity of what the unnamed Sandbox Sheik wanted from them.

They wanted high-profile soft targets, the favorite among them being the children of elected officials, who wandered through their lives unprotected. The plan was pretty simple: snatch the kids, drug them, and hand them off to a designated foreign official who then shipped them home as diplomatic baggage. The diplomatic status was a particularly brilliant touch, Spike thought. And man, was the pay good!

A few months ago, the plan took an odd turn when the sheik demanded that the US complement of al-Amin expand into a new line of business, one that Spike considered to be reckless, but that he was nonetheless honor-bound to execute for fear of being outed by his Middle Eastern masters. They wanted a real terror strike somewhere in the heartland of the United States, the kind that would shake the country to its knees.

It was one thing to drop the Twin Towers and make a hole in the Pentagon, but those were symbolic strikes that Mr. and Mrs. Mid-America had difficulty bonding with. People who chose to live in big cities accepted the risks that came with it. In the Heartland, people felt comfortable that they lived their lives under the radar, perpetuating the illusion that the War on Terror churned in areas that didn't concern them.

But suppose a bomb detonated in the middle of a high school football game in Iowa? The panic—the *terror*—would be sublime. The stock markets—the symbol of American wealth that seemed to piss off the camel jockeys worse than any other—would plummet. The government would be overwhelmed with demands for action that they could not possibly respond to, and when the people lost faith in the political system, chaos would rule. And if there was one condition in which history had proven that zealots could thrive, it was in the midst of anarchy.

Since the end of World War Two, it had been the *il-*

lusion of American invincibility that had driven American power. Once the nation was shown to be as vulnerable as any other nation, then American leadership would dissolve. One cannot lead, after all, when no one is willing to follow.

Spike had feared that his troops would consider such a high-profile operation to be distasteful, too reminiscent of a suicide mission, but much to his surprise, they had embraced it with verve. The challenge, they all agreed, was to inflict the greatest possible damage while at the same time provide the greatest opportunity for evasion and escape. If the scope were large enough, and they left a big enough hole in the fabric of the community they attacked, then this would by definition be their last mission in the United States. No one on Spike's team carried the suicide gene of the average jihadi.

As they reviewed their options, they determined that the Iowa model, as they called it, was unworkable. Being in the middle of the country made escape to the border far too difficult. That meant that it was important to stay near one coast or the other. Since their home base was located in Virginia, the East Coast was the most logical point of attack, and the Old Dominion the simplest location from which to launch it. As they reviewed their options, they concluded that Northern Virginia offered the best of all options. It was the part of the state where the police were most constipated by matters politically correct, and where the local law enforcement agencies were enjoined from performing the kinds of stop-and-question operations that the rest of the country found instinctively appropriate.

That invited even more questions for consideration. Close-in jurisdictions like Fairfax or Arlington Counties teemed with federal law enforcement types and enjoyed a tax base that allowed them to deploy armored personnel carriers and massive firepower with only minutes' notice.

As they looked farther south and west, the population densities thinned to the point that even a massive strike could only do so much damage—until you got to the military-dense Tidewater areas, where the federal presence again became a problem.

All things considered, they'd determined Braddock County to be the best compromise. Real estate agents liked to call it a Washington suburb, but that was a stretch. It had a police department, but it was short on technology thanks to a tax base that could not afford to live closer in. The fire departments in the county were still volunteer, and the back-up long guns in most of the police vehicles were pump-action shotguns. Some of the units had AR-15 variants, but they were spread wide throughout the area. Superior firepower meant everything to Spike and his team.

Until a couple of days ago, Spike believed that all systems were go, and that they were closing in on a D-day that was maybe three weeks out. Now, though, with one operator dead, and a Haji team encroaching on their turf, he had an uneasy feeling about things on a number of fronts.

The parking lot in the back of the lodge looked fairly full as Spike nosed into a spot two spaces away from the nearest vehicle. There was a strong argument to be made that a man in his line of work should drive only the most inconspicuous vehicles, but as far as he was concerned, there was nothing quite as suspicious as a single man under forty who chose to drive an inconspicuous car. Besides, he was a car guy, and the seventy-four 'Vette was a slice of engineering beauty. He always figured that he would die young, and with that being the case, he was going to die happy.

Entering the lodge building required entering a twelve-digit random cipher and turning an eight-inch dead bolt. No one was allowed to answer a knock at the door. You either remembered the cipher or you were done. Short of using explosives—and quite a lot of them at that—police or anyone else would have one hell of a time serving any warrants in this place. And as soon as they arrived to try, the occupants would disappear though a network of tunnels that led to various friendly basements throughout the area.

The perfectly balanced door pulled easily considering its four hundred pounds, revealing an interior that looked pretty much as Spike imagined it did back when moose roamed free. It could have been a time capsule from 1985. Ceiling fans churned the air below suspended acoustic panels, and beige linoleum tiles covered the floor. A sagging Formica bar stood in the far right-hand corner, its face constructed of the same knotty pine paneling that covered the walls. The assembled members of al-Amin in America sat in random clusters, either at the bar or at the long folding tables that were lined up cafeteria-style, as if to play a rousing game of bingo. Everyone Spike saw at first glance was nursing some kind of beverage, mostly beer, but a few were enjoying hard liquor. On a day like this, Spike fantasized about beer. Herb Townsend even read his mind as Spike entered, and was already pulling a Blue Moon from the tap to hand to him.

"Good afternoon, gentlemen," Spike said after a generous tip of the plastic stadium cup. "Thanks for being timely."

"This is a bad idea, Spike," said Ace Reinhold, a former wet-work contractor for the CIA. "All the feds have to do is follow one of us to get all of us."

"I understand that, Ace, and when we break this thing up, we're going to have to watch our backs for the next couple of days. But this meet is necessary, trust me."

Spike pulled one of the wooden spindle-back bar stools into the center of the room and spun it so that he could see all the faces. They numbered twenty in total, and they ranged in appearance from stereotypical biker to Boy Scout. All of them were strong as oxen, but a few of them had been away from the gym for a few weeks too long. The lighter guys tended to fall back to skinny, and the bigger guys grew guts.

"We have a problem," Spike said. "And I need to know what the hell is happening."

"You talking about Bill Jones falling off the grid?" asked Vince Caplan, the smallest man on the team, a former boonie rat with the disposition of a cobra.

"Not yet," Spike replied, "but I'll get to that in a minute. Right now, we've got some Hajis screwing up a snatch and grab that I didn't even know about." He explained about the foiled efforts to kidnap the Johnson kid. "I'd be interested in hearing any theory on just what the hell is going on in our backyard that we don't know about."

Drew Jackson raised his hand. Mid-thirties and sharp as a needle, Drew was the unofficial head of intel for the group. "I think it's a trust thing. Hajis prefer to work with their own, just like we do."

"Any idea who those guys were?"

Drew made a face. "What difference does it make? They all fly under the same radar. My prediction is that they were loving children from fabulous homes whose families are shocked—*shocked*, I tell you—to find out that their little darlings had been radicalized by that nasty Internet." His comment drew a laugh from the group.

Spike clarified his question. "I guess what I really want to know is why did the sheik feel compelled to hand this off to a group of amateurs? Does it mean that He's losing confidence in us?"

"Who gives a shit?" Vince asked. "It's not like we don't have other ops to plan. Judging from the results, the sheik can't be very happy with his selection. Those boneheads blew an easy op. How did the cops find them?"

"They didn't," Drew said. "The rescue wasn't done by the police. They're treating the incident as a triple murder, though not very energetically. They kind of get the point that it was a rescue, but they have no clue about the details."

"You're getting this from your BCPD sources?" Spike asked.

"Yes, and they're completely stymied over who the shooters were."

"Do we have any idea?"

Drew shrugged. "I don't."

Spike scanned the room and got unison blank expressions.

"I've got more," Drew said. "And you're not going to like it."

"I hate preambles like that," Spike said.

"I think Bill Jones is dead," Drew said. "He's the contractor who—"

"I know who he is," Spike snapped. "Why do you think he's dead?"

"He never checked in after he picked up the drop. I figured he was taking his time, practicing tradecraft or some such, but my police contact asked me if we were missing anyone. I told him no, and asked why he wanted to know. Apparently, there's a John Doe in the morgue, and the kid who killed him says he was a kidnapper."

Spike gaped. "Finish the story."

"Okay, we *know* that Bill Jones is dead," Drew said. He seemed nervous. "I told the mole to send me a pic just for the hell of it. It's him."

"Did you say that?"

"Of course not. But a face is a face. It's him."

Spike weighed the details. "And your source told you that a *kid* killed him?"

"Well, not literally a little boy. Early twenties. Made coffee for a living. Says he recognized the guy from when he was kidnapped when he *was* a little boy. Only my mole says there's no record of that ever happening. And you want to hear the rest?"

"Don't play the game this way," Spike warned. "Say what you have to say."

"The kid—the guy who killed him—tells a story of being rescued by a team of two guys, but there's no record of that, either. What they *have* found is an un-solved case from somewhere in Ohio in which a few people were killed in what looked like a hostage res-cue."

"Like what happened with the Hajis," Spike said.

He wanted to make sure that he actually heard the story the way it was told.

"Except in this case, the dead were all white guys."

"So, it's possible that Bill Jones—the John Doe in the morgue—was involved in a kidnapping . . . How long ago did this happen?"

"Eleven years."

"Are you suggesting that Bill Jones was involved in a kidnapping eleven freaking years ago that was foiled by the same guys who broke apart the deal down near Quantico?"

Drew looked more nervous, and Spike appreciated it. A little bit of fear among killers never hurt. "The alternative would be one of the wildest coincidences in history."

"It's already one of the wildest coincidences in history!" Spike said. "What the hell is going on here?"

Around the room, the assembled team exchanged glances and mumbled unintelligible comments.

Spike's mind raced. When two or more things went to hell at the same time, they were always connected. *Always.* And it was always for a reason that created the most danger.

"The sheik must think we're a bunch of bumbling assholes," Vince said.

Spike wanted to be pissed at the comment, but the truth was the truth. "Would you blame him? I *know* we're not, but I still think we look like bumbling assholes."

He pressed at the air with both hands, a physical effort to calm himself down. He needed to find the logical string to pull that would set this all right again. He told himself that he needed to break events down to their component parts. With Bill Jones dead—and what a ridiculous pseudonym, barely better than his current one of John Doe—that meant there were loose ends that needed to be tied.

"How does a kid who pours coffee for a living kill a trained killer?"

"You tell me. The cops say he just jumped him in the parking lot and stabbed him."

"I don't buy it," Spike said. "Coincidence on top of coincidence always means bad things. The kid belongs to somebody. All these screwups are related somehow, and it's time for us to start flexing. I want to find a way to take that kid out. There's no way that some teenager could kill Bill Jones with his bare hands."

"He had a knife," Drew reminded.

"I don't give a shit," Spike said. "It's just not possible. If he—" Spike paused in mid-sentence as a new nightmarish thought occurred to him. "Was Jones killed before or after he serviced the dead drop?" Spike asked Drew.

Drew's face showed instant distress. "I don't know. We need to check."

"I'll take care of that," Spike said. "Are there any other problems out there that I need to know about?"

Drew prepared himself with a loud, noisy breath. "Actually, there is."

Spike felt his chest tighten.

"Again, this comes from my guys at BCPD."

"Jesus, what's going on over there?"

"Well, wait," Drew said. "It's a good thing that they stepped forward with this one. It turns out that there's a civilian employee there named Cletus Bangstrom, who's—"

Spike choked on a laugh. "Wait. Did you say Cletus?"

"Right."

"What is he, a horse?"

"Name like that, you gotta be tough," one of the other guys said.

"Do you want to hear this or don't you?" Drew snapped.

"Excuse *me*," Spike said with exaggerated deference.

Drew's face reddened. "Cletus Bangstrom works in the property office, and he's been noticing the equipment we've been skimming."

"Of course he has," Spike said. "His job is to count things, right? If the numbers are wrong, it's his job to notice."

"Yeah, but he's asking the kinds of questions that make our contacts nervous. He's starting to link events that could expose our plans."

Spike settled farther back into his chair. "What events are we talking about, exactly?"

"He told my guy the he suspects a terror move, that people are going to dress up like police officers and start shooting people."

This was the most disturbing news yet. "Are those your words or Cletus's?"

"Those are the words of my contact who says they're Cletus's words. That's too damn close for comfort if you ask me. My guy told me that he brought it up with the chief of the department."

"What did he say there?"

"I don't know. It was a closed-door meeting. But I know the chief never mentioned it to my contact, who would be the person to go to if they were planning to defend against an attack on the station."

Spike scowled as he considered that. "Isn't that a good sign?"

"My contact doesn't think so. He thinks he's not in the loop because he's being watched. He wants us to move up the strike date."

"Does he, now?"

"Before things get locked down too much. Before this Cletus character can stir up too much trouble."

"Okay, well, for sure, we make Cletus go away," Spike said. "You and Vince take care of that. Nothing flashy, just effective." He looked over to Vince and got a satisfied nod.

"There's another reason to hit the police station soon," Drew said, clearly not ready to move on. He smiled. "The kid you want us to hit? Apparently he got himself beat up in the jail, and they've moved him to the holding cells in the police station itself. If we move in the next few days, we get a two-fer."

Chapter Nineteen

Jonathan didn't get up to Brookville very often, and among those few times, he'd never been to the historic district. The antebellum buildings here in the little town square had an undeniable charm about them. Built around a traffic circle that displayed a statue of a Confederate soldier manning a Napoleon gun, this section of Braddock County had been the site of several skirmishes during the Civil War, as well as a training ground for elements of George Washington's troops during the American Revolution.

The park he and Boxers sought lay two blocks off the circle, in a slot between two tall, narrow row houses that had been converted to businesses. Jonathan wondered if the lot had been the site of a fire back in the day, and that the town fathers just decided not to rebuild. The park—if that's even what you could call it—was fully accessible from the front and the rear, and was really just a spot to display a few trees and flowers surrounding a couple of park benches.

"Doesn't look like much to me," Boxers said as he piloted the Batmobile down the narrow street.

Up ahead, just beyond an intersection with a perpendicular street, the road widened to allow angled parking. "We've got a good parking place," Boxers said, pointing.

"Not yet," Jonathan said. "Let's take in the whole block. I want to see what's on the other side."

Boxers complied without objection. In a perfect world, they would have driven around the block a few times, but the Batmobile was such a conspicuous vehicle, more than twice would draw attention. "Okay," Jonathan said. "Pick a spot you like for doing surveillance."

The original slot Big Guy had spotted was still open. It was located in front of an auto supply place that had a CLOSED sign in the window.

With the engine turned off, Boxers activated the ventless air conditioner, and they moved into the back of the vehicle to begin their survey of the area. This would take some time. Jonathan's biggest concern was that the cops had viewed the same patterns from Stepahin's cell phone, and that they might be scoping out the area as well.

Generally, local police did a crappy job of hiding their surveillance operations. It was as if they had all attended the same classes, and then did the same things. The taxpayers bought the police a vehicle, and they might as well have painted the words *Surveillance Van* on the side. The other strategy would be to observe from a distance, but from what Jonathan could tell, there were no commercial or residential windows that would give observers a great view of the area. A scan of the park with thermal imaging showed no one hiding behind bushes or trees.

"I don't see a soul, Boss," Boxers said, looking up from the thermal scope. "I call this one clear."

"Let's get down to business, then," Jonathan said.

"How are we handling it?"

"First of all, I want you to stay here and keep your eye on the monitors. Thermal and visual. I don't want to wander into something that surprises me."

"You know I don't like you doing these things on your own," Boxers objected.

"I promise I'll be careful, Dad," Jonathan said with a chuckle. He appreciated Boxers' sense of protection. "There are couple of things working here. First of all, it's entirely possible that there is active surveillance of the area that we haven't yet seen. Thanks to my meeting last night with Detective Hastings, I have plausible deniability if I'm caught on somebody's video. In the company of the very giant that the kid remembers from his rescue—no offense—that would be hard to explain."

"I don't like you being that exposed," Boxers said. "There's something bad in the air, and over here, I'll be too far out of place to give you any hands-on help."

"I have a solution for that, too," Jonathan said. "I'll clip on a body cam so you can watch, and wear an earpiece so you can tell me if it looks like I'm going to get company."

Boxers still didn't like it.

"It's just not worth the risk, Big Guy. I promise I won't take any chances." Among the kit stored in locked compartments in the Batmobile—along with a stash of cash, a selection of small arms, both long and short, and a small assortment of explosives and primers—Jonathan stored various outfits for both him and Boxers, different looks to meet different applications. The tactical gear was inappropriate for the current mission, so he changed into a flannel shirt that was specially cut to conceal not only his Colt, but also an encrypted radio that would allow him to stay in contact with whomever he needed to stay in contact with. A tiny bud in his right ear would allow him to both transmit and receive radio transmissions hands-free. The body cam looked for all the world like the top button of his shirt.

When he was dressed out and ready to go, he placed a phone call to Venice back in Fisherman's Cove. After it rang six times and went to voice mail, he cursed lightly under his breath and hung up. "Where the hell is she?" he asked to no one in particular.

"Did you ask her to wait by the phone?" Boxers asked.

"No, but—"

The phone rang. Venice. He let it ring three times just to be difficult, and then answered, "Joe's Pizza, can I take your order?"

"Hello, Scorpion," she said with a groan. Despite the encryption, they used only avatars on the air. "I was helping the little one with his homework, but if phone games are the order of the day, I'm sure his grade point average can suffer." A single mother, Venice was devoted to her thirteen-year-old son, Roman, but worried that her job—both the nature of it and the long hours—got in the way of her mothering duties. The good news was that she had the fallback of Mama Alexander, who specialized in making Roman feel great, and occasionally made Venice feel small. Mama didn't know what the covert side of Security Solutions did, but she clearly had her suspicions, and she even more clearly did not approve.

"Sorry for the interruption," Jonathan said, "but this one is official. We need your help monitoring the video feed from my body cam. I need you to record it."

"I can do that," she said. "When are you going hot?"

"Approximately now," Jonathan said. "I'm leaving Big Guy in the van to monitor the area real time for intruders, and I don't want him looking away from his scope to watch the screen."

"Might I ask where you are?" Venice asked. In the background, Jonathan could hear her shifting into position and booting up equipment.

"We're in the land of the big red dot," Jonathan said. Since she had forwarded the images from the phone tracker, he knew she'd figure out what they were talking about.

"Do we have suspicions?" she asked.

"Not that we should discuss over the air. Let me know when you are set, and I'll head out."

"I'm all set," Venice said.

Jonathan disembarked from the vehicle on the left side, the side opposite the park. The plan was to stroll around the block the opposite way, and maybe pop into a few shops to look around. In the unlikely event that people were indeed watching, his theory was that a long stroll would make them lose interest, whereas walking a straight line from the Batmobile to the park would draw attention.

As he drew near the first corner, the grumble of a muscle car caught his attention, and he turned to see a red Corvette, top down, stopped at a traffic light. The driver, in his thirties, had that operator wannabe look, complete with a battle beard and a fitted ball cap perched just so, the Oakley sunglasses straddling the brim. Jonathan chuckled. The guy looked fit enough, so maybe he was the real deal, but Jonathan never understood the drive to look badass all day every day. If the guy in the car had walked the walk, Jonathan stipulated that he had the right to look the look—unlike the pudgy gun nuts who liked to pretend. He just never understood it. He knew better than most that some moments called for toughness, but to be in that space all the time had to be exhausting.

The car was twenty-five yards away, but the driver seemed to sense that Jonathan was watching, and he looked over. Jonathan gave him a little five-finger wave, which the badass returned with a single finger. *Dickhead.*

Jonathan chuckled. Nothing pissed off those guys as quickly or as badly as a show of disrespect. If Mr. Badass Soldier Boy wanted to pick a fight, that'd be fine. But he'd better hit first and hit hard. The confrontation defused when the light changed and the Corvette swung a turn away from Jonathan, toward the coffee shop.

"Did I just detect some dick-knocking, Boss?" Boxers said in his ear. Jonathan could hear the smile in his voice.

"He seems young for a midlife crisis car," Jonathan said.

Finally turning right at the corner to head down the far side of the block, Jonathan saw a storefront that intrigued him. Miriam's Miscellany. If nothing else, it was a great name for a store. A spring-loaded bell announced his entry through the stout front door, clearly a replacement for its original. The frame was made of steel—did they have steel doors in the nineteenth century?—and the glass behind the mullions was more suitable for a bank teller's cage than a store full of miscellany, whatever the hell that meant.

Two steps in, Jonathan realized that miscellany did not mean recently dusted. The place was like the attic of a haunted house. Lots of weather-worn mannequins and parts of mannequins, an old rocking chair that might have held the body of Norman Bates's mother, and a menagerie's worth of mounted game heads. In a single glance, Jonathan noted a boar, a bison, and a deer-like beast with four-foot corkscrew horns. Intrigued, he stepped farther into the store, turning sideways to get past the assembled crap on the floor. A glass counter displayed an assortment of Nazi memorabilia, at which point Jonathan decided it was time to move on.

"Can I help you?" a voice called from the back.

Jonathan never saw the guy's face, so he didn't bother to answer.

"Oh, don't go yet," Boxers said in his ear. "Don't you want to see if they've got a mummy?"

Jonathan exited to the sidewalk and pushed the door closed behind him. "With that door, I figure they're either running a bookie operation or they're cooking meth in the basement," he mumbled.

The rest of the block had lots of storefronts, but very little retail. He saw a tax adviser, an attorney, another coffee shop, and a contracting outfit. He continued to walk. At the next corner, he turned right again. Looking casual.

"Break, break," Boxers said. "Your buddy from the Corvette is coming this way. From his eye lines, it looks like he might be scoping the same park we are. You might want to pick up your pace."

"Is he a cop?" Jonathan asked.

"How the hell do I know?"

"How far out is he?"

"Call it seventy-five yards. But his eye lines are hard. I give it a ninety percent shot that's where he's going."

Jonathan picked up his pace to a jog.

"Okay," Boxers said, "I'm ready to declare him not a cop. He's too nervous. Too much time looking over his shoulders. How far out are you?"

"Nearly to the corner," Jonathan said.

And then he was at the corner. Across the street, in the middle of the block, he saw the guy with the battle beard and the attitude. The guy walked casually, his hands in his pockets. Just like nothing was wrong, nothing on his mind. Jonathan recognized the posture all too well, and he slowed his pace so as not to attract attention.

"He's gonna get there first, Boss," Boxers said. "I've got an eyeball on you, too."

"Don't look at me," Jonathan said. "Keep an eye on what he's doing."

Battle Beard took the tactical look the whole way, as it turned out. Now that the man was out of the car, Jonathan could see the desert tan tactical pants and boots, and untucked khaki shirt that no doubt concealed a firearm.

"Do you think he's servicing the dead drop?" Venice asked. So she'd figured it out.

"It'd certainly shorten the learning curve," Boxers said.

Jonathan wasn't sure how to handle this. If he hung back and just watched the guy do whatever he was going to do, they'd have a recording of it, and then maybe they could follow him. That seemed inefficient as hell. On the other hand, to confront the guy out here would likely cause a fight, and nobody wanted that. Certainly not out in the open like this, though the street was empty.

He decided to keep walking and play it by ear.

Battle Beard seemed to know exactly where he was going. He made no feint or diversionary move. Instead, he made a beeline to a plot of garden in the center of the space, where he stooped to his haunches and started poking around the blooming flowers.

Jonathan had closed the distance to only a few yards, but Battle Beard was so engaged in what he was doing that he didn't notice. This was why it was always best to work in a team. It's just not possible to watch two things at the same time and pay any attention to what you're seeing.

Jonathan was almost on top of him when he saw the guy lift a rock from the dirt and from beneath it excise a piece of paper. He still had it in his fingers as he stood.

"Good afternoon," Jonathan said.

The guy jumped a foot and whirled, his feet set in a fighter's stance.

"Whoa," Jonathan said. "Didn't mean to startle you. What you got there?" He kept his tone light as he pointed to the paper.

"You need to back off," Battle Beard said.

"Why? What's going on? What's on the piece of paper?"

Battle Beard slipped the paper into his front right

pocket. "Nothing for you to be concerned about. Just leave and there'll be no trouble."

"Well, I certainly don't want any trouble," Jonathan said. He widened his stance. "But I'm not going anywhere. I really need to see what's on that paper."

Battle Beard's eyes hardened. "You really think you're ready for a fight, old man? Because that's where this is headed."

Jonathan smiled. "Tough talk for a guy who drives a big penis." He'd been called way worse things than *old man,* but he pegged this guy as one who took his wheeled penis very seriously.

Battle Beard reached behind him, and Jonathan's hand twitched toward his Colt. When the other guy's hand reappeared, it held a wicked-looking T-grip knife with maybe a three-inch blade protruding from the space between his knuckles.

"Oh, shit," Boxers said in his ear. "I'm on my way."

Jonathan didn't think he'd need Big Guy's help, but he didn't turn him back, either. Knife fights could get very messy very quickly.

"Is it really worth this?" Battle Beard said.

"You're setting the price, pal," Jonathan said. "And if I were you, I'd think twice before you get in way over—"

The guy made his move. Fifteen, maybe twenty feet separated them when he initiated his lunge, leading with the knife. Jonathan reacted instantly, pivoting a half-step to his left, even as he drew his Colt from its holster. The trick to surviving a knife fight was to stay out of the blade's arc while punishing the hand that was wielding it. Jonathan used the steel muzzle of the Colt to smash the knuckles on Battle Beard's knife hand, loosening his grip on the T-handle. Jonathan took control of the attacker's hand with his left hand, and then brought the muzzle of the pistol hard across the man's exposed ear and temple. Battle Beard's legs wobbled a bit, and then Jonathan sealed the deal with a hard blow to the back of his head. Out and done.

Total combat time: less than five seconds.

"Are you okay?" Venice asked in his ear.

"I think so," he said. "Big Guy, get the Batmobile fired up. I want to be out of here like now." Dropping to his knees, Jonathan rolled the unconscious man onto his side to expose his front pocket. He fished out the piece of paper and stuffed it into his own pants. He could read it later. For now, it was time to disappear.

"Old man, my ass," he mumbled as he headed back to the street.

Chapter Twenty

Ethan gingerly fingered his swollen lower lip while his tongue explored the wound inside his cheek, which had begun to ulcerate, adding a new layer of discomfort to the general body ache that had settled over him since his fight in the jail. He didn't actually remember a lot of it. Just the first couple of punches, and then waking up on the floor with a mouthful of blood.

According to the deputies who had managed his travel over here to the police station—to the *holding cells,* as he had been told—the psychiatrist lady, Wendy, had engineered his transfer because she was afraid he wouldn't survive the environment of the jail.

"Looks like you've got her in your court," the deputy had said. "Seems silly to me. Our little Adult Detention Center is nothing compared to the state penitentiary, so why not give you some experience to toughen you up a little?" The deputy laughed at his own joke.

Ethan didn't. He thought the guy made a good point, although it was moot. Ethan had no intention of going to the state penitentiary. If it came to that, he'd figure out a way to off himself. He'd come close before.

The interview rooms were nicer in the police station than they were in the detention center. Padded chairs that moved made life easier. And the security was way less paranoid. They didn't make him wear the leg irons or the waist chain, and they cuffed his hands in the front, eliminating the agony of the nose itches that always tormented him as soon as he lost access to his hands.

Dr. Adams sat across from him, her legs crossed, with her chair turned sideways so she could rest her notepad on the table. She looked a lot more comfortable in here, too. They'd already plowed through the introduction niceties. He thanked her for her role in his transfer, and he assured her that while still sore, he was recovering from his beating.

They'd been meeting like this every other day for about an hour, and Ethan was beginning to feel that maybe she truly was in his corner—that she was one of the handful of people on the planet who weren't working some kind of angle against him.

"Today, I want you to talk about the aftermath of the assault against you," she said. "Not this one, but the one when you were eleven." Ethan noted that he was no longer the victim of kidnapping and rape, but rather the victim of an assault. He wondered if that was to make him feel more comfortable or if it was for her benefit. Some things, he supposed, were hard for even psychiatrists to talk about.

"What about it?"

"You tell me. I know about what they did to you in that basement, and you've told me details about your rescue. I know about your life before the incident happened, and now I want you to talk about the aftermath."

Ethan scowled. "It's been eleven years," he said. He wasn't being difficult. He just didn't know what she was looking for.

"Let's talk about the day you got home," she said. "What was that like?"

"It was happy," he said.

She gave him an impatient look. "Can you go a little deeper, please?"

"Okay, it was *very* happy." He smiled, and was pleased to see that she got his joke. "Actually, it was weird," he explained. "After something like that, you expect a big deal. I don't know, maybe a cake and reporters and family and stuff, but there was none of that. My dad met me and the priest guy in a parking lot of some shopping center. He hugged me and he thanked the priest, and then we drove home."

"What time of day was it?"

Ethan shrugged. "I have no idea. It wasn't dark yet, but it was getting there. And I remember feeling cold."

"Is that significant?"

"What, the cold? I don't know. You're the doctor. Is it?"

"Go on," she said. "I shouldn't have interrupted."

Ethan's mind took him back to territory he hadn't explored in a very, very long time. When he was finally alone in the car with his dad, the atmosphere felt thick. Dad was on the verge of tears—something Ethan had never seen before—and when they were finally rolling toward home, he said, "Did they hurt you, son?"

Ethan remembered taking his time answering. What

was he supposed to say? He didn't want anyone to know what had been done to him. That was gay stuff, and he didn't want anyone to know that he'd done that. He didn't want to think back on it himself, and he sure didn't want anyone else to think of him that way. God, what if the kids at school found out? They couldn't know. No one could ever know.

"I'm fine," he said.

Silence then dominated for what must have been two or three miles of driving. "What I mean to ask, Ethan, is, did they . . . Were you . . ."

See? No one could even say the words. And what's the point of saying them anyway? It couldn't be undone. Nothing that had happened to him could un-happen, so what difference did talking about it make? Why make everyone uncomfortable?

"I don't want to talk about it now," he said. "I'm tired."

"That's fine," Dad said. And he looked relieved. "In your own time." They didn't say another word as they drove back to the house. It was a long drive, too. Probably a couple of hours. Ethan slept some, but the images in his head wouldn't go away. The sounds of the gunfire, and pictures of the dead bodies. The smell of the blood.

The smell of the shit and piss from the bucket, the taste of his own blood, the taste of awfulness, of fear, of shame. The disgust.

He watched in silence as they finally drove through territory that he recognized, hoping that Dad would think he was asleep. When they finally pulled into the driveway, Dad reached over and jostled Ethan's leg to wake him up. Ethan reflexively jumped and pulled away. He saw that he'd hurt his dad's feelings and he said he was sorry.

"You have nothing to apologize for," Dad said. "I just wanted you to know that we're home. Your mom will be thrilled to see you."

Ethan knew that probably wasn't true. It wasn't that she wouldn't be happy to see him, but rather that she probably wouldn't be awake. It was way too long after dark for her to be up. Come sundown, Mom was all about taking her "medicine," and within a few hours after that, there wasn't much communication to be had. Ethan had known for years that the medicine was actually booze—and he was pretty sure she knew that he knew—but it made her more comfortable to call it medicine. What difference did it make?

He was surprised, then—shocked, really—when the front door opened even before he was out of the car and his mom came running out to meet him. She was a little unsteady on her feet, and she was wearing her pajamas and robe, but she was there. She gathered him into her arms and hugged him hard, swinging him back and forth in an oscillating embrace.

"Oh, my God," she said. "I am so happy to see you. Ethan, Ethan, Ethan, I love you so much. Welcome home. Are you okay?"

Ethan hugged her back and tried to ignore the musky smell of the medicine. "I'm fine," he said. "I'm really fine."

Mom let go of him, and then held him out at arm's length, her hands still on his shoulders. "Are you sure?"

"Hey, Marian," Dad said. "I think we should take this inside. No sense stirring up the neighbors."

Ethan didn't know at the time how long he'd been gone—it turned out to be a little over eight days—but it felt like it had been forever, and as he stepped across the threshold into the foyer, he was struck by how little anything had changed. It was as if time had stopped for Mom and Dad, while it moved with the speed of a tornado for him. So much had happened.

"He said he doesn't want to talk about anything right now," Dad said. "He said he's tired and I think he should go to bed."

"But I want to hear what happened. My God, Porter, he was kidnapped! God only knows what—"

Dad put his hand on her shoulder and gently shook his head. A silent warning about something that shouldn't be said. At first, Mom looked confused, but then she seemed to get it. "It's okay if you need to go to bed," she said. "We can always talk later."

That was code, he realized over time, for not talking at all.

"Would you like to take a bath first?" Mom asked.

He hugged himself without knowing it until after he'd done it. "No," he said. "That's okay." He was afraid of what bright light and a mirror might show.

Instead, he went straight to his room. He closed the door, and paused, hovering near it for a good thirty seconds. Then he locked it. It was a long-standing rule in Falk household that doors remained unlocked all the time. He supposed it had something to do with his parents being able to check in on him at night after he was asleep, but on that night, the one guarantee he craved more than any other was that no one would come into his room. Ever. He climbed under his covers still fully clothed in the secondhand rags he'd been given in the car as Scorpion and Big Guy had driven him away from the hell house. As far as he could remember, he fell asleep immediately.

The next morning—okay, it could have been several mornings later, but within the same sleeve of time— when he was getting ready to go back to school, his parents sat him down at the kitchen table. They looked serious, sad.

"Ethan, we have something very important to talk to you about," Dad said. It was about seven in the morning, close to the time when the school bus would be arriving, and a good half hour past the time when Dad normally went to work. Nothing about this was right. "What I'm about to tell you is entirely unfair, and I want to apologize to you for it right up front."

Ethan remembered his heartbeat racing at those words. He anticipated something about somebody having cancer, or some horrible thing that was going to hurt him even deeper than he'd already been hurt. The words made him feel light-headed, but he hung in there. He said nothing, choosing instead to let them fill the silence.

"This stuff that happened to you," Dad said. "You can't tell anyone about it. Not any of it. Not about being taken, not about how . . . you were treated, and certainly not about how you were rescued."

"Why?" Not that he was straining at the leash to share his ravaging with the rest of the world, but it was an odd order, delivered in an even odder way.

"It's complicated," Mom said. She looked like hell, like she hadn't slept all night. He wondered if they'd been up around the clock talking about him.

"Ethan," Dad said, "the truth is that I'd rather not go

into all the details. We did some things that we're not very proud of. We broke the law, in fact, but we broke it for the sole purpose of getting you back."

"We didn't know that people would be killed," Mom said.

Dad clarified, "Well, we knew it was a possibility, but we sort of talked ourselves into believing that it would go another way."

Ethan was lost in the conversation. He remembered looking at them, confused, wondering what the hell they were talking about.

"During your rescue," Dad explained. "We didn't know that people would be killed. That's the part that's against the law. If word of that got out, then your mom and I could go to jail."

"For *rescuing* me?" Ethan couldn't believe he was hearing the words. "How is that against the law?"

Mom reached out a hand, just sort of into the air, more or less in his direction. "That's where it gets complicated."

"I was *happy* to see them killed," Ethan said, his voice rising in both pitch and volume.

"You don't mean that," Dad said.

"Yes, I do! I prayed that someone would kill them. You don't know what they did."

"We have a good idea," Dad said. "I fear that I have a *very* good idea, but that's not the way the law works. You can't just kill bad people."

"I didn't kill anybody," Ethan said. Suddenly, he felt that he was on the wrong side, that they were angry with him.

"No, we know you didn't, honey," Mom said.

"But Scorpion did," Dad said. "And his friend."

"Big Guy," Ethan explained. "The police."

Mom and Dad exchanged another significant look. A lot of those going around now. "I don't want to confuse you," Dad said. "And I don't want to load you down with details you don't need to know, but those men were not police officers."

But Ethan had seen them. He'd seen their clothes and their guns and the way they operated. "Sure they were," he said.

Dad shook his head. "No. We couldn't involve the police," he said. "Our instructions were very specific. Those men were people we hired to rescue you. They're not police, and what they did was against the law."

"How can that be?" Ethan asked.

"Just trust me on this, son," Dad said. "That's the way it is. And because I was the one who hired them, I broke the law by doing so."

"But they saved my life."

Mom and Dad held each other's hands. "Yes, they did," Dad said. No one held Ethan's hand. He wasn't sure he wanted them to, but it was a detail he remembered. "And we will always be grateful to them for doing that. But that doesn't change the facts. If you talk to anyone about this—ever—you will be exposing your mom and me to legal action. To jail. I don't think you want that to happen, do you?"

Ethan's memory of the conversation was that he just stared, but he must have nodded, because they both looked relieved by whatever they saw.

"Okay, then," Dad said. "Do I have a cross-your-heart pinky swear on that?"

Ethan crossed his heart. But the pinky swear was baby, so he didn't do that.

"There's one other thing," Dad said. He looked really uncomfortable. "I know you don't want to talk about what happened, but I need to know one thing."

Ethan felt tears pressing behind his eyes. There was nothing about any of that that he wanted to share.

"I need to know if you're bruised," he said.

Ethan didn't understand the question.

"I need to know if there are marks on your body."

Even today, Ethan felt the press of the tears. "They were worried about the cosmetics," he said to Wendy. "After all the shit I went through, after all the violation, they were worried that if I went to gym class and somebody saw bruises on me, that they would call social services or something."

"Were there?" Wendy asked. "Bruises, I mean."

"Jesus Christ, of course there were bruises! How could there not be bruises? And you know what? They wrote me an open-ended excuse not to go to gym class. I don't know what they put on the excuse, but it was good for two, three, four weeks. However long it took for all the colors to go away."

Wendy said, "I'm sure—"

"No," Ethan said, cutting her off. "No, before you say anything, do you want to know the one thing they never did?"

She waited.

"They never took me to a goddamn doctor. Christ, looking back, I could have been bleeding to death on the inside, but they were so embarrassed about what had happened, that they were willing to roll the dice on that one."

"I'm sure that's not what they were thinking."

"Oh, yeah? Then what's your theory?"

"I think it's probably just exactly what they told you. They were worried about going to prison as accessories to murder. Once that door is opened, it's not an easy one to close. They cared enough to send someone after you, Ethan. Did they ever tell you why they didn't just call the police and let them handle it?"

Ethan shook his head. "No," he said. "But I'm not sure I ever asked."

"And why is that?"

"Because they didn't want to talk about it. Hell, I didn't want to talk about, either. Nobody did. Everybody wanted it just to go away so we could pretend that none of it ever happened. If you didn't think about it, it couldn't hurt anymore."

"It doesn't work that way," Wendy said. Her tone was much softer.

"No shit, Sherlock," Ethan said. "You know we're talking in a jail, right?"

Wendy took her time paging through her notes. Finally, she said, "Your parents got divorced shortly after that."

He blinked, unsure whether his voice was trustworthy.

"Can you tell me about that?"

The cliché is that children always blame themselves in part for the separation of their parents. Ethan had read a few articles on it, and he'd seen the oh-so-earnest doctors talk about it on television. The emphasis there was that children needed to cut themselves a break. Mommies and daddies just fall out of love sometimes, and it's possible for parents who don't like each other anymore to still love their children equally.

The doctors and article writers should have spoken to Ethan before they went out on such a narrow limb. Because Ethan was, in fact, the reason why his parents' marriage fell apart. He was the one who decided to break the rules and go on that stupid bike ride. He was the one who ignored the clanging warning bells of stranger danger and allowed the perv to shove him into that car. And then, while he was stuffed down in that dank, stinky basement, he was the one who allowed the violations. He could have fought harder. He could have gouged their eyes or he could have bitten, he could have done *something* other than simply let himself be frightened into allowing them to do that.

While the nightmares of the specific violations, the replaying of the pain and the images had decreased over time, other nightmares had intensified. It was the faces of the other boys that had shared his prison basement, though for such short periods. Even after over a decade, Ethan felt shame for the elation he'd felt when the others were chosen for selection and he was not. He remembered the terror in their eyes and he wondered what came of them. As he got older, and he read more and more about human trafficking and sexual slavery, he knew that he was reading about those other kids. He hoped they got away, and if they didn't, he hoped they died quickly.

It wasn't possible to make people understand the horrors he'd endured. And rather than try, Ethan said nothing. He thought at the time that he was doing everybody a favor, but looking back, he realized how fundamentally he had changed as a boy. As a human being. Happiness became a charade for him, the thing you fake when people are looking, but never quite exists. And the thing is, you never know that you're not happy. You just think that everyone else in the world is clueless.

You'd never be able to convince Ethan that people didn't know about what he'd allowed to be done to him. Somehow, people knew, and they judged him for it. He could see it in the eyes of the other kids in school, the way they stopped talking when he passed. He heard it in the guidance counselors' voices as they sat him down and urged him to explain what was going on inside his head. Why were his grades falling? Why was he fighting with other boys so much?

He'd come close to saying it. *So* close to saying it, just to punish those earnest assholes for asking questions they really didn't want to hear the answers to. Then he realized that with all the shit that was piled on his life in layers without any icing separating them, he really didn't need the burden of having sent his parents to prison. For murder.

So, yeah. Ethan caused his parents' divorce. From the overheard conversations—the screaming matches that even the deaf could hear—he figured out that each of them blamed the other for *the incident.* That was the euphemism they'd settled on, sort of unofficially. *The incident* left out all the unpleasantness of reality. If the other had kept better watch on Ethan, if they hadn't have been so tough on him, if they'd done the right thing and called the police, if sun spots didn't happen and if pigs flew, then their son would still be the happy little boy who he used to be. Ethan didn't bother telling them that he'd never been all that happy to begin with, but that would have felt like piling on.

He remembered vividly the night when the truth clarified for him. He lay in bed, listening to the row between his folks, and he realized that it was simply easier for them to hate each other than it was to embrace what had happened to him. Shame does that to people.

When he was done, Wendy wouldn't make eye contact with him. She just concentrated on her notes. He was a breath away from chastising her for being no better than the others when he saw her wipe away a tear.

Chapter Twenty-one

The paper worth killing for—and dying for—contained an address. A Mr. Peter Appleton who lived on Illinois Street in Arlington, Virginia. Venice's Internet scour for the address turned up nothing of note. Mr. Peter Appleton of that address was an employee of the US Department of State, who listed him as a senior data analyst. It was the kind of meaningless job title that drove Jonathan crazy. A GS-14, he earned a solid low six-figure income, and that was the kind of money that could fund an upper middle-class lifestyle even in the close-in suburb of Arlington.

Alice Appleton, Peter's wife, was the executive director of the Organization of Waste and Recycling Businesses, an unpronounceable acronym (and therefore not an acronym at all) that lobbied for laxer rules on the disposal of waste and the handling of recyclable materials. No stranger to that industry—Jonathan's father had once run a scrap yard as a cover for his mob connections—the irony was not lost on him.

Brookville, in Braddock County, was less than an hour from Arlington, so Jonathan decided to go directly there to see what the connection might be. During the drive, Venice tore the Interwebs to shreds trying to find some connection between the Appletons and . . . well, anything, but all she found was vapor.

"They're visible enough to be legitimate," she proclaimed at the end of her search, "but not visible enough to be a problem. I don't know what to tell you."

"Well, we have to follow it to ground," Jonathan said. And that's what they were doing now.

Jonathan had a theory that the streets in Arlington, Virginia, had been laid out with an eye toward some Cold War plot to keep enemies from navigating the roads. Addresses such as South Persing Avenue West were at an entirely different geographic grid than South Persing Road North. In the days before reliable GPS navigation aids, Arlington had been known to swallow tourists whole, only to spit them out ten years later, exhausted and craving sanity.

Illinois Street was relatively easy to find, provided you started at Interstate 66 and realized that the only way to get to it was to follow the signs for Washington Boulevard. Then, you just had to have enough street smarts to get off of Washington Boulevard onto a street that even GPS didn't know about. Then it was immediately on your left, noticeable only after you'd passed it. Jonathan hated this part of Northern Virginia. Nowhere near as much as he hated the District of Columbia, but it was close.

The Appletons' house was quintessential Arlington. Built in the late 1940s, it was small, but had a lot of the character that was attendant to that era of high-quality construction. As Boxers pulled the Batmobile to a stop across the street, he looked across the console to

Jonathan. "What do you think we're getting into? What do you think this address is all about?"

"I can only assume that it's the next target for kidnappers," Jonathan replied.

"Why would somebody want to kidnap an analyst for the State Department?"

"I have no idea," Jonathan confessed. "But we've rescued our share of people who had no immediate need to be kidnapped."

Boxers chuckled at the absurdity. "Fair enough," he said. "How do you want to play it?"

"Given how little we know, I suppose we just go to the front door and knock. See what happens."

"Are we going together?" Boxers asked.

Jonathan said, "Yeah, normally I'd have you cover the back, but it looks like they have a fence all the way around their property. I don't want you climbing stuff and attracting attention. Let's knock and see what we find."

"Firepower?"

"Just side arms," Jonathan said. "Concealed."

"I'm ready, then."

As they climbed out of the vehicle, Jonathan scanned the horizon for threats. Whoever he'd knocked out at the park had had no usable identification, which was no surprise, and the fingerprints Jonathan took had come back negative. The owner of the fingerprints had valued this address enough to threaten him with death, though, so that meant something important resided here. Jonathan needed to know what that was.

Typical of a neighborhood that was nearly seventy years old, the sidewalks were crumbly, and the steep, narrow brick steps that led from the street level to the elevated lawn should have been replaced ages ago. The yard was easily six feet higher in elevation than the sidewalk, prompting Jonathan to again scan the horizon for threats. The additional elevation introduced an entirely new target package for anyone inclined to be looking for a target.

Jonathan and Boxers had done this drill enough over the years that Big Guy knew to hang back in the yard while Jonathan knocked on the door. Given Boxers' height and girth, Jonathan considered it a bad idea to have him in the same visual frame when someone answered the door to a stranger.

With Big Guy in position, Jonathan walked to the door and rapped with his knuckle. When no one answered after thirty seconds or so, he scanned the area around the jamb and found the doorbell button. He pressed it. If he used his imagination, he could convince himself that he heard a ding and a dong from the space beyond the door. A few seconds later, footsteps approached. Jonathan caught movement behind the curtains that lined the jamb, and he knew that he'd been eyeballed by someone. That was a ritual that he'd never really understood. If the visitor were a bad guy—someone intent on doing harm—then he'd shoot at the movement and be done with it. On the other hand, if the visual check revealed someone known, but whom one didn't want to see, how would the homeowner explain the fact that he peeked, yet didn't open the door? As a third alternative, if one peeked out and saw a stranger, yet opened the door anyway, what was the purpose of checking in the first place? When Jonathan was elected king, things would make a lot more sense than they did today.

A lock slid and the door opened to reveal a scrawny young black man, perhaps twenty years old, who looked like he needed a nap. "Good afternoon," he said. The words rang as strangely formal to Jonathan's ears.

"Hello," Jonathan said. "Mr. Appleton, I presume?"

The young man scowled. "Who are you?"

"Mr. Appleton?" Sometimes, the best way to avoid answering a question was to ask one of your own.

"No," the young man said. "Good day." He moved to close the door.

Jonathan kicked out his foot to block it, the old salesman's trick. "Please don't," he said. "I need to ask you a few questions."

"You need to answer one first," the kid said. There was a toughness to him that surprised Jonathan.

"Who am I?"

"That's the one." The kid stood with half his body bracing the door, as if expecting Jonathan to attempt to crash through. That spoke of training.

"Well, okay," Jonathan said. He reached into his back pocket and produced his FBI badge. "My name is Special Agent Horgan. Richard Horgan." If the kid had checked the details of the credentials, he'd have seen a matching name. But people rarely saw past the badge.

The kid looked at the creds, and nodded, but he didn't move to let Jonathan pass. Definitely, he'd been trained. "Okay, Agent Horgan, how can I help you?"

"You can tell me where I can find Mr. or Mrs. Appleton," Jonathan said.

"Last I heard, they were in Peru," the kid said.

Jonathan narrowed his gaze. "And who are you?"

"My name is Prince Albert, and before you give me

a bunch of crap about it, yes, that's my real name. I've hated my mother and father for it my whole life."

Jonathan stifled a chuckle. What would possess parents to do such a thing to their child? "Okay, Mr. Albert—"

"Call me Prince."

"Sure," Jonathan said. "Why not? Okay, Prince, I'd appreciate it if you could tell me who you are, why you're here, and what happened to the Appletons."

"Not a problem," he said. "You already have my name. The Appletons were transferred to Peru, and my boss is renting their house for the next couple of years. I am the au pair for my clients' two daughters."

"May I ask who your client is?" Jonathan asked.

"May I ask why you're asking?"

This was a way chattier interview than Jonathan normally encountered, especially after he'd badged someone. Usually people saw the gold shield and just babbled out words. This guy—this *Prince*—seemed not the least bit cowed by the presence of the power of the federal government.

"I can't go into the details," Jonathan said, "but we have good reason to believe that the occupants of this house—that you—may be the target of people who are trying to do you harm."

"Who?" Prince asked. "Who would want to do harm to this family?"

Recognizing that this was going to be a harder sell than he had anticipated, Jonathan decided to swing for the fences. He reached into his pocket and produced the crumpled piece of paper with the Illinois Street address on it. "A man tried to kill me today to prevent me from getting my hands on this piece of paper." He let Prince hold it in his fingers, and then motioned for it back.

"That's this address," Prince said.

"I know that," Jonathan said. He held out his arms in a silent *ta-da!* "So here we are."

"But the Appletons don't live here anymore," Prince said.

"I believed we've established that," Jonathan said. He felt his patience ebbing. "What we keep dancing around is, who *does* live here. Other than Prince Albert, of course."

Prince offered a smile that looked more like a wince. "Yeah, well, my boss is Ariana Baker," he said. "Senator Ariana Baker, of California."

Jonathan's heart skipped. What were the chances of randomly interacting with the families of two members of Congress over the course of the same week? This wasn't good. "Where is Senator Baker now?" he asked.

"At the Capitol, I presume." His face became a mask of concern. "What is going on?"

Jonathan's mind ran through about ten thousand options in the span of a couple of seconds. Senator Ariana Baker lived in a house that Venice's data said belonged to the Appleton family. He supposed it was possible that Battle Beard was after the Appletons but got the Bakers instead. However, on the heels of the incident with the Johnson girl, he didn't believe that for a second. Somehow, Battle Beard had better intel than Venice did, and that was at its face unsettling.

"You said you were the au pair," Jonathan said. "That means there are children in the house?"

Prince's scowl deepened. "I think it's time for you to tell me what this is all about," he said.

"May we come in?" Jonathan asked.

For the first time, Prince realized that there was a second man, Boxers, who continued to stand in the yard. "No, you may not," he said.

As standoffs went, this one was feeling pretty solid. Time for a different approach. "I feel as if we've gotten off on the wrong foot," Jonathan said.

"Would that be the one you stuck in my door?" Prince asked.

Jonathan smiled in spite of himself. He had a role to play here, but it was hard not to be amused by Prince's adherence to whatever protocol he'd been taught. "Actually, that's my right foot," he said with a smile. It was a statement of fact.

A shadow of a smile appeared on Prince's face. "Please just tell me what you want."

"The bottom line," Jonathan said, "is that I believe the residents of this house to be in danger, but before I can explain the specifics, I need to know who I am speaking to. Other than merely your name and job description."

Prince eyed Jonathan for a full ten seconds, then said, "I am the manny. That's male nanny. I'm a student at American University, and this is the gig that pays my bills and gives me a place to sleep."

Jonathan checked his watch. Two-thirty. "Are the children in school now?" he asked.

"Yes."

"Age and sex?"

"Twin girls," Prince said. "Nine years old."

"And what school do they go to?"

"Our Lady of Sorrows," Prince said. "It's just a couple of miles from here." He checked his watch, as well. "They'll be getting out in a few minutes, at two forty-five."

The entire scenario crystalized for Jonathan in a flash. This was another kidnapping attempt in its infancy. "Please listen to me very carefully," he said. "Is Our Lady of Sorrows one of those private schools that lots of wealthy kids go to?"

Again, Prince recoiled. It was the kind of cheap question one would expect from a *Washington Post* reporter.

Jonathan picked up the pace. "What I'm really asking is if the school has a higher level of security than your average public school."

"It *is* a private school," Prince confirmed. "The teachers are priests and nuns, but the curriculum is more secular than you would think."

"I don't care about that," Jonathan said. "Listen to the question. Do they have a high level of physical security there?"

Prince looked confused. "There aren't armed guards, if that's what you're talking about."

That was exactly what Jonathan was talking about. Perhaps he should have asked the question that way. His mind raced to formulate some kind of plan. It wasn't as if an attack were imminent, or that the children were even in immediate jeopardy, but the evidence was mounting, so he was willing to take the leap of faith. Besides, if the whole thing turned out to be bullshit, no one had any idea who he truly was.

"Okay, Prince, I need you to listen to me carefully,"

Jonathan said. "The girls are in danger. So are you and the senator."

"What's going on?" For the first time, Prince's face showed real fear.

"Just listen to me," Jonathan said. "I need you to call the school and tell them to hold the girls past dismissal. Tell them whatever you'd like—up to and including that they are in danger, but try not to trigger a lockdown of the entire campus."

"Who's causing the danger?" As he asked the question, Prince craned his neck, as if to spot a gunman in the street.

"I can't tell you that," Jonathan said. That sounded so much better than, *I have no idea*. "I can tell you, though, that another member of Congress's daughter was recently kidnapped—"

"I didn't hear anything about that," Prince said. "I'm sure the senator would have told me."

"The sheer weight of what senators don't know should shift the orbit of the planet," Jonathan said before he could stop the words. In the hierarchy of flora and fauna, Jonathan harbored more respect for honeybees than he did for members of Congress. At least honeybees worked for what they got. "This kidnapping attempt no doubt happened outside her sphere of knowledge."

"How do you know about it, then?"

"Really?" Jonathan snapped. "I just told you that the girls are in jeopardy, and you want to knock dicks over our relative intel resources?"

That seemed to take Prince off balance. "I'm going to have to tell the school *something*," he said.

"Like I said, figure that out. And after you talk to the

school, you probably should call the senator and tell her what you're doing. None of this needs to be public knowledge unless you want to make it so."

"And are you going to the school to protect the twins?" Prince asked.

Jonathan knew that the smart move here was a lie, but nontactical lies did not come easily to him. "No," he said. "I'll leave that part of the security to you and the senator."

"But I don't have any experience with that sort of thing," Prince objected.

"There's more," Jonathan said. "After you call the school and the senator, I think you need to make plans to be somewhere else for a while. We're confident that the threat exists, but we only suspect that the children are the targets. It could be the senator as well. And if not her, then just a target of opportunity, which would be you."

Prince looked like he'd been beaten, a combination of exhaustion and confusion. "But *why*?"

Jonathan made a show of looking at his watch again. "Ticktock," he said.

Chapter Twenty-two

Ethan explained, "After they split, I stayed with my mom for a while, but she was hitting her medicine pretty hard, so Dad took me to his place."

"How did that work?" Wendy asked.

"I think he tried," Ethan said. "But I also think he was as lost as I was. There was always the unspoken thing in the room. And he changed, too. After the incident, he'd let me get away with shit that he'd never have let me get away with before. It's like I was made of glass."

"Emotionally, you probably were."

"Okay. So letting me get away with shit was a good thing. Fine, I can agree to that."

"And you tested your boundaries pretty aggressively," Wendy said.

"Yeah, I kind of became a shit." Ethan said that with a trace of a smile.

Wendy referred to her notes. "You vandalized your school, you were picked up for underage drinking—three times. After you sold marijuana to a classmate, you were expelled from middle school. Five fights of record, and you were caught with a deadly weapon. All before you were sixteen."

"The deadly weapon was a pocket knife," Ethan said. "It was a tool, not a weapon. It's not like I tried to stab anybody with it. But on the others, yeah. I did all that."

"And other things?" Wendy asked. "Events where you didn't get caught?"

A shrug. "Of course."

"Tell me about them."

Ethan had anticipated this question, and he'd been waffling on how to answer it. There were a lot of other petty infractions, from smoking more pot to illegal drinking to petty shoplifting, but he didn't see how she needed to know any of that. It wasn't like he was torturing cats or setting fires. He said, "No, I don't want to get into that. It was just more of what you talked about. Same shit, different day."

"Did you have friends during this period? People you'd hang out with?"

"Probably not in the way you'd think about them. Everybody's got an angle, you know. I'm no different. When somebody says they want to be your friend, what they're really telling you is that they want something. You've got it, they want it, and the way to get it is to be nice."

"What did people want from you?"

"It depends. When I was selling drugs, it was the drugs. When I was filching beers, it was the beers."

"What about other times?"

Ethan prepared himself with a giant breath, and smiled as the memory bloomed. "You know, there's a lot of fame that comes with being a designated bad kid at school. The nerds are all afraid of you, the cool kids think they're hot shit because they're not you. They might be utter shitheads, and might treat other people like crap, but at least they're not Ethan Falk. I'm sure they pointed to me a lot when their parents were talking about grounding them.

"And then there are the invisible kids, the ones who think that if they hang out with you—if they stay in the shadows of a bad kid—their street cred will somehow grow. Those are the kids who egg you on to do shit, and then either don't show up, or they screw it up and get you caught. Then, when I didn't rat them out I became an even bigger deal. It's not a bad gig when you've got nowhere else to be."

Wendy scowled. "I don't understand," she said. "What do you mean by 'when you've got nowhere else to be'?"

"I'm not talking about a physical place," Ethan clarified. "Actually, I'm not sure what I mean. It's like we all have these roles to play. When you're little, I guess you get to experiment, but by the time you get to high school, those roles are set. Mine was to be the bad kid. I think I was pretty good at it."

"But you weren't happy."

"I thought I was. Shit, by then, I didn't even know what happiness looked like. Even now, I'm not sure I do. This isn't it, that's for sure." He made a broad gesture with his cuffed hands to indicate the entirety of the room.

"Tell me about the scars on your wrists," Wendy said, pointing to his hands with her forehead."

"I think you already know," Ethan said.

"I want you to tell me."

* * *

People who don't understand it want suicide to be an act of insanity. They want it to be an impulsive over-reaction to a single bad thing, or a series of bad things that make a person go mad. The reality for Ethan was exactly the opposite of that, or nearly so. When the day comes that every hour hurts, when every new day is an exercise in endurance, there's that moment when you realize that ending it all is the only rational choice. Who wouldn't choose peace over warfare? And when the war is being fought between your ears, all sides of the conflict are the same person. The winner *is* the loser. And vice versa.

Not to get all melodramatic, but what difference would it make? Really, what difference? As the source of pain for so many people—himself among them—he'd be doing the world a favor by not being in it any-more.

Ethan didn't know why he did the things he did. He'd gotten a little contemplative about it all in recent years, but back then, five, six, seven years ago, when it was all very real and very raw, he'd find himself in the midst of an act of thievery or an act of violence that he didn't even understand at the time. He'd tried to explain that to a school counselor once, but she just got angry. She thought he was sandbagging. That was her word, *sand-bagging*. At the time, Ethan didn't know what the term meant, but he knew it was yet one more thing to be ashamed of.

To hell with all of them. To hell with their judg-ments, and double to hell with the tens of thousands of things about him that people didn't like. Every one of us has an Eject button beating beneath our breastbone, and every one of us has perfect control over how to activate it.

Once the decision was made, all that remained was the selection of method.

Ethan had witnessed a guy overdosing once, and he wanted nothing to do with that. The guy's name was Jay, and he was one of Ethan's earliest customers, back when they were both still in eighth grade. Jay moved on to bigger and better drugs—and became the kid that scared the hell out of Ethan—but they still partied together in ninth and tenth grades. They had a special spot near a train trestle where they figured no one would find them. But of course they *were* found, because Ethan was the designated bad kid, and every bad kid in training wanted to be with him.

Ethan wasn't sure what Jay was taking the night when he OD'd, but he knew he wanted nothing to do with it. Jay started twitching all over, and he launched a column of puke that spattered for five feet. A few seconds later he pissed and shit himself, and Ethan ran. Let the bad kids in training get a taste of their own medicine. That kind of trouble brought not just cops, but ambulances and fire trucks, too.

Ethan never found out the details of what happened after he ran away, but somebody must have called someone, because Jay survived. He was thrown out of school because of the overdose, because it made sense to some dickhead administrator that the best way to help someone up from the bottom was to send him to a strange place to make a whole new bunch of friends among strangers. Ethan had been there, done that, gotten the scars, and in case anyone was interested in his thoughts, it was a stupid goddamn idea.

So, drugs were out. He considered jumping off a building or some other tall place, but that brought with it the same problems that attended hanging or crashing his car into a wall. He lived in terror of being paralyzed. And since he knew that he had no luck that wasn't bad luck, there was a virtual certainty that he'd snap his spine and end up a quadriplegic, like that detective in the Denzel Washington movie.

The more he thought about it, and the more he researched the topic—there's all kinds of stuff about suicide on the Internet—he became convinced that the best way to push your own button was to slice an artery and just bleed out. The experts said in the articles that it would be like falling asleep. As your blood leaked out, your oxygen levels would dip, and you'd feel tired—and a little cold—and then you'd go to sleep. Next stop: The Other Side.

The radial artery was the vessel of choice because of its ease of access. The femoral artery would drop the blood pressure faster, but it was hard to get to. The body is pretty well designed to protect the parts that'll kill you if you insult them. And the cuts needed to be made lengthwise, parallel to the line of the arm. Otherwise, the bleeding is too easily stopped. The longer the slit, the harder it would be to undo the damage.

He did worry about the mess, though. Arterial spray was well known to cover a wide area, but even at that, it couldn't be more disgusting than Jay's puke spray, could it?

* * *

"I didn't eat anything on the day I did it," Ethan explained. "I didn't want to shit myself. I didn't want that humiliation, and I made sure to take a leak so my bladder was empty. I'm telling you, Wendy, I had thought this through from the first moment to the last. After school that day, I stopped by a 7-Eleven to buy brand-new razor blades because I wanted them to be sharp. You know, that was one of the happiest, most focused days of my life? It was like I had a purpose, something important to do, and I was the only one who could do it. Do you hear that a lot?"

"It's not uncommon, but I don't want you to digress." She hadn't moved during the entire time Ethan was telling his story. She sat with her legs crossed, her hands folded across her knee. She didn't even take notes.

"It's funny the things you remember," Ethan went on. "The label said that the blades were for a *safety razor,* but the blade had two equally sharp edges. And how stupid is this? As I prepared to kill myself—to open these huge wounds on my arm—I wrapped one edge of the blade in Kleenex so I could hold it without cutting my finger. I mean, this made *sense* to me."

He shook his head as the memory passed. Then he felt tears again. It wasn't like he was going to cry, but it would be close.

"I hung up all my clothes in the closet—or put them in the hamper, depending—and I made my bed. I knew I was going to make a mess, but I guess I didn't want it to be a big mess. I put on a pair of swim trunks, and then I sat down on the edge of my bed. There was this reading lamp clamped to my headboard, kind of a spring-loaded articulating arm thing that I would use to read before going to sleep. It had a really bright light, and I wanted to be able to see what I was doing.

"I remember being fascinated at how tough my skin was at first, and then at how once I started, the edges of the cut separated just like you were trimming a piece of beef."

Chapter Twenty-three

The cut over Spike's ear took four stitches to close, and as he sat in the passenger seat of Drew's van, he had to force himself not to mess with the scar. The rest of his team knew what had happened to him at the park, but they knew better than to talk to him about it. He'd let himself be beaten by someone who didn't have half his skills. Spike had tried to deconstruct those final few seconds a hundred times, and he still didn't know how he had awakened from unconsciousness without that blue-eyed bastard's body lying next to him.

Spike wasn't sure what it meant that Blue Eyes had taken the slip of paper with the address, but after thinking it through from every angle, he'd decided that it didn't matter. The sheik was expecting al-Amin to do a job, and the job needed to be done. He'd already lost too much credibility as it was. His Yemeni masters were and were not many things, but one category on which they had an undeniable stranglehold was reliability. Spike had promised a cadre of exceptional operators, and by all evidence he had seen, he had delivered.

Yet these outside forces that he didn't understand threatened to undermine everything.

The kid with the knife from the coffee shop was perhaps the most perplexing of the setbacks they'd encountered. That wasn't the kind of thing that just happened. And Spike felt an immediate need to settle that account. The failure of the second string team to snatch a kid was not his fault, and he was ready to defend that, but when all was said and done, the Yemenis were going to have a bad taste in their mouths about the events of the last week or so, and Spike and his team had enough money on the line that it was important not to let the handlers down.

The government had labeled groups like al-Amin to be "lone wolves"—unaffiliated teams of mayhem makers—and the Yemenis had jumped on it right away as the recipe for success. The unwitting architects for their impending success were a hapless pair of snipers who created real terror in the Washington, DC, suburbs in 2001 or 2002. The public had just finished enduring the 9/11 attacks with national days of mourning, combined with a general sense of invincibility. Lots of verses of "God Bless America" were sung in public places, and many a pundit stood in front of God and everybody to expound on the bravery of Americans and the strength of American spirit.

Then, after one person was shot at a gas pump, and then a second, like the flip of a switch, all that brave swagger was replaced by house moms cowering in their cars while the dial on the gas pump spun, only to dash out, remove and replace the spout, and then duck back under cover again. For those three or four weeks, in a community of three million people, couples stopped going out for dinner, and soccer practices were canceled, all because a team of two guys with a gun—at the time, everyone thought it was one guy with a gun—was shooting a person a day. The chances of getting hit were literally three million to one, yet that was enough to evoke mass cowardice among those of indomitable spirit.

The significance was not lost on the murderous minds in the Sandbox. Shutting down the wheels of the Great Satan didn't require toppling great symbolic structures, after all. All it required was instilling a bit of discomfort in the lives of middle class families. Do that, and by God the people will overthrow the government. It was what the rest of the world hated most about the United States: While others fought for their survival, Americans came to blows over the untimely death of a whale or a lion.

Spike no longer had a card in that game. He'd sold his soul and his patriotism for money, and now he intended to earn it. He had this one last snatch to take care of, and then the Big Show, and he'd be on his way to the easy life on a Caribbean island somewhere, his bank account swollen by an extra $2.2 million. The rest on his team would have $2 million apiece, the delta explained by his planning and supervisory responsibilities. None of them fooled themselves into believing that all of them would survive long enough to collect, but likewise, none of them presumed that they would be among those who would not.

Spike figured that he had two, maybe three days before he was off to his island paradise, even though he had no idea yet where he would go. His passport was current, and he had cash. It made no sense to get an early reservation and telegraph to the world where he intended to go.

Some of his troops had done that. They'd made reservations, most for Saturday morning or afternoon, the very days that every port of exit would be crawling with feds. Spike had tried to talk them out of it, but you know how it is with yay-hoos who think they know everything. In Spike's mind, after the Big Show was over, he'd have to go to ground for a couple of weeks—maybe a couple of months—before he could safely make his move. Even then, he planned to get out via Canada, where the borders were way softer than Mexico—unless you were coming in from Mexico, in which case the equation was reversed. Spike considered himself an atheist without a country. His loyalty lay entirely with the man in the mirror, and as far as he was concerned, there was no shame in that.

Today's mission was a simple one, at two levels. The first level was to not screw up. Just getting it done would be an accomplishment against the backdrop of the past few days. The second was to grab the Baker twins, sedate them, and get them to the Yemenis, who would handle the details of getting them shipped to the powers that be in ISIL. At that moment, his involvement in this would end. After that—whatever the shit-heads did with them after the fact—the fallout was all on the heads of killers in the Sandbox.

At two forty-five sharp, the doors to Our Lady of Sorrows burst open, and children swarmed from every orifice. The spray of kids was omnidirectional, targeting every compass point.

"How are we going to pick out two kids from among all of these?" Drew asked.

"We don't have to worry about all of them," Spike explained. "The Baker girls are walkers. This is the route they have to take." When they eyeballed the girls, they wouldn't attempt to take them here in the driveway of the school, but rather, they would wait until they were on the road out front and take them there. Spike intended to invoke the clichéd ruse about helping him find his lost dog.

For a solid ten minutes, children of all ages from seven to eighteen poured from the building. Drew and Spike sat in their van at the base of the hill along with the dozens of parents waiting for their little darlings, invisible among the crowd of vehicles. The kids moved in flocks, swarming around and between cars in groups of two through fifteen, all of them engaged in the discussion of whatever the hell kids talked about.

One by one, the other cars in the queue swallowed their loads and pulled away from the curb, headed toward home, or the orthodontist, or soccer practice. By 2:55, the van was one of only six remaining vehicles, and as such they were no longer invisible.

"Did we miss them?" Drew thought aloud.

"Couldn't have," Spike said. He used an authoritative tone to mask his own doubts. Maybe they went to a friend's house or something, driving them to use a different exit from the building. If that was the case, they could always take the kids at their residence, but that was many times more complicated and all but guaranteed a violent confrontation. Not the best way to go.

"We could do it tomorrow," Drew said.

Spike shook his head. "No, something's not right here. If it's not right today—"

He stopped speaking as he saw the parade of three police cars approach them down the hill and then pull into the school driveway. No lights or sirens, but they weren't moving slowly, either.

"That doesn't look good," Drew said.

The cars drove all the way up to the main entrance to the school, where they parked nose-to-tail at the curb. Each car carried a single officer, and the three of them converged on the sidewalk before climbing the concrete stairs in unison.

"Like I said," Spike grumbled, "something's not right here. Time for us to go."

"Wait, wait," Drew said, pointing back to the road in front of them. "There's more."

This time, the single vehicle was unmarked, though it very clearly was a government sedan. They watched as that vehicle—Spike guessed it was a Ford—pulled in behind the last police cruiser in the line. The guy who climbed out of that one pulled a suit jacket out of the backseat before heading up the stairs. During the transition, Spike spotted the pistol on the man's hip.

"FBI?" Drew guessed.

"Us being embarrassed again," Spike said. This snatch had been a high priority for the sheik. So far, it had cost the life of one operator, along with the reputation of al-Amin in America. How could it be that he and his team could be no more capable than a bunch of local thugs in Woodbridge? "Just get us out of here," he said. "This might not even be about our plan, but the smart money says it is." He smacked the dashboard with his open palm. "Dammit!"

Gone were the days when Cletus Bangstrom would toil away past quitting time—on his *own* time—making sure that all of the equipment was secured and accounted for. Yes, he knew he was a broken record, but things were *different* now. People were *different*. And he was a dinosaur. Every single day was a new reminder of how it truly was his time to retire. If other people didn't care about doing a good job, then why should he?

Soon it would be just him and Abby growing old together.

As he drove toward home, he again ruminated on his conversation with Chief Michaels, and on how much he admired the man.

Going over the heads of two levels of supervision to speak directly to the chief of the department was so wildly out of line that Cletus imagined that if he wasn't already on his way out, he'd have been fired. Chains of command existed for a reason, and to violate them was an unforgivable offense. He told Chief Michaels as much.

"I know this is a huge violation of protocol," Cletus had said.

The chief looked a little surprised. He shot a look to Lieutenant Hackner, who gave an uncomfortable shrug in return.

"Come on in, Cletus," the chief said. (Cletus caught him glancing at his ID badge for the cue to his name, but he wasn't offended. He thought that using his first name was a classy touch.) "A man who's been working here as long as you gets an occasional bye on protocol."

The chief ushered him to the little conversation corner he'd just vacated when the previous guests were leaving.

"Do you want me to stay?" Jed asked.

The chief looked to Cletus, and then said, "No, I think just the two of us will be fine. I tell everybody that I have an open door policy, so I guess I have no business being surprised when someone takes advantage of it. Come on in, Cletus."

Cletus flushed with a feeling of warmth. It wasn't every day that you were invited to a one-on-one with the chief of police.

The meeting lasted a while—probably twenty minutes. Cletus shared everything with the chief. He told him of the missing uniforms and equipment, and of Sergeant Dale's apparent disinterest in any of it.

"Sergeant Dale seems to think it's nothing," Cletus said. "He writes it off to routine losses, but I don't think that's true, sir. Think of it. Eight uniforms have been lost in the past ten months. The service company swears they don't have them, and I know for a fact that we don't. I worry, sir."

Chief Michaels pursed his lips as he considered what he'd heard. "Tell me what you worry about." he said.

Wasn't it obvious? "Chief, there's only so many things you can do with a police uniform. Every Halloween we lose a few, but then they mostly come back. I get that.

Somebody's teenager wants to go to a party. I think it's wrong, but I get it. But in all my years, we've never seen losses like this."

"You look like you have a theory," Michaels said. "Share it with me."

"I'll be honest with you, Chief, I don't have a theory so much as I have fears. Terrorism fears. I mean, let's be honest, there are a lot of people out there who want to do us harm. Dress a bunch of them up in police uniforms, and you never know what might happen."

"Wouldn't it be just as easy to buy uniforms from a costume shop somewhere?" Chief Michaels asked.

That was the question that made Cletus's heart fall. The chief didn't want to believe him, either. "Yes, sir, I suppose it is," he said, and he started to stand.

The chief reached out and put a hand on his arm. "Where are you going?"

Again, wasn't that obvious? "I assumed—"

"Have a seat," the chief said. "Seriously, sit back down." It sounded more like an invitation than an order.

Cletus sat.

"You look like I offended you," the chief said with a deep scowl. "I wasn't doubting you. I was just test driving the idea. Why *wouldn't* it be easier to just rent a costume? You know, from a company that does high quality stuff, the kinds of costumes a movie company might use?"

"Because they won't look like BCPD uniforms," Cletus said. "Remember, the shirts they stole were the ones that have the badge embroidered on the breast. Anybody who puts one on is going to look official."

Chief Michaels raised a cautionary hand. "Again, not to argue that you're wrong, but please don't refer to them as the stolen shirts. Not yet, anyway." His face wrinkled as he seemed to sink into deeper thought. When his eyes came back to Cletus, the chief smiled. Then he stood. "Thank you for bringing this to my attention, Cletus."

Cletus took the hint and stood with him. "If you don't mind my asking, sir, what are you going to do with the information?"

"Truthfully? At this moment? I have no idea. I need to talk it over with some of my staff."

"Are you going to mention it to Sergeant Dale?" Cletus asked.

The chief didn't seem to like the question. "Is there a reason I shouldn't?"

Should he answer or shouldn't he? He decided, what the heck. "Well, sir, to be perfectly honest, he's not going to be happy I came here. I've still got thirty-one days to go, and I don't want them to be miserable, you know what I mean?"

The chief grinned. "I know exactly what you mean," he said. "If I speak with Sergeant Dale, I'll make it clear that I appreciate your inquiry, and doubly clear that he should appreciate it, too."

"He's likely to suggest to you that I took them," Cletus said. There, it was out.

"I think you and I both know that that's absurd," the chief said.

That meeting had happened nearly twenty-four hours ago, and as far as he could tell, the world had not left its axis. He was almost certain that the chief had talked to

Sergeant Dale, because shortly after their meeting ended, Cletus saw Lieutenant Hackner head toward Dale's office, and then together they walked back toward the chief's office. If there had in fact been a meeting, it didn't last very long. Ten minutes later, the sergeant walked back toward where he'd come from. It might have been Cletus's imagination—probably was—but it seemed that Dale was making a real effort to not look in his direction.

He didn't like these unsettling times. He didn't like the feelings of paranoia. Cletus wanted to be happy again, to laugh again in the middle of the day. Honest to God, it used to be that way. Maybe he should have mentioned that to the chief as well.

As soon as that thought crossed the threshold of his mind, he dismissed it. They'd just think he was being sentimental, just being old. And he *felt* old. Maybe it wasn't wrong that they thought of him that way.

What it really came down to was showing some damned respect. He hadn't been on the receiving end of that in a long, long time.

And then it was all clear to him.

The reason why Dale's meeting with the chief had been so short was because they all dismissed Cletus's concerns as crazy. Chief Michaels probably told Dale to keep an eye on Cletus. You know, to make sure he didn't do something stupid. The reason why Dale didn't look at him was because he couldn't trust himself not to laugh.

Good Lord, he hated himself sometimes. Hated the way he thought. Yeah, retirement couldn't get here soon enough.

As he pulled into his driveway, he laid out a plan for Abby and him tonight. He'd open a bottle of wine, cook up a couple of those steaks he'd had in the freezer out on the barbeque. And he'd grill those fresh ears of corn that Blake Thorpe, his next-door neighbor, had brought up from the farmer's market they'd shopped coming back from their trip to Florida. Then, armed with about two thousand calories of good food apiece, they could settle down and blast through all the shows they'd recorded but hadn't watched.

He pulled his Camry as close to the garage door as he could without denting anything and shut off the engine. One day, he was going to get around to clearing out enough crap to actually get the car *into* the garage, but getting Abby to part with her various collections was like putting light back into the sun. A waste of time.

A nice breeze greeted him as he walked to the front door, making him look even more forward to his time in the backyard with the grill. He had his key out, but saw that it wouldn't be necessary. Abby had left the door open a couple of inches. Cletus was going to have to say something to her about that. There were security issues to think about. These days, things being as they were, you couldn't be too—

He froze on the tile floor of the foyer, one foot in and one foot still holding the storm door open. "Abby?" he said. She sat in a chair straight ahead of him, in front of and facing the stairs. It was a dining room chair, one of the end chairs where you could rest your arms while eating. "Abby, what are you doing?"

She didn't answer.

"Hey, babe, are you all right?" He hurried forward to help her. "Do I need to call—"

Three strides into the house, he sensed a shadow. Before he could react, he felt an arm cross his face from behind, and then white and red lights erupted inside his head.

Chapter Twenty-four

Jonathan sat in the darkest back corner of the Maple Inn in Vienna, Virginia, his back to the wall, watching across the bar for the arrival of his dining companion. Located on Maple Avenue, just six miles south of CIA headquarters, the Maple Inn had long been a spooky place, a kind of gastronomic Switzerland, where intelligence assets from all sides could meet in peace to take care of the kind of business that seemed beyond the abilities of politicians and their appointees. More than a few world crises had been defused in this dank little place and others like it, dotted throughout the Washington Metropolitan Area.

The place was packed as it always was. Literally, always. Home of the best chili cheese dogs on the planet, as well as damn good breakfast selections, it was a favorite of the locals. Jonathan couldn't imagine how much money this place generated per unit of time, but it had to be spectacular.

He arrived early to claim his booth of choice, and his waitress, Brittany, was more than happy to move the nearest table a few feet away in order to provide him with more privacy. One quirk of the Maple Inn was the placement of the television, elevated on a 1980s-vintage metal platform immediately over Jonathan's head. If you kept your voice low, nothing you said could be audible past more than a few feet.

Irene Rivers's bodyguards entered the place first. Thankfully, they'd changed into polo shirts and khaki pants, but the rod-straight posture and razor-sharp creases announced their true identities to anyone who knew what to look for. They flanked the door while their boss entered, and then took seats at the bar, where they would have the best view of the room.

Irene smiled as she approached. She, too, wore casual clothes—a plain white blouse tucked into off-the-shelf blue jeans.

Jonathan stood as she approached the table. She proffered no handshake, so neither did he. She looked pissed. In fact, Dom had told him she sounded pissed when she'd called him to arrange the meeting. The fact that she demanded it to be held right by God now sort of confirmed the supposition. She'd suggested Saint Matthew's again as the meeting spot, but Jonathan pushed back and told Dom to relay that he would meet her in the middle here in Vienna. Jonathan liked Irene, and he had undying respect for her, but it was important for her to know that he harbored no fear of her. They'd collaborated on far too many clandestine projects. Each had been for the right reasons, but in Washington, rationality was almost always trumped by transient political priorities. Hey, *somebody* had to keep politicians from destroying the world. Ask anyone who'd occupied this back booth over the years.

"Nice outfit," Jonathan said, taking a pull from his beer mug. "You going on vacation?"

"When in Rome," she said. She leaned in close, her forearms crossed on the table. "What were you thinking?"

Jonathan ignored the bait. "Right now, I'm thinking about how good the chili cheese dogs are, and wondering if I have chili tracks on my cheek." He flashed his smile, but she clearly wasn't in the mood.

"I'm talking about your antics involving Our Lady of Sorrows," she said.

"Oh, that," Jonathan said. He knew damn well that's what she meant, but why give her the satisfaction? "How did that go?"

"Don't be an ass," Irene seethed. "You had no authority to go to Senator Baker's house. You terrified her staff, who in turn terrified everyone in the school."

"Are the daughters safe?" Jonathan asked. He took another bite out of his chilidog.

"That's not the point."

"It's kind of important though, isn't it?" Jonathan asked around his mouthful.

Irene glared. There were times when she enjoyed the banter. This clearly was not one of them.

"Oh, give me a break, Wolfie," he said after the swallow. "Those kids are on a target list, and Big Guy and I saved their asses. We saved Senator Mom's ass, too, along with some guy named Prince. Honest to God, who would name a kid that?"

"Focus, Dig."

Jonathan put the chili dog down and planted both hands on the table, as if to demonstrate that he was unarmed. "Tell you what," he said. "Why don't you have yourself a good rant? I'll listen politely and then tell you the scary shit that's happening." He sold it with a smile that was not intended to be all that friendly.

"You misrepresented yourself as an FBI agent. You stirred a hornet's nest. Senator Baker wants to know the names of the two agents responsible for this. What am I supposed to tell her?"

"Tell her to blow it out her ass," Jonathan said. He felt heat rising in his ears, and it was a struggle to keep his voice in check. "Then tell her to give those little girls a hug for her Uncle Dig who saved them from being shipped off to their deaths."

Irene's features blanked for a few seconds, and then morphed to a look of concern. He had her attention.

"And, if I might remind you, the badges we used were given to us by you."

"For very specific purposes," Irene said.

"And I would number saving lives among those purposes." Jonathan told her about the dead drop. "The address led us to a house belonging to a Mr. Appleton," he explained. "We went there because Appleton was a nobody as far as we were concerned, so we wondered why would the address be part of a dead drop."

"So, you didn't know that it was the senator's house?"

"Not a clue," Jonathan said. "I know I'm an insensitive pain in the ass, but if I'd known that, I believe that even I would have given you a heads-up."

Irene took a moment to process it all. As she was thinking, Brittany approached, but then retreated from the subtle shake of Jonathan's head. This was not the time.

"Your suspicions were correct, Irene," Jonathan said. He'd wrested control of his tone again, and hoped that he sounded as earnest as he felt. "Al-Amin is targeting the families of congressmen and senators. How else to explain the Johnson girl and then the Baker girls? I don't know if they're focusing specifically on girls, but this is a big deal. I also don't know what their end game is. I don't know what they plan to do with those they kidnap, but we both know it's nothing good. In the best case, it's a ransom demand. In the worst case, it's a video record of them being decapitated, drowned, or burned alive."

"Jesus."

"I'm confident that of all the prophets who have a vote in this madness, Jesus is not among them," Jonathan said. "Let me tell you about the guy who inadvertently led me to the dead drop. Okay, we'd actually sort of figured it out on our own, but the guy who tried to kill me to keep me from getting the address—"

"Someone tried to kill you?"

Jonathan waved off her concern. "He wasn't nearly as good at it as he thought he was. But I'm willing to bet the dog that he's a former operative of ours."

Irene recoiled from the thought. "Oh, come on—"

"He had the look," Jonathan said. "Desert kit, battle beard, Oakleys. The whole nine yards."

"You just described ninety percent of the people who attend gun shows," Irene said with a dismissive wave.

"He also had the neck and the shoulders," Jonathan said. "And the knife skills." He grinned. "Sometimes, though, really good is just not good enough." He turned serious. "Trust me when I tell you that he was the real deal. And I'll tell you something else. This guy was born in Ohio as a Presbyterian. Or in Kansas as

Methodist. There's not a drop of Islamic blood in this guy's veins."

Irene's scowl deepened. "Don't make me guess, Dig," she said. "What are you trying to tell me?"

"I'm telling you that we've got a terrorist cell of the highest American order working right here in Virginia. You lean on your intel assets to give you the details, but I'm not making this shit up. The incident in Woodbridge is linked directly to the stabbing incident in Brookfield, which is directly related to the *foiled* kidnapping in Arlington. Notice the emphasis on the word *foiled*. That part was me. The guy you came here to yell at."

"Don't pretend that you are a sensitive man," Irene said. "What am I supposed to do with that?"

"If you're looking for a recommendation, I'd tell you to tell the Baker family to stay away from their home, and to keep their kids away from school."

"How can I do that?"

Jonathan leaned in very close and lowered his voice to almost a whisper. "You're the director of the Federal Bureau of Investigation. You're good friends with the director of every alphabet agency in the world. I'm guessing that between all of you, you can find a way. Especially when you consider the alternative."

"Which is . . . ?"

"Congressional children being held hostage," Jonathan said. "It's a brilliant plan, if you think about it. We don't provide security for members of Congress or their families, and most of them couldn't possibly afford it on their own. It's not exactly as if Congress does anything for the country now, but can you imagine the political constipation if there were real personal consequences for their actions? Holy crap, the mind boggles."

Irene stewed over her options for the better part of thirty seconds. "Where's the end point?" she said finally. "When can I tell them that it's safe to return to their home? And what do I tell the other five hundred thirty-four members from the two chambers about their families?"

Jonathan didn't bother to answer because he had nothing to offer, and he didn't imagine that she expected anything from him.

When a solution finally occurred to Irene, she sat a little straighter. "I have another job for you," she said.

"Does this mean I'm forgiven?" Jonathan asked.

"You're being an ass again," she said.

He laughed. Hey, when you're right, you're right.

"I want you to find him and follow him."

"Who?"

"The man you accosted in the park."

"You know he was the one with knife, right?"

"Like it matters," she said. She smiled. "You're alive, he's hurt, everyone is happy. I want to know what he's doing."

"Didn't we already discuss that you're the director of the FB friggin' I?"

Irene looked at him for a few seconds, telegraphing that he was an idiot. "And what, exactly, would I tell my agents? How would I justify that budget entry? I may be the director of the FB friggin' I, but I still have to answer to congressional and presidential oversight. Is that really your preferred route?"

Jonathan chuckled. "You know, when you put your mind to a buzz kill, there's nobody better than you."

Irene gave him a little grin. "So, that means yes?"

"It means I'm going to speak to Mother Hen, and she'll get pissed. But yes, that all translates to yes."

Irene extended her hand. "It's always a pleasure doing business, Scorpion," she said.

He returned the gesture. "Why do I have the feeling that by the time this is all over, I'm going to get shot at?"

"It's what you do," she said.

"Put the drinks down," Spike Catron demanded as he stormed through the door of the Moose lodge. He didn't know for a fact that anyone was drinking, but he followed the smart money. He heard plastic mugs hitting the surface of the bar and the various tables. This was the second time in three days that he'd gathered everyone into one place, and the exposure made him nervous as hell.

Vinnie met him halfway to the first bank of chairs. Clearly, he'd been waiting for the confrontation. "Hey, Boss, you want to tell us what the hell is going on?"

"Sit down, Vinnie. This isn't the time for your power play. There's too much to do."

Vinnie had made no secret of his desire to oust Spike from power, but it had always been an unstated undercurrent. He seemed unnerved by Spike's direct address of his ambition. He returned to a stool at the bar and sat down.

"Give me a report," Spike said.

"Bangstrom is dead," Vinnie said.

"And?"

"He told us that he told the police chief and a lieutenant who works for him."

"Told him what?"

"About the missing uniforms," Vinnie said. "Bangstrom pretty much figured out what we're planning. I told you that this would be a—"

"Save it," Spike said. What had or had not been said prior to this made no difference. "What else do we hear from our friends in the police department?"

"Our primary contact doesn't think that the chief bought it," Vinnie said.

"What does that mean?"

Vinnie shrugged. "It means that I think we still have time."

"And what do you think will be the case when they find out that you killed Bangstrom?" Spike asked.

"You told me—"

"Answer the question," Spike said. "Do you think that maybe when they find out that the guy who blew the whistle on an attack is dead they might draw the conclusion that he was right?"

Vinnie arose again from his bar stool. "If they do, you can't lay that on me," he said. "I was following your orders."

"What did you do with the bodies?" Spike asked.

Spike cocked his head, the way a dog does when it's confused. "What are you driving at?"

"It's a simple question, Vinnie. You killed Cletus Bangstrom. What did you do with his body?"

"I killed his wife and his dog, too," Vinnie said. There was defiance in his tone. "And as far as I know, they haven't moved from the spot where I dropped them."

"So, they'll be found," Spike said.

Vinnie took a step closer. He seemed ready for a

fight, and he seemed to think a fight was inevitable. "I suppose they will, if someone comes looking for them. How about you tell us all what happened at the school? And in the park, if you're ready to talk about that."

Spike felt himself flush.

"I'm not here to do battle with you," Vinnie said, "But I think we can all agree that bad shit is happening, and we need a plan to figure out what it is."

Given the personalities in the room—and their talent for homicide—it was difficult for Spike to think of any of the assembled team as anything but dangerous, but he owed them an explanation. He prepared himself with a deep breath. "Okay, here it is," he said. "The guy who coldcocked me at the park got the paper with the address on it."

"Who was he?" someone asked.

"I have no idea," Spike confessed, "but he had skills. Look at my face. But he didn't kill me, which makes me believe he's a cop."

"Oh, shit," someone else said.

"I don't know the details, but the fact that the Baker girls never left the school, and that cops swarmed the place leads me to believe that they're figuring things out that we don't want them to know."

Vinnie took another step closer. This time, though, it was less threatening than it was an expression of interest. "Where does that leave us with the sheik?"

"In a delicate spot," Spike said. "Al-Amin wants terror. At the end of the day, that's the goal. The fact that his own people couldn't pull off a snatch actually helps us. He understands that success will be harder than he originally thought."

"What about our money?" asked another voice. It belonged to a guy with the avatar Avery.

"Well, that's the key, isn't it?" Spike said. "Our purpose on the planet, as far as the sheik is concerned, is to deliver terror. The big play is Operation Armageddon. I fear that that's been blown by the property office clerk, but I think the way to make it work is to pull the trigger now."

"Excuse me, Boss," Drew said, "but we're not ready."

"I disagree," Spike said. "We've got the uniforms, we've got the weapons. The only reason we've been waiting this long is for the kidnapping bullshit, and God knows that hasn't been working."

"The money," Bill repeated. "You're talking ephemeral bullshit. I just want to get paid."

"And that will happen," Spike said, "after we hit Mason's Corner and the police station. We go on Friday night. Tomorrow. The sheik told me that half of our payments have already been deposited in whatever accounts you provided. I checked and mine was there."

"How much?" Vinnie asked.

"One million," Spike said.

"That's a hundred short of half," Drew said.

Spike waited a beat, hoping that they would catch on without him stating the obvious. "We didn't deliver the kids," he said. "There's got to be a penalty. Trust me, the sheik wanted it to be more of a penalty than that, but I told him we wouldn't do the rest for any less than two million apiece. Finally, he agreed."

"Who said you can talk for the rest of us?" said Alfie Burdick, a long-ago agency contractor.

"The rest of you," Spike said. "I've been speaking for you from the beginning."

"From the beginning, it was two point two million for each of us. I didn't approve no cut in pay."

"Then walk away," Spike said. "Take your money, disappear, and never sleep soundly again. Remember these are the guys who like to burn people alive."

"We're not the ones who screwed up the kid snatch," someone else said.

"No, we're not," Spike said. "That guy is dead. We hired him, and he let himself be killed, so yeah, it was us."

Spike crossed his arms and strolled among the assembled team members. "I can't stop you from doing whatever you want to do, but we signed up for this, and the sheik has played it pretty straight with us from the beginning. Do what we're told, and we get paid for it. He's always been good on his word. He paid us for the three cop shootings in the Midwest, and he paid us for the judge we killed in Arizona. Those were our auditions, and we knew that from the beginning. The kidnappings were a distraction, and they didn't work out.

"Y'all need to make your decisions now, though. If we get to H-hour and you're not where I've been counting on you to be, then al-Amin will be the least of your problems. You might be good at what you do, but you don't want the rest of this team hunting you down. So, what'll it be? Do you do this and retire with two million bucks, or do you walk away? I need final answers right now. Alfie, I'll start with you. Are you in or out?"

"How do we know we'll get paid the rest?" Alfie asked.

"In or out?" Life came without instruction manuals or guarantees. He saw no reason to answer the question.

Alfie took his time. He scanned the room for an indication of what others were going to do, but it was room full of poker faces. Spike admired that. Professionals never showed what they were thinking.

Finally, Alfie said, "I'm in."

"Good," Spike said. "Thank you." From there, Spike polled the room. Twenty people present, twenty people in.

They were good to go.

Chapter Twenty-five

Venice gathered the team into the War Room.

Jonathan and Boxers had been in the basement armory when she told them that she had news. She said it was big, and that they should come up right away. While known for an expansive sense of drama, Venice was never one to bluff, so Jonathan was anxious to hear what she had to offer. By the time he and Big Guy arrived in the War Room, Venice was already ensconced at her command module. Occupying the end of the long conference table, opposite the enormous LCD television monitor/computer screen, she was surrounded with multiple keyboards and mice, a cornucopia of toys that rendered all doors useless and all secrets moot.

"What've you got, Ven?" Jonathan asked as he entered. Boxers was right behind him and he closed the door.

"You said Wolverine wants you to find and track down your friend in the Corvette."

"Indeed." Jonathan could tell from the set of her smile that something big was on the way.

Venice explained, "I thought to myself, how in the

world will I ever be able to trace down a random red Corvette and tie it to a particular person? I suppose I could have dredged up a list of all Corvettes sold, but my God, that would take forever. So I got to wondering—"

"Do I have time to make a sandwich before you make your point?" Boxers asked.

Venice glared, but she barely broke stride. "So I got to wondering what other options were available to me. And then I remembered how we knew about the Corvette in the first place." She looked expectantly at Jonathan, clearly waiting for him to connect his own dots.

"You know I don't like this game, right?" he said.

"Your body cam!" she said. There was a triumphant tone in her voice. "I remembered how it was that I saw it in the first place. I saw it on your body cam! So I was able to replay the video, and with a little manipulation, I was able to find his license plate number."

Jonathan recoiled. "You mean it was that easy?"

She scowled. "No, of course not."

"Of course not," Jonathan parroted. How could he have thought that anything would be easy? "But you're still smiling. I presume that means you've taken another step."

"I have," she said, and she started typing. Up on the screen, computer stuff happened. Lots of screen movement and numbers, and finally a list of license plate numbers, addresses, and makes, models, and years of automobiles.

She used the arrow pointer of her mouse to highlight a particular line. "Here's the license plate you found on the car. It's a Missouri plate."

"Is this public record?" Jonathan asked.

She looked offended. "Of course not. This was actually a very tough get."

Boxers growled.

"And as you'll see," Venice went on, "the license plate in question does not belong to the car it's attached to. Unless he was able to turn a Dodge Viper into a Corvette."

"The Viper is a good car," Boxers said. "I'd prefer one of those over a 'Vette any day." When Jonathan gave him an impatient look, Big Guy feigned surprise. "Oh, I'm sorry, I thought we wanted to talk about irrelevant shit. My bad."

Venice's jaw set, and Jonathan stifled a chuckle. "Go ahead," he said. "I'm listening."

Venice held the glare for another second or two to sell her point, and then returned her attention to her screen. "That plate—that Viper—belonged to a Samuel Deffenbaugh out of St. Louis. He passed away earlier this year at the age of eighty-two."

"I didn't even know he was sick," Boxers grumbled.

"Please give it a rest, Big Guy," Jonathan said. "What's the significance of him being dead?"

"I thought it was interesting," Venice said. "Think about it. Our guy has license plates that belong to someone who died. Now look at this." She zoomed her picture in closer on the license plate. "Look at the date on the tag. It's new. He's got another two years to run on those plates."

She clicked to a different screen. "Now, if you look at the transfer records for the Viper—"

"You're kidding, right?" Jonathan interrupted. Exasperation had morphed into pure admiration. Who thought of dong this level of research?

"I thought it was important," she said, but her eyes stayed on the screen as she searched for what she was looking for. "There it is, right there." She navigated the mouse arrow to the right spot. "In the transfer record, the plates are listed as lost."

Jonathan cocked his head. He wasn't getting it.

"Not stolen," she said, her voice gaining more excitement. "But *lost*. That means our man has two years to use someone else's plates free and clear. No record is going to show anything stolen."

"Suppose he gets pulled over?" Boxers said. "Won't that be a problem?"

"Thank you for asking," Venice said with an even bigger grin. "So, I looked up Mr. Deffenbaugh's driver's license." More clicks, and a new image. "Gentlemen, meet the new and improved Samuel Deffenbaugh."

"That's my guy," Jonathan said. He'd recognize that jawline anywhere. It amused him to think of what it might look like now.

"I thought that might be the case," Venice said. "Now here's the bit of bad news. I ran the image through all the facial recognition software—and as you know, we have the best available—and the image came back negative."

"What does that mean?" Jonathan asked.

"Well, on the large scale, it means that there's no record of him. He's as invisible as our Mr. Stepahin. And before you ask, yes, I looked for all Samuel Deffenbaughs—there are more of them than you think—and none within the correct age range look anything like your guy."

Truth be told, Jonathan wasn't going to ask that because it hadn't occurred to him. This was the way

Venice's mind worked. Her logic stream tunneled her into some wild, unexpected places.

"But there's good news within the bad news," she said. "All indications are that these off-the-grid guys are some kind of government contractors."

"How can that possibly be good news?" Boxers asked.

"Because it's data," Venice said. Like it was the most obvious thing in the world. "Now we can say with a pretty high degree of reliability that the government is somehow involved in whatever is going on. The question is, why would the United States government be trying to kidnap congressmen's and senators' children?"

"We've seen worse," Boxers said. "Sometimes I really hate what we do for a living."

Jonathan made a waving motion with his hand. "No. I think that's a step too far," he said. "Wolfie told me a story that I haven't passed on to you guys yet."

Boxers shot him an angry glare. "You keeping stuff from us, Boss? That's not the way we do things. At least it never has been."

"It's not like that," Jonathan said. "At least, that's not the way I'd intended it to be. It's a pretty big deal, and she asked me to promise not to spread it around. Even to you guys."

"You could have said no," Boxers said.

"Yes, I could, but no, I didn't. And I apologize. The gist of it was that over the years, our alphabet agencies have had to hide the identities of a lot of wet-work contractors in order to protect them from prosecution by the Justice Department's witch hunt. That's what happened to Stepahin. There's no reason to think that the same thing didn't happen with this guy—Deffen-baugh or whoever." He looked to Venice. "So, what

I'm saying is that government-level cover does not necessarily mean current government-level involvement."

Venice scowled deeply. "So, we just created these monsters and then unleashed them on the world?"

"Wolverine assures me that it seemed like a good idea at the time."

"You know this is madness, right?" Venice said. "This is no way to run a world."

"Depends on where you sit in the equation," Jonathan said. "We hired these guys to do a job that needed to be done, and we did it on good faith. You can't change the rules after the deal is done. And if I sound a little defensive, it could be that I'm talking about myself."

"You're not an assassin," Venice said.

"No, I'm not," Jonathan said. "And I never would be. But the finer distinction would likely be lost on the families of the people I've killed in pursuit of the greater good."

"Can we please move on?" Boxers said.

Jonathan nodded for Venice to continue with her presentation. "Forget about his true identity. How are we going to find him?"

Another coy smile from Venice. "That's my biggest get of all," she said. "I mean, think about it. There's only about a bazillion cars on the road, right? Finding the one out of the masses was a daunting task. I wasn't sure how to tackle it until I remembered that Fairfax, Braddock, Prince William, and Loudoun Counties all photograph license plates."

"They do?" Jonathan said. "How?"

"If you look around, you'll see cameras on the back of police cars. There are pole-mounted cameras as well. They're not supposed to keep the data, but the Virginia attorney general doesn't enforce the rule, so the counties keep it anyway."

"Why?"

"To track people," Boxers said. "Big Brother is watching." Deep inside Boxers' body, there had long been a conspiracy theorist trying to break out.

"He's mostly right," Venice said. "It's part of a post-nine-eleven security package—the same one that gave Braddock County an armored personnel carrier. The idea is to be able to search back after a terrorist event to find the perpetrators."

"It worked pretty well after the Boston bombings a few years ago," Jonathan said.

"Different system, same idea," Venice said.

Jonathan thought about that for a few seconds, about the ramifications for him and his operations. "So, you mean that every time Box and I roll out with the Batmobile, there's a photo record of it, and our license plates are tracked?"

Venice chuckled. "Not a problem," she said. "I went into the system back when I first found out about it. There's a back door that allows national security assets to hide from Freedom of Information requests. It was a pretty easy hack. Every time the system registers your tag, it automatically erases it."

"So, is it safe to say that you put the system to work for you?"

"Indeed it is," she said. She stroked some more keys, and more data popped up on the screen.

"Also not public information?" Jonathan asked.

Another glare.

"Do I want to know how you got the password information?"

"Would you understand what I told you if I did?"

"Probably not. Pardon me for interrupting."

"So, I searched the database and got a total of six hundred thirty-seven hits on his license plate."

"Holy crap," Boxers said.

"Not unexpected," Venice said. "These are passive devices. They suck in everything, and once sucked, it gets categorized and it just sits there forever. But those six hundred-plus sightings go back quite a ways." She tapped some more. "So I copied all those locations into mapping software, and I got a pattern."

The screen turned into a series of lines, squiggles and circles. "Here's where your buddy in the Corvette has traveled over the course of the past four weeks," she explained. She clicked again, and time and date stamps appeared, overlaying the image of the travel routes. "Like most of us, he's something of a creature of habit. We all spend most of our lives within the same few-mile radius—well most of us, anyway. Our man nee Deffenbaugh has a few outliers, but not many. That line there"—she indicated with her mouse arrow—"that's his trip to Brookfield, where you spotted him and beat him up. You can see the date stamp."

"Got it," Jonathan said. The phrase *beat him up* rankled him a little because it seemed juvenile, but he let it go. "So, we know where he's been. How does that help us—"

"Just listen," she said. "I'm getting to it. "So, let's take that data and gray it all out." More clicks, and the once-green lines faded and turned gray. "That there is his historical data. Now, if we lay in his travel for the past five days, this is what we get." The lines around the park in Brookfield turned green again, and so did others.

"Here's where we got lucky," Venice said. "We've got seven hits since your fight. If we put them together from oldest to newest, we get a travel path. So, let's isolate that." All but one line faded back to gray. "That's where he's heading."

Jonathan scowled and leaned into the table for a better view. "I don't get what I'm looking at," he said. "It looks like it ends in the middle of nowhere."

"But nowhere has an address," Venice said. She tapped some more. "Look. There's a picture of him turning into what turns out to be a former Moose lodge."

"How did you get that photo?" Boxers asked. He, too, was leaning in to see better detail.

"From a pole-mounted camera," she said. "And if I bring back the historical data, look what we get." The image on the screen changed again. "He goes out here with fair frequency."

Jonathan exchanged looks with Boxers. Impressive work.

"Is he still there?" Big Guy asked.

"I'll keep checking, but as of about fifteen minutes ago when I finished putting together this presentation, he had not left."

Jonathan stewed over the data. "What is that, about an hour's drive from here?"

"Maybe if you're driving," Boxers said. "I can get us there in forty-five minutes."

* * *

They took the Batmobile because it had the tools and toys. Boxers drove, as always, and bravado and bluster aside, it took every bit of an hour to make the trip. The Moose lodge sat by itself on what must have been an acre of parking lot, maybe fifty yards down the road from a strip mall that featured a barber shop, a UPS store, and a Sheetz gas complex, and seventy-five yards up the road from a Methodist church. Surrounded by a locked chain-link fence, the place looked abandoned. They drove past the front, but couldn't see anything out of the ordinary.

It was nearly five o'clock, and the sun had begun to sink toward the horizon, taking the temperatures with it. As they pulled into the church parking lot, Jonathan lifted his portable radio from its mount in the center console and keyed the mike. "Mother Hen, Scorpion. Are you on the net?"

Five seconds later, squelch broke and Venice's voice said, "Present and accounted for."

"Run your records again, will you? Tell me if our boy has left yet."

"Stand by."

"What's the plan?" Boxers asked, looking at Jonathan across the center console.

"I don't have one yet," he said. "If he's still here, we'll wait and watch, I guess."

"Want to try and take them here?"

"No, not yet. Correlation and causation are two different things. We don't know what they're up to yet— if they're up to anything at all."

"We could always go in and ask them."

"Oh, that couldn't possibly end badly," Jonathan said with a laugh.

"Worst case, they shoot and we shoot back. We might not know what they were up to, but they'd be dead and I don't think the world would care that much."

Jonathan suspected that Boxers was just pulling his chain, but sometimes it was hard to tell. "Think like a professional, Big Guy," he said.

"Scorpion, Mother Hen."

Jonathan keyed the mike. "Go ahead."

"There's no record of them moving."

Jonathan scowled. "I hear a hedge in your voice. No record of them moving is different than still here."

"Yes, I suppose it is," she said. "And that's the best I can do."

It really wasn't good enough. "Okay, I copy," he said. "Stay close." He turned to Boxers. "What do you think?"

"I think we don't know anything," Big Guy said. "And we need to know more."

Jonathan knew immediately what they should do. "Want to play with the drone?"

Boxers replied with a grin and started his climb over and past the seats to get to the cargo bay. It was a comical thing to behold, but Big Guy showed impressive flexibility as he navigated the tight spaces.

Not that long ago, Jonathan had to use stolen military technology to get a decent set of eyes in the sky. Jonathan's favorite had been a Raven UAV. It looked like a sleek model airplane and performed with state-of-the-art capability. Unfortunately, they'd had to leave it behind after an op in Detroit, but even if he still had it, he'd be embarrassed to use it. Like so much other technology, what used to be cool was now big and clunky. For a tenth of the cost, he'd been able to pick up a replacement drone that looked more like a flying saucer than an airplane. Roughly hexagonal in shape, it got its lift and control corrections via six powerful little rotors that together made the sound of an angry bee.

Boxers had named the drone Roxie, presumably after an old girlfriend, and he'd gotten pretty damned proficient with it. It had a stout lifting capacity, easily capable of hoisting a camera and the electronics necessary to transmit images real time to a laptop.

After fifteen minutes of prep time, Roxie was ready to go.

"Need me to do anything?" Jonathan asked.

"Just stay out of the way," Boxers said. "Actually, you can take her outside and lay her on the ground. Then stay out of the way."

All that separates men from boys is the size of their toys. Jonathan had heard Mama Alexander say that a thousand times when he was growing up.

Jonathan exited the Batmobile through the back, and when he had his feet on the ground, he turned back for the drone. Almost four feet in diameter, it was made of composite material that made it lighter than its size would suggest. Jonathan carried it carefully, keeping it in front, and taking special care not to damage the camera equipment that dangled underneath. While not the best one to run equipment such as this, he was the only one qualified to buy it, and he knew all too well how expensive the internal optics were for a lightweight camera such as this. He carried it thirty feet into the vacant parking lot and set it on the pavement.

He hadn't taken five steps back when the electric rotors spun up and Roxie shot into the air. The speed of it startled him and he jumped. In the distance, he heard the rumble of Boxers' deep-throated laugh through the open door to the Hummer.

"Sorry about that, Boss," Big Guy said as Jonathan climbed back inside. "Didn't mean to scare you."

"Bullshit."

"Got that right." He laughed again. "Hey, before you get back in, check again for overhead power lines, will you?"

Jonathan had already looked, but he did it again anyway, confirming that no one had built power poles in the past three minutes. "Still good," he said, and he climbed back inside and closed the door. He slid in behind Big Guy and watched the show unfold on the computer screen.

"I'm going to go in high and use the optics," Boxers said. "Less chance of someone noticing it."

"How high is high?" Jonathan asked.

"I'll start at three hundred feet and see what we can see."

He took Roxie straight up to altitude, and then moved her forward. Of all the arsenal improvements over the years, this drone technology was in Jonathan's mind the most dramatic. In days past, he had to rely on eyeballs for this kind of intel, and that meant getting in close, which in turn meant greater risk, planning, and expense. And with the high-quality optics that were available even to hobbyists, much of what used to require satellite imagery he could now see on his own, through Roxie's eyes. The only limitations now were control distance and power supply. Roxie was a particularly advanced version of UAV, capable of being sent to a position in the air and remaining in place without human intervention, beaming continuing pictures to the ground. As it ran low on power, it would, on its own, return to the precise map grid from which it was launched.

It was also possible to attach a tracking locator to a target, which would allow Roxie to follow the target automatically. It was a feature designed primarily for extreme athletes who couldn't afford a camera crew to record their suicidal antics on whitewater rapids or insane ski runs, but the possible application in Jonathan's line of work were both obvious and exciting.

As the world fell away on the screen, Jonathan saw the Batmobile diminish in size, and then come back closer into view. "Are you landing?" he asked.

"Zooming," Boxers said. "I want to establish the focal length over friendly territory." As Big Guy worked the controls on his keyboard and mouse, the picture blurred, then cleared, and Roxie was ready to go.

In the computer monitor, the parking lot became the road, and then they saw woods. The woods gave way to another parking lot, this one crumbly and neglected. Alongside the image on the monitor, a series of electronic dials and gauges showed Roxie's altitude, airspeed, compass direction, her orientation to the horizon and her geospatial location. Jonathan found all of it fascinating. And Boxers' skill with the controls rivaled his skills with all other forms of flying machines.

Boxers zoomed the image out a bit, and the flat roof line of the Moose lodge came into view. He tapped keys, and the image changed to infrared, revealing that heat was emanating from the structure. "At least we know somebody's home," he said, and the image switched back to standard.

The roofline fell away again, and in the back of the building, they could see a bunch of cars parked, angled in such a way as to be invisible from the front road.

"I count eighteen," Jonathan said.

"And there's your buddy's 'Vette," Boxers said, pointing to the screen. "Now watch this." He maneuvered the controls to zoom in tight on the Corvette's license plate. "The numbers match," he said.

"Are you recording this video?" Jonathan asked.

"Of course."

"Then get a look at all of the tags and beam them to Venice. Get her to see what she can get on identities."

"Do you think any of them will be legit?"

Jonathan shrugged. "Probably not, but it's worth checking."

The request wasn't a big deal, just a quick pass over the back lot to capture license plate images that could later be digitally enhanced for a clear view of the numbers. They could get all but two, because those two were parked in a way that blocked the view.

"Sixteen's better than nothing," Jonathan said.

As the image was zooming out again, a shadow crossed the frame, so close that it gave Jonathan a chill—so clear was the imagery. And then there were more shadows. "Pull out, pull out," Jonathan said, hammering Boxers' shoulders.

Big Guy zipped the image all the way out gaining hundreds of feet of altitude in just a second or two. "Almost makes you dizzy, doesn't it?" he said.

Below, the back door of the Moose lodge had opened, and people were streaming out of the building and heading to five different vehicles, all of them vans and SUVs. To a man—and there appeared to be only men—they carried duffel bags of varying sizes, along with other equipment cases. They appeared to be leaving their individual vehicles in the parking lot. For later, perhaps?

"This doesn't look good, Boss," Boxers said.

"Looks like they're mobilizing, doesn't it? Do you think those are weapons cases?"

"I can't say they're not, so that means I think they are."

"Copy that," Jonathan said. "Come on in a little closer."

The image zoomed down another hundred feet or so, to a level where they could make out faces.

"Do you see your guy?" Boxers asked.

It was a good question. The angle was so much different than it had been before, and, truth be told, Jonathan saw much more of the man's knife than he did of his face. He did notice, however, that there were commonalities to each of the faces he did see. There were far more broad shoulders than broad bellies, and that Special Forces bearded look appeared to be a meme.

"I think we just found al-Amin," Jonathan said. "I think this is the nest of bad guys we've been looking for."

"You know, it might be that they just had a meeting," Boxers said. "This doesn't have to be the launch." He looked at his watch. "Christ, it's after eight o'clock. A little late for doing lots of damage, don't you think?"

"Depends on what the target is," Jonathan said. "Let's keep watching for a while."

"It looks like they're carpooling," Boxers said.

"Concentrating firepower, maybe?"

"Sure, why not?"

In reality, there were as many possible reasons to combine cars as there were wild guesses to be considered.

"Maybe they're launching multiple, simultaneous assaults," Jonathan said.

"Or that, too," Boxers agreed.

"There he is!" Jonathan said, pointing at the screen. "That's the guy I hit. Unless someone else would be wearing a big ass bandage over his right ear." The man Jonathan pointed to wore the battle beard, and the correct high-and-tight hair style, but more than that, he wore a distinctive white gauze bandage on the exact spot where Jonathan had opened him up. He appeared to be the last one to leave.

"Some of the vehicles are leaving," Boxers said, pointing to the screen. "We're gonna lose somebody if I don't bring Roxie back home."

"A few more seconds," Jonathan said. "I want to see where my guy goes."

"What about the others?"

"Zoom out all the way," Jonathan said. "We'll watch them for as long as we can."

As the image fell away farther, and the vehicles started to move, Jonathan's attention was drawn from the video world to the real one as the first in the line of vehicles passed by them out on the street.

"We're gonna have to make a decision here soon, Boss," Boxers said.

Jonathan didn't reply. Instead, he watched as Battle Beard put his duffel into the back of a white Grand Cherokee and climbed into the shotgun seat. Outside, another vehicle passed by them.

"Okay, bring Roxie back in now. We're following

the Cherokee. If he's the leader then we'll find the others. If he's not, then we'll still have the guys in the Cherokee."

The image on the screen reacted immediately, as if to Jonathan's voice command. Boxers had pushed the abort button, which automatically brought the UAV back home. "Suppose I'm right and they're separating?" Big Guy asked.

"Then we'll know what one part of them is doing."

The Batmobile appeared on the screen again as Roxie hovered overhead and eased down to the ground on the pavement outside.

Boxers opened the door to retrieve it, but paused when Jonathan grabbed his shoulder. "Let's let the Cherokee go by first," he said. "You get ready to drive, and I'll bring your electronic girlfriend back inside."

Jonathan watched through the tinted window as Battle Beard and his crew drove by in the Cherokee. That vehicle's windows were also tinted, but Jonathan was pretty sure that he saw at least two others in the vehicle in addition to Battle Beard and his driver.

"Hey, Scorpion, are we gonna go or not?"

Thirty seconds later, Jonathan had pulled Roxie into the back of the vehicle with him, and he was making his way back to the front. Boxers' foot found the gas and they were on their way before Jonathan was even close to his seat.

Chapter Twenty-six

The megaplex movie theater at Mason's Corner was a relatively new addition to an old shopping center that had recently undergone a massive renovation. According to people who had grown up and grown old in Braddock County, Mason's Corner had literally been an unpaved crossroads as recently as the Johnson administration. With the completion of the Capital Beltway in the sixties, places that were barely dots on the map had grown over the years into massive suburban sprawl. Nowadays, real country folk were hard to find in Northern Virginia because they'd all made millions selling their land to developers who'd spun those millions into billions. Now Mason's Corner was home to some of the biggest corporate names in the world, and residential real estate had shot through the stratosphere.

It wasn't a corner of the county that Pam visited very often, but it offered the greatest variety of dining and entertainment options short of traveling into the District, which she avoided at any price. But if an evening at the movies and dinner to follow would get

Josh Levine to stop tormenting her for a date, then this was an evening well spent. They'd gone to the seven o'clock showing of some comic book shoot-'em-up action thriller—Josh's choice, of course, absent consultation with his date—and now they were in Silvio's, a reasonably high-end tapas place.

They'd asked for and had received a quiet corner in the back room of the restaurant, separated by distance and shielding from the cacophony of the mall. Mason's Corner management had decided to place six popular restaurants all in a cluster near both the movie theaters and the massive bookstore. Most of the "eating" establishments were in fact geared to the hard-drinking sports bar crowd, and the result was a constant drone of noise that was driven even higher by the presence of live music in two of the venues. Pam didn't understand how the employees could stand it, or how OSHA didn't require them to wear hearing protection.

Here in the back room, though, the atmosphere was calmer, but a table full of Korean businessmen was driving the decibels higher here, too.

They'd ordered their drinks—Josh a Corona beer with lime, and Pam a screwdriver—and they were both working hard to salvage the date from disaster.

"I've always wondered why we don't post DWI checkpoints outside of bars," Josh said. "It seems like it would be such low-hanging fruit."

Pam chuckled because chuckling was the thing to do. "I believe the chief would find himself at war with the Chamber of Commerce," she said. "Remember that overreach ten, twelve years ago in Fairfax County, when the cops raided the bar in Herndon and had people blow for public drunkenness?"

Josh screwed up his face. "No. Really? Is there a threshold for public drunkenness?"

"Of course not," Pam said. "It was during the holidays and a couple of flatfoots decided to be Grinches. The cases were thrown out. I don't know what happened to the cops. I'm just saying your suggestion has sort of already been tried."

Uncomfortable silence.

"So, how was your trip to Ohio?" Josh asked.

"How did you hear about that?"

"BCPD is a pretty small club. I hear things."

"And what did you hear?" Pam didn't mean for her tone to sound as defensive as it did, but Josh clearly felt it.

"Nothing bad," he said. "Just that you were going."

"That detail being prompted by what?"

"You're getting pissed," he said. He looked unnerved.

"Not pissed," she said. "But I'm getting tired of feeling watched. I'd like for you to tell me what kinds of things are being said about my trip to Ohio."

He broke eye contact. "Just that, you know, you were going."

"For what reason?"

"To check up on details of that parking-lot murder case."

"Was it considered to be a noble mission?"

Josh grew visibly uncomfortable and shifted in his chair. "Look, I'm turning this into a really crappy evening, aren't I? I just wanted to go out, get to know you better, and I chose the wrong movie. Now this."

Pam felt bad for him. She put out her hands in a halting motion—whether to stop him or herself she wasn't sure. "No," she said. "That's more me than you,

I'm sure. I've been a weird headspace the past couple of weeks."

"Personal headspace or job headspace?" His expression showed real interest, not superficial, small talk interest.

Pam took a sip of her drink. A little more OJ than she liked, but still pleasant. "You don't want to go there," she said. "We won't know each other that well."

The waiter approached—his name was Juan and he'd be their server for the evening. While Juan waited patiently, she and Josh agreed that they would split a roasted roma tomato flatbread, and that she would have the ahi tuna tartare appetizer for her entrée while Josh would have the rack of lamb. A two-thousand-calorie delta, and what do you bet that he wouldn't gain an ounce while she put on another half-pound?

Of course the Italian bread slathered in olive oil didn't help.

"You know," Josh said, "when I put myself in your position, I think things could be pretty difficult." He added salt and pepper to his plate of olive oil, and swirled a slice in the green pool.

Pam waited for it, girded for something inappropriate and patronizing.

"I know how tough it is being accepted into the *blue line*"—he used finger quotes—"as a middle class white guy with a law degree. That alone makes it hard for me to blend in. Being a smart, articulate woman—"

"Wait," Pam interrupted. "You have a law degree?"

He nodded.

"How old are you?"

He grinned. "Kind of a rude question, don't you think? First date and all?"

Pam felt herself blush.

"I'm twenty-four," Josh said. "But I'm very smart. Smarter than I look." When his smile was genuine, it was a pleasant thing to behold.

Pam did the math in her head. She was thirty. There were no statutory issues, but six was a lot of years. "How did I not know this?" she said. "About the law degree, I mean?"

He blushed a little. "I don't hide it, but I don't lead with it, either. I figure I've got to earn respect just like everybody else, and the second somebody thinks I'm trying to get an edge, I'm screwed. You know how it works."

"Do I?"

"How could you not? Shit, Pam, you've got so many protective shields, you're like the Starship Enterprise." As soon as the words were out, he winced at the sound of them. "Yeah, and I'm also a nerd," he said. "Anyway, I'm really not trying to pry. Hell, at this point, I'm just trying to not dig myself into a deeper hole."

Pam smiled and reached across the table to grasp his hand. "Relax," she said. "You're absolutely right. I have shields on shields. What was it that Bob Cratchit said? We wear the chains we forged in life. I guess I'm carrying more than my share."

"That was Jacob Marley," Josh said through a smirk. "Bob Cratchit was Tiny Tim's father."

"And you worry about showing off."

They shared a laugh. And then silence prevailed again.

"Some of the officers are pissed that you're working too hard to get the Falk kid acquitted," Josh said.

That got her attention.

"You asked," Josh reminded. "That's how your trip came up in conversation. Some of the cops think that you're working for the wrong side."

"There is no *side* to justice," Pam said. "That's an absolute."

"Okay."

She couldn't read his tone. "What does 'okay' mean?"

"In this case, it means that I more or less don't care," Josh said. "I arrest people all the time, and I don't give them a second thought. I put the cuffs on, fill out the paperwork, and take the cuffs off. Rinse and repeat. That's one of the reasons I'm not champing at the bit to become a detective. I like staying above the fray."

Pam appreciated the honesty. A good part of her missed the neutrality that came with patrol work. "I get that," she said.

"So, how did it go?" Josh said. "Ohio, I mean."

She hesitated, yet she didn't know why. Again, what angle was he working? Finally, she decided that she had nothing to hide. "Do you know about Ethan Falk's backstory? What he said happened to him in his past?"

"Just what I heard there on the scene when we arrested him. He'd been kidnapped, right?"

"Exactly," Pam said. "At first, we all thought his stories were outlandish, but then his lawyer brought in Wendy Adams—"

"The psychiatrist?"

"Right. And she worked with him and he was consistent in his story and very passionate about it." Pam told him about how she connected the dots to the cold case in Ohio. "What I found there all supported his story. I think he was rescued completely off the record by some kind of mercenary team. That's why there was no record."

Josh's eyebrows knitted together. "Mercenaries? Really?"

Pam pointed at him. "And that reaction right there is the biggest problem Ethan Falk faces. There were no useable prints on the scene after the shootings."

"Not even the kid's?"

"They kept him in a sub-basement with a dirt floor and concrete walls. The techs couldn't lift anything useable. So, all we've got is an eleven-year-old story from someone who was eleven years old when it all happened. And the rescuers all wore masks—balaclavas, I guess. So all Ethan can testify to is a man with no face and blue—"

Pam stopped herself in mid-sentence. *Blue eyes.* Jesus Christ, could it really be that?

"What's wrong?" Josh asked. He seemed genuinely concerned.

"Holy shit," Pam said. "I think I met the guy who rescued him."

Wendy Adams jerked her Prius to a stop in a space marked "Official Vehicles Only," jammed the transmission into Park, and threw her door open. She left her coat in the car as she rushed through the front door of the Braddock County Police headquarters building. The public space of the police station was pleasant yet Spartan, decorated in plastic and Naugahyde.

Five people in their fifties sat in three clusters, clearly distraught, no doubt awaiting news on the disposition of their recently arrested loved ones.

Wendy paid them no mind. She made eye contact with the duty officer who sat in an open window that was reminiscent of a medical office reception station. He reached for the button that buzzed her past the inner door that led to the guts of the police station. This part of the building hadn't been built for heavy security, so there was nothing remarkable about the construction materials. The door and everything that lay beyond might have been any other business office—until you turned the angle in the hallway up ahead and walked down a much longer hallway, where the Sheetrock and stud work gave way to concrete block, and then finally to reinforced concrete. Halfway down that hallway, a hard right took her to a heavy steel door that had no handle.

Wendy strode to the door, pressed the call button, then looked straight into the camera lens. The heavy door buzzed and a heavy bolt slid out of place. She pushed, and the well-balanced door moved out of the way with virtually no effort. When she was on the other side, a hydraulic piston pushed the door closed again. In here, there was no pretense of an office environment. Gray and dull yellow were the dominant colors, and the furniture and fixtures made the Spartan elements up front look like luxury. She walked to the bottom of the stairs.

"I'm here for Ethan Falk," she said to the first face she saw.

The officer pointed to the other end of the prisoner processing spaces. "I think they put him in the medical exam room."

"How is he?"

"I don't know," the officer said. "All I know is that he stopped screaming."

A half hour ago, around eight o'clock, and only moments before she was on her way to the bathtub and then bed, she'd received a phone call from the police station that Ethan was in the middle of a "psychic episode"— meaning, she presumed, a psychotic episode—which itself was a diagnosis that lay far beyond the expertise of any custodial cop. Ethan had created a huge ruckus by screaming incoherent things and throwing himself around his cell. It took more than a few officers to subdue him, and even at that, they had to use a Taser before they could put him in restraints.

That's all she knew because that was all they had at the time of the call.

As she approached the closed door to the infirmary, she slowed her pace and steeled herself. She would have sworn that they'd made better progress, that Ethan was coming to terms with his past—and with the glimmers of hope for his future. Life had put him on a terrible path, and he'd done everything he could, it seemed, to make it as bad as it could possibly be. Outbursts like the one reported by the police officer who called her did nothing to help his case in the future, and in fact might have done it a lot of harm.

It was her job, over the course of this visit—over the course of the next hour or so—to explain these realities to him without triggering more panic.

With her hand on the door latch, she stopped, inhaled deeply, and let the breath go slowly. *Showtime.*

Ethan Falk lay in a semi-reclining position on his back, wearing only a pair of county-issued boxer shorts. His hands were cuffed to the bed's side rails, and his ankles were buckled into padded hospital restraints, which had in turn been fastened to the bedframe. Another restraint around his waist kept his middle tied to the bed as well. The restraint buckles were themselves locked.

Her patient had lost a noticeable amount of weight since he'd first been arrested, weight that he could not afford to lose. She'd not seen him unclothed like this before, but she doubted that on their first meeting she'd have been able to count each of his ribs as she could now. Angry red marks on his chest and his gut marked the locations where the Taser probes hit.

Ethan needed a shave and his hair was a mess. He stared at the ceiling, and he didn't bother to turn his head to acknowledge Wendy's entry.

"It appears that you've had an exciting evening," Wendy said. She wanted to start things light, if only to gauge the depths of his angst.

"Why don't they let you commit suicide in jail?" Ethan asked the ceiling. He still had not acknowledged her.

And hell would freeze over before she went along with that game. He knew the rules. If he wanted to speak with her, he needed to speak *to* her. She waited him out.

After ten seconds, he rocked his head to the side and made eye contact. "That was a real question," he said.

"And I believe it's one to which you already know the answer," Wendy said.

"I can't do this, Doc," Ethan said. His eyes glistened red. "There's just no way I can do this. Not for another day, and certainly not for years. I just can't. I didn't do anything wrong."

She let the words hang for a while, fully aware that she could make no response that would counter the awfulness he saw ahead. "Tell me what happened," she said at last.

"I got to ride a lightning bolt," he said with a forced chuckle. "That Taser is a pretty special experience."

"Tell me about what led up to that."

"Did you know that you can actually *see* electricity when it's slamming through your body? It sets off blue lights behind your eyes. And it tastes like blood."

She waited.

Ethan sighed and looked back at the ceiling. "I know you like eye contact, but honest to God, my neck is sore. It's hard to look to the right. Come to my left and maybe we can do the eye contact thing."

Wendy didn't know if the request was in reality a passive-aggressive power play, but she bought that it was not unreasonable. So she moved to the other side of the bed. The whole room wasn't eight by ten feet, so the distance separating them remained the same.

Ethan followed her with his eyes until he could rock his head to his left. "Yes, that's better," he said.

"Good," Wendy said with a smile. "Now tell me what happened."

He took an enormous breath and held it as his jaw muscles worked hard and his face turned red. He was fighting a losing battle over a wave of emotion. "I think I went a little crazy," he said.

*   *   *

Warren Michaels looked up as Jed Hackner knocked on his open door. "It's going on nine o'clock, Warren. It's Friday. Why aren't you at home?"

"Asks the man who's at my door at nine o'clock on a Friday."

"You have a life," Jed said. "I don't."

Warren knew that to be more true than false. Jed had always been drawn to troubled relationships. "I just want to clear the decks for the mountain of crap that's going to arrive over the weekend when I'm not here. I won't be a lot longer. What about you?"

"Another half hour, max." Jed turned to leave.

Warren said, "Hey."

Jed stopped and turned.

"What's the rumble in the jungle over housing the Falk kid here?"

Jed shrugged. "I haven't heard anything, but I haven't asked, either. Want me to put out feelers?"

"No, that's okay. No sense kicking a nest. Have a good weekend if I don't see you before one of us leaves. You're still planning to come over Sunday for the 'Skins game?"

"What, are you kidding? Life wouldn't be the same without my weekly dose of perpetual yet futile hope."

"They're splitting up," Boxers said, pointing through the windshield. "Who do you want to follow?"

"Let's stick with the Cherokee," Jonathan said. When faced with a binary choice, pick one and make it sound authoritative.

"It looks like two vehicles are going left," Boxers said. "No, three. The Cherokee has only one companion."

"I'm making this up as I go along, Big Guy. For all we know, they're going home to sleep."

"You don't believe that for a second, do you?"

"Of course not. But if something is going down, I figure one vehicle will lead us to the others." Saying it out loud made it sound even more correct.

"The good ol' whiskey indigo plan," Boxers said with a rumble of a laugh. Whiskey indigo equaled "wing it."

They followed the Cherokee at a distance, working hard to keep at least two vehicles between them. The route took them back into the deep center of Brookville, past the Old Town city center, and then through a low-rise industrial section until finally they were in the middle of what appeared to be the county government complex.

"Open up a little more distance," Jonathan said. At this hour, traffic in and around the government center was practically nonexistent and the Batmobile was not what one would call inconspicuous. It helped that it was black and that the area was dark, but it never hurt to be careful.

"I don't get it," Boxers said. "Are they paying parking tickets or what?"

As soon as Big Guy asked the question, Jonathan knew exactly what they were about to do. "That's the police station up there," he said. "I think they're going to hit it."

Boxers laughed. "Oh, now that should be a hoot to

watch. That's like picking a gunfight at a gun show. Can you say circular firing squad?"

Jonathan reached for his radio and keyed the mike. "Mother Hen, Scorpion," he said over the air. To Boxers, he said, "Do you forget how many people we saw pouring out of that Moose lodge?"

"They're not here," Big Guy said.

"Go ahead, Scorpion," Venice said.

"Hey, Box, I want you to launch Roxie again. Put her in a hover over the police station. Just park her there so we can see what's what." He keyed the microphone. "Mother Hen, I think we may have stumbled into something hot here. We're at the Braddock County Police station. See what you can pull up from their video feeds, and if you can, get me a floor plan."

"Please tell me you're not breaking that boy out of jail," Venice said.

Boxers and Jonathan exchanged glances. Jonathan said into the radio, "Ethan Falk is inside the police station?"

"Affirmative," Venice said. "I thought I told you that."

Maybe she did, but sometimes he got distracted during long discussions with Venice.

"And don't forget about the property officer who was found dead," Venice said. "I don't know if that's significant, but it would be a heck of a coincidence if it wasn't."

"Copy that," Jonathan said. "Let me know what you can get on the police station and get back to me ASAP, okay?"

"Will do."

In the back of the Hummer, while Boxers got busy bringing Roxie back online, Jonathan opened the storage locker in the vehicle's floor.

"What are you doing, Boss?" Boxers asked.

"Once you get Roxie up and running, I want us to kit up and be ready to go hot."

"To do *what*?" Boxers looked at him as if he'd grown a new nose. "You know that police stations are full of cops, right?"

"I think that explains the *p* word on the door," Jonathan quipped.

"And you know we break a lot of laws," Boxers said. "The police station is pretty much number one on my list of places I don't want to go."

"I'm not all that keen on it, either, but if these guys launch an assault, I can't imagine just sitting here and watching."

"Then let's leave," Boxers said. "That way we won't know."

The lightness of Big Guy's tone sold the suggestion as a joke, but Jonathan had to admit that it made some sense.

"Hey, Dig, listen to me," Boxers said. "There's already a million cops in there as it is. Those two cars hold, what, maybe four, five guys apiece? We can't bring anything to that fight that won't already be there. Not to mention the fact that we're going to be on the round end of the cops' weapons if we come in behind the bad guys. If the bad guys go in at all."

"I can't argue with any of that," Jonathan said. "Maybe we won't have to do anything. But let's kit up anyway, just to be on the safe side. You can make fun of me later."

"Something to look forward to," Boxers said. He unlatched the back door and stepped out into the night with Roxie. "No, you stay in where it's warm," he said. "I got this."

Chapter Twenty-seven

Drew and the rest of the mall team parked in various corners of the three enormous parking structures that served Mason's Corner. They left the vehicles one at a time, at an interval that shouldn't draw any attention. And if it did, they were just cops on a routine patrol. In a perfect world, they would have been able to get their hands on a police vehicle, but that most assuredly would have attracted attention.

When this one was over, the whole game was over for Drew. Over the course of the past few weeks, so many things had gone wrong with virtually nothing going right that he was going to take his share of the sheik's money and retire. He'd been a shooter in one form or another for nearly twenty years now, and while he was damn good at it, the time had come for him to realize the obvious: that this was a young man's game.

He had also realized that killing on home turf was a lot harder than killing overseas. He'd never personally invested in the politics that underlay what he did, and he had no compunction against taking lives for money, but after today he and his team would be vilified by the entire free world. The plan was so simple in its design that Drew couldn't understand why it hadn't already been thought of by others.

The uniforms were the key to it all. People expected to see police officers mingling about in crowds. While the M4s that each of them wore slung across their body armor would surely draw attention, the worst that might happen was that people would bitch about the militarization of American law enforcement.

Boy howdy, wait till tomorrow.

Drew was last to leave his vehicle, a Honda CR-V. He left it unlocked, with the key fob in the center console. Whoever got to it first—if, in fact, it made sense to get back to it at all—would be able to drive it to the rally point, and from there, the focus would shift to escape and evasion.

The teams had trained for this for weeks. They'd toured the mall, they'd identified shooting lanes and areas of responsibility. For the entire plan to work, they needed to keep the attack hot for at least ten minutes. Fifteen would be better. Each member of the team carried a minimum of four hundred rounds of ammunition for their long gun, and then whatever they opted to carry for a sidearm.

The first seconds of the attack would by far cause the most damage. The first gunshots would startle mingling shoppers, but then within ten seconds or so, the reality would kick in, and they would head for cover. From there, the initial round of spray-and-slay would transition to aimed shots. Sniping. And that's when the panic would fold in on itself. As the real police arrived, each member of the team would decide when it was time to blend in and leave. That wouldn't be possible for everyone, of course, but each loss of a team member meant an expanded share of money for the survivors.

Drew entered the mall through the airlock leading to Parker's Department Store, a chain of high-end clothing and knickknacks headquartered in Seattle, but with anchor stores in countless malls in the Mid-Atlantic that catered to customers who perceived themselves to be richer than their neighbors. It was an egocentric marketing strategy that Drew imagined sold tons of stuff to people who flat-out couldn't afford what they bought. And for those, there was always the store credit card account, through which already-bilked customers could finance their purchases and wind up spending two or three times the already-inflated prices for the things they didn't need to begin with.

Drew held no animus for those who participated in the Northern Virginia nouveau riche competitions that fueled BMW and Mercedes dealerships, but he understood why the rest of the world so hated Americans. When starving kids in Africa were drinking out of shit-contaminated mud puddles, the "poor" people of America suffered through clean tap water instead of bottled designer water and they complained. Drew lamented that his lazy countrymen who had never wandered more than fifty miles from their birthplace moaned about inner-city poverty which looked to the rest of the world like a thriving middle class.

And then there was Mason's Corner, a monument built at the feet of money. Five–and-dime stores were not welcome, thank you very much. No barber shops, no trinket stores. Nothing that might attract the hoi polloi that was truly the American middle class. Absolutely not. If you couldn't afford a fifteen-dollar burger, you had no business being here. Yet it was the place of places to be. Kids were here, teenagers spending their parents' money, pretending that it was theirs. Young parents were here, too, pushing their kids in strollers through a mall easily an hour after said kids should have been tucked into their own beds.

If ever there was a group that needed an introduction to reality, it was this one. And he was the vector for it.

As he walked past the jewelry counter, toward the cosmetics counter and the mall that lay beyond, Drew was keenly aware of the looks he attracted, especially from children, especially from boys. Something about the universal attraction to rifles, he assumed.

While he was in the space that separated jewelry from cosmetics, a thirty-something man who had clearly never seen a gym yet warranted a "department manager" name tag from Parker's, approached him from the left. "Excuse me, officer?" he said.

Drew stopped and addressed the man. He placed his right hand casually over the grip of the Glock 17 that rode in his holster. If he did it right, the posture would look natural. "Yes, sir?"

"Is there something going on in the mall?" the manager said. His name tag identified him as Darrell Kent.

"I'm not sure I understand your question," Drew said. As he spoke, he plotted out firing lanes inside the store, in case it came to that.

"I'm just coming off my break," Darrell said, "and you're the third cop I've seen in here carrying a rifle and all kinds of ammunition. We don't see that very often. In fact, I don't think I've ever seen it before. Is there some kind of elevated threat level or something?" Darrell's tone betrayed fear. Drew wondered what the department manager would do if he shared the reality of what was coming in the next few minutes. In the next six minutes and fifty-three seconds, if the truth be known.

"We call it a show of force," Drew said, parroting the line they had rehearsed. "You never know when trouble might strike, so periodically we like to step out with a little extra firepower. If bad guys are casing the joint, as they used to say in the old movies, we hope we'll give them reason to second-think their desire to hit Braddock County."

"So there's no immediate cause for concern?"

Drew took his time on this answer, savoring his smile. "No, sir," he said. "It's all just routine."

"Good," Darrell said. He held out his hand. "And thank you for your service."

Drew shook the man's hand. "You're welcome," he said.

Past the cosmetics counter, a wide doorway opened into the rest of the mall, where hundreds of sales people in hundreds of stores would be more than happy to separate you from your money. Want a cigar? There was a store for that. How about a pretzel double fried in a vat of artery-clogging fat? There was both a store and a kiosk for that. Across the way, pictures of mostly naked teenage boys beckoned customers into a store where boys and girls alike could spend a hundred dollars for pre-torn jeans and fifty dollars for a T-shirt that Drew's mother would not have let him wear in public. He passed by the kiosk that offered three-dollar cups of coffee, and another where you could spend thirty dollars for a purse for your six-hundred-dollar smart phone.

As far as Drew was concerned, this was a turning point in the history of the world. And he was the tip of the spear. There was a better than average chance that he would not survive the next thirty minutes, but if it came to that, then by God his final hour on the planet would have been well spent.

Mason's Corner Shopping Mall lived on two levels, around a towering atrium that featured glass artwork across the ceiling that reminded Drew of the famed lobby of the Bellagio Hotel and Casino in Las Vegas. Travel between the two levels was made possible not just by the elevators inside the anchor stores, but also via five sets of escalators, multiple ornate stairways, and two sets of glass elevators in the body of the mall.

Drew took his station on the second level, outside a designer shoe retailer, at the corner where the mall angled out at about forty-five degrees. From here, he had clear lanes of fire down nearly the entire length of the mall, plus an unobstructed view of the shoppers below. The rest of his team members were similarly installed in other strategic locations. He checked his watch.

Fifty-five seconds till H-hour.

Drew steeled himself for what was coming. He watched the old couple who held hands while the husband held on to the atrium's guard rail for support. The young moms and dads with their strollers and with their toddlers who clearly wanted to be anywhere else but here. The teenage couples young and in love. The teenage marauders who saw the mall as an amusement park without an admission fee.

He smiled at those who made eye contact, but mostly he watched how they handled themselves. The law of averages dictated that there would be a few off-duty law enforcement officers, and maybe even a few on-duty ones. This being Virginia, where all God's children were born with a right to carry firearms, there were likely to be a few civilians who would try to shoot back. This being autumn, where more people wore jackets than didn't, it would be harder to identify the concealed carriers than it would be if it were summer. But he knew they were out there.

Thirty seconds.

Two teenaged boys made eye contact, and Drew knew right away that they were going to be a problem. They approached with anger etched into their faces. Both white and skinny with hair that could have used both a pair of scissors and a pint of shampoo, the one on the right wore a Che Guevara T-shirt, and the other wore a polo that came from the designer store that featured kiddie porn in its windows.

"Hey, Officer," said Che-boy as he approached. "Really? You've got to have a goddamn machine gun in a shopping mall? Seriously?"

"Shouldn't you be chasing real terrorists instead of playing tough killer here?" said the other kid. "Don't you guys kill enough people as it is?"

Drew didn't respond. He looked past them, so as not to get distracted.

"What?" Che-boy said. "Did your masters forget to program your robot brain to answer questions?"

Drew felt his lips draw back into an unintentional smile.

Ten seconds.

* * *

Venice had been able to pull up a floor plan for the Braddock County Police station, and had successfully hacked into the building's video surveillance feed—apparently one of her easiest hacks ever. Jonathan didn't understand the technical ins and outs of such things, but he figured it made sense not to have multiple layers of security over footage that was readily accessible to the media. The feed showed a building that was more occupied than Jonathan would have imagined, given the time of night on a Friday. Venice had been watching the feed for more time and with more intensity than Jonathan had, and she'd been able to cross-reference some of the faces she'd seen with various other records. Most important, she'd been able to identify the chief of police, and to confirm that he was still in the building. Jonathan wasn't sure why that was an important detail, but it felt like it was.

On Boxers' screen, the continuing image from the hovering Roxie showed a Jeep Cherokee in which multiple men had gathered, none of whom seemed in any hurry to get out.

"What can they be doing in there?" Boxers wondered aloud. He and Jonathan had both pulled black coveralls over their street clothes, and they'd prepared their assault gear in case it needed to be deployed.

"I have no idea," Jonathan said. "But let's assume that they're planning to assault the station. How would you do it?" He spun his laptop so Big Guy could get a better view of the floor plan Venice had sent. The footprint of the building bore a striking resemblance to a fat pistol, with the vertical part of the grip running north-south and the barrel assembly running east-west. The

public entrance and reception areas were in the grip at
the westernmost extreme of the building. Jonathan
could see the light through those doors straight ahead,
though partially concealed by trees.

In the door (think slide rod on the pistol image) and
turn left (toward the front sight), you'd find the chief's
office and other administrative services clustered in
the northwest corner. Halfway to that corner, the single
main hallway—a long one—split off to the right. Down
that hall lay evidence rooms, men's and women's locker
rooms, the armory, the patrol briefing room, and then a
hard stop at a security door that led to the secure prisoner processing areas, which were downstairs. The detention cells lay on the lower floor at the farthest
northeast corner of the building.

Boxers leaned in closer. "How many troops do I
have?"

"Let's say ten."

Boxers gave a low whistle. "What's my mission? Is
it merely to create mayhem, or am I after something?"

"Let's say you're trying to kill a prisoner." That
comment earned him a concerned look. "Just for planning purposes," Jonathan said.

Boxers' face took on a serious concentration as he
planned an imaginary attack. "How good is my team?"
he asked.

"Very."

Boxers growled as he studied the plans.

Jonathan decided to take the first shot at his own
question. "Going in from the east end is a nonstarter,"
he said. "Any walls that are designed to keep killers in
will work just as well to keep attackers out."

"Agreed," Boxers said. "The softest point of entry is

going to be the front door. With ten guys who are good at what they do stacked up on the door, they'll be able to spread out pretty quickly to contain any threats."

"What about here?" Jonathan pointed to a spot on the south wall, roughly where the trigger would be, carrying on with the pistol metaphor. "That's their 'public safety training room,' whatever that means. It's got a big window. That might be a great breach point."

Boxers scowled, then nodded. "Either way, once they get to that security door in the center of the long hallway, everything's going to choke. If they can't get through, they'll be trapped. It'd be a damned firing squad wall."

"And what about when they get to the other side?" Jonathan added. "People on the other side of that wall will have had a lot of unintentional advance notice. They'll be loaded for bear."

"Do they allow firearms on that side of the security door?" Boxers asked. "The smart move for them might be to just boogey out and run."

Jonathan thought about that. "Actually, I think I've got it," he said. "Simultaneous entry from both the west and the south. The team from the west can confront and control shooters while the team from the south works its magic on the center security door."

"Hey, Boss? Tell me again what you see our role to be in this imaginary firefight between cops and bad guys."

Jonathan clapped him on the shoulder. "You'll be the first to know as soon as I figure that out," he said.

* * *

"Any sign of the Hummer?" Spike asked. Of all the members on his team, the one who called himself Tomlinson was by far the most paranoid. He'd talked himself into believing that they were being followed by a big black Hummer. Tomlinson made it his habit to ride turned backward in the seat, perpetually looking for signs that they were being tailed. Spike had never drilled into the origins of his paranoia—he didn't care— but there were advantages to having someone on the team who worried all the time. In the world of alpha male shooter teams, that kind of perceived weakness was hard to come by. Spike didn't doubt the fact that Tomlinson had seen the Hummer both of the two times he reported, but this was a crowded part of the world, and most roads led to thousands of places, of which this was only one.

"I don't see him," Tomlinson said. He had a reedy, squeaky voice that served only to perpetuate the perception of weakness. "But I saw lights behind us as we pulled in, and no vehicle ever passed us. They could be hiding in the shadows back there, and we'd never know."

"Could be Apache warriors," said Watkins, another member of the team. He considered himself the alpha of alphas.

"Pygmies." That from Simpson.

"Har, har," Tomlinson said. "Judge as you wish. I'm just tellin' you what I'm seein'."

The ball-busting continued among the team as Spike considered his options. Part of him imagined that paranoid people lived longer than non-paranoid people. As the thought passed through his head, he realized he was gently stroking the bandage over his right ear. That guy in the park had skills. And maybe a guy with skills would go to the effort to follow them for their assault on the police station.

There were a million reasons why that concern was preposterous—start with the fact that this was Braddock-freaking-County, Virginia, not Westchester County, New York. This little burg was nowhere on anyone's list of probable terrorist targets. Add to that the security they'd built into their operations. But then there were the breaches. The death of Bill Jones. The mugging in the park. The black Hummer.

"Here's what we're going to do," Spike announced, effectively cutting off the banter among the team members. He looked at his watch. "In ten seconds, the show starts at the mall. Figure five minutes max for these idiots to get the word, and then we're off and running. Tomlinson, I want you and Watkins to move backward when the balloon goes up. If your Hummer is there, kill everyone in it, and then join the attack."

"Oh, come on," Watkins protested. "Are you serious?"

"Those are my orders," Spike said. "And feel free to scalp any and all Apache warriors you run into."

Chapter Twenty-eight

"Let me share a secret with you," Drew said to his new smartass friends. "Listen carefully."

One crossed his arms, the other planted his hands on his hips.

"Three, two, one, zero." Drew raised his M4 to his shoulder and shot them both in the face, point blank. It was on.

Automatic weapons fire opened up from every compass point within the mall. At first, predictably, shoppers froze, some in a half crouch, but most stood cluelessly upright. With his right thumb, Drew switched the selector from single shot to full-auto, and he fired a full thirty-round mag down the length of the mall to his left, and as he dropped the empty and replaced it with a full, he pivoted on his own axis and fired down the length of the mall to his right.

Through the window of the designer shoe store, he saw a teenage clerk standing stock still, frozen in place as she tried to comprehend the incomprehensible. Drew waved at her and motioned for her to get down. His good deed for the day.

The thunder of gunfire translated to vibrations in the floor as his team members did the jobs they were being paid so handsomely to perform. Drew found it thrilling at a visceral level. It tapped the same corner of his brain where sexual pleasure resided. He felt himself growing erect. The air itself transformed into a smoky haze that smelled of gunpowder and blood and fear.

He emptied another full magazine in each direction, and then he switched his selector to single fire. From here on out, his shots would be aimed. Fifteen seconds into the attack, those who were able to move to save themselves dove for cover inside the nearest store, oblivious to the fact that those doorless, wide-open spaces offered virtually no cover at all. Soon, he would begin his stroll to prove the futility of their actions in the most vivid way he and they could imagine. Up close and very, very personal.

But first, they had to make it that far. Only thirty feet away, a young husband enveloped his bride in a protective hug as he tried to hustle her out of sight, but Drew killed them both with the same bullet through two set of lungs.

Slaughters in real life don't happen the way they do in the movies. First of all, nothing is in slow motion, and there are rarely eruptions of blood as shown on the screen. In real life, people just fall, and the blood comes later, sometimes bright red, sometimes darker red, but always red.

People screamed, he supposed, because they believed it to be the thing to do in a stressful situation, but it made no sense to him. Screaming accomplished nothing. Worse, it took up valuable real estate in the brain. Real estate that would be better dedicated to escape and evasion and even retaliation.

Just for shits and giggles, Drew chose the farthest target he could see, a dark-haired woman in some kind of retail uniform running directly away from him. He settled his red dot sight on a spot between her shoulder blades and pressed the trigger. She fell facedown and slid along the tile floor as she died.

"Holy shit, that's gunfire!" Pam declared. She jumped to her feet and drew her off-duty weapon, a 9 millimeter Glock 26, spilling her water and sending her mini key lime pie crashing to the floor. Opposite her, Josh was on his feet as well, brandishing his 9 millimeter Glock 19. Diners saw the weapons and panic rippled through the room.

"We're police officers!" Josh yelled. "Everybody stay put and get down."

Outside in the mall, it sounded like a war. People rushed away from the open front wall of the restaurant and started packing into the back. Moving against the flow, Pam and Josh tried to push their way to the front.

"Make way, please," Pam said, trying her best to keep her voice modulated. "Move to the back and stay down. Take cover." She held her badge in one hand, poised over her head, and her Glock in the other. "I'm a police officer," she said again and again. "Nobody panic. I know it's hard, but nobody panic. Go to the back of the restaurant. We'll protect you." She cringed as she heard her own words. She'd just made a promise she had no idea that she could keep.

Among the throngs of pushing humanity, Pam caught sight of Juan-their-server-this-evening. She grabbed a fistful of his vest and pulled him out of the flowing stream. "You remember me, right?" she said. "We were at your—"

"My table, yeah. What do you want?"

"I need you to lead these people to the back door. Show them where it is and direct—"

The kid looked terrified. "What if there's a guy with a gun back there, too?"

"Work the odds," Pam said. "The world is coming apart out there beyond the front door. You *know* there's a shooter out there. And it sounds like he's getting closer. Against that, there *might* be a bad guy in the back hallway. Which sounds like the smarter move, staying or going?"

She saw the darkness lift from his eyes. He got it.

"Okay," Pam shouted to the gathering crowd of panicking shoppers. "Listen up! I am Detective Pam Hastings with the Braddock County Police Department. I want you all to follow—"

"You!" a lady yelled. "You're the police!"

Pam turned to the voice.

The lady rushed her, threw a punch that missed by a foot. "God *damn* you!" the lady yelled. Her face and her blouse—a beige flannel shirt, really—were both spattered with blood.

Pam recoiled from the attack, feeling unbalanced by the violence of it. The *anger* of it. "What the hell is wrong with you?"

"It's you!" the lady yelled. "You're the killer!"

Josh had joined Pam now. He'd slung his own badge—a silver one while Pam's was gold—from his shirt pocket, and he seemed ready to tear apart the lady who had accosted his date.

"*We're* the killers?" Pam pressed. "What are you talking—"

"The police are shooting everybody. They're shooting everybody they see!"

A memory rumbled deep in Pam's brain. Casual talk about stolen uniforms. Her stomach seized.

Outside, the shooting continued. The screaming, the running. The panic continued. The slaughter continued.

"I don't understand what you're saying," Pam said. She dared to grab the woman by both shoulders and gave her a hard shake. "Tell me. Tell me what you saw out there."

The woman seemed surprised that Pam wasn't getting it. Annoyed. "They're cops," she said. "Police officers. I saw four of them, but I think there are more. They're everywhere and they're just executing people."

"No," Josh said. "That can't be right."

"Doesn't matter," Pam said. To the blood-spattered woman, she said, "Join these people. Get out of here." She raised her voice and addressed everyone. "Follow Juan here, and he will lead you to safety. Don't slow down, don't turn back." She looked to Josh. "We'll take care of this."

The MIA box on Warren Michaels's desk squealed at the same instant that his phone buzzed an SOS in his pocket. The MIA system—Major Incident Alert—was an outgrowth of the old Plectron system that told the chief of police that it was time to go to work with extreme prejudice. Triggered by dispatchers in the EOC—Emergency Operations Center—a MIA tone preceded the dispatch of something earth-shattering, and alerted everyone from the county executive down through the newest public safety employee that whatever plans they thought they'd made for the day had been canceled. During the six years that Warren had been chief, this was the first time that the system had been implemented outside of a drill.

Warren's head pivoted to the box on his desk and his heart stammered at the sound of stress in the usually implacable dispatcher's voice. "Attention all units, attention all units. Emergency traffic. All available units respond to multiple active shooters at Mason's Corner Shopping Mall. We are receiving dozens of calls reporting multiple casualties and multiple shooters. All available units respond."

In the space of a heartbeat, the world changed. Warren could almost feel a vacuum being drawn on the headquarters building as more than a dozen officers ejected themselves from whatever corner or cubical they'd been occupying and dashed for the doors.

Warren rose from his desk and yelled, "Long guns!" He had no idea if anyone had heard him. Being the chief puts you in a corner office beyond the smaller office that held his administrative assistant, who was now at home, enjoying a peaceful evening. Or so he hoped. As long as she wasn't shopping at Mason's Corner. He hurried past her desk to confront the flow of exiting officers.

He was pleased to see that many of them were already ahead of him. They swarmed the armory down the hall, where Cletus Bangstrom's temporary replacement seemed utterly swamped by the demand for rifles and magazines. In the middle of it all, trying to bring order to the chaos, was Jed Hackner, among whose many talents was an impressive knack for calming people down. This wasn't the place Warren wanted him to be.

"Jed!" Warren called.

The lieutenant turned.

"I want you on the scene. Now. Take charge and be my eyes until the van gets spun up. I'll be in the CTC." Crisis Tactical Center. When the command van was staffed, Warren would move from the CTC in the basement of the police station to the MCTC—the Mobile Crisis Tactical Center. If the incident grew large enough, there'd be a lot of people inside that van—a converted RV, really—and about forty percent of them would want to be in charge. For now, though, and for the next ten minutes or so, no one would challenge Warren's authority in what was known to his command staff as the bunker.

Warren left the scene in the hallway to head to the CTC. As he passed the various cubicles and hallways, he noted that all but a few of the department's civilian employees were gone for the night. One of the exceptions was a young IT genius named Yolanda Pierce, who Warren wasn't sure he'd ever seen in the building past 5:30. On a different night, he'd have asked if everything was all right. Tonight, however, he knew for a fact that a lot of things were very wrong.

When he got to the door to the basement, he passed his ID card over the reader in the wall and the heavy steel door buzzed. He pulled it open and glided down the stairs into the gloom that housed the CTC as well as the prisoner processing and holding areas. While the new building was under construction, Warren had suggested to the Board of Supervisors that there might be dividends in making the basement spaces less dank, but none of them wanted to hear it. Prisoners were criminals, and they deserved to be treated as such. The fact that police officers needed to work in that space too seemed beyond their grasp.

The CTC looked like a poor man's version of the White House Situation Room—lots of computer terminals arranged around an eight-foot-long rectangular conference table. The cables from the computer equipment all snaked into holes designed for that purpose into a space below the table that Warren had never cared to look at. He wouldn't have known what he was seeing even if he had.

He was the second person to arrive, after Janey Brothers, the night-shift proprietor of all things electronic. The speakers in the walls hummed with radio traffic as various police units marked responding.

"Are we up and running?" Warren asked.

"Radios and phones are functional," Janey said. "But there's no video to show yet."

"I want an open line to the EOC." Emergency Operations Center—fancy name for the dispatch center.

Janey pointed to the headset that hung from a hook on Warren's designated terminal at the end of the table. "Already established," she said. "You can use that dial there to switch between the EOC and radio traffic on the scene."

Warren sat in his chair, donned the headset and turned the dial from mute. "EOC, this is Michaels. Anybody there?"

"Right here, Chief," said the familiar voice of Ray Boyd, the man who ran the night shift—the knife and gun club—at the EOC.

"Excellent," Warren said. "Let's get to work."

"Scorpion, Mother Hen. Emergency traffic."

Jonathan shifted his eyes from the windshield to the computer feed from Roxie while he pressed the transmit button in the center of his ballistic vest—the very vest onto which he had affixed a Velcro panel that read FBI.

"Go ahead."

"I've been monitoring Braddock County police and fire radio traffic. They just dispatched a major shooting incident. Multiple active shooters in Mason's Corner. Oh my God, I do Christmas shopping there every year. I was going there next weekend."

"Whoa, look at that," Boxers said, pointing ahead through the windshield. Police officers swarmed out of the headquarters building like bees leaving a hive. Most were heavily armed, and all of them were headed for parked cruisers.

"The dispatcher is calling for all personnel and issuing a recall of off-duty officers," Venice went on.

"Please tell me we're not going to join that fight," Boxers said off the air.

Jonathan ignored him and keyed his mike again. "Okay, we can't wait any longer," he said. "Use a blocked burner phone to call the Braddock County Police Department. Tell them that it's very likely that they are about to be swarmed by terrorists. They're going to want to know who you are and how you know. Just tell them that you are a reliable source, and that they need to take action."

"Suppose you're wrong?" Venice asked.

"Then I'll be wrong and they'll have spent some time being overprepared. But I'm not wrong."

"Okay," Venice said. But Jonathan could tell that her heart wasn't in it. At times like these, when there were so many moving parts to monitor, making a phone call based on an assumption was a pain in the ass.

Jonathan looked back to the feed from Roxie. The car he'd been following sat still, its doors closed. While he didn't have eyes on the other two cars, he could only imagine that they, too, were being patient.

"Tell me what you're thinking, Boss," Boxers said.

"I think that the attack on the mall is a diversion from the attack here, on the police station," Jonathan said. "And vice versa. I think they're using a mass shooting to drain the station, and then they're going to come in strong and take out everyone they can."

"And then what?" Big Guy asked. "What do you do with a captured police station?"

"Spray and slay and get away," Jonathan said. "Terror isn't about capturing ground, it's about making everyone feel unsafe."

"Scorpion, Mother Hen." Venice again. Ahead, the exodus from the headquarters building had slowed to a trickle.

"Go."

"This is getting worse," she said. "The BCPD dispatcher just said that the mall shooters are police officers."

Jonathan and Boxers exchanged glances. "The uniforms," they said in unison.

Over the air, Jonathan said, "Have you gotten through to them yet?"

"Not yet."

"Well, when you do, tell them not to shoot the guys in the FBI tactical gear."

"Say again?"

"Oh, shit," Boxers said. He pointed to the Roxie feed, where heavily armed men poured out of the doors of the Cherokee. "Here they come."

Chapter Twenty-nine

Pam kept the doorjamb pressed to her shoulder as she dared a look into the mall, down to the left, down toward where the shots were coming from. What she saw sickened her. Bodies of the dead and wounded lay everywhere. She could see ten of them in a single glance. People moaned, and the usually white tile glistened red and wet.

But she saw no shooters. She could *hear* them—hell, the whole world could *hear* them—and there was definitely more than one. She fought the temptation to call 911 and report what she saw. They'd be flooded with calls as it was, and she had plenty to do.

"I don't see a shooter," she said to Josh. "We need to find them and try to end this."

Josh looked terrified. His face had grown pale, and his hands shook. But he said, "Okay. Do you want to split up?"

This was new territory for Pam. She'd gone through the motions of active shooter training, but she wasn't a SWATer and had never wanted to be. On the one hand, she supposed they could cover more ground separately, but there was a reason why SWAT guys stayed together.

"No," she said. "Stay on me. If you see a shooter, shoot him."

"But they're cops," Josh said.

"Not today, they're not."

"But real cops will be here soon."

And that was the nightmare: blue-on-blue shooting. "Then be careful," she said. "And try real hard to be sure."

The gunfire never stopped. It was no longer the full-auto sound that she'd heard in the first volley, but it was a sustained rate of single-shot fire. It seemed to be coming from everywhere, but as she eased out into the wide-open spaces of the mall, she realized how impossible it was to *see* everywhere. She kept her Glock in the number-three position, drawn and in a two-handed grip, but in tight to her body. From here, she could push out to shoot a target at any level, but as she passed doorways, no one could reach out and snatch her weapon from her.

She advanced at a low crouch, bent deeply at the knees, moving in exactly the opposite direction of the dozens of fleeing shoppers that swirled past her.

"Get under cover!" she yelled to the fleeing victims, and she made wide sweeping motions with her left arm. "Don't stay in the open! Get inside a store!"

Two of them sprawled face-first onto the tile floor as two rifle reports reverberated off the walls. Those shots were twice as loud as the others, and Pam knew that a gunman was coming this way.

Josh darted out from behind her to help one of the fallen shoppers, but Pam grabbed his belt and pulled him back. "The wounded wait till the shooters are accounted for. They're for EMS to handle, not for us." Of the lessons that stuck from the SWAT-lite training she *had* received, that was the one that resonated loudest, because she imagined it was the one that the general public realized least. In an active shooter situation, the victims were likely to be on their own for a long time.

"Can you see him?" Josh asked.

"Negative, but he's close." They were crossing in front of a store that catered to teenaged girls. *Rich* teenaged girls, whose tastes even in the wintertime tilted toward covering as little skin as possible. Inside, it appeared empty save for the mannequins, but Pam assumed that people were cowering behind the display cases.

She was startled, then, when a female mannequin spoke. In a male voice. "He's up there," the voice said.

Pam whirled on him. He was a kid himself, maybe twenty years old, and he held his hands up at chest level. In his right, he held a pistol. Looked like an M&P Shield 9 millimeter. Nice weapon, not your typical thug gun.

"Please don't shoot me," the kid said. He seemed calmer than the circumstances warranted. "It's been a bad enough day already." And a silver shield dangled from his shirt pocket.

Josh nodded to it. "You a cop?"

"Firefighter," the kid said. "David Boone. The badge is a little something to keep me from being shot as a bad guy."

"That's impersonating an officer," Josh said.

"Yeah, like that's my biggest damn problem," David said. "Want to see my carry permit?"

"No," Pam said. This was a stupid conversation, and she wanted to get past it. "Just know that if you shoot, somebody's going to shoot back."

"After this is over, I'll take you back to my apartment and show you my bronze star," David said. "Not my first rodeo."

Apparently, he was older than he looked. Or he was lying his ass off. Pam didn't care either way. "Pam Hastings," she said. "This is Josh Levine. We're cops. Real ones, not the ones who are shooting. You said you know where he is?"

David pointed downrange. "One of them, yeah. He wanders around down there. Pacing, kind of. Like he's got an assigned AO. Sorry, area of operation. I haven't been able to get a clean shot, and with the discrepancy in firepower, I didn't want to give my position away."

There was no quibbling with his logic. It was a particularly strong argument since he thought he was all alone.

"So do you want to come with us on the hunt, or do you want to hunker down?"

"Hunkering is not all that it's hyped up to be. I'll come along."

"How many rounds do you have for that thing?" Josh asked.

"Eight plus one."

"Any spare mags?" Pam asked.

"The mall management doesn't want me to carry a gun in here in the first place. Didn't you see the sign on the door?"

Pam took that as a no. She looked to Josh. "Spares?"

He winced his answer.

She did the math aloud. "I've got eleven. Josh, you have sixteen, and David's got nine. What is that, a total of thirty-six? Against a bunch of AR-fifteens. Oh, yeah. We've got this. Well, here we go. Stay low and shoot straight."

"I've seen two of them," David said. "Looks like they've got ballistic armor."

Pam's shoulders sagged. "Of course they do. Then go for pelvis and head shots." Combined with center-of-mass, those were the most devastating locations to be shot.

She led the way closer to the shooter, who continued to pound away at targets she couldn't see and from a location that was invisible. Her team advanced as a cluster of three, staying in physical contact with each other—another lesson from SWAT-lite, and apparently one that was taught to soldiers as well. By keeping the shops to their left, only half a world needed to be covered.

The rifle fire got louder, as if the shooter had turned a new direction, toward them instead of away.

Pam saw the muzzle flash before she saw the rifle, but only by a second or so. And there he was, wrapped in the uniform of her colleagues, committing murder at random. The uniform had its desired effect, trigging that hard-wired hesitation.

The gunman saw her. He swung his rifle to cover her. To kill her.

Pam settled her front sight on his head.

Two gunshots from inches away rattled her, and the

distant gunman dropped, his brain circuitry fried by
bullets from David Boone's gun.

Pam was still trying to make sense of it when David
said, "Weapons and ammo. Cover me." And he was
off.

"Holy shit," Josh said, and he stood.

Pam stood, too. She watched in awe and terror as
David Boone dashed into the open expanse of the mall
and headed straight for the body.

From her new vantage point, Pam could see another
shooter on the far side of the mall. He turned and
aimed his weapon at David. Pam got the shooter in her
sights and pressed the trigger. Again. Again and again.

At this range, snap-shot pistol fire had little chance
of hitting its target, but it was guaranteed to break the
concentration of the person being shot at. The shooter
dropped out of sight behind a couple of faux beer bar-
rels that anchored a faux hitching post that was supposed to entice people to buy leather goods from the
store behind it. Pam didn't know if he'd been hit or if
he was just ducking out of the line of fire. On the one
hand, it didn't matter because he wasn't shooting anymore. On the other, if he was alive he could get up and
shoot again.

"I'm keeping an eye on that guy over there," Pam
said. "Josh, keep scanning for targets."

"Gotcha," he said.

Pam didn't bother to see what he was doing or how
he was doing it. She wasn't his training officer, and
now, in the thick of things, he either knew what he was
doing or he didn't. She kept her concentration on the
spot where her target had dropped, but couldn't resist

the urge to watch through her peripheral vision as David stripped the dead shooter of his rifle.

Clearly working from muscle memory, David dropped the magazine out of the well, pulled another one from a pouch on the shooter's vest, and slid it into place. He threw a glance over his shoulder, flashed a thumbs-up to Pam, then pointed to the spot where the other guy had dropped.

Pam didn't know what he was trying to tell her.

He pointed again, then pointed at himself, and then pointed back at the man they couldn't see. Surely, he was not going—

David spun away from Pam, brought his new rifle up to his shoulder, and then advanced on the hidden bad guy.

"The hell is he doing?" Josh asked. His voice squeaked an octave higher than normal.

Pam broke her aim lest she accidentally shoot David, and watched, stunned, as he charged the barrel at a crouch, firing single shots as he moved, launching 5.56 millimeter bullets through the barrel and through whatever lay behind it. A man in a police uniform—the shooter—slouched onto the floor from behind the barrel. When David was three feet away, he shot the dead man in the head.

With these two down, the sound of gunfire seemed distant. Still present, but concentrated at a different part of the mall.

"We need to help the wounded," Josh said.

"Not yet."

"But they're dying!"

"What are you going to do?" Pam snapped. "You don't have—"

"Hey!" David yelled from across the mall.

Pam's head snapped around.

"Weapons and ammo! Jesus!"

Pam felt embarrassed. He was correct, of course. The fight wasn't over yet, and they had a diminishing opportunity to level the odds for themselves. At least a little. "Cover me," she said.

She holstered her Glock and ran to the first man David had killed. Her skin crawled with the certainty that she was being watched and that a bullet would pierce her at any minute. She arrived at the body. The fake cop's sidearm was a Glock 19—standard department issue—and rather than deal with the firearm itself, she relieved him of his full magazines, sliding them out of their pouches on his gun belt, four in total, plus the full mag still in his pistol, bringing the total to five.

And she realized that she didn't have enough hands. "Josh!" she called. "Come here!"

Five seconds later, he slid to a stop next to her.

"Take this guy's mags. You've got what's in the gun plus two more. The other two are for me." One thing Glock had going for it was that all magazines of a given caliber fit into any other gun of a similar caliber. Thus, the fifteen-round mags from the dead guy's Glock 19 fit perfectly in the grip of her own pistol, which was designed for only a ten-round mag.

"Don't forget his vest!" David called from closer than he was before. He was a fast worker. Somehow, he'd already donned his guy's vest and gun belt, and he carried two M4s.

"You look like Rambo," Pam said.

"I don't believe you just did that," Josh said. His admiration was palpable.

"A sergeant major told me once that in a gunfight, the best way to live is to kill. Who gets the other vest?"

Pam pointed to Josh. "Him. The rifle, too."

Josh looked stunned. "What about you?"

"I'll get another one," she said. She caught the look that passed between the two men, but she pretended not to. She was the senior cop, which meant that the junior cop got the better gear. It sucked, but it was a better alternative than living with the grief and second-guessing that would follow if Josh got hurt and she was wearing the only set of body armor—that was obtained for them by a civilian, no less.

"Who do you want to be in charge?" David asked.

"That would be me," Pam said. She felt a flash of anger. Defensiveness, maybe.

"Fine by me," David said with a grin. "Lead, and I will follow. It's been too long since I've been in a good shoot-out."

Pam looked over her shoulder, and Josh was finishing with the last of the Velcro straps on his vest. They were ready to go hunting.

Ray Boyd considered cell phones to be simultaneously among the best and worst inventions ever created. And on a night like this, when the EOC was erupting in telephoned reports of a terrorist attack at Mason's Corner, combined with the terrified reports from the wounded seeking medical assistance, the nonstop action made the building feel like a living organism.

In a way that no one outside of emergency services could ever understand, these were the moments he lived for, the moments that made the average days of routine drudgery seem every bit worth the cost. He sat at an elevated console surrounded by an arc of computer monitors from which he could keep track of the activity of each of the fourteen call taker/dispatchers, who themselves sat behind a computer console that fed to a master status screen that was mounted on the wall.

Right now, that master screen showed every police vehicle and ambulance from three counties converging on Mason's Corner Shopping Center. Television monitors flanked the status screen, each of them tuned to a different local news station. In a far corner a college intern monitored Twitter and Facebook for postings there.

On a night like this, Ray Boyd did not field emergency calls himself, but rather dictated the order of dispatch, and coordinated the dispatch of fill-in units who would stage in the fire stations and cruise the police corridors that had been stripped of emergency responders. The public had no idea how exposed they were at times like this. With such a rush to the site of multiple active shooters, anyone who had a heart attack right now would either die or find a way to drive himself to a hospital. And good luck finding a bed when the emergency rooms were being flooded with trauma victims.

Despite the swirl of activity, and the urgency of it all, Ray's mind recorded it as time slowed to half speed. He sensed that his hearing was better and that his comprehension skills were at their peak. And he knew that when this finally ended, he would be utterly exhausted.

And fulfilled.

"Ray!"

He heard his name shouted from somewhere across the room and his head snapped up from his plan to backfill ambulances. He didn't know where the shout came from, and frankly, he was annoyed by the violation of protocol. He did not permit shouting in the EOC.

"Ray!"

It was Devon Jefferson, a seven-year EOC veteran, and he was waving his hand to get his attention.

"Pick up two-two-four-four. You need to hear this."

It was the kind of request that didn't happen very often. He fought the urge to ask for an explanation, knowing that the explanation would present itself as soon as he answered the phone.

"Emergency operations center, Boyd."

The female voice on the other end of the phone was both pleasant and businesslike. She spoke in clipped words that projected urgency. "You need to warn the people inside the Braddock County Police Department that an attack force is on the way into their building," she said.

Jonathan watched the infrared Roxie feed. Heavily armed men, clad all in black, streamed from the car they'd been following and from two more. Call it thirteen, fifteen people. They swarmed toward the front of the police station, weapons up and ready to go, but they moved carefully.

"Definitely a planned operation," Jonathan said.

"If we're going to engage, let's engage now," Boxers said. "Hit them from the rear and then flank them."

As he spoke, he lifted his 7.62 millimeter Heckler & Koch 417 rifle and snapped its lug to his sling.

Jonathan pointed to the screen, and then looked out through the front windshield. "Doesn't look like we're going to have a choice," he said. Two members of the assault team were heading toward the Batmobile, weapons to their shoulders.

Jonathan slapped the computer closed to bring blackness to the space, and he rocked his night vision goggles down over his eyes. The four-tube array gave him near panoramic vision. His vision flared a bit from the streetlights, but the additional detail outweighed the inconvenience.

"Mother Hen, we're going hot," Jonathan said. "Big Guy, you've got—"

"The one on the left. Yep."

In unison, they threw open their doors. There was no interior light to give them away, but the sound startled the approaching attackers. They stopped and each dropped to a knee.

Jonathan extended the barrel of his suppressed M27—a Marine Corps variant of the 5.56 millimeter Heckler & Koch Model 416—through the space between his bulletproof windshield and bulletproof door frame. It would not be a fair fight, but Jonathan worked very hard *never* to participate in a fair fight. To his left, Boxers mirrored Jonathan's position and stance.

Jonathan settled his infrared laser sight on his target's head and fired a single shot at nearly the same instant that Boxers' suppressor barked a louder and equally deadly report. Both attackers fell in unison. Given the spray of bone and brain, there was no reason to confirm that they were kill shots.

"Two sleeping," Jonathan said. That was for Venice's benefit. On assaults like this, Jonathan never used the body cam. Those were for collecting information they could use, not evidence that could be used against them.

Up ahead, the sound of unsuppressed rifle fire drew Jonathan's attention to the front of the police station building, where the invading phalanx of terrorists had ambushed a straggler cop who had exited the doors. The number of gunshots at that range meant certain death. Jonathan's blood boiled.

"What are we gonna do, Boss?" Boxers asked over the air. Their radios were set to VOX, which meant that every word they said was transmitted.

Jonathan's head raced. He knew they were going to get into the fight, but there was too much distance between himself and the opposition to simply open up from here. Plus, there was the issue of the background. You couldn't shoot through windows and walls when you knew there were good guys among the bad guys on the other side.

Jonathan closed his eyes to recall the diagram he'd studied of the layout of the police station. "Mother Hen, the power supply and the backup generator are both on the black side, is that correct?"

"That's correct," Venice said. "In the rear of the building near the right-hand corner."

"I copy. Come on, Big Guy. We need to even the odds."

"Scorpion, Mother Hen."

"Go."

"Be advised, I got through to Braddock County's

nine-one-one system. I told them, but I'm not sure they believed me."

Ethan kept his eyes on Wendy as he told his story. He didn't know if a panic attack was an actual thing, but that's how he described it. He'd been sitting alone in his cell, cross-legged on the padded concrete slab they called a cot, trying to read a novel about dragons and shit he didn't care about when the reality of his future piled in on him again.

He'd tried to concentrate on the positive—on the fact that he wasn't guilty until he'd been proclaimed such, and that there was always a chance that his luck would turn—but then the reality of the discomfort and the stale air and the concrete walls creeped in. He tried to find that damned dock again, the one that his previous shrinks told him would be a sanctuary from the traumas of his past, but it wouldn't show itself. Perhaps it had been consumed and torn from its moorings by the vines of misery that only grew stouter and stronger.

His heart raced, his breathing huffed, and as his vision went sparkly, the walls had started to move—literally, they started to move. They closed in tighter and tighter. He couldn't breathe. He panicked. He pounded on the doors and he screamed, but the assholes wouldn't let him out. Couldn't they see that he was going to be crushed?

"And then when they finally opened the doors, I thought they were letting me out," he said, recounting the story. "I swear to God that's what I thought, so I dove out of the door and the struggle started. I couldn't

go back in. I just couldn't. I tried to make them understand, but they wouldn't. Hell, maybe they couldn't.
Shit, now that I hear myself telling the story I think I'm
bat-shit crazy myself. They tazed me, and here I am."

Through the entire telling of his tale, Wendy never
once looked up from her notes, never once made eye
contact. Ethan didn't know how to read that. Was she
pissed? Was she believing him, or did she think he was
bullshitting? Did she even care one way or the other?
When he was done, he waited. He had no place to go,
and couldn't go there even if he did. Waiting out her
response at least prolonged the time during which he'd
have company.

It took her a while. When she made eye contact, she
looked tired. "Ethan," she said, "you're not helping yourself with outbursts like this. Pushing aside the physical
damage you're causing to your body and your psyche,
there's the damage you're doing to your case. Remember that we're trying to paint a picture of you being a
victim forced into an instantaneous rage that could
qualify as temporary insanity. In a perfect world, we'll
be able to spin that further into the picture of an innocent young man who merely defended himself after the
fact. I'm not a lawyer, so I don't know the legal ins and
outs, but that's the gist of it. Antics like the one you
pulled tonight do serious harm. The prosecutor is sure
to show the video feed to the jury. I haven't seen it. I
don't know what it looks like, but I know it can't be
good."

"I couldn't help it," Ethan said. He felt tears pressing.

"Yes, you can," Wendy said. "You can and you
have to. If you hope to avoid a life sentence—or a

death sentence—you have to start living a script. Do you understand that?"

"What kind of a psychiatrist are you? You want me to live a lie?"

Wendy smacked her notepad against the flesh of his bound foot. An act of frustration, not malice. "No, I don't want you to live a lie. I want you to live to live. You can share your angst with me, and with no one else. Everything you say can and will be used against you. Remember those words? Between now and your trial—and up to and including any appeals if they're necessary or forthcoming—consider yourself under a microscope. There are levels of honesty which you simply cannot afford. We can agree that it sucks, but that's the deal. Can you wrap your head around that?"

Ethan tried to sit up, but the straps wouldn't permit it. "How am I supposed to do that, Wendy? How am I supposed to keep the walls from closing in?"

"Coping skills," she said. "You've got them. We've talked about them. Use them."

"I can't help what my mind does!"

"Bullshit, Ethan. Bull, period. Shit, period. You have to find a way out of the spiral of making yourself the victim in your own tragic narrative, and start seeing yourself as the architect of your own future. If that future involves years in prison, then you need to find a way to turn that into something that is not awful. Find God, get a degree, teach people how to sew, or raise a pet bird in your cell. Whatever it is, you have to find it, and you have to look forward to it. That is the only secret to survival in a situation like yours."

Ethan's mind raced. How could he make her understand—

"And I'm not done yet," Wendy said. "As you search for your silver lining, you have to stop getting in your own way. These violent outbursts have to stop. That's not optional. I can't give you the kinds of drugs in here that will help you do that. On the course you're tacking now, you're guaranteed long stretches in isolation, and trust me, young man, that is not a route you want to take."

Ethan had never seen this kind of passion from his doctor before. He wasn't sure what to make of it. On the one hand, her words pissed him off, but the presence of tears in the corners of her eyes did not escape him. "You really do care about me, don't you?" he said. He winced at the corniness of his words.

"You're my patient, and I'm your doctor," she said, but he read the lack of commitment in her words. "I feel for all of my patients. But some have had a much lousier deal than others."

Somewhere in her words and in her eyes, Ethan found a sense of peace, a source of hope. Maybe she was right. If this terrible hand was the one he was destined to be dealt, then maybe he could—

A series of *bangs* startled him. He and Wendy jumped together. "Oh, God," Ethan said. "Were those gunshots?"

Chapter Thirty

Warren listened to the words Ray Boyd spoke, but he wasn't sure he comprehended them. "Who was this person?" he asked.

"She wouldn't identify herself," Boyd explained. "She implied she was with the government—an alphabet agency, I presume—and she stated it as fact. You're going to be attacked. And she said not to shoot the people in FBI vests."

Warren looked to Janey, who of course had no idea what was being said because Warren was on a headset. "Okay," Warren said into his phone. "Let me know if you hear anything else."

He clicked off and shifted his gaze to his computer screen, where he pulled up the extension for Yolanda Pierce, the IT lady who was burning the midnight oil. She answered her phone on the second ring.

"Yolanda," Warren said. "Chief Michaels. I need you to do me a favor and I need you to not ask why."

"Sure, Chief," she said.

"I need you to lock this facility down. Every lock closed, inside and out."

"It's too late," she said. Was that a smile he heard in her voice? "They're already here."

Through the phone, and through the walls, he heard the sound of gunfire.

The others in the CTC heard it, too, and in unison they turned to Warren. He didn't understand the details, but he understood that simultaneous attacks did not happen coincidentally. He spun in his chair and pointed to Janey. "You. Lock this door. Nobody gets in and nobody leaves till I say so. I don't care if it's the county executive or the president of the United States, *nobody* gets through that door."

Janey spun out of her swivel chair and dashed to the door, where she typed in the requisite four-digit code. Her body language said it all. Her shoulders sagged as her hands began to shake. She tried the code again.

"It won't work, sir," she said. "I can't lock the door."

Warren rose from his chair to join her at the door. "Do it manually," he said.

"We can't," Janey declared. "This building is state-of-the-art. Everything's controlled by electric locks."

"There's no manual override?"

"There probably is, but I don't know where or how." Janey looked embarrassed. "I'm sorry, Chief, but this has never come up before. Tom Castriotta will probably know. He's the day shift guy. He gets all the training."

"Get him on the phone," Warren snapped. "Now."

More gunfire, this time louder. Closer.

"Um, Chief?" Janey said. She held the telephone out, as if offering a sacrifice. "The phones are out."

* * *

Jonathan and Boxers moved with practiced speed and agility as they glided across the parking lot as a single entity, a shooter team whose rifles covered every compass point and whose feet never tangled. Jonathan led the way, walking forward and sweeping the forward 180 degrees, and Boxers moved backward, sweeping the six o'clock half of the horizon. The police compound was a sprawling structure, covering what must have been an acre or more of footprint.

Inside the station, gunfire kicked up. From the rhythm of the shooting, it sounded like a two-sided battle.

Jonathan picked up his pace. Halfway down the red side of the building—the right-hand side—he saw the big windows for what he knew from the drawings to be the training room. He stopped and grabbed a fistful of Boxers' vest. "Big Guy, stay here and set a charge that will get us in through that window. I can blow the electricity and the generator. When it's dark, I'll come back and we'll make the breach."

He walked away without waiting for a response. He moved faster now, nearly at a run, as he approached the red-black corner.

He nearly lost his shit when he saw two of the bad guys already back there, finishing work with a pair of wire cutters. His approach was quiet enough that they didn't see him until he was only a few yards away. They reached for their rifles, and Jonathan killed them both with a single shot apiece.

"Sitrep," Boxers demanded over the air. "What the hell was that?"

"Two more sleeping," Jonathan said. "Looks like they cut the phone lines."

"Were they going for the electricals, too?" Boxers asked.

"Negative." That would have been significant if they had. That would mean the bad guys were equipped with night vision, which was the single big advantage Jonathan and Big Guy had over them.

Jonathan stepped over the bodies and dropped to one knee while unslinging his rucksack. He could have done what was coming blindfolded. He found the GPC among others that he always carried in an outside pocket of his ruck. A general-purpose charge was a premade block of C4 explosive with a tail of detonating cord (literally, a tube stuffed with PETN explosive) and two initiators already taped into place. As imprecise as they were deadly and effective, Jonathan typically used them to make entry, but this one would be more than enough—way, way more than enough—to sever the electrical connections.

The cool weather worked against him as he did his best to mold the GPC to the electrical feed. When he was done, it was ugly, but it was functional. Boxers had designed the ignition chain himself by taping electric matches to the ends of twenty seconds' worth of OFF—old-fashioned fuse. Powered by a watch battery, the match leads were separated by a piece of plastic, which, when pulled out of the way, completed a circuit and lit the match, which would in turn light the fuse.

Timing was important now. Once the fuse was lit, a big boom followed. It made sense, then, to kill the back-up generator first. "I'm shooting the generator," he said for Boxers' benefit. Then he emptied what was left of his thirty-round magazine of 5.56 millimeter bullets through the metal walls of the generator. Whatever he hit caused a shower of sparks, which in turn triggered a fire. Even if the whole assembly ignited, Jonathan didn't think the fire could propagate to the building.

He pivoted and returned his attention to the GPC. "Fire in the hole, fire in the hole, fire in the hole," he said, almost as one word, and he pulled the pin. He got the spark and the burning fuse he wanted, and it was time to go.

While the fuse burned, Jonathan ran back to join Boxers, whose posture screamed impatience. He stood off to the side of the window, pressed against the brick. "Aren't we in a hurry anymore?" he asked.

Twenty seconds seemed like a very long time.

The world shook as Jonathan's charge erupted, plunging their surroundings into darkness.

Boxers laughed. "Jesus, how much did you use?"

"A GPC."

"For an electrical box? I don't ever wanna hear crap from you again about me using too much dynamite." He was amused. "You might want to step a little closer to me," he added.

Jonathan got the subtext and pressed against the wall next to Big Guy. Two seconds later, a smaller blast eliminated all of the glass from the window to the training room.

"Time to go?" Big Guy asked.

"Tallyho," Jonathan said. He buttonhooked to the left, heaved himself over the fractured sill, and dropped into the darkness of the police station. He noticed that the shooting had stopped. "I think we got them thinking," he said.

* * *

Pam Hastings felt woefully under-armed, despite the spare magazines she'd found, and the act of ignoring the pained cries of the wounded seeking assistance had begun to eat away at her soul. This was a nightmare, and the shooting continued. She couldn't begin to imagine how many hundreds or thousands of rounds had been dumped into this crowd of preholiday shoppers. The thought of it sickened her. But it also steeled her for bringing more of these assholes to justice.

As Pam led the way, she could not escape the terrible feeling that she was living beyond her ability. She'd never hunted a shooter team before. Hell, she'd never shot at anyone before—not *really,* outside of a simunition drill—and here she had a combat veteran and a whelp of a police officer counting on her to know what was the right thing to do. This was madness.

This was reality. Her reality. Her present and her future. A world where her past didn't matter.

They moved as a three-sided creature, each of them having no choice but to trust both of the others. She walked forward while the others walked a combination of backward and sideways.

"David, am I doing this right?" she asked. It was better to admit weakness and be alive than it was to ride your charade to the grave.

"You're doing great, Detective," David said. "The trick is to not hesitate. Do me a favor and don't shout out any of that 'don't move' shit. If you see a shooter, take him out. If it comes to that I promise I'll testify that you gave him a chance to surrender."

"There's a dogleg up ahead," Pam reported. "It turns

to the right, and I think that's where the next shooter is."
The shooting sounded louder as they approached.

"Roger that," David said.

"You still there, Josh?" Pam asked.

"This is our first date," he said. "A gentleman always escorts his date to her door at the end of the evening."

Pam smiled. "Just so you know, your chances of getting lucky tonight are something south of zero."

"Noted," Josh said.

"You know I'm still here, right?" David asked over a chuckle. "At least we can all die horny."

The words tickled her and Pam laughed.

The distance to the shooter was getting ever shorter. God, she wished she had a rifle. Soon.

The shooting stopped.

"What's that?" Josh asked.

"That's silence," David said. Although, considering the wailing of the wounded and the grieving, the mall was anything but silent. In fact, it was a cacophony of pain.

Pam didn't like it. The absence of gunfire felt like a trap, a lure to pull them into a killing zone. But how could they—and who the hell were *they*?—even know that Pam and her team were present?

"Stay sharp," she said. "We're approaching the turn."

Outside, beyond the walls of the shopping mall, the sound of sirens crescendoed.

"You know that arriving officers are going to see us as the shooters, right?" Josh said.

"Look innocent," David quipped.

The wounded and dead lay everywhere, among shards of glass and abandoned shoes, spectacles and handbags.

Bullets had shredded everything and everyone. Pam tried not to see the heads without faces, the shoulders without heads. The bloody blobs of unidentifiable tissue. They were not her responsibility. Moreover, she did not *want* them to be her responsibility. Right now, hers was a mission of vengeance, not mercy. She sensed that it would be years before room opened in her heart again for mercy.

An Oriental pagoda marked the pivot point in the center hallway of the mall. Designed as the retail space of wasabi paste, folding fans, and any number of borderline racist artifacts of the Japanese culture, its primary feature tonight was the lifeless body of the very blond, very not-Asian corpse of a teenaged salesman whose spine glimmered white through an exit wound just above his shoulders.

"Look past it," David said from behind. "He's gone, and we're still here. Focus on that."

Practical words for a very impractical time. They helped.

"We're about to pivot right," Pam said to her team. And that's what they did. Up ahead, where she expected to encounter gunmen, she saw only more of the dead and wounded. There was no one to shoot at, and no one shot at her.

She stopped.

"What's up?" David asked.

"Where are the shooters?" Joshed said.

Pam scanned all compass points, ready to shoot anyone in a police uniform, or anyone who dared to point a firearm at her. All she saw were victims. "I don't know," she said. "Stay on me. We're moving."

It was hard not to get cocky, not to get lazy. If there were a target to shoot, it would be shooting at her, right? It was hard not to get distracted by the suffering, the crying, the pleading.

She led her team down the wide hallway to the place where the floor was littered with hundreds of spent shell casings. This was the spot where the shooter stood, but where was the shooter?

"Oh, my God," Josh said.

His words got Pam's attention, and she turned to see him pointing to the ground, where a police uniform shirt, a ballistic vest and an M4 had been dumped in a pile.

"They're gone," David said. "That's brilliant." He recoiled from the looks he got from the others. "Hey, I'm on your side," he said. "But this is friggin' brilliant."

Pam wanted to disagree, but she couldn't. Instead, she reached for her cell phone and dialed 911.

Chapter Thirty-one

Bedlam reigned in the basement holding area of the police station. Uniformed officers swarmed everywhere out in the hallway. "Lock us down!" someone yelled. "Lock us down! Lock us down!"

"Unlock the guns, for God's sake," someone else shouted.

Ethan felt the panic rising again, and he struggled against the shackles that held him to his bed. "Let me out! I don't want to die like this."

"Nobody's going to die," Wendy said, and she winced at the stupidity of her own words. Of course people were going to die. They were dying right now. People were shooting and yelling and dying. "I think we're safe," she said. "There's a lot of security down here. A lot of doors." She knew, though, that she looked every bit as terrified as she felt.

"The doors won't lock!" a voice yelled from the hallway.

The gunfire edged closer.

Ethan rattled his bonds. "Let me out of these!" Everything held fast. "Please!"

An explosion rocked the building and the lights went out. Only the dim glow of emergency lights remained.

An instant later, a second explosion might have actually moved the foundation. The shooting stopped for a bit, maybe ten seconds. When it resumed, it did so with double the ferocity.

Spike and his team had been able to fight their way into the middle of the police station with relatively little resistance. It helped immeasurably that so many of the cops were on the road heading toward the shopping mall, which by now should be empty of assaulters if Drew was able to hold to the plan. The operation was going perfectly. In just a few hours, they would all have shit pots of tax-free money, and the United States would be a different place.

They'd entered through the front doors and moved all the way down the front hallway, engaging only three officers along the way, not counting the one they killed on the front sidewalk. They'd driven down to the chief's office, only to be disappointed that no one was there.

"Did anybody see the chief leave?" he asked the assembled group.

"He's downstairs," said a female voice from down the hall.

Ten rifles shifted toward her simultaneously.

"No!" she said. "I'm Yolanda! Yolanda Pierce. I'm working with Sergeant Dale. The command staff is either all downstairs in the CTC, or they're on their way to the mall."

"The CTC?" Spike asked.

"It means Crisis Tactical Center."

"The jail cells are downstairs, too, aren't they?"

Yolanda pointed behind her, toward a big metal door. "It's down there. I've disabled the locks. Every lock in the building is out of service"

"You did that?" Spike asked.

She beamed.

"Why?"

"We have to take our country back from the police," she said. "I only work here to do as much harm as I can from the inside. Sergeant Dale and I have been working on this for months."

"Is Sergeant Dale here?" Spike asked.

"No, he went home. He didn't want to risk being here." Yolanda seemed proud of her bravery.

"When you think about it," Spike said, "that was probably a good move." He raised his rifle to arm's length, holding it like a pistol, and fired a single round through Yolanda's chest.

"Jesus!" someone yelled.

"No choice," Spike said. "If she'll betray her boss, she'll betray us, too. There's no better way to keep a secret than to kill the bitch who holds it."

Others on his team seemed shocked.

"Hey, it's war," Spike said. "People die in war."

An explosion shook the building, followed a few seconds later by a second one. Bathed in instant darkness, someone yelled, "What the hell was that?"

Spike didn't know for a fact, but he had his suspicions. The cops were somehow mounting a counterassault. "Light!" he shouted. "Give me light!" He twisted his muzzle light to life, and the rest of his team followed

suit, their white beams cutting wedges through the dust
that had been knocked free by the blasts.

The blasts came from the red side of the building.
Spike worked the problem in his head in seconds. There
was only one reasonable path of access from there. The
counterassault had to come from the front hallway.

"I want a defensive line halfway down this hallway," he said, indicating the green-side hallway with
the beam of his light. "Four people. Haddon, you
choose. I don't care. Move quickly. The rest of you on
me. We're going to raise some hell downstairs."

The words had barely cleared his throat when someone opened up on them from the far end of the green-
side hallway.

Jonathan didn't move from his low crouch until he
was certain that Big Guy was with him. Movement
was awkward thanks to the weight of their firearms, ammunition, and ballistic armor. They went full-soldier, as
Jonathan called it, which meant Kevlar lids and plates in
their armor that would stop rifle bullets up to 5.56 millimeter.

"Scorpion, Mother Hen," Venice said over the radio.
"Be advised that with the power down, I'm blind here. I
can't help you."

"Understood," Jonathan said. "Keep the channel
clear, please."

With his NVGs in place, the darkness looked like
green daylight. To increase their advantage, he and Big
Guy had each outfitted their long guns with infrared
muzzle lights, which worked just like any other flash-

light, but with a beam that was visible only to those wearing night vision.

"Moving," Jonathan said, and he duck-walked to the door that led to the hallway. Each step of the way, he felt Boxers' enormous frame in physical contact with him.

"Covering right," Jonathan said.

"Covering left."

"Two, one, now." With his rifle pressed to his shoulder, Jonathan swept out into the hallway and broke right, while Boxers mirrored his motion to the left.

"Clear."

"Clear."

"I think the action is on the white and green sides, Boss," Boxers said.

For sure, that was where the shooting was coming from. Jonathan scooted past Big Guy to lead the way. As the shorter man, it made no sense for Jonathan to be in the rear. He led the way to the corner of the front hallway, where he shifted his rifle to his left hand, and peeked around. He saw two bodies on the floor, the warmth of their blood glistening a brighter green in the infrared image, but no one was moving.

"Big Guy, we've got a shitload of offices between us and the green-side hallway where the action is. I say we don't bother to clear them. The bad guys are making an assault, and the only people we'll find hiding are good guys. You concur?"

"So long as they don't shoot at me, we'll be fine."

Jonathan started down the front hallway. "Watch for cops," he said. "We're not shooting those."

"No kiddin'."

As they got closer to the battle, the concussions of

the gunfire grew steadily louder. "The war's around the next corner," Jonathan said. "Remember we're feds. When we turn the corner, I want to bang 'em. Anybody not in a police uniform but holding a gun gets one chance to drop, and then we kill him."

A flashbang grenade was a tube of explosive that was designed as a distraction device. As the name implied, a flashbang launched no shrapnel, but it created a blinding flash and a teeth-rattling bang, the combined effects of which generally scared the shit out of everybody in the vicinity. He pulled one from the pouch on the right side of his vest and let his M27 fall against its sling.

They arrived at the white-green corner, and Jonathan could see the strobes of muzzle flashes reflected off of the recently painted walls of the brand-new building. "Okay, here we go," Jonathan said. "Flashbang away." He pulled the pin, peeked around the corner to make sure it wasn't going to land in some innocent's lap, and was startled to see that the bad guys had formed a skirmish line across the hallway. More accurately, they were still in the process of forming, dragging desks across the tile to provide themselves with cover. These guys knew what they were doing, and that was never a good sign. They worked in the dark with flashlights, and two shooters already had sights downrange. They lit up Jonathan, flaring his NVGs.

They yelled. Jonathan heard two shots.

The darkness in the CTC was absolute. Warren heard the breath catch in Janey's throat, and he knew he needed to act quickly to keep her from crossing over into panic. He pulled his cell phone from his pocket and swiped it open. It wasn't a lot of light, but it was enough to illuminate the way to the door and pull it open, introducing the dim glow of the battery-powered emergency lights.

Out here, chaos reigned as cops and civilians alike tried to make sense of events. "Everybody calm down!" Warren shouted.

His words seemed to have no impact. People swarmed and swirled in the darkness. They shouted at one another, but no one was listening.

"Hey!" Warren bellowed, and this time people stopped. "This is Chief Michaels, and I want everyone to calm the hell down! Who's the night shift commander down here? I want a status report!"

"Computer controls have all been overridden," said a voice from the dark. "Every door in the place is unlocked."

"Is that Sergeant Tobin?" Warren asked. "Everyone else shut up!" He walked toward the source of the voice.

"Yes, sir, this is Tobin." Neither short nor tall, Tobin had been with the department longer than Warren. He sported a giant gray walrus mustache.

"How many prisoners do we have in custody?" Now that they faced each other, they could speak at a conversational level.

"Just three. Two DUIs and the kid we have to keep long-term. Are we under attack, Chief?"

Upstairs, he heard a gunshot. And then a lot of gunshots.

"It would seem so," Warren said. "Cut the DUIs loose.

Keep an eye on the Falk kid. What is our status on weapons?"

"Weapons lockers are locked shut," Tobin said. "No one is allowed in here armed, and now we can't get access to the guns officers brought in with them. What few remain, anyway. Most of them are out on the Mason's Corner thing."

Warren surveyed the area and ran through his options.

"So, you're telling me that my gun is the only firearm down here?"

"Oh, we've got plenty of guns."

"But the lockers are locked."

He didn't need an answer from Tobin. "Well, shit," Warren said.

Blinded by the flare of his NVGs, Jonathan jumped back as the skirmishers fired. Their rounds went wide, but now they knew where he was, and these walls wouldn't provide any protection against a rifle bullet.

"Full-auto," he said to Boxers, and then he lobbed his flashbang grenade down the hall without exposing himself.

The confined space of the hallway compounded the loudness of the explosion as sound waves hit solid surfaces and reflected back. When dealing with untrained, unprepared bad guys, the effects of a flashbang could last for twenty, thirty seconds as people struggled to figure out what had just ripped their world apart midseam. Against professionals, the disorientation was measured on a far shorter scale, and that time marked the period of Jonathan's maximum advantage.

"Now!" Jonathan said, and he and Big Guy rolled out of concealment and into the hall. They shot the guys with the flashlights first, dropping them both in the first two seconds of the firefight. With the lights out of play, and darkness back on their side, they swept the hall with their IR flashlights and laser sights, and two more men with guns died with a three-round burst.

Less than ten seconds into the fight, the keepers of the barricade were all dead. Jonathan wasn't sure that any of them fired a defensive shot. But past the dead men, Jonathan saw someone duck behind a door. If he remembered the floor plan correctly, that was the door to the secure areas of the basement.

"FBI!" Jonathan bellowed. "Everybody down! Show me your hands!" It was the ruse that would, in theory, keep them from getting nailed by the good guys. He and Big Guy advanced in unison, guns up and ready.

"FBI! Don't move!"

Ahead on the right, the heavy door to the basement had been propped open. As he approached, Jonathan sensed movement from offices on either side of the hall, but all he could afford was a casual glance to see if they were friends or foes. None of them made threatening movements, so he left them alone.

The decision not to confront the occupants and secure them was a huge departure from tactical doctrine. Any one of them could be a bad guy, after all, and if so, all he would have to do was wait till Jonathan and Boxers passed and then step out and whack them from behind. Jonathan hoped that the fact that he was on the side of the angels would work to his benefit with whoever ran God's luck department, and he'd get a break.

"Don't any of you shoot me in the back," Big Guy shouted, "or I swear to God I will tear you in half and sell you for parts!" Leave it to Boxers to take a more direct approach.

When they arrived at the heavy door, Jonathan opened it a little wider, and dared a peek. "We've got two more shooters at the bottom of the steps. They're waiting for us."

Warren realized that his options had boiled down to one. "Sergeant Tobin," he said, "I want everyone out of here."

"Excuse me, sir?"

"Out," Warren said. "Cut the prisoners loose, and get everybody else outside to safety. Go out through the sally port."

When Tobin didn't respond in half a second, Warren announced his decision to everyone else. "Everybody out! Right now! I want this station cleared of all personnel, cops and civilians alike." It was the smart play, perhaps the only one. Bad guys taking over the police station was bad press no matter how you cut it. But fear of bad PR was no reason to let innocents die.

"Sergeant Tobin here will lead the way. Take nothing with you. Just get out." As he spoke, he spread his arms wide, as if to scoop people along. "Quickly, now. This station is under attack, and I want you all to get to safety."

More gunfire erupted upstairs, and then, from behind, he heard commotion on the stairs, as if people were hurrying down them.

Warren pushed harder. "You need to move quickly," he said. "Sergeant, I want this area cleared right by God now."

His stomach churned as he realized that his was the only available firearm to repel the invasion, if only for long enough to buy people time to get out.

He turned and walked backward, facing the threat that announced itself as narrow white lights bouncing up and down on the wall opposite the stairs. They were here.

Warren retreated farther down the hallway, closer to the sally port. He had to find cover.

When one of the muzzle lights swung the corner at the end of the hallway, which was now an easy thirty feet away, Warren looked back over his shoulder and confirmed that the hallway behind him—his route to safety—was clear of people. Sergeant Tobin had done his job well.

When the invaders lit Warren up with the light, he snapped off three quick shots and then hit the deck. The return fire was wild and uncoordinated, all of which inured to his benefit. At least for a few seconds. He belly-crawled backward, keeping his aim on the invaders.

They lit him up again, and he fired three more rounds.

"Sounds like more than two shooters to me," Boxers said. "Let's bang them, too. You'll probably bitch if I say frag 'em."

"Aimed shots," Jonathan said. "We roll out and take them from here." If they used a flashbang now, they'd give away some element of surprise. "I'll take the one on the right, you have the left. Are you ready?"

"Born ready."

"Two, one . . ." There was no need to count the rest of the way. Boxers reached over Jonathan's head and pulled the door wide open. Jonathan rolled into the opening, M27 to his shoulder, and nailed his man with a three-round burst to his head. The guy collapsed. Somehow Boxers' man dropped even faster.

In an operation like this, there was no deadlier, less defendable space than a stairway. In a war zone, where everyone who wasn't on your team was on the other team, you tossed a couple of fragmentation grenades to clear the way, and then you streamed in with guns for mop-up. Here, they couldn't do that because of the number of good guys presumably mixed in with the bad.

That meant crossing a space where everyone knew you had to go.

Three more shots—they sounded like pistol fire—resulted in another extended fusillade of rifle fire.

Jonathan led the way down the stairwell, pausing five steps from the bottom. The outgoing gunfire came from very close by.

"Boss, if we step out there, we're going to get ourselves caught in the crossfire."

Spike heard the suppressed bursts of gunfire from the top of the stairs, and when he turned, he saw his men down. This spot had become untenable.

"Give me covering fire," he said. "We need to disburse. We've got shooters behind us."

* * *

Jonathan heard the man's commands, and he knew what he needed to do. If he could take the good guys out of the fight, that would leave only bad guys to worry about.

"FBI!" he shouted. "Put your weapons down or I will—" His last words were lost in the eruption of covering fire down below. His enemy was moving. That meant they weren't paying close attention. At least that was his story and he was sticking to it.

"I don't think that scared 'em, Scorpion," Boxers said, his smile evident in his voice. "How do you want to go? Just fast and hard?"

There weren't a lot of options. Until Jonathan realized that he was missing the obvious. Three steps ahead, and six feet up, an exit light glowed in the darkness. He shot it, and the vision through his NVGs improved immediately.

"Nice one," Big Guy said. "We restack the deck."

"I don't think surprise is an element anymore." Jonathan reached into his vest pouch again. "Flashbang away." As before, he tossed it around the corner without looking.

"Did he just say FBI?" Warren asked the air around him. That was what Ray Boyd had told him, wasn't it? *Don't shoot the FBI.*

Warren nearly left his skin as a brilliant white light and a deafening explosion rattled the world and loosened ceiling tiles. He wasn't expecting the blast, but he recognized it as a flashbang, and he said a silent prayer that his hearing would return to normal one day. It was the distraction he needed. Keeping low, he rose to his feet and started hauling ass toward the sally port. Down to the end of the hall, a sharp right turn, and then he'd be out.

He didn't know what this FBI team was all about, but if there was a gun battle, he didn't have nearly the firepower he'd need to survive it. The only option was to get the hell out.

"Help us!" someone shouted from the darkness. It was a female voice, and it sounded familiar to him.

"Who is that?" he said, sliding to a halt. He dropped back down to one knee and pressed himself against the wall.

"Chief?" the voice asked. "It's Dr. Adams. Wendy Adams."

"Help us!" yelled another voice. Male.

"Where are you?"

"In here," they said together.

"I'm tied to a bed. I can't move."

Jonathan lifted his NVGs out of the way as he again shot left-handed to kill the banks of emergency lights and exit signs. A blind enemy was a helpless one.

After darkness fell, the muzzle lights all went out. Nobody wanted to be a target.

"FBI!" Jonathan yelled again. "We can see you, but you cannot see us. Put your weapons down, or we will shoot you just as dead as we've already shot so many of your friends. You cannot win!"

As he and Boxers stepped away from the opening of the stairs into wideness of the hallway, they paused and took inventory. Other than the two corpses that they had created, there appeared to be only one additional body in the hallway. It looked like a friendly.

"We're not really cutting these assholes a break, are we?" Boxers whispered.

"The rules are the rules," Jonathan said. "If they surrender, they live. But they've received their last warning."

When people lose the advantage of sight, their hearing becomes more acute, and while the flashbang ruined that for everyone for the foreseeable future, Jonathan had no intention of giving them a target by shouting another warning. He stood still as he scanned for targets, not wanting to risk them sensing his movement and firing a lucky shot.

"I see one," Boxers whispered. "Twenty feet on the right. His breech is still hot."

"Take him and move."

Boxers' 417 popped, and then he and Big Guy advanced ten feet and went to a knee. Suppressors were not the *silencers* of movie fame. In a closed space like this, it reduced a rifle report to the sound of a pistol shot, but it was still loud, and it reduced the muzzle flash to nearly nothing. A bad guy down on the left ducked back into the hallway to return fire, and Jonathan killed him before he could fire a shot.

The secret to victory was to confuse your opponents and then make them pay with their lives.

"How many were there, total?" Boxers whispered.

"I have no idea."

"Do you think that was the last one?"

"No."

"Neither do I."

"Time to move," Jonathan whispered.

* * *

"Good God, what did they do to you?" Warren asked. The world inside this room had returned to absolute darkness, save for the dim rectangle of light cast by the emergency lighting. He didn't dare use his phone for illumination again.

"He was unruly," Wendy whispered.

Warren pushed the heavy door closed. Now the only illumination came from the window in the door.

Ethan rattled his bonds again. "Get me out of here. Please get me out of here."

"Shh!" Warren hissed.

"I don't want to die here," Ethan whined. "Not here and not alone."

Warren's shoulders sagged. "You're not going to die alone, Ethan," he said. "I'm not going to leave you. I don't suppose you have the key by chance, do you, Dr. Adams?"

"We wouldn't be here if I did."

Outside another volley of gunfire reverberated through the hallway.

"Oh, God," Ethan said. "Oh, God, oh, God."

Somewhere beyond the walls of this kill zone, Warren heard the distant sound of approaching sirens.

"Reinforcements?" Wendy asked.

"It won't matter," Warren said. "With our doctrine, it will take ten minutes minimum to get set with a SWAT raid in here. Longer, probably, because they're already deployed to the mall."

"We don't have ten minutes, do we?" Wendy asked. Her voice cracked at the words.

"We're not entirely alone," Warren said. "I think

there's a team from the FBI here as well. That's who the attackers are exchanging fire with."

"Unlock me!" Ethan insisted.

"I can't!" Warren hissed. "And be quiet!"

Spike followed the right-hand wall in the darkness until he found the turn in the hallway and swung it. At least now he had some measure of cover from the FBI team. Who the hell called the FBI? How were they here so soon? Not that it mattered.

He was finished with this shit. Whoever and however, this counterassault team was damned good. When he did the math in his head, he didn't even know if he had any team members left. With the sound of sirens blooming in the distance, he was out of options. Without a doubt, the people who had fled were gathered outside. Even if they were not lying in wait, they now posed a near-insurmountable problem. The original plan had called for them to breeze through, kill as many as they could, and then escape. The total time on site was to be less than six minutes.

Now this. At least the emergency lights were still working on this leg of the hallway. That gave him something.

The window of opportunity for any chance at survival was closing quickly. He needed to get the hell out, or make a stand. Either way, he figured he was going to die.

Better to die fighting than die hiding. If he could find one of the holding cells, he could take refuge in there and then kill whoever opened the door, however long that took. It wasn't much, but in this narrow space, he option of moving and shooting made no sense at all—especially since his adversaries had night vision and could easily make this as dark as the other hall.

Someone said, "Get me out of here! Please get me out of here!" And it was very close, coming from behind a closed door on the left. There were more voices, too. Over the course of just a few seconds, he thought he picked up the sounds of two males and a female. Much of it was sotto voce and therefore undiscernible, but it gave him direction. He heard the stress, he could smell the fear.

And then one word rose above all the others. Someone mentioned the name Ethan.

So the mission wouldn't be a complete waste after all.

Warren heard movement beyond the door, and he placed his left hand on Ethan's shackled ankle in hopes of communicating the need for total silence. In his right, he kept his Glock tucked in close to his body, facing the window.

"Wendy, get on the floor."

"What's—"

"Get on the floor!"

Wendy stooped to a squat, and then lay down on the tile.

"What about me?" Ethan said.

"They've got to go through me first," Warren said.

The movement had stopped. In Warren's mind, someone was staging himself on the other side of the door, waiting for—

The door burst open, and Warren was blinded by an impossibly bright light that hit him straight in the face. He dove for the light, swatting it to the side at the same instant that rifle muzzle to which it was attached fired a shot into the ceiling. Warren fired, too, but apparently to no effect. As the chief focused on not letting the muzzle come back around, the attacker had a crushing grip on Warren's gun hand. Warren pulled the trigger again, but nothing happened. The struggle must have unseated the pistol's slide just enough to take the bullet out of battery.

Warren let go of his pistol. If it didn't fire once, it wasn't going to fire now, and he wanted both hands for his struggle with the rifle. He threw an elbow at the attacker's face, but he knew that he didn't land solidly.

Stars erupted behind Warren's eyes as the attacker pistol-whipped him with his own pistol. He reeled, and in that instant, he knew that he'd lost the fight.

Jonathan jumped at the sound of the gunshots, and then he realized someone was in a lot of trouble. There's a sound to hand-to-hand combat that is unlike any other, driven by grunts and growls and shouts that sounded much like any animals fighting to the death.

Those were precisely the sounds Jonathan heard pouring from the room down the hall, and he quickened his pace. Anticipating the closest of quarters, he let his M27 fall against its sling and he drew his 1911.

The temptation was to run in, but it was always a mistake to overcommit. Instead, he slowed to a brisk walk, and then pulled to a stop just outside the open door. He peeked around the corner in time to see a man in body armor deliver a stunning punch to a man in a suit.

The bigger man stood and shouldered his M4.

Jonathan reached out one-handed and shot a .45 caliber bullet at point-blank range into the attacker's ear.

It was over.

Chapter Thirty-two

Jonathan reholstered his Colt. "Is everybody okay?" he asked. He lifted his NVGs out of the way, then reached into a pocket on his thigh and withdrew a visible-light light stick. He tore open the packet, cracked the stick and shook it. The green light made everyone look ill, but at least they could see.

He stooped to see if the guy in the suit was conscious, and he was. Blood streamed from a cut over his eye, but it didn't look like a big deal. "Thanks," the guy said, and he extended his hand.

He might have just been looking for a handshake, but Jonathan decided to help him up instead.

"FBI?" the man said.

Jonathan said nothing.

"Warren Michaels. I'm chief of police here. Or I was, anyway. How bad is the carnage upstairs?"

"It's pretty bad," Jonathan said. "You lost a few, but the bad guys are all dead."

"How did you know?" Warren said. "I mean, you called ahead."

"Holy shit!" Ethan shouted. "It's him! It's you! Holy shit!" Jonathan knew without looking that Boxers had entered the room.

Big Guy helped a lady to her feet.

"Wendy, these are the guys who rescued me! Ask them. They know what happened."

Jonathan smiled. "Hello, Ethan. It's been a long time."

"See?" Ethan said. "He knows!"

The woman named Wendy stared, her mouth open a little. It was the kind of expression that Jonathan imagined people would have if they met an alien.

"Is that true?" Warren asked.

"I'm afraid it is, Chief," Jonathan said. "Your John Doe in the morgue is really named James Stepahin, and I can't think of anyone who more deserves to be on a slab."

The chief shifted his gaze between Jonathan and Boxers. He wasn't entirely buying what they were selling. "What are your names?"

"That one's Scorpion, and the other one is Big Guy," Ethan said. "Just like I've told you a thousand times."

"Those aren't names," Warren said.

"They'll do for tonight, Chief."

"You're not really FBI, are you?"

"Sure we are," Jonathan said. He pointed to the three gold letters embroidered onto the shoulder of his vest, near his knife. "It says so right there. Want me to show you a badge?"

Warren glared, not saying a word.

"Tell you what," Jonathan said. "I need to get going,

and you have some very long days ahead of you." He extended his hand and Warren shook it. "Chief, I am terribly sorry for your loss."

"You're under arrest," Warren said.

"No, I'm not. Trust me, Chief. I'm really not. Tomorrow, if you get a chance, call Irene Rivers at the FBI."

"The director?"

"Yes, sir. She'll take the call, or if not, she'll find a way to contact you. She'll tell you everything you have a need to know. Sorry to be so cryptic. As for my old friend Ethan there, cut him a break, will you?"

Warren glanced over to the shackled young man. "We'll do our best."

"Now, I do need a favor from you," Jonathan said.

Warren arched an eyebrow.

"I need you to vouch for us as we leave," Jonathan said.

"That's kind of a bold step, don't you think?" Warren said. "Especially after you *refused* to be arrested? I'm not sure that's ever happened before. And I'm definitely not sure that I'm going along with it."

Jonathan pointed to the dead man on the floor. "Be a sport," he said. "You owe me."

A few minutes later, Jonathan and Boxers walked with purpose through the sally port back toward the Batmobile. It was a good bet that people saw them, but no one seemed to notice. There were way more important sights to see than two FBI agents leaving a police station.

* * *

Jonathan suspected that he knew details about the horrors of the shooting at Mason's Corner before the chief of police did. As soon as he and Boxers were back on the road, Venice caught them up on every-thing that she'd picked up from listening to the radio channels and tracking developments on ICIS.

Apparently, after firing hundreds of rounds into the crowd, the shooters abandoned their hardware and their police uniforms and blended in with the fleeing victims. The plan was perfect in both its execution and its simplicity. Two of the bad guys had been killed by off duty officers on the scene, but the others were just gone.

"Not yet, they're not," Jonathan said.

Big Guy looked at him across the center console. "The Moose Lodge?" he asked.

Jonathan smiled.

Chapter Thirty-three

This time, Irene's security detail parted without comment to let Jonathan enter the Our Lady Chapel. Wolverine wore a wool business suit and seemed engrossed in a sheaf of papers she was reading. He stood still, waiting to be recognized.

After fifteen seconds or so, she said, "Are you going to take a seat or not?"

Jonathan helped himself to a chair one row ahead of hers, and he turned sideways, his leg cocked on the adjacent chair. "Am I in trouble?" he asked.

She had her mad face on. "You're getting harder and harder to cover for, Digger. And I don't appreciate you dragging my name into things."

"Are we talking about the Braddock County thing?"

Irene slapped her papers down on the seat next to hers. "Yes, we're talking about the Braddock County thing. You had no right to bring my name into that."

"This would be the same night when Box and I saved a whole bunch of lives?" Jonathan knew that he could do cocky better than most, and he also knew how much it pissed Wolverine off when he played that card.

"Don't you even," she said.

"I've read the news reports," Jonathan said. "Undercover FBI agents whose names cannot be revealed. I think that sounds pretty strong."

"The press is pushing hard."

"It's what they do," Jonathan said. He was not going to be repentant for having done a very good deed at no small risk to himself. "What about Ethan? Are they still planning on prosecuting him?"

"No," Irene said. "But he's going to a hospital. Inpatient treatment for a while. That young man has issues."

"But he has a pass to get out?"

"When the doctors say he is ready. It won't be tomorrow or next month, but there's hope for a good future."

It was a better outcome than Jonathan had expected. "So, why don't you tell me why I'm *really* here?" he asked.

"The Moose Lodge," she said. "Was that you?"

"I have no idea what you're talking about," Jonathan said.

"Nine dead, zero wounded," Irene said. "Ring any bells?"

He looked at the ceiling, pretended to search his memory. "No, I'm pretty sure I would have remembered that."

"I understand that it was quite a shootout," Irene said.

"Maybe it was street gangs," Jonathan offered.

"Pretty high-end ammunition for street gangs."

"Well, you know what they say about kids these days," Jonathan said.

"Do you still have a heavily modified Hummer?" Irene asked.

Jonathan didn't like the way this was going. He watched his poker face. "Maybe," he said.

"Look anything like this one?" She pulled a photograph out of an inside pocket and handed it to him. It showed a black Hummer in a body shop with lots of bullet damage in the armored plating and glass. "It's interesting that this particular vehicle has your fingerprints all over the inside."

Jonathan handed the picture back without comment. She'd get to her point soon enough.

Wolverine put the photo back into her pocket. "Don't ever forget that we share many of the same clandestine assets," she said. "The locals are really hot on this one. Nine fatalities in a shoot-out and no leads. That's the kind of story that has legs for a long time."

"Are you coming to a point where you put handcuffs on me or something?" Jonathan asked.

She scoffed. "You know better than that," she said. "Just tell me that you're sure it was them."

Jonathan ran his options. Generally, he avoided any form of confession to Irene, but it seemed important to her. "They were the mall shooters," he said.

"You're certain," she said.

"One hundred percent."

"How can you know that?"

Jonathan scowled. "That's a step too far," he said. "You couldn't use it if you knew, so there's no reason for you to know."

They sat in silence for nearly thirty seconds. "Did you get all of them?"

"I can't say that for certain," Jonathan said. "We got all who were there, but I don't know how many I might have missed. So I guess you'll have to keep looking."

"You bet your backside we have to keep looking," Irene said. "The good news is that we've been able to tie three sets of fingerprints to the mall."

"What was the final death toll in that?"

"I thought you said you watched the news."

"Twenty-four dead, a hundred twelve wounded," Jonathan recalled. "Is that a real number?"

"I'm afraid it is," she said. "And given some of the wounds on the survivors, I expect the fatality number to grow. The public wants someone to prosecute. They want closure."

"They have it," Jonathan said. "They just don't know."

"Tell me they suffered," Irene said. "I don't want to think of those bastards dying easily."

"Big Guy and I talked about that," Jonathan said. "We decided no head shots unless absolutely necessary. They screamed a lot, actually."

ACKNOWLEDGMENTS

It's been twenty years since I wrote my first published novel, *Nathan's Run*. The world was a very different place in 1995. As a practical matter, the Internet did not yet exist for everyday citizens. Correspondence between writer and agent or writer and publisher depended on telephones, fax machines, and envelopes with stamps affixed. Every new iteration of a manuscript meant physically printing a couple of pounds of paper and FedExing it for $25 a pop. The subject of that first novel, Nathan Bailey, would be thirty-two years old now if he were a real person. It was a thrill to bring him back in *Friendly Fire*, if only for a short time. It was equally thrilling to spend some time with his adopted father, Warren Michaels, one of the noblest characters I think I ever created.

For all that change, however, it's the constants that keep me going. First and always, there's my lovely bride Joy, still my best friend and still my smartest ally, even after thirty-three years of togetherness. Holy crap, that's a third of a century! My, how the time flies.

Then there's our son, Chris, who somehow will have passed his thirtieth birthday just weeks before this book hits the stands. Keep an eye on that kid. He's already setting the world on fire. We couldn't be prouder.

Once per month, I meet with a group of very talented, very honest authors, and we critique each other's work in progress. Every get-together is a monthly master class in fiction, and it is one of the events that I look most forward to. Because we meet in my basement—my *rumpus room*—we call ourselves the Rumpus Writers (Rumpi for short). Those four mentors—Ellen Crosby, Allen Orloff, Art Taylor, and Donna Andrews—do more than they probably know to keep me on the path I need to follow to squeeze the best story possible out of the ideas in my head. Thanks also to my buddy Reavis Wortham for giving the manuscript an early read and providing valuable input.

I'm blessed to have a growing Rolodex filled with subject matter experts who always help me out when I need a solution to a problem. It's always risky to name a few for fear of missing some, but I'd be remiss if I did not shout out to a few. On things munitions-related, thanks to Chris Grall, Jeff Gonzales, Steve Tarani, Rodney Sanchez, and Barry Witt. On the police procedural side, thanks also to Lee Lofland, Brian Gaynor, and every member of the FDLE SWAT Team that let me observe (and play a little) for three exhausting days. Thanks also to Terri Lynne Coop and Margie Summers for sharing with me their knowledge of chairs.

Just because mine is the only name on the front of this book, don't assume for a moment that it is the product of my work alone. I've got an impossibly strong team behind me in the form of Kensington Publishing. My editor, Michaela Hamilton, has been a part of the

Jonathan Grave series from the very beginning, as has the guy in the big office, Steve Zacharias, whom I've known since those first *Nathan's Run* days. Filling out the team are Alexandra Nicholajsen (a real-life Venice Alexander), Vida Engstrand, Morgan Elwell, and our publisher, Lynn Cully.

Finally, there's my longtime agent and friend, Anne Hawkins, who makes all of this cool stuff possible in the first place.

Don't miss John Gilstrap's next compelling
Jonathan Grave thriller

Final Target

Coming from Kensington in Summer 2017

Keep reading to enjoy a sample excerpt . . .

Chapter One

Jonathan Grave heard the sounds of ongoing torture a full minute before he arrived on the scene. An approach like this in the middle of the night through the tangled mass of the Mexican jungle was an exercise in patience. He was outnumbered and outgunned, so his only advantage was surprise. Well, that and marksmanship. And night vision.

Ahead of him, and too far away to be seen through the undergrowth, his teammate and dear friend Brian Van De Muelebroecke (aka Boxers) was likewise closing in on the source of the atrocity.

The last few yards, the last few minutes, were always the most difficult. Until now, the hostage's suffering had been an academic exercise, something talked about in briefings. But hearing the agonized cries above the cacophony of the moving foliage and screeching critters of this humidity factory made it all very real. The sense of urgency tempted Jonathan to move faster than that which was prudent. And prudence made the difference between life and death.

The slow pace of his approach was killing Jonathan. It was 02:15, the night was blacker than black, and that victim who no doubt was praying for death had no idea that he was mere minutes away from relief. All that had to happen was for Jonathan and Boxers to get into position, read the situation for what it was, and then execute the rescue plan. There was nothing terribly elegant about it. They would move in, kill the bad guys who didn't run away, and they'd pluck their precious cargo—their PC, a DEA agent named Harry Dawkins—to safety. There was a bit of yada yada built into the details, but those were the basics. If past was precedent, the torturers were cartel henchmen.

But first, Jonathan had to get to the PC, and get eyes on the situation, and he had thousands of years of human evolution working against him. As a species, humans don't face many natural predators, and as a result, we don't pay close attention to the danger signs that surround us. Until darkness falls.

When vision becomes limited, other senses pick up the slack, particularly hearing. As he moved through the tangle of undergrowth and overgrowth, Jonathan was hyperaware of the noises he made. A breaking twig, or the rattle of battle gear, would rise above the natural noises of the environment and alert his prey that something was out of the ordinary. They wouldn't know necessarily what the sound was, but they would be aware of *something*.

Alerted prey was dangerous prey, and Jonathan's two-man team did not have the manpower necessary to cope with too many departures from the plan.

Another scream split the night, this time with a slurred plea to stop. "I already told you everything I know," Dawkins said in heavily accented Spanish. The words sounded slurred. "I don't know anything more."

In time, the magnified light of his night vision goggles, NVGs, began to flare with the light of electric lanterns. "I have eyes on the clearing," Boxers' voice said in his right ear. He was barely whispering, but he was audible. "They're yanking the PC's teeth. We need to go hot soon."

Jonathan responded by pressing the transmit button on his ballistic vest to break squelch a single time. There was no need for an audible answer. By their own SOPs, one click meant yes, two meant no.

As if to emphasize the horror, another scream rattled the night.

Jonathan pressed a second transmit button on his vest, activating the radio transceiver in his left ear, the one dedicated to the channel that linked him to his DEA masters. The transceiver in his right ear was reserved for the team he actually trusted. "Air One," he said over the radio. "Are you set for exfil?"

"I'm at a high orbit," a voice replied. "Awaiting instructions." The voice belonged to a guy named Potter, whom Jonathan didn't know, and that bothered the hell out of him. The Airdale was cruising the heavens in a Little Bird helicopter that would pluck them from one of three predetermined exfiltration points. He was a gift from the United States Drug Enforcement Administration as an off-the-record contribution to their own employee's rescue. For reasons that apparently made sense to the folks who plied their trade from offices on Pennsylvania Avenue, this op was too sensitive to assign an FBI or even a US military rescue team, yet somehow it could support a government-paid pilot, and that inconsistency bothered Jonathan. A lot. It was possible, of course, that Potter was every bit as freelance as Jonathan, but that thought wasn't exactly comforting. All too often, freelancers' loyalty was as susceptible to high bidders as their skills were.

"Be advised that we will be going hot soon," Jonathan whispered.

"Affirm. Copy that you're going hot soon. Tell me what you want and I'll be there."

Jonathan keyed the other mike. "Big Guy, are you already in position?"

Boxers broke squelch once. *Yes*.

Jonathan replayed Dawkins's plea in his head. *I already told you everything I know*. The fact that the PC had revealed information—even if it wasn't everything he knew—meant that Jonathan and Boxers were too late to prevent all the damage they had hoped to. Maybe if DEA hadn't been so slow on the draw, or if the US government in general had reacted faster with resources already owned by Uncle Sam, the bad guys wouldn't know *anything*.

The bud in Jonathan's left ear popped. "Team Alpha, this is Overwatch. Over."

"Go ahead, Overwatch," Jonathan replied. He thought the "over" suffix was stupid, a throwback to outdated radio protocols.

"We have thermal signatures on Alpha One and Alpha Two, and we show you approaching a cluster of uniform sierras from roughly the northwest and southeast."

Somewhere in the United States, Overwatch—no doubt a teenager judging from his voice—was watching a computer screen with a live view from a satellite a couple hundred miles overhead. As Jonathan wiped a dribble of sweat from his eyes, he wondered if the teenager was wearing a wrap of some kind to keep warm in the air conditioning. "Uniform sierra" was what big boys wrapped in Snoopy blankets called unknown subjects.

"That would be us, Overwatch," Jonathan whispered. He and Boxers had attached transponders to their kit to make them discernible to eyes in the sky. Even in a crowd, they'd be the only two guys flashing here-I-am signals to the satellite.

"Be advised that we count a total of eight uniform sierras in the immediate area. One of them will be your PC. Consider all the others to be hostile."

In his right ear, Boxers whispered, "Sentries and torturers are hostile. Check. Moron."

Jonathan suppressed a chuckle as he switched his NVGs from light enhancement to thermal mode and scanned his surroundings. It wasn't his preferred setting for a firefight because of the loss of visual acuity, but in a jungle environment, even with the advantage of infrared illumination gear, the thick vegetation provided too many shadows to hide in. "How far are the nearest unfriendlies from our locations?" he asked on the government net.

A few seconds passed in silence. "They appear to have set up sentries on the perimeter," Overwatch said. "Alpha One, you should have one on your left about twenty yards out, call it your eleven o'clock, and then another at your one, one-thirty, about the same distance. Alpha Two, you are right between two of them at your nine and three. Call it fifteen yards to nine and thirty to three. The others are clustered around a light source in the middle. I believe it's an electric lantern."

Jonathan, Alpha One, found each of the targets nearest to him via their heat signature, and then switched back to light enhancement. Now that he knew where they were, they were easy to see. The concern, always, were the ones you didn't see.

As if reading his mind, Venice (Ven-EE-chay) Alexander, aka Mother Hen, spoke through the transceiver in his right ear. "I concur with Overwatch," she said. The government masters didn't know that Venice could independently tap into the same signal that they were using for imagery. She was *that good* at the business of taming electrons. He liked having that second set of eyes. While he knew no reason why Uncle Sam would try to jam him up, there was some history of that, and he knew that Venice always had his best interests at heart.

On the local net, Jonathan whispered, "Ready, Big Guy?"

"On your go," Boxers replied.

Jonathan raised his suppressed 4.6 millimeter MP7 rifle up to high-ready and pressed the extended butt-stock into the soft spot of his shoulder. He verified with his thumb that the selector switch was set to full-auto and settled the infrared laser sight on the first target's head. He pressed his transmit button with fingers of his left hand and whispered, "Four, three, two . . ."

There was no need to finish the count—it was the syntax that mattered. At the silent *zero*, he pressed the trigger and sent a two-round burst into the sentry's brain. Confident of the kill, he pivoted left and shot his second target before he had a chance to react. Two down.

From somewhere in the unseen corners of the jungle, two more bursts rattled the night, and Jonathan knew without asking that the body count had jumped to four.

Time to move.

Jonathan glided swiftly through the undergrowth, rifle up and ready, closing in on the light source. They were ten seconds into the fight now, plenty of time for the bad guys to react. If their weapons were on them and they were trained, they would be ready to fight back.

An AK boomed through the night, followed by others, but Jonathan heard no rounds pass nearby. Strike the training concern. Soldiers fired at targets, thugs fired at fear. Barring the lucky shot, the shooters were just wasting ammunition.

Jonathan didn't slow, even as the rate of fire increased. His NVGs danced with muzzle flashes. The war was now fifteen seconds old, the element of surprise was gone, and that left only skill and marksmanship.

Three feet behind every muzzle flash there resided a shooter. Jonathan killed two more with as many shots.

And then there was silence.

"Status," Jonathan said over the local net.

"Nice shooting, Tex," Boxers said through a faked southern drawl. "I got three."

"That makes seven." With luck, number eight would be their PC. "Mother Hen?"

Before Venice could respond, the teenager said, "Alpha Team, Overwatch, I show all targets down. Nice shooting."

Jonathan didn't bother to acknowledge the transmission.

"I concur," Venice said. She could hear the teenager, but the teenager could not hear her. Of the two opinions, only one mattered.

Jonathan closed the distance to the center of the clearing. A naked middle-aged man sat bound to a stout wooden chair, his hands and face smeared with blood, but still alive. Dead men surrounded him like spokes of a wheel. This would be their PC, Harry Dawkins, and he looked terrified.

"Harry Dawkins?" Jonathan asked.

The man just stared. He was dysfunctional, beyond fear.

"Hey, Dawkins!" Boxers boomed from the other side of the clearing. At just south of seven feet tall and well north of two hundred and fifty pounds, Boxers was a huge man with a huge voice that could change the weather when he wanted it to.

The victim jumped. "Yes!" he shouted. "I'm Harry Dawkins."

As Jonathan moved closer, he saw that most of the man's teeth had been removed, and with all the blood, it was hard to verify his identity from the picture they'd been given. "What's your mother's maiden name?" Jonathan asked.

The guy wasn't patching it together.

"Focus," Jonathan said. "We're the good guys. We're here to take you home. But first we need to know your mother's maiden name. We need to confirm your identity."

"B-Baxter," he said. The hard consonant brought a spray of blood.

Jonathan pressed both transmit buttons simultaneously. "PC is secure," he said. Then he stooped closer to Dawkins so he could look him straight in the eye. He rocked his NVGs out of the way so the man could see his eyes. Dawkins hadn't earned the right to see Jonathan's face, so the balaclava stayed in place. "This is over, Mr. Dawkins," he said. "We're going to get you out of here."

Boxers busied himself with the task of checking the kidnappers' bodies for identification and making sure they were dead.

The kidnappers had tied Dawkins to the chair at his wrists, biceps, thighs, and ankles using coarse rope that reminded Jonathan of the twine he used to tie up newspapers for recycling. The knots were tight and they'd all been in place long enough to cause significant swelling of his hands and feet. Several of Dawkins's fingernails were missing.

Jonathan loathed torture. He looked at the bodies at his feet and wished that he could wake the bastards up to kill them again.

"Listen to me, Harry," Jonathan instructed. "We're going to need your help to do our jobs right, understand? I'm going to cut you loose, but then you're going to have to work hard to walk on your own." It was good news that the torturers hadn't made it to his feet yet.

Jonathan pulled his KA-BAR knife from its scabbard on his left shoulder, and slipped its seven-inch razor-sharp blade carefully into the hair-width spaces between rope, skin, and wood. He started with the biceps, then moved to the thighs. The ankles were next, followed last by the hands. Dawkins seemed cooperative enough, but you never knew how panic or joy were going to affect people. The edge on the KA-BAR was far too sharp to have arms flailing too early.

"Who are you?" Dawkins asked.

Jonathan ignored the question. A truthful answer was too complicated, and it didn't matter. Dawkins surely understood that leaving this spot was better than staying, regardless of who the rescuer was.

"Listen to me, Harry," Jonathan said before cutting the final ropes. "Are you listening to me?"

Dawkins nodded.

"I need verbal answers," Jonathan said. After this kind of ordeal, torture victims retreated into dark places, and audible answers were an important way to show that they'd returned to some corner of reality.

"I hear you," Dawkins said.

"Good. I'm about to cut your arms free. You need to remain still while I do that. I could shave a bear bald with the edge on this blade, and I don't need you cutting either one of us up with a lot of flailing. Are we clear?"

Dawkins nodded, then seemed to understand the error of his silent answer. "Yes, I understand."

"Good," Jonathan said. "This is almost over." Those were easy words to say, but they were not true. There was a whole lot of real estate to cover before they were airborne again and even more before they were truly out of danger.

The ropes fell away easily, and in seconds, Harry Dawkins was free of his bonds. Deep red stripes marked the locations of the ropes. The man made no effort to move.

"Do you think you can stand?" Jonathan asked. He

offered a silent prayer with the question. He and Boxers were capable of carrying the PC to the exfil location if they had to, but it was way at the bottom of his list of preferred options. He glanced behind him to see Boxers continuing his search of the torturers' pockets, pausing at each body long enough to take fingerprints that would be transmitted back to Venice for identification. Uncle Sam had not asked him for that information, but if a request came, Jonathan would consider it.

"I think I can," Dawkins said. Leaning hard on his arms for support, he rose to his feet like a man twice his reported age of forty-three. He wobbled there for a second or two, then took a tentative step forward. He didn't fall, but it was unnerving to watch.

"How long have you been tied to that chair?" Jonathan asked.

"Too long," Dawkins said with a wry chuckle. "Since last night."

Jonathan worked the math. Twenty-four hours without moving, and now walking on swollen feet and light-headed from emotional trauma, if not from blood loss.

"Scorpion, Mother Hen." Venice's voice crackled in his right ear. "Emergency traffic."

Air One beat her to it: "Break, break, break. Alpha Team, you have three—no, four victor-bravo uniform sierras approaching from the northwest." Vehicle-born unknown subjects.

"If that means there are four vehicles approaching your location, I concur," Venice said. She didn't like being upstaged.

Jonathan pressed both transmit buttons simultaneously. "I copy. Keep me informed." He turned to Boxers, who had heard the same radio traffic and was already on his way over. Jonathan opened a Velcro flap on his thigh and withdrew a map. He pulled his NVGs back into place and clicked his IR flashlight so he could read. "Hey, Big Guy, pull a pair of boots off one of our sleeping friends and give them to the PC. The jungle is a bitch on bare feet."

"What's happening?" Dawkins asked.

Jonathan ignored him. According to the map—and to the satellite images he'd studied in the spin-up to this operation—the closest point of the nearest road was a dogleg about three-quarters of a mile from where they stood.

"Alpha Team, Overwatch," the teenager said from under his blanky. "The vehicles have stopped and the uniform sierras are debarking. I count eight men in total, and all are armed. Stand by for map coordinates."

Jonathan wrote down the minutes and seconds of longitude and latitude, and knew from just eyeballing that the bad guys had stopped at the dogleg.

"Air One, Alpha," Jonathan said to the Little Bird pilot. "Are the bad guys walking or running?"

"I'd call it strolling. Over."

"So, they're not reinforcements," Boxers said, reading Jonathan's mind. He handed a pair of worn and bloody tennis shoes to Dawkins.

"I'm guessing shift change," Jonathan said.

"What, people are coming?" Dawkins had just connected the dots, and panic started to bloom.

Jonathan placed a hand on Dawkins's chest to calm him down. "Take it easy," he said. "We've got this. Put those on your feet and be ready to walk in thirty seconds." To Boxers, he said, "Let's douse the lights. No sense giving them a homing beacon." It was a matter of turning off switches, not exactly a big challenge.

With the lights out, Dawkins's world turned black. "I can't see anything," he said. His voice was getting squeaky.

"Shoes," Jonathan snapped. "You need to trust us. We're not going to leave you, but when it's time to go, you're going to need to move fast and keep a hand on me. I won't let you get lost or hurt."

"Are we gonna fight them?" Boxers asked. Ever the fan of a good firefight, his tone was hopeful as Dawkins's was dreadful.

Jonathan pressed his transmit button. "Air One, Alpha. Give me the bad guys' distance and trajectory. Also, are they carrying lights?"

"I show them approximately three hundred meters to your northeast, still closing at a casual pace. They have white light sources. I'm guessing from their heat signatures that they're flashlights, but I can't be certain."

Jonathan started to acknowledge the information when the pilot broke squelch again.

"Alpha, Air One. Before you ask, I cannot engage from the air. This is not a US government operation."

Jonathan and Boxers looked at each other. With the four-tube NVG arrays in place, Boxers looked like a huge creature from a Star Wars movie.

"What the hell?" Big Guy said. "Where did that come from?"

Jonathan had no idea. The last thing he wanted was an overzealous chopper driver shooting up the jungle from overhead. He'd spent too many missions receiving air support from the best in the business to trust his life to an amateur.

Jonathan didn't want to take a defensive position and have a shoot-out with a bunch of unknowns. It wasn't the risk so much as it was the loss of time. In a shoot-out, it's easy to identify the people you've killed, and if the wounded are screamers, they're easy, too. It's the ones who are smart enough to wait you out who you have to worry about. When he was doing this shit for Uncle Sam, he could remove all doubt by calling in a strike from a Hellfire missile. At times like this, he missed those days.

Waiting out a sandbagger could take hours, and their ride home—the Little Bird—didn't have hours' worth of fuel.

"We're going to skirt them," Jonathan announced.

Boxers waited for the rest.

Jonathan shared his map with Big Guy and traced the routes with his finger. "The bad guys are coming in from here, from our two o'clock, a direct line from their vehicles, which are here." He pointed to the dog-leg. "We'll head due north, then double back when we hit the road. If we time it right, we'll be on our way in their truck before they even find this slice of Hell."

"We're gonna pass awfully close," Boxers observed.

"Fifty, sixty yards, probably," Jonathan said. "We'll just go quiet as they pass."

"And if they engage?"

"We engage back."

"And we're doing all of this with a naked blind man in tow," Boxers said.

"Hey," Dawkins snapped. "I'm right here."

"No offense," Boxers grumbled.

"Let's go," Jonathan said. He moved over to Harry,

taking care to make noise in his approach so he wouldn't startle the guy. "Hold your hand out, Harry," he said.

The PC hesitated, but did as he was told.

"I'm going to take your hand," Jonathan said as he did just that, "and put it here in one of my PALS loops."

"Your what?"

"They're attachment straps for pouches and other stuff," Jonathan explained. "Stuff you don't need to worry about. You think of them as finger rings."

Dawkins yelped as he fitted his wounded fingertips through the tight elastic. "Hurts like shit."

"Better than dyin'," Boxers observed.

No response. None was needed.

"Okay, here we go," Jonathan said, and they started off into the night. He keyed both mikes simultaneously and relayed their plans. "I want to know if anybody wanders off or drifts toward us. My intent is not to engage. But more important than that is not walking into an ambush."

"I copy," the Overwatch teenager said. "I'll let you know if I see anything."

For three, maybe four minutes, they moved as quietly as they could through the thick underbrush. The approaching bad guys were so noisy and clueless that Jonathan's team could have been whistling and not be noticed. Then, like flipping a switch, all that talking and jabbering stopped. The beams turned in their direction, painting the jungle with a swirling pattern of lights and shadows.

Jonathan and Boxers took a knee, and Dawkins followed.

"What's happening?" Dawkins whispered.

"Shh," Jonathan hissed.

The bud in his right ear popped. "Break, break, break," Venice said. "The other team seems to be turning in your direction."

Jonathan's stomach knotted. This was wrong. Why would they do that? It was almost as if they'd been informed of Jonathan's presence.

He keyed the mike to the Little Bird. "Air One, Alpha," he whispered. "How are we doing?"

"Alpha, Air One, you're doing fine," the pilot said in his left ear. "You're close to the approaching hazard, but they are staying to their course."

"That's a lie!" Venice declared in his right ear. "They're closing on you."

"Overwatch, do you concur?" Jonathan asked. But apparently the teenager had taken a soda break.

"Scorpion, Mother Hen" Venice said. "I smell a trap."

"So it looks like we're going to have a gunfight after all," Boxers said with a chuckle on the local net. "Maybe two if the dickhead in the sky is trying to get us hurt."